"TELL ME WHAT YOU THINK," JOANNA WHISPERED.

He swung about, gripping her face between his callused palms. "About touching you," he said. "About taking more and more. Very dangerous."

Warm currents brushed Joanna's skin beneath the clinging silk. "Touching you would never be dangerous."

His hands went rigid on her cheeks. "Better for us to stop. Now. Before we . . ."

Her lips blocked his words. Cursing, he gripped her hips through the thin veil of wet silk.

Joanna shivered with a rush of desire as the mist rose. She swallowed slowly. "Kiss me, Alexei. Touch me. Dangerous or not, I want this . . ."

CHRISTINA SKYE

KEY TO FOREVER

AVON BOOKS  NEW YORK

My deepest appreciation to Tom Egner, for his inspired designs and a book cover of rare beauty. And warmest thanks to all booksellers who keep books alive through their singular enthusiasm, especially Kevin Beard, Jenny Jones, Mary Bullard, Thea Mileo, Beth Ann Steckiel, Julie Kim, Cindi Streicher, Mark Budrock, Wanda Groves, Patricia Groves, and Jeannie Heikkila.

AVON BOOKS
A division of
The Hearst Corporation
1350 Avenue of the Americas
New York, New York 10019

Copyright © 1997 by Roberta Helmer
Cover art by Paul Stinson
Inside cover author photo by Bill Morris Studio
Published by arrangement with the author
Visit our website at http://AvonBooks.com
Library of Congress Catalog Card Number: 96-96871
ISBN: 0-380-78280-4

First Avon Books Printing: March 1997

AVON TRADEMARK REG. U.S. PAT. OFF. AND IN OTHER COUNTRIES, MARCA REGISTRADA, HECHO EN U.S.A.

Printed in the U.S.A.

RA   10 9 8 7 6 5 4 3 2 1

Prologue

Sussex, England
1984

"No, no, and *no!*" Smoke drifted and billowed in the spring air, and the snap and hiss of embers filled the clearing. "He is son of ugly pig farmer and I *hate* him. I do not stay more in big English house!"

Alexei Andreiivitch Turov Cameron was seventeen, and his hair was long, the color of Russian forests stretched against unending hills of snow. His eyes were filled with restless hunger as he stamped out an ember that had fallen near his worn leather boot. When his sleeve caught on a piece of smoldering wood, he stripped off the too white, too new shirt and tossed it onto the grass. "Learn English," he mimicked. "Why? Learn business. Why again? Is work for men with little brains and too soft hands." His voice hardened. "Learn *manners.*" This was clearly the worst of all. "Manners!" Alexei made a rude gesture with one calloused hand.

A fire blazed in a stone-lined pit, tended by an old man with sharp eyes and hard, scarred fingers. He frowned as he stirred the embers hissing beneath a metal blade laid horizontal against the flame. "He is your father, Alexei Andreiivitch."

But Alexei Cameron, son of the earl of Greywood, was also the son of the pure-blood daughter of Estavian Gypsies, and he slammed a branch of wood against his

1

thigh. "Is blood father. *You* are father of heart, Constantin." He cursed and switched to the deep Slavic syllables that came far more naturally. "For now and forever, I swear this to you with my life. Though we are come here to this foreign land, I will never forget you."

"This foreign land," the old man said gently, "is your home."

"Bahh."

The old Gypsy swordmaker smiled, and there was both pride and sadness in his weathered face. "You see the metal, how it glows?"

Alexei nodded.

"You see how in a second it stirs and shifts?"

Alex watched intently and then nodded. Beneath him, layers of steel glowed, expanded, bonded.

"You are like the steel. We are *all* like the steel. We are pieces of yesterday and last week and tomorrow, fragments of every place we have been and everything we have touched." Constantin Stevanov turned the blade with deft fingers and nodded, pleased. "And you, Alexei Andreiivitch, you are the earl's son. This does *not* change." He turned and his fist slammed against the boy's powerful chest. "That makes you *English,* though your heart remains Gypsy."

Alex's eyes were stormy, those of an animal caught in a cage, searching for doors where no doors existed. "I spit on English manners and English tradesmen. I will learn the way of the blade with you, Constantin. I will sweat by the fire and burn my hands raw, learning as you have learned with your father and his. This is what I want, I swear."

The old man stiffened. He shoved Alex back from the fire, his face suddenly as hard as the steel he tended and cursed and loved. "The English earl gave up much to bring you and your mother back from Estavia. Then he paid more still to bring us here. There was only mud and hunger for us in the old country. The flat eyes followed us, waiting for the first slip when our backs were turned. Remember that, Alexei."

"How could I forget?" The boy who was not quite a man, the boy with powers he could not control or even understand, glared down at the fire. "At least in Estavia we *knew* our enemies. Here all is false. People smile at you with their eyes, then stab you with their mouths. And who can understand this cursed language they speak!"

Gently Constantin worked the rim of glowing steel. Where the metal resisted, he was ruthless. Yet when a fragile corner required it, his hands were as soft as a lover's. "There is no looking back, Alexei. That door is closed. Whether you choose to open new doors remains up to you. We are here now. England is our future." He made a hard, stabbing movement into the fire. "So from now you will do as the English earl says."

Silent and tense, Alexei folded powerful arms across his chest.

"No more running away or I will beat you with my own hand. Is this understood?"

The boy's face darkened with rebellion.

"Do you *understand* this?"

Anger stretched the skin over Alex's high, exotic cheekbones. A bead of sweat slid down the sculpted curve of his strong biceps. "And if I do not obey?"

"Then I cut you from my teaching. I give you no more of my secrets."

For a moment, there was such raw anguish on the boy's face that Constantin looked away. His jaw hardened, and he gave a merciless jab to the glowing blade, which rang out with a clear tone.

"You would do this. To *me?*" The boy's defiance gave way to disbelief.

"I would."

Alex's jaw worked up and down. "And I must do as he says in all things? Wear the ugly clothes? Eat the ugly food? Sleep in the ugly room?"

"You are his son, Alexei. You will be earl one day. You dishonor yourself and your Gypsy blood when you rebel against him."

"I shall always *hate* him," Alexei hissed, his hands closing to fists. "He made my mother cry. I remember very little about the time before we left this country, but this I do know."

Constantin looked into the fire—and beyond. "Nine years is a long time. You were still a child. Memory can play tricks, my son."

The last phrase registered upon Alex like a gentle touch. "I remember the sound of things dropping and angry words that hissed back and forth in the silence of night. Then one morning our bags were packed and the big car was waiting. My mother's face was cold and white, and I knew she had been crying again. But he— he, the great earl—said nothing." The boy spat out the words.

"It is the English way, Alexei. They do not speak of the heart. They are not like us."

The boy snorted. "When I cut my thumb, I curse and kick something. When I am happy, I throw out my hands and dance. But these people, they gnaw each moment like little seeds. They chew and swallow them down like food, revealing nothing. Bahhh!"

Constantin smiled faintly and looked into the fire. "One day you, too, will be this way."

"Never."

"Yes, oh yes." Constantin's gaze narrowed on the flames, on the bar of steel that fought his mastering vision. "You will walk amid them like a shadow, among them but not of them. You, too, will learn to chew each moment and watch their eyes while you hide your feelings beneath a cool smile. You will be more English than the English, my son, and this will cause you great pain."

Alexei's calloused hand fell, striking the anvil nearby. "Your vision lies!"

The Gypsy went on as if he had not heard. "And the fire that now gives you joy will turn, darkness in its light. It will bring you the greatest pain you have ever known, a testing to measure all I have taught you. But by then I will be gone."

Alex's head shot up sharply. "No!" His voice was anguished.

The swordmaker fell silent, swaying slightly as he looked into the fire's heart.

"And then what? Tell me how it ends, Constantin."

The Gypsy gave himself a slight shake. His hands flexed. "How it ends? You will choose, my young fool. You will choose the fire or the darkness. All you have learned will be forgotten, as will be my lessons."

"I will forget nothing," Alex said fiercely.

"Oh yes, you will forget. Even this you will forget, and it is the only lesson that matters. This blade we make reproduces the old sword of the Camerons. It is as true as we can make it. But I tell you that a blade is made not by hand or tongs or fire but by the heart. Your heart goes into every blow of every sword. If the heart is weak, the blade will snap."

"But—"

Constantin threw up a hand. "Enough! You are too lazy. Too much talk when you should be working." He gave the boy a thump on the back. "Bring me the bellows and draw a tub of water. We have much to do." His voice rose. "Dimitri!"

A stocky boy with guileless eyes rose eagerly from his watching place on a nearby pile of logs. "Yes, Father!"

"Another dozen logs for the fire. We are near the sword's heart now. If the flame wavers even for a second's second, the steel is ruined. Do you understand this, Dimitri?"

"Yes, Father." There was doglike devotion in the boy's soft eyes.

"And you, Alexei, do you understand this also?" The two pairs of eyes met, so alike and yet so different. One pair was young and muddied with a storm of emotion, the other fierce and focused by three score years of scorn and hatred and unrelenting toil. There were different lessons offered here, lessons on a level that the guileless Dimitri could never understand.

Alexei frowned. "Not entirely. But I will try, my uncle and teacher."

"It is enough," the old man said. "Now be quick. The steel waits for no man, my lazy little bears!"

"I worry about him, Andrew." She stood by the window, her hair a dark storm around her shoulders.

Andrew Cameron, the ninth earl of Greywood, gazed at his wife and felt his throat tighten with love. It still hurt to look at her after all these years. "Alexei is nearly grown, Tatia. He must make his own way."

The woman made a sharp, exasperated sound. "Outside, he is man. Inside, he is only frightened, angry little boy!"

Her English was awkward. Hardly surprising, Andrew thought, considering the nine years she had spent shut away in her homeland. Even now they did not discuss the horrors she and her son had endured in Estavia. Tatiana Turova Cameron had put all that behind her when she turned her back on her native land.

Andrew put one hand gently on her shoulder. He felt the bones, far too close beneath the skin, and wondered when her pride would bend enough for her to tell him something of those harsh years.

He did not think he could bear it if she did. *She* was the strong one, not he. Again the almost painful wave of love engulfed him. "Tatia—"

"No. He is lost, my Alexei."

"*Our* Alexei."

Her fingers covered his. "Yes. How I forget. Now we are back. This beautiful, quiet house is same. The roses nod and bees sing, and all before seems like bad dream. Except I know that my—*our*—son hides a great pain. Can you do nothing for him, Andrew?"

"He doesn't trust me. I don't even think he likes me."

"He does not know you. We have been gone so long, and Alexei has forgotten everything. Maybe . . ."

"Maybe I should be easier on him?"

There was a sudden tension, and both knew that some fine and dangerous line had been crossed.

"I do not challenge, Andrew, I only question. There is so much I do not understand."

"The boy *must* become English, Tatia. Greywood and all its possessions will one day be his. Such as they are," Andrew Cameron added dryly.

A frown marred his wife's brow. "But you have so much. The china. The paintings."

Her husband laughed. "The rot darkening the walls, the unmended tapestries. The faded spots where the Impressionists used to hang."

She caught a breath. "I did not know. How terrible and selfish of me. How did this happen?"

Cameron shrugged, and the sun picked up the gray hairs scattered amid the black. "A little here, a little there. It began with my obsession for my headstrong Gypsy wife and her young son half a continent away. Finding you was my only thought, and the estate suffered. Business suffered. *Everything* suffered." He looked grim. "Damn it, Tatia, what I'm trying to say is that there isn't much left. Oh, we'll get by. But there won't be half what I wanted to give you and not one-tenth of what I wanted to leave young Alexei."

His wife made an impatient gesture. "What is here is here. Is *you* we come back for, not house or things inside it." She put a hand awkwardly over his heart. "But how do you manage to find us? It cannot be easy. The pig on the county committee makes eyes at me, and after that they bury us where no one can find."

Something dark came and went in her husband's gaze. "I found you. That's all that matters. As for Alex, he's got to stop running away from the future. He's got to stop flying to the Gypsies." His voice hardened. "To this man Constantin especially. I forbid it."

"You are jealous."

"Of course I'm jealous. The man has far too great a hold over Alexei."

And over you.

The words lingered, unsaid. Suddenly, the silence in the room seemed almost painful.

Tatiana Turova Cameron sighed. "You let your mind make too many shadows, Andrew. Between Constantin and I is nothing, only shared Gypsy blood and the ties of our home. It is same with Alexei, for now Constantin teaches him the way of sword."

"Sword? Damn it, he needs to learn to speak properly. He needs to learn manners and business and—"

His wife covered his mouth gently. "Enough. I should never have left England, I admit this. We fight, there is much pain between us, but I should have waited."

"No, Tatia. Your father was dying back there. You wanted to see him, to show him the grandson he had never known. Do not blame yourself now. How could we have known the Estavian government would break its word and not let you return?"

His wife sighed. Her eyes held a sudden vulnerability. She took Andrew's hand and raised it to the waist that was still as narrow as it had been when she was a young girl. "I need to know, Andrew. Is it still same or did you bring us out to break things off, to tell me you find someone new? You are decent man. You would feel you owe me this much."

For a moment, shock filled the earl's eyes. "Is *that* what you believe?" Anger flared. "Do you *want* it to be done between us?"

"I . . ."

"No, it's *not* done, Tatia. Do you think I wasted nine years to find you just so I could say good-bye?" His hands gripped her hair, and he made a low, harsh sound in his throat.

"Andrew. Sweet and decent Andrew. So very English you are."

For haunted moments neither moved. Too much lay between them, too many shadows cast by years of separation. Then Tatiana's hand opened. A heartbeat later it was encircled by Andrew's strong fingers.

"For me nothing has changed, Tatia. But for you— it was many years and you had to survive. No matter what happened, you lived and kept our son healthy. The price . . ."

A shudder went through the proud Gypsy woman.

Slowly she leaned against his chest. "Is this truly you I feel, Andrew? Is this truly *us*?"

"Never doubt it," her husband said fiercely, angling her face up for the kiss he had dreamed about in the sad silences of every night since she had left Greywood.

Outside the window, the air was rich with the heady spice of moss roses. Red blooms, heavy laden, scraped against the old stone walls. A kestrel cried shrilly from the cloudless sky.

"Now, Andrew." Her hand trembled. "To close the dark memories. To bring alive all that will become our future."

Their shadows wavered, eased together, and as the curtains fluttered, they finally became one.

"Dirty Gypsy."

The words were curt, filled with disdain.

Alex stood on the edge of the clearing, his hands throbbing after six hours bent over the flame. His bare chest was streaked with charcoal and sweat, and his black hair hung in a wild tangle.

But he did not move.

The disdainful English beauty slid down from her horse, flicking her riding crop against one perfectly polished boot. "Dirty Gypsy," Penelope Hewitt Fowler said again, her full lips very red. Her beautiful face could have been carved in marble.

Something snarled inside Alexei's chest, something that threatened to claw free and explode. "Why you come here?"

She laughed, goading. "Your English is terrible, boy."

"Your Estavian more terrible than my English." He looked at her through narrowed eyes. "Why do you come here?" he repeated.

Two angry spots of color filled her cheeks. She could not seem to pull her eyes from his naked, sweaty chest.

"Answer me."

"You are on my land, boy. I came to order you off."

"Ahhh." The word was dark, richly accented. He

mocked her now. "This where we stand is Draycott earth. Gypsies come only with right of owner, Lord Draycott."

The crop flicked against polished leather. "So you say."

His full lips curved. He was learning quickly, young Alexei, sensing his power, measuring his enemy. "So I say." It was a challenge that the experienced woman five years his senior was quick to sense.

Her hand slid to one hip. Her shoulders straightened to offer a clearer view of high, full breasts.

None of this Alexei missed. "Give me hand," he ordered.

"My hand?" She sniffed. "Why should I?"

"Because I tell you."

He watched the two angry spots of color grow. There was something she wanted. Something she thought only *he* could give her.

"I could make you go, boy. I could beat you with this crop again and again until you bleed. You're just a dirty Gypsy and no one would believe you."

But Alex was in many ways already older than she was. The life he had led had made him so, forging him like Constantin's bright steel.

So he did not rise to her bait. "Hold out your palm," he said imperiously. "Or leave."

She hesitated. "Why should I obey you?"

"Because I am Alexei Andreiivitch Cameron and one day I am earl of Greywood."

Her breath puffed out in shock, and Alex felt a cold tingle of power. So this title of his could make things happen, could it?

Curiosity slowly overcame her distaste. She shoved out her palm.

Alex took it firmly. "I tell you fortune. All the secrets you whisper alone in night."

He traced the lines on her white, perfumed skin and watched her eyes darken at his touch. Another piece fell into place. "You look for something dangerous. A man perhaps."

She shivered and leaned closer. "Do I?" she whispered.

Alex smiled slowly. His father had ordered him to learn everything about the English. He would start with the arrogant beauty before him. "Palms do not lie. Lines here and here show heart. *Secrets* of heart." He spread her soft hand and traced the full mound at the base of her thumb. "Two lines so mean men follow you with eyes. And you like very much."

Her tongue swept her lip. "No." But the word was hoarse.

"And now I touch you. My hands rough. They excite you, no?"

Her nostrils flared. *"No."*

Slowly he found the hard, tight point of one breast. "With mouth you lie. Not here, I think." He breathed a silken phrase, dark, mocking words of passion.

"Damn you," she said. Her crop rose sharply.

Alex waited, unflinching. His eyes ran over her flushed face and heaving chest. "Now you beat me?" His laugh was goading.

Her breath caught, and the crop dropped to the dark, wet earth behind her. "Dirty Gypsy," she whispered hoarsely.

And then her sharp red nails pulled his head down against hers.

Andrew Cameron looked down at his sleeping wife, then eased silently from their bed. Moonlight pooled through the tall, mullioned windows as he tugged on a worn robe and padded down the hall. Some instinct made him stop at Alexei's room. The door was ajar, the room in darkness as Andrew crept inside.

His son's dark lashes were a veil against his cheeks, frosted by moonlight. One arm lay at a slant, and his legs were bent, as if he had been running in his dreams. The earl shook his head. Once again the boy was asleep on the floor in a sprawl of sheets and blankets.

Andrew tucked the blanket closer around Alexei's chest. As he did, his heart clenched painfully. But he did not tarry. He had letters to write, words that would not be easy to put to paper.

The house was quiet as the earl made his way to the study two floors below. On one wall hung an unimposing landscape. Andrew frowned at the ugly cows, then ran one hand along the bottom of the frame.

The painting sprang free of the wall. Deftly, Andrew twirled the calibrated metal face behind the painting, entering a sequence of four numbers. When he heard the faint click of metal, he eased open the heavy gray door.

Behind stacks of trade documents, bank statements, and estate receipts, the earl found what he was searching for. The notebook was small, its leather worn with age and handling.

Andrew traced the delicate gilt shape of a key etched on the red Moroccan leather, remembering the night his own father had presented him with this book. He had been twenty, on his way to Korea, and his father had guided him away from a tearful family dinner into the quiet shadows of this study.

The old earl had not said a word, only pressed the leather book into Andrew's strong, young hands. Andrew had studied the fragile, yellowed pages in confusion while the door closed softly behind him.

Then he had read and read.

The world fell away. Perhaps even time fell away as he sat in the circle of light cast by a single lamp, reading of hard men with desperate pride, secrets that each Cameron son for centuries had been granted upon his maturity.

Andrew Cameron felt the same wonder and shock squeeze through his chest now as he lifted the stiff leather cover, careful not to force the fragile binding. His gaze slid to the opening words written in an elegant and ancient hand. He did not need to see to remember them. His Latin returned, scavenged from his schoolboy days.

I am dying. There is little question of it now.

My hands shake. My breath growls against my throat like a hungry dog. At least the burning of my skin has waned since the call to Evensong. Now darkness is my only companion. I do not fight to keep this tired heart alive.

But before I go, the riddles must be given and old secrets passed. Snow blankets the high keep, and beside me in the shadows I find half-forgotten shapes that press upon my page. Where do I begin?

With words of warning for the seeker. Remember, you of Cameron blood, that he who would hold the sword must be pure of heart. If darkness stain the steel, then the magic will be turned. Only those who are pure may understand the three keys, which are both truths and lies.

The soldiers and their dogs are at the gate. Howling fills the night. The time is short.

If you are pure in heart and seek the sword, read on.

Here begins the test.

The first riddle of the three: The Sword, which is the Key to Yesterday.

Hidden but not hidden.

Whole but not whole.

Its tale is old, begun in days long gone. All I know I have set down here in this book cut and stitched by my own hand. I could trust no other to the task, for men have killed to find my secrets.

And they will kill again.

By the wish of God, they will not succeed.

My hand wavers. Pounding fills the silence of hall and hearth. There is so little time left.

The rushlights shift. Even now the metal dances before me, oddly sleek. Coldly silver. Its steel rouses at my glance, smooth as water in moonlight, alive as the pool from whence I first raised it.

The great blade of Cameron burns and shimmers, heavy with old magic that tests men's souls, as mine was tested. Beside it lies the jeweled sheath. When these two are one, together paired, the enchantment will begin, bound by oath, linked for all eternity.

God protect you if your heart is not true when that day comes and their power is linked. The Cameron treasure will be yours then, with all its pain and joy.

Heed me well, you who are Cameron. And if you bear no Cameron blood, may your heart freeze and your breath end as you read these stolen words.

The earl of Greywood studied the fragile sheets from a time long past. The book was worn by the hands of many Camerons, carried next to the body when dangers were near. Each word had been fought for, guarded with Cameron blood.

And here that first Cameron had set down the riddles one by one. When it was time, those secrets would be given to young Alexei, the earl swore.

But not yet.

Andrew turned to the back of the book, finding the first of the remaining blank pages. Ignoring the tears that lay silver on his cheeks, he picked up his pen and began to write.

1

Greywood House
Sussex, England
Twelve years later

THE SWORD seemed alive.

The swordsman stood shirtless and sweating in the empty ballroom. A vast cut-crystal chandelier spilled light over his powerful shoulders and long blue-black hair. He lunged sideways and hefted the broadsword in a swift, lethal crosscut that would have left any attacker reeling.

Or dead.

Without pausing, he braced his legs and swung the heavy shaft upward in a clean attack guaranteed to finish whatever life his first stroke had missed.

His face was bathed with sweat as he shoved back his hair and studied the fine, honed blade of the sword. The hilt was perfectly curved and the heavy pommel carefully designed to balance the long, thirty-inch blade. The sword was that rare instrument, a warrior's blade as well as an artist's delight, in which use and design met perfectly.

Alex Cameron's lips curved as he turned the sword to read the line of fine gold script incised along the blade. The words were Gaelic. "When the heart is true, the blade is sure."

Was *his* heart true? Alexei Cameron wondered.

He touched the warm hilt of the Cameron replica he'd begun years ago with Constantin. The grip felt slightly uneven. He would have to unwrap the braided leather and refit it tomorrow.

He permitted himself a smile of triumph. Over six months of work had gone into producing this weapon. He had learned many of the old man's secrets in the process.

Alex raised the broadsword and studied its glowing length beneath the chandelier. Each movement made light splinter and bounce over the fine blade, giving it a strange sheen.

The glow of Alex's own spirit was captured within the metal, just as his old teacher had told him.

His fingers moved over the pommel, taking primitive pleasure in the product of his sweat and skill. He laughed softly, finding a sensual delight in every curve of the finished sword.

Yes, the weapon was good.

He turned slowly, studying the oil painting that dominated one wall of Greywood's ballroom. A Highlander stood against sullen mountains, clad in a length of bright cloth. One long fold lay draped over his shoulder. His hands were huge, and his eyes held the same tawny specks that Alex's did. But it was the sword that commanded the picture, its huge blade raised high to catch sparks from a distant bolt of lightning.

The *claidheamh mór* of the Cameron clan. A claymore that was now priceless. Or it would be if it still existed.

Alex's eyes narrowed. His father had told him the painting was by Van Dyck, and Alex saw no reason to doubt him in spite of the pale and precise young scholar from Oxford who had published a paper sneering at the theory.

The scholar's theories did not matter. Nor did the artist in the end.

Only the sword mattered. As Alex studied the huge canvas, his hands curved unconsciously, moving to fit the shape of the broad grip crisscrossed by finely braided leather. He drew a slow breath, almost able to feel the dense weight slap against his palm. If the painting was accurate, the claymore was wonderfully balanced, its wide hilt a perfect counterweight to the long blade. This was the painting Alex and Constantin had used to make their replica years before. Alex smiled, remembering how his father had been struck speechless by the gift.

That had been the first moment of true communication between them since Alex's return from Estavia, and the gift had begun the journey to bridge their years of separation. The voyage had not been easy. Alex had been raw and rebellious, and often their discussions had turned to shouts. Whenever Alex had come to apologize, he had found his father here in the ballroom, frowning up at the portrait, his eyes filled with sadness. He had always cleared his throat, rushing off to some urgent appointment. On the day Alex had finally found the courage to ask him about the sword, the earl had sighed, looking away. Alex still remembered the moment clearly. There had been heat lightning climbing Greywood's hills above the dark woods bordered by roses.

The earl's explanation had been terse. The old claymore, he explained, was long lost, vanished in the days of Mary, Queen of Scots. An early Cameron had served the queen well, following her into captivity at Hardwick, then briefly at Draycott Abbey. This same Angus Cameron had been involved in a desperate plot to free the queen, but the effort had failed.

Alex's father would say no more than that.

Now Alex stood before the priceless portrait, feeling oddly uneasy. Maybe it was his Gypsy intuition that made him look down at the great scabbard lying by his ancestor's foot. Its surface was embossed with gold studded by a dozen pearls and one huge ruby. Van Wyck had worked these details from sketches made by a family retainer, Alex had been told. At one time there had even been talk of a diary describing the events leading up to the sword's disappearance.

Alex knew there was much his father had kept hidden from him. There had been respect but never an easy relationship between the two men. And when his father died two years before, no diary had been found among his papers.

Alex looked up, awed by the skill of the craftsman who could forge such a great weapon—and the strength of the warrior who could wield it. "What do you know that you do not tell, Angus Cameron? What secrets are hidden where you lie? Is the great sword even now clutched beside you in the cold earth?"

There was no sound in the still room. Alex shrugged. Was he actually talking to a man who had been dead for four hundred years?

There were far more important matters he should be considering. By single-minded focus and relentless attention, Alex had built up the Greywood enterprises in a dozen countries. First had come microchip technology in Ireland, then the petrochemical drill bits and seismographic software sold in China, Japan, and the Middle East. Now that Alex finally had the funds to indulge his own passion for collecting, he found himself locking horns with one man over and over.

Jacques St. Cyr.

The arrogant Frenchman had challenged Alex again and again in fierce auctions in Paris, Geneva, and Rome. The two men had driven the price of the world's finest swords far beyond precedent. Sometimes Alex had won, but more often St. Cyr had taken home the prize, for the Frenchman had unlimited funds and an obsessive need to acquire the finest pieces for his huge collection. The contest had grown more personal of late.

Alex frowned, pushing aside unhappy memories. He had made his share of mistakes, and Jacques St. Cyr was only too well aware of them.

The earl of Greywood laid the replica back in its case and tossed a towel over his shoulders. Twice in the last six months his gallery at Greywood House had been broken into, and Alex had a keen suspicion that another collector was to blame.

If St. Cyr hoped to steal the Cameron replica, he was dead wrong. Alex's newest security system would see to that. It was high time the Frenchman learned that some things were beyond buying.

Or stealing.

Even if he'd been starving, Alex would never sell any of his work to St. Cyr. As usual, Constantin had been right. Every sword carried a piece of his soul, claimed through fire and pain and sweat during long months of design and construction. Alex had sworn that his blades would go only to owners worthy of their power, and Jacques St. Cyr would *never* be that.

Frowning, Alex traced the sword's blade. Abruptly, his finger slipped. He looked down to see blood on the glinting steel. As Alex watched the dark drops, something stirred in his chest, an old intuition that came without words. The sight born of his Gypsy heritage whispered to him now of danger, a shadow that would come where and when he least expected it.

Footsteps crunched behind him and Alex spun about, feeling cold dig at his neck. But it was simply his white-haired butler. "Blast it, Metcalfe, I didn't hear you come in."

"Hardly surprising, my lord. When you're caught up with your swords, a troupe of male gorillas couldn't rouse you." The servant shook his head in dignified reproach. "You've had three phone calls from London and another from Paris." He cleared his throat. "There is also a gentleman waiting for you in the blue parlor."

"Another real estate agent keen to turn Greywood into a corporate convention center, complete with golf course and spa? Or is it Jacques St. Cyr, come to offer me the Taj Mahal in exchange for a sword I have no wish to sell?"

The butler laughed. "Neither, my lord. I'm afraid it's someone interested in researching a documentary. He wants to ask you a few questions. About . . . the sword."

"Not again."

Both knew which sword. There could be only one weapon mentioned in the same breath with Greywood and the Cameron legacy.

Alex turned, studying the old portrait, wondering yet

again what dark secrets his ancestor had carried with
him to the grave. "I tell them it is lost, Metcalfe. I tell
them the truth again and again, but they think it's clever
marketing, the trick of a man who wants to stir the
curiosity of his audience." He pulled the leather thong
from his hair, frowning. "Tell the man I don't *have* what
he wants!"

Metcalfe's brow rose.

"Oh, all right, I'll talk to him. No need to give me that
haughty glare you perfected when I was a teenager."

"I will do exactly that. After all, I *did* promise your
father that I would keep you in line."

Alex muttered, starting for the door.

The butler cleared his throat again. "Another person
is waiting to see you, my lord. Ms. Vail."

Alex's brow rose. "Here?"

"She said to tell you she would make herself comfortable down by the pool, my lord."

"You don't like Samantha, do you, Metcalfe?"

"It is not my place to hold opinions of your female—
er, acquaintances, my lord."

"Why not? You hold opinions about everything else.
Maybe *you* should have the discussion with the research-
er. Tell him that you're a long-lost Cameron ancestor
and you've finally succeeded in tracking down the old
Cameron claymore. Tell him any bloody thing you
want."

"But—"

Alex's eyes took on a measuring glint. "I'll be down by
the pool."

There was only one thing better than the sight of
Samantha Vail in clothes, Alex decided as he moved
through the gathering twilight.

That was the sight of Samantha Vail taking off her
clothes.

He set down two crystal goblets and reached for the
Krug '72, watching his uninvited guest reach to her
form-fitting silk chemise and pop open two buttons.

"You work too hard, Alex. You need other interests."

"Like?"

"Me." Another button slid free. "Interested?" she whispered.

"I'm getting there." Alex moved toward the edge of the swimming pool. Water lapped softly as he set down his goblet on the flagstone rim. The other he held out to Samantha.

But it was a warm night and his red-haired visitor had other pleasures on her mind. She tossed back her shoulder-length hair and fingered the single diamond at her throat. The movement sent her extraordinary breasts thrusting against the lace design that sold for an extortionate sum in one of London's finest lingerie boutiques. Alex knew, because he had bought it for her a month ago.

He frowned. Was it already a month? Of course there *had* been his two business trips to Asia, then the final work on his sword.

"Alex?"

Her skin was perfectly tanned, her breasts exquisite. All things considered, Alex should have been far more interested than he was.

Maybe it was the memory of the warning light on his security panel that was distracting him. The red light had gone on and off for the last two days in spite of his efforts to find the glitch. The new voice recognition codes had malfunctioned twice this week without any apparent reason. On top of that, he had received a curt fax this morning from Jacques St. Cyr, demanding a meeting to discuss the Cameron claymore and its replica.

When hell freezes over, Alex thought.

"Alex, why do I have the feeling you're not listening to me?"

The earl of Greywood took a sip of champagne, watching two luscious coral nipples slide free of their restraining lace. He felt a momentary stab of desire, but the feeling quickly fled.

Damn it, this was unnatural. Samantha Vail had to be one of the most beautiful women in England. Her body was superb, her voice was exquisite, and her singing career was just about to explode.

Judging by the look on her carefully made-up face, her career wasn't the *only* thing about to explode, Alex realized.

"You've raised distraction to a bloody art form, Alex. I don't think you've heard a *word* I've said."

"Sorry, Sam. I'll be more focused, I promise."

She made a little moue of discontent. Her eyes narrowed as she shimmied out of her dress, leaving it in a heap by the pool. Long, slender thighs rose to a lacy thong. Her scrap of a bra went flying into the pool.

Alex wondered what his housekeeper was going to say in the morning when she came across the cast-off clothes. Actually, that thought interested him more than how the evening was going to end.

He looked at the diamond at Samantha's neck and calculated how long the attraction had lasted. Eight weeks—or was it nine now? Suddenly the time didn't matter. To his amazement, Alex realized he had absolutely no interest in the exquisite and nearly naked body poised on the edge of his swimming pool.

As he stood scowling, the champagne goblet clenched in his hand, he felt a prickle at his spine. Again came the sense of danger. He tensed as shadows closed around him.

"Alex, come and play."

Dimly he felt teeth nip at his ear. A warm, sleek body left an erotic friction against his chest and thighs. "Stop thinking about those expensive swords of yours, damn it." A jeweled finger tugged at his belt. "Tonight I'm only interested in feeling this particular blade."

Alex didn't move.

Perfectly manicured nails inched beneath his waistband. With exquisite care, they circled his shaft and eased him free.

At the same moment, the lighter-sized beeper in his chest pocket began to screech.

"Not again. Damn it, this is beyond enough!" Samantha hissed.

Alex frowned as he snagged his beeper. "I quite agree. That's the third time my security alarm has been triggered this week. I've had enough."

"What about *me?* Here I am, naked and ready, and all you can think about is a bloody *security* alarm!" Samantha stood glaring at him, entirely furious.

Alex refrained from reminding her that the art collection inside the fifteenth-century house above the pool was worth somewhere in the vicinity of twenty million pounds. Something told him that wasn't likely to impress her right now.

"I've got to go, Sam." He strode toward the stone steps that led up to the house. "I'll have Dimitri drive you back to London."

"If I go now, I'm not coming back, Alex!"

He barely heard. He broke into a run, struck by the premonition that something inside was very, *very* wrong.

"You'll be sorry for this, Alex Cameron!" Behind him, Samantha's curses filled the air.

But Alex was at the edge of the grass, frowning up at the new, glass-walled wing. A single light on the ceiling glowed red, and he could see that one glass case had been shattered. All the contents had been removed, right down to the rare Colt Lightning slide-action carbine.

And along with it the Cameron claymore replica.

"Bloody, bloody hell."

"*Look* at me, Alex!"

Not even the wet lace thong slamming down against the flagstones made him turn back.

"Lord Greywood?" The police officer who answered Alex's call was overweight and overworked. He picked his way over a sea of shattered glass, his pale green eyes bored. "You called about a theft."

Alex stopped pacing. "It happened thirty minutes ago as close as I can determine. They came in through the far glass window."

"You have an alarm system?"

"Updated two months ago. But I've had several false alerts in the last week."

The officer flipped open a worn leather notebook. "Who did the installation?"

Alex gave the name of a security firm in London.

"And exactly what was stolen?"

"An Arab *saif,* seventeenth century. Matching scabbard with gold mounts."

"Approximate value?"

"Eight thousand pounds. More or less."

"Anything else?"

Alex's face darkened. "A Colt Lightning carbine. It was a gift from the president of Mexico to my grandfather."

"Rare?" The eyes were still bored.

"Less than forty Lightning medium-frame rifles were made by Colt. Only three of those were carbines. This piece is the only one that carries a factory-engraved serial number." Alex laughed harshly. "Yes, you could say it is rare."

All he got was a shrug. "Value?"

"Whatever price the seller asks."

The officer flipped the notebook shut and studied the chaos that had once been an elegant exhibition area. "Was anything else taken, Lord Greywood?"

Alex frowned at the glinting glass. "A replica of an old family sword."

"Value?"

"It's a modern piece, but to me it is priceless," he said grimly. "They also broke into my study."

The officer slid the notebook into his pocket. "If they try to pass your pieces off to a reputable dealer, we'll have a shot at them. If not . . ."

"If not, I might as well kiss everything good-bye."

The officer's face was impassive. "Do you have any enemies, Lord Greywood?"

Alex sighed. "Probably as many as you do. The usual rival collectors. A few irate business competitors."

"Anyone who would do this? Out of personal vengeance perhaps?"

Alex thought for a minute. "Possibly."

The officer's shoes squeaked as he rocked from side to side. "I'm not sure you're being very helpful, Lord

Greywood." He fingered his thick belt and looked around him. "Any idea what else these people might have been looking for in your study?"

Alex thought of the wall safe hidden behind a very ugly painting by Turner. The cows had always looked like overgrown squirrels to Alex. Tonight the cows looked worse than ever because they had been slit in three places by a very sharp razor. Most of his father's personal papers were inside that safe along with Alex's research notes on the missing Cameron claymore, painstakingly gathered over the last three years. "I'll go through my papers to be sure."

"You do that. Meanwhile, we'll be in touch."

Right, Alex thought. *When the Thames freezes over, you will.*

He watched the officer amble out, as bored as when he'd arrived. No help there.

He picked up a piece of chipped glass. Someone had wanted something from Greywood. That person had gotten past two microwave motion sensors and a voice-protected code box. The same person or persons had then gone to his study and forced open a safe holding papers of no conceivable financial worth. All around were rare weapons and antique armor worth several million, yet they had taken only one period sword, one Colt carbine, and the Cameron replica.

Rare restraint. Or possibly they had come with a shopping list.

Alex turned the glass chip restlessly in his fingers. His intruder had up-to-date information about every detail of Alex's house and alarm system. Now he had the replica of the Cameron claymore, too.

The intuition that had been bothering Alex for a week turned into a silent scream.

2

IT WAS going to be one of those days.

Joanna Russell picked up the twelve-pound metal helmet and frowned. There was a slender but defined muscle in her forearm from yoga and hard jogging with weights three days a week. She had finally come to like her body, and she meant to keep it that way. She also liked the sense of control that being in good shape gave her.

But right now Joanna wasn't feeling in control of anything. Her pet angora rabbit was trailing gray hairs all over the red tapestry sofa, she was late for an important appointment at the county museum, and she had a nagging suspicion she had just put a run in her last pair of stockings.

When had she ever thought she was in control?

Sighing, the slender American shoved a mass of straight cinnamon-colored hair from her forehead and looked down at the restoration project spread across her oak worktable. Behind her, the rabbit left a tuft of fur on a paisley cashmere throw, hopped onto the arm of the floral chintz sofa, and continued on a collision course with a vase full of white peonies.

Joanna sighed when she heard the crack of shattered china.

"Down, Winston."

The rabbit looked at her with melting brown eyes, then proceeded undaunted toward a row of portraits in silver frames. Joanna managed to snatch three out of harm's way just in time. As she slid the rabbit back down onto the floor, she felt a run tear down the other stocking.

Nothing to do about it now. She had exactly six minutes to finish her report for the museum. After her appointment there, she had to go directly to Draycott Abbey for the afternoon tour.

Joanna fingered the small tape recorder on the table and began to speak. "Flemish armor. Eighteenth century. Fine to excellent condition. The close helmet with plume holder contains two hairline cracks in the left temple. The breastplate shows signs of discoloration and possible rust damage. On closer examination, the helmet reveals extensive renovation, beginning with the addition of a modern visor. This work considerably reduces the value of the piece. I recommend that you pass on this item."

Behind her another picture frame toppled from the Malaysian lacquer table. Joanna caught the rabbit firmly and slid him into a cage wedged between two shining metal gauntlets. "Stay."

The rabbit looked back at her, twitched his nose, then turned to gnaw on a fresh carrot.

Behind her, sunlight spilled over oak cabinets and bright tapestry squares in the airy, open kitchen. Red and white roses brightened a tulip-shaped vase near hand-painted teacups.

Joanna closed her leather case, picked up a cup that read "Scotty, beam us *all* up," and finished her cold Earl Grey tea. As she did, the phone began to ring. She glanced at her watch, then snatched up the receiver. "Hello?"

There was no answer.

"Hello?"

The silence held. Muttering, she put down the phone. She shoved a blue suede jacket over her linen dress, combed back her hair with her fingers, and scooped up her keys from a basket of correspondence at the end of her worktable.

Fourteen minutes to get to the museum.

She looked back at the room and breathed in the lush scent of fresh peonies mingled with damask roses.

"Thank you," she said softly to no one in particular. "Thank you again and again."

She looked down at the rabbit. "Guard, Winston. Blood, sweat, and tears, remember."

A carrot peel hit the cage wall.

Joanna smiled and closed the door behind her.

April sunlight shone on a pink marble statue of Venus and Cupid. "This is one of the viscount's favorite sculptures."

Wearing navy linen and a single strand of matched pink pearls, Joanna guided her tour group through Draycott Abbey. "The ruby in Venus's hand is said to be a gift to the Draycott family from Queen Elizabeth I. Supposedly, the huge gem was granted in exchange for political services rendered. But what I'd really like to point out is this beautiful suit of sixteenth-century armor." Joanna's voice warmed as she spoke. "Legend holds that this set was created for one of the early Draycott ancestors."

A tall lady with a southern accent raised her hand. "Ms. Russell, honey, would you be speaking about the *Evil* Viscount?"

Joanna sighed, well used to this line of questioning after nearly a year leading tours at the magnificent fourteenth-century English manor known as Draycott Abbey. The abbey's famous ghost consistently drew more visitors than the house's priceless paintings and exceptional collection of armor. Every group seemed spellbound by legends of the notorious guardian ghost, who had recently been dubbed the Evil Viscount after a female journalist felt phantom hands on unmentionable parts of her anatomy.

The name had stuck.

"If you mean the eighth viscount, you're correct. That suit of armor did belong to Adrian Draycott at one time." Joanna turned away, only to be interrupted by the same visitor.

"I read he gambled away ten thousand pounds in one hour of gaming, then finished two bottles of claret and took his rapier to fight three consecutive duels. He'd been caught with the men's wives, you understand." The woman pursed her lips. "In a *very* compromising position."

Two elderly gentlemen muttered disapprovingly. A pair of German students studied the far wall, where a stern man in black satin and pristine white silk stared with palpable arrogance from a gilt-framed portrait.

Joanna brushed back her thick bangs and smiled faintly. "His record was said to be four duels in one night. He was a terror with a sword as well as a pistol. But I suspect you already know that."

"Oh yes. I also know the Evil Viscount haunts the abbey still," the woman said eagerly. "He paces the roof on moonlit nights, and he is always seen with a cat. Or with something that takes the *shape* of a cat."

The two old gentlemen sniffed while the rest of the tour group crowded around the portrait.

"Have *you* seen him, Ms. Russell?" This came from a little girl with bright red hair. "The ghost, I mean."

"If a ghost had been drifting about this abbey, I would have noticed him," Joanna replied calmly. "I'm afraid this is pure gossip."

The little girl frowned. "Like the legend of the Scottish queen who was held prisoner here?"

"No, Mary was real enough, and she *was* held captive here for a short time. The plot to free her failed because there was an informer, or so I have heard."

The girl's eyes widened. "Do *you* believe that?"

A gust of wind ruffled Joanna's hair. She watched a curtain stir gently at the window. "I'm not sure. She was a tragic figure, a woman who could trust no one. She had neither home nor happiness. People like that always inspire legends." She patted the girl's shoulder and smiled. "Let's get back to our tour. I'll bet you like knights and dragons, don't you?"

The girl nodded shyly.

"Well, this old house has some *awesome* armor. You can even touch it." Joanna moved to stand beside a suit of polished steel. "Can you see the slight dent here on the right arm? Family records say that this piece was damaged after one of the Draycotts took a fall from his horse."

The visitor from South Carolina interrupted again. Her drawl was heavier now. "That was *him*. The Evil Viscount, I mean. He was on his way to Scotland when he was attacked by a traitor to the Crown. I read all about it when I was just a girl." Her voice fell to a dramatic whisper. "And you can't tell me he wasn't on a diplomatic mission. He was only *pretending* to take part in that medieval tournament."

Joanna sighed. "Adrian Draycott was wearing this suit of armor when it was damaged, but abbey records state that his horse was frightened by a cat. And there is no mention of any diplomatic mission being held during that part of the mid-eighteenth century."

"You think they'd tell everybody? It had to stay absolutely *secret,* honey."

Joanna realized this was her last chance to regain control. "Since you are so interested in the eighth viscount, perhaps we should make our way to the second floor. There is a very fine pair of his dueling rapiers up there that you might—"

"The second floor? Lord, isn't that where the *bedrooms* are?"

Joanna nodded, all too aware of what the next question would be.

"Can we see the Evil Viscount's mahogany bed? The one where he held an orgy with fifty innocent virgins on All Hallows' Eve?"

Not the orgy again.

Joanna muttered beneath her breath as the eager group surged toward the staircase. Nothing made a tourist's heart race faster than legends of the Evil Viscount's ghost.

Unless, of course, it was the hope of visiting his bedroom.

At the back of the gallery, beyond the portraits and the elegant Regency furniture, light swirled up and drifted over Draycott Abbey's elegant marble staircase. A faint gust of wind rustled the perfect white roses arranged in bowls above the two mantels.

As the last of the tour group left, low laughter spilled through the room.

White lace took shape, clustered richly over sleeves of black satin. Slowly, the hard features of the abbey ghost took form. Cynical gray eyes measured the room above a full and sensual mouth.

"So now I'm the *Evil* Viscount, am I? I knew I should have thrown that whey-faced female into the moat when she first came poking about with her questions." Lace fluttered as Adrian Draycott's powerful fingers stroked his jaw. "Perhaps the name is suitable, however, considering my lamentable past."

A gray shape ghosted over the polished marble floor. Amber eyes burning, the great cat moved to the spectral figure pacing beside the far wall.

"There you are, Gideon. What do you think of my new title?"

The cat's tail flicked sharply.

"You don't like it?" Laughter drifted past the cut roses and the priceless old tapestries. "Don't tell me you are becoming prosy in your old age, my friend."

The cat hissed once.

"No, you are probably right. *Prosy* was the wrong word to use." The guardian ghost of Draycott Abbey frowned as he bent to stroke the cat's back. "Besides, there weren't anything close to fifty females here on the evening in question. And there certainly wasn't a single virgin among them."

The cat meowed sharply.

"Of course, I had them checked! What do you take me for?"

The great amber eyes blinked.

"Is that so? Well, if *I'm* an arrogant, black-hearted rake, what does that make *you?*"

The amber eyes blinked again.

"The unquestioning friend of an arrogant, black-hearted rake?" Adrian laughed suddenly. The rich sound spilled through the room, filling every dark corner with light. "Yes, a true friend you have been, Gideon. Century after century. What amazing adventures we have had." His black boots gleamed as he walked to a fine centifolia rose and inhaled its musky scent. "Tell me, what do you think of our fair tour guide?"

The cat sat back on his powerful haunches. His whiskers twitched.

"Too good to be true. Aye, that's exactly what I was thinking. Why should such a beautiful female live alone in that old stone cottage across our valley?"

The cat's whiskers moved again.

"I am well aware that times have changed! I am also aware that Miss Russell is some sort of expert on hilt weapons." Adrian snorted. "Weapons indeed. Outrageous! In my time, women knew their place. You didn't find them rushing about brandishing swords while garbed in outlandish costumes." His lips pursed. "She's also a specialist in historical reenactments. Hardly suitable work for a woman."

The cat's back arched.

"Oh, so you think her figure is quite nice, do you? Especially in doublet and hose. Wicked cat." After a moment, the ghost sighed. "You are right, I suppose. Times *have* changed. Females even hold the right to vote now. Perhaps it is all for the best, given the general muddle we males seem to have made of things." He moved to a photograph of a woman with golden hair smiling up at a man with admiring eyes. Between them sat a small girl caught in midgiggle. "Yes, things are much better now that Kacey is here to keep an eye on Nicholas Draycott and our old abbey."

The cat rubbed against his boot.

"I know that they are safe and well in France with their friends. It's just . . . hang it, I miss little Genevieve. She could *see* me, you know. And it's been ages since anyone has been able to see me."

The cat's tail arched.

"All right, I *do* admit it. It's damnably lonely without the three of them. The halls are far too quiet and it's no good trying any of my usual tricks. If you ignore the tour groups—and I generally do—there is no one to shock except for that shrewd butler, and he pays no attention to *anything* I conjure up."

Abruptly, Adrian's dark eyes took on an inner softness. "Of course, *she* could see me from the very first. Gray and I were meant to be together. I'd been waiting here for her." His voice turned husky. "It seems as if I'd been waiting for all of time."

Dim light played over the nearby paneling.

"Gray, is that you?"

Instantly, the light vanished.

"Blast it, Gray, I *know* that's you." Adrian strode to the wall. When the light did not return, he melted through the polished wood into the adjoining study. But that room, too, was empty. "Where has she gone, Gideon?"

The cat blinked.

"But why? Angry about what? I've done *nothing!*" Adrian frowned. "What do you mean, all that talk about orgies? That was ages ago."

His feline companion managed to look sympathetic and disapproving at the same time.

"It's hardly *my* fault that I've suddenly become notorious with the locals. It's all because of that meddlesome woman who insisted on dredging up the old scandals. Still, I suppose I had better find Gray and apologize. Deucedly unfair, given that I've done nothing *really* notorious for several centuries now."

The cat's eyes gleamed with sudden warning.

"Of course I remember the Scottish queen. How could I forget? The abbey was a cold, silent place during her months here. But that's long buried, Gideon. The sword and its great scabbard are no more than legends now. I mean to see that the past *stays* past. I'll have no more talk about this."

The cat nudged his booted foot.

"That episode with Lord Sefton and the lost urn? That was rather exciting, I admit."

Gideon coiled around his other foot.

"Yes, I remember our adventure with the hidden wine,

too. I'm not likely to forget a great man like Mr. Jefferson, am I?" The abbey ghost stared out at the bars of sunlight slanting over the green lawns. "The truth is I'm unutterably bored, Gideon. That's the beginning and end of it. We have walked these grounds for so long, unseen and unthanked. Then Gray came at last . . ." He frowned down at the lace spilling over his cuff. "I'm being a black-hearted fool again, but after all these centuries, there is so little left that is new. And now I'm in Gray's bad graces because of all this talk about my lamentable past."

The cat purred softly.

"I know she only says it because she loves me. And I love her, too. But hang it, even a spirit can grow tired of walking the same halls and seeing the same faces." Abruptly his gray eyes narrowed. "But this tour guide quite intrigues me. I'm convinced there's something very odd about our Miss Russell." He ran his hand along Gideon's back. "She quite clearly deserves more of our attention."

His eyes took on a wicked gleam as footsteps hammered over the corridor above. "But I think we should look in on our latest visitors. It's the least we can do, given their sordid interest in my misspent life."

Adrian's eyes seemed to shimmer. At his feet, the cat went very still.

"What am I going to do? A little manifestation or two. Perhaps I'll riffle a book or twitch someone's scarf."

The cat's eyes blinked.

"Come now, Gideon, it's expected. Draycott Abbey is known for its ghost, and we can't let our visitors down. It will be the only interesting part of a remarkably boring week."

In a swirl of light, the two figures walked into the heavy Flemish tapestries lining the front hall.

And there they vanished.

"But it's true! He was caught in the act right there on that table with a princess of the royal blood. I wouldn't lie about a thing like that, would I?"

Joanna Russell rubbed her forehead. "Miss—Hayes, isn't it?"

"That's right. Elizabeth Victoria Hayes. I was named after the dear queens. I was spoon-fed on English history," the woman said proudly. "Oh, the things I can tell you. Even the other legends about the great Scottish sword that was buried here at the abbey."

Joanna sighed. The Cameron claymore was a frequent topic during her abbey tours. It seemed that anyone with a smattering of interest in English history had heard about the lost sword and its jeweled scabbard. The fact that the pair of objects were said to carry the curse of Mary, Queen of Scots, only added to the persistence of the legends.

"Is there not a painting of this sword in the Great Hall?" An elderly Frenchwoman with manicured hands and a voluminous turban looked at Joanna. "This thing I read about in Paris. Very famous."

"No, the only painting of the Cameron claymore is at Greywood House."

"It is nearby, yes?"

"Ten miles or so. But the house is not open to the public." Joanna knew after twice trying to see the portrait herself. Both times she had been turned away by a politely intractable butler who had told her to apply to the earl of Greywood upon his return from Asia. But Joanna never had, since other research projects had always been more pressing.

"A pity." The woman toyed with one glove. "And this sword, she is lost, *non?*" The young blond man at her side frowned, and his hand circled her arm.

A current of air nudged Joanna's neck. Suddenly, she shivered, wanting to be out of this room. "So it is said. The sword's owner does not invite public interest in his family's possessions, however."

"That would be the earl of Greywood," the old woman said softly. "This I have heard, too. Very rich, he is. And all this for one who is Gypsy."

"Gypsy?" Joanna hadn't heard that before.

The woman shrugged. "So his mother was." She smiled faintly. "I, too, have my pieces of history, *non?* My husband, he was diplomat, you understand." She looked at the young man beside her and her smile grew. "But *mon fils,* he does not like me to chatter of it."

The diminutive Miss Hayes cleared her throat, eager to steer things back to her real interest. "What about the Evil Viscount and *his* room?"

Joanna shook her head. "Not possible." As she spoke, a page of the Draycott Bible near her right hand fluttered in the wind. Odd, all the windows were supposed to be kept closed in this room. Climate control was absolutely essential for the priceless Old Master paintings and the three very fine Whistler landscapes.

Joanna made a mental note to discuss the problem with Marston, the abbey's unflappable butler, as soon as she finished with the tour. "As I explained, the bedrooms are not open to the public. We are going to the ballroom now," she said firmly. "There you can see a remarkable collection of tapestries and a pair of gilt—"

"You mean we *can't* see the Evil Viscount's bed?" Miss Hayes looked heartbroken. "And here I've come all the way from America!"

Joanna felt a pang of regret, but rules were rules. "I'm afraid that won't be possible. The current viscount and his family keep some parts of the house private, so that they can lead a normal life."

As normal a life as possible in a house with such awesome beauty and extraordinary history. Joanna had felt a nearly tangible sense of life about the abbey from the first moment she had set eyes on it. That almost magical sense of presence was one of the reasons she had decided to accept the viscount's offer to rent his renovated stone cottage for use as her studio. The low rent she paid in exchange for her tour duties was an added incentive.

Draycott Abbey wasn't haunted, Joanna firmly believed. It was *alive,* rich with living, breathing history. That was the next best thing to being haunted.

The pages of the Bible fluttered once again. Joanna

noticed the book now lay open at the family births. This particular page recorded the appearance in the world of the eighth viscount.

She frowned. Next she would be imagining the hard features of the Evil Viscount taking shape in front of her. "The ballroom is down this corridor," she said.

Miss Hayes pouted. "No bed?"

"No bed."

"Not even a peek?"

Joanna shook her head. "Afraid not."

Her visitor sighed. "Why are all the really interesting places off limits?"

"Perhaps we can include a visit to the abbey's roof. You'll find the view is—"

Now it was the little girl's turn to interrupt. "Didn't the English hang everyone who tried to help that Scottish queen escape?"

Joanna took a calming breath. "Some of them were hung. Now if you'll just come with me, I believe you'll enjoy—"

"Wasn't there a Bible connected with that plot?" Miss Hayes said.

Joanna eyed the woman with new respect. Not many amateurs knew of that particular legend. "So it is said, but no proof has ever come to light. With the sword lost, we may never know the truth."

"If it truly is lost," the Frenchwoman murmured. "What is lost may sometimes be found, *n'est-ce pas?* Unless there is a true curse that lies over the sword and scabbard."

"I'm sure there is no curse." Joanna steered Miss Hayes toward the door. "And I'm also certain that you'll find the view from the parapets very romantic."

"But why can't we have one look at the bedroom before we—" Suddenly the tiny woman gasped. "Who did *that?*"

"Did what?" one of the elderly gentlemen asked.

"Someone p-pinched me. On a *very* sensitive spot."

"Well, it certainly wasn't I," the elder Mr. Piggott-West said sharply.

"Nor was it I," said his brother, edging away.

"*Someone* pinched me." Miss Hayes's eyes widened. "Or something."

The pages of the Draycott Bible lifted, fluttered slowly, then fell open to a new spot. Great illuminated letters began the page: "For the price of wisdom is above rubies."

Joanna stiffened, aware of being watched, almost as if a new presence had entered the room.

She cleared her throat. "I'm certain it was someone bumping into you, Miss Hayes. The viscount insists his spatial sense is disturbed here in the abbey. Things seem farther away than they really are. Lord Draycott believes it comes of the varied lighting, when sunlight gives way to deep shadows in the same room. You can see that play of light and dark around us right now, and I've always felt it was part of the abbey's charm. Now if you'll come this way, we'll finish our tour up on the roof."

As Joanna held open the door for the group, she looked back into the Long Gallery. A single beam of sunlight slanted through the windows, radiating around the imposing portrait of a man with stern eyes and a chiseled nose.

The eighth viscount, she realized with a little stab of surprise.

And she could have sworn, just before the door closed, that she saw a sleek gray cat pad across the old Persian rug.

But that, of course, was impossible.

Two hours later, Joanna dropped her keys with a sigh and stood in the middle of her sun-filled workroom. Light glinted off three-hundred-year-old Spanish blades and French jousting swords. A polished suit of armor hung on a dress form by a floor-to-ceiling bank of windows. Beyond the wooded gorge, Joanna could just make out the high towers of Draycott Abbey, her nearest neighbor.

She tossed down her jacket tiredly. The cottage seemed far too empty.

Winston looked up expectantly in his cage.

"Hungry, little guy?"

The rabbit's pink nose twitched and Joanna scooped him up into her arms. He was soft and restless against her, one long ear nudging her cheek. "Everything looks safe. No broken locks. No damaged armor. Good job, guy. You really know how to guard a perimeter."

Joanna set the rabbit down and kicked off her shoes. She loved this cottage overlooking the tree-filled valley. She loved the way sunlight played through the clean contemporary windows set floor to ceiling above the valley. She loved having her life spill around her while she worked, in framed pictures, cabinets full of books, and tables full of potted herbs.

Most of all she liked the life she had made here, quiet and steady, rich with the work of restoring old weapons. Always before, that work had been enough to rescue her from any temporary bouts of depression.

But now something dark pressed at her mind. Joanna had felt it begin in the Long Gallery at Draycott Abbey.

Nonsense, she told herself, flicking on her phone message machine.

Sounds of clapping filled the air. "Joanna, my dear, we've found something really *awesome* this time." The voice was lost in a series of high-pitched beeps.

She recognized her father's voice, calling about some new relic unearthed at the nearby Roman dig site where he worked with Joanna's mother. The beeps came from the radiometric sensor he used to check for magnetic anomalies caused by underground iron. Even at sixty, Harrison McTiernan could still outdig, outtunnel, and outexcavate any archaeologist half his age.

"Come out today and we'll give you the guided tour," the hearty voice continued. "Unless, of course, you've found a knight in shining armor to sweep you off your feet. In that case, by *all* means stay away."

Oh, Dad, don't I wish. Joanna frowned at Winston, who was gnawing on a green shoot of chives. These days, Winston was the only creature sweeping her off her feet.

The message machine beeped again.

"Halloo, be-u-ti-ful!" a fluid Welsh voice boomed. "Don't forget that we have a date tonight. Pack the long skirt and padded vest. Yes, I *know* it split the last time we practiced. That's why I made you another and hung it in your workroom over your latest suit of armor. That way I know you'll see it."

Joanna chuckled. Sure enough, the padded linen vest was just where he said it was. Nigel Llewelyn was a big burly Welshman and her partner in their part-time business of historical performances. Joanna certainly hadn't forgotten the evening's engagement or their generous fee. Her costume was already packed.

She straightened a pair of eighteenth-century dueling swords as her reenactment partner called out to someone in the background. "No, not *those* lights. The new ones." He returned to the phone. "These university students don't know their—well, never mind. Just don't be late tonight, or we're sunk." Nigel laid their success at Joanna's door, but it was really due to his organizational skills and unflagging enthusiasm. The fact that his father was a famous Shakespearean scholar hadn't exactly hurt either.

Joanna sighed as she studied a claymore laid against a velvet pad on her worktable. The ornate hilt was broken along one corner, and the pommel was badly rusted. Carefully, she lifted the old Scottish sword and tested its balance against her palm.

A fine weapon should feel heavy and light at the same time, perfectly balanced with a life of its own. Only one man made such swords, a genius whom Joanna had met once. The man known as Constantin would certainly have known how to shape a hilt to refit this beautiful old weapon. Where he had worked from instinct, Joanna worked from textbooks and scientific analysis. That had seemed to suit Jacques St. Cyr perfectly.

The wealthy French collector had offered Joanna her first job and helped her through the lean years after her training, but she had finally needed to stand on her own two feet. Despite his protests, she had relocated here to this cottage and put out word that she was available for independent appraisals.

At first other collectors had been wary. Her prior connection with St. Cyr was well known, and Jacques was not an easy man to like. He rarely walked away from an auction without the prize, and he flaunted his victories on every possible occasion. He was irascible, supercilious, and unforgiving. But he was also *right* most of the time, and he had taught Joanna things she could never have learned in an academic setting.

Across the sunny floor, Winston pushed a toy truck filled with sunflower seeds toward Joanna. A potted lavender plant swayed perilously as he passed, and the air filled with pungent fragrance.

"Heel, Winston."

The rabbit's ears twitched. He stopped to sniff at a pile of mail dropped through the letter chute. As the pile toppled, Joanna saw an envelope bearing Jacques's distinctive scrawl. She hesitated for a moment, then tore it open.

Two sheets were folded inside. The first carried five words.

"Come back. Name your price."

Attached was a check made out to Joanna. The amount was left blank.

Joanna's hands began to shake with anger. How typically high-handed of Jacques, who coolly assumed that money was the answer to all problems. Maybe it was for him.

When the phone rang, Joanna caught it up irritably. "Yes?"

"Joanna, it's Nigel."

"Oh. Sorry. Nothing's wrong about tonight, is there? Not a cancellation, I hope."

"Never fear, everything is go. I just wanted to be certain you got my message."

"If Winston doesn't trash another pot, I'll go dress right now."

Nigel laughed. He was a big, dark bear of a man, as hard outside as he was marshmallow-soft inside. He had been Joanna's friend, supporter, and business partner for nearly two years now.

But he had never been more than that, which was exactly what Joanna wanted.

"Shall I come by and pick you up?" Nigel asked.

"Why? It's only a few miles to Greywood."

"These last few days you've seemed restless. Not your usual self. If it's money that's bothering you, maybe I can help."

"Nigel, I—"

"Just hear me out, all right? I know you've got big expenses right now. I also know that you're doing well but not *that* well in your appraisal work. St. Cyr's lingering influence, no doubt. I could manage a loan for a month or two."

Joanna felt a burning behind her eyes. "Nigel, you don't have to—"

"I *want* to. I owe you for all you've done for our group. I'm not silly enough to think it's my doing that we're in such demand. We were nothing until you took us in hand and badgered us into doing our best work."

Joanna blinked back tears. Winston was perched beside an armchair, looking at her curiously. She thought about last month's unexpected bills and the new equipment she needed to upgrade her studio. She thought about the skyrocketing price of precious metals used in her work. "I'll be fine, Nigel. I've got four swords to finish, and three new boxes came in today. Sometimes I wonder if I'll ever catch up."

"Quality, not quantity, remember? That's what you tell me when I'm gnashing my teeth."

"True."

The Welshman laughed darkly. "By the way, have you heard the news? The absentee landlord of Greywood has returned in full splendor. It appears he'll be on hand tonight for our performance. Quite an honor, since no one has seen him here for months."

Joanna watched Winston bite off a lavender shoot. So the earl of Greywood was back, was he? Maybe she should ask him for a look at that portrait of the claymore. The worst he could do was say no.

Then she could hold him at sword point and threaten to carve him into little pieces.

Or maybe she could just sic Winston on him.

"Who is this man? These titles can be so confusing."

"Alex Turov Cameron."

Joanna put down the carrot she had been holding. "Did you say . . . Turov? As in Alexei Turov?"

"Know him, do you?"

"Not exactly. But *he* is the earl of Greywood? I don't understand."

"His father died quite suddenly. Two years ago, I think it was. His mother was a pure-blood Gypsy from somewhere near Russia. An unusual background."

Alexei.

Joanna swallowed hard. There was a crack in the polished floor. Somehow she couldn't take her eyes away from it, even when the ringing in her head grew louder and louder until she thought she would scream.

Alexei. No, not here. Not tonight.

"Joanna, is something wrong?"

"Wrong?" She frowned. "Why should there be?"

"You sounded odd, that's all."

After all these years. Tonight he would be at Greywood, a few short yards away. Close enough for me to see, to touch.

Joanna's hands tightened. She could handle a casual meeting. Five years was a long time after all.

Nigel cleared his throat. "Joanna, are you sure?"

"I'm sure. See you at nine, Nigel."

She hung up blindly. Winston had blurred to a white streak.

Her hands trembled as she sank back against the cold glass window.

Tonight. After all these years.

"What in heaven am I going to do now?" she whispered.

3

ALEX CAMERON braced a broad shoulder at the mullioned window, watching crimson streaks stain the western sky. Daimlers, Bentleys, and Jaguars purred up the drive, disgorging women with too many diamonds and men with too much groomed hair, their laughter drifting up through the night.

He scowled.

"You need help with bow tie, Alexei?"

"What I need is my head examined. Why did I agree to host this event, Dimitri?" He watched another limousine nose up the circular drive.

"Examine head? What is this? For size of hat maybe?"

"Never mind." The curtains lifted around Alex, caught in a current of wind. "Is the security team in place?"

"For one hour already. You wish to speak to chief?"

Alex's eyes moved restlessly over the arriving guests. "In a few minutes. Are the scenery pieces and lights in place?"

His old friend nodded.

Another car spilled out another sleek pair of visitors. "I guess I'd better go." Frowning, Alex pushed away from the window and slid the ends of his black satin tie expertly into place.

"You worry about exhibition, no?"

Alex smiled grimly. "Only every second. But it would

44

take a fool on Halcyon to target this place now that it's as heavily guarded as Fort Knox."

Dimitri frowned. "Halcyon? And Knox—what is this thing?"

"The place where the Americans stow their gold."

"Ah, yes, gold. Now I understand this Knox. But if you worry, why do you make such a night for people to visit?"

Alex's eyes narrowed. "Because I'd rather have my enemies out in the open where I can see them. All week my instincts have been whispering, Dimitri. I'm certain they will be here tonight."

"They?"

"The ones who stole the replica." Alex smoothed the bow tie into place, then snapped on a pair of beaten gold cuff links that had belonged to his father. "They'll be back. They won't be able to resist a second crack at my safe." Alex's sharp eyes swept the lawns. "And if they're here, I'll know it."

"Ah." The word slid from Dimitri in a whisper. "The gift, it works tonight?"

"It works," Alex said tightly. Even as he spoke, the tingle of awareness crawled up his neck and tightened his shoulders. He recognized the warning stab of danger, a primal, blood-deep scream of the senses learned long ago in an icy forest while a knife nudged his neck.

He had won then, a skinny boy who learned to obey an instinct of danger.

He would win again tonight, Alex swore.

They were out there somewhere. His Gypsy vision never stirred unless the danger was very close. The gift was nearly as old as he was, part of the blood heritage of his mother's people. It came sometimes as a sharp pain in the chest, other times as a blur of shadow rising at the edge of his vision.

Right now, there was no mistaking the edgy, driven feeling that made Alex as tense as a hungry wolf on very thin ice. And tonight he would track that feeling to its source.

He did not move from the window, wise enough to let

the instinct take its own shape. He neither coaxed nor courted the old knowledge that came burning up from his blood. He simply allowed it until the certainty of danger screamed and pumped in every vein.

Here. Definitely here.

"You wear gun?"

"Not tonight. Destroys the lines of the tuxedo."

Dimitri snorted. "Not to joke about this, Alexei. Is too dangerous for joking."

"It's not a joke. All I need are my two hands."

"But why——"

Abruptly, Alex stiffened at the window. "Who is *that?*"

Dimitri bent forward, studying the shadowed courtyard. A slender figure in midnight-blue silk moved along the flagstone path toward the gardens. Her hair glinted honey gold in the light of hundreds of lanterns hung from the trees, and she walked with the controlled grace of a dancer. It was that power that had caught Alex's eye and continued to hold Dimitri's now. "I do not know this one. A pity, I am thinking."

"A very great pity." Alex saw the glint of crystal. She was holding a glass, but she was not drinking and her eyes were on the house instead of the other guests. The tension working through his gut increased. "I want a complete rundown on her, Dimitri," he ordered. "Find out her name and who she works for. I want to know where she lives, how much she earns, and who she's currently involved with."

"Involved with?"

"Sleeping with," Alex said tightly.

"But how you know——"

"A woman as extraordinary as that is *bound* to be sleeping with someone." Alex kept his eyes on the window as he pulled on his jacket, then slid a flat black receiver into his breast pocket. "Tell Metcalfe to get on it right away."

"Is done soonest." Dimitri frowned as Alex strode toward the door. "But, Alexei, the security chief is below. He wants you to——"

Alex frowned. The old gift was burning into his mind and making his nerves tense. "He'll just have to wait."

Joanna could have sworn someone was watching her. She pushed past a row of flowering orange trees and snagged a goblet of champagne from a passing waiter, telling herself not to be an idiot. No one would be watching her in *this* crowd.

Greywood's broad lawns were filled with distinguished men and bejeweled women. The dresses were sleek, timeless creations by Chanel and Anouska Hempel and the jewels were strictly Bulgari or family heirloom.

Tonight no one was watching her. They were all waiting for their host to make an appearance.

A waiter in a jacket and a tartan kilt passed. His silver tray of Baccarat crystal rattled softly. Discreetly. Everything was discreet tonight. The air was warm, rich with designer perfume and confident laughter.

Probably Joanna was the only person here who wasn't feeling confident. Her hands were shaking and her throat was dry.

Nigel loomed out of the twilight. "Glad to see you made it."

"Right on time." Joanna made sure her hand was steady before she lifted her glass. "To you, Nigel." She smiled tightly. "Here's to good friends and fine swords."

"Fine enough for me." The Welshman raised his glass and drank slowly. One brow rose. "Roederer Cristal, no less. Damned smooth. You've got to admit, the earl of Greywood knows how to throw a party."

Joanna watched a London collector argue with a Saudi prince while the publisher of a German art magazine took discreet notes. Nearby a French rock star with a shaved head checked possible purchases in a catalog of rare Winchester rifles. Lights burned in dozens of mullioned windows, illuminating Greywood's graceful stone towers and arched turrets. Candles flickered along the broad front drive leading up to the massive stone steps.

Maybe the legends about the house *are* true, Joanna

thought. Elizabeth I was said to have visited secretly whenever the intrigues of court grew too burdensome, and it was whispered that Mary, Queen of Scots, had arranged a clandestine visit to Greywood in hopes of negotiating a truce with her cousin.

Through all the succeeding centuries, Greywood remained as it had always been: intimate, exquisite, and full of legends.

"Don't look now," Nigel said tightly. "I think Hunsford's seen us." The Welshman snorted as a short man with gray hair strode toward them. "Time for me to go check some scenery."

"Chicken," Joanna muttered.

"Joanna, dear, how *are* you?" James Everington Hunsford was pushing fifty and desperately trying to look thirty. The signs of repeated cosmetic surgery were definitely beginning to show. The director of the largest museum of antique arms in the British Isles, Hunsford knew every public and private collection of swords and fine guns—along with a few illicit ones. As he kissed Joanna's cheek, he managed to scowl at Nigel's retreating back. "Where's Llewelyn going?"

"Er—work."

"Really. I can't stand *him,* either. But you're looking lovely as ever, my dear. Blue quite becomes you."

Joanna raised a bare shoulder, and light shimmered over her midnight-blue gown. "Ever the diplomat, James."

"Not diplomatic enough." His patrician mouth thinned. "Why won't you come back to the museum, Joanna?"

"Because I don't want to do museum work full-time. Not even for you, James. Besides, I already have more conservation work than I can possibly finish this year."

Hunsford sniffed. "You're fast as they come and you know it. Any faster and you wouldn't be the best. Yet you find time for these other interests. Damned dangerous if you ask me."

Joanna smiled tightly. "Exacting, not dangerous. And I don't believe I *did* ask you, James."

Hunsford smoothed his Hermès tie. "I simply hate to see you waste your skills on pointless amusements, my dear."

"Pointless?" Joanna's eyes took on a blue-green glitter. "My amusements, as you call them, are every bit as educational as the cheerless displays in your museum. And people don't fall asleep when Nigel and I are working."

Hunsford swirled his champagne. "Only because they're hoping to see blood, my dear girl." His eyes narrowed. "Have you seen Greywood, by the way?"

"Greywood?"

"Our host, darling."

Joanna swallowed. "I don't think so." Her hand began to shake again and a knot of tension formed at her neck.

Alex.

Any second she expected to hear his low voice and feel the probe of his gray eyes. Why had she come here tonight?

Simple. You need the money and you love your work. Also because you can't let Nigel down.

Joanna took a slow breath and watched a lantern rock peacefully in a beech tree over her head. "Let's agree to disagree for once, shall we? It's far too lovely a night to waste arguing." Up the hill, light spilled from the gallery at the end of Greywood House. After downing generous amounts of champagne, caviar, and grilled salmon canapés, the jeweled throng would head for that spacious new wing, which contained one of the finest weapon collections in the world. All contributions from the evening's guests were earmarked for Lord Greywood's favorite charity, though no one seemed to know what that was.

With *this* setting, no one needed to know.

Hunsford pursed his thin lips. "I'm bloody glad that I don't have to handle the security tonight. There must be three hundred people here."

A stocky man with impassive features ambled past. Though he wore a dinner jacket, he carried no drink and his sharp eyes slid continually over the crowd.

Security, Joanna thought. The wealth of Scottish claymores, Renaissance fencing rapiers, and Viking swords on display up the hill made protection essential. Though few people had seen the Greywood Foundation collection, enough photographs had surfaced to hint that every piece was the very finest in its class. At any other time, Joanna would have been fighting for a glimpse.

Not tonight.

Tonight she was counting the minutes until she could leave. Tonight she would do everything possible to avoid the exhibition and the reclusive earl who had assembled it.

"Are you feeling quite the thing, Joanna?" James Hunsford frowned at her. "You've gone dead pale, my dear."

"It must be the shadows from these lanterns." Joanna forced herself to smile. "I'm fine, see?"

"Nerves, no doubt." Hunsford said coolly, one eye on the new arrivals. "Jacques coming tonight?"

"I wouldn't know."

"Really." Hunsford's lips pursed. "This is just the kind of event he loves. I thought you two were still close."

"I don't have access to his personal calendar, James."

"Maybe he won't show. The word is he and Greywood have been at each other's throats in every auction from here to Singapore." Hunsford's frown grew to a scowl. "Speaking of Greywood, where is the bloody man? You'd think he would condescend to make an appearance at his own party." Hunsford snared another glass of champagne from the tray of a passing waiter. "Then again, he is known to be rather strange."

"Strange?" Joanna's throat went dry and scratchy. "You—you've met him?"

"Two months ago. He brought in an exquisite Manton dueling pistol and offered to make a gift of it to the museum. Then he turned eccentric and refused to have his picture taken afterward."

"Modesty is not necessarily eccentric, James."

Hunsford frowned. "What does the fellow have to be

modest about? Besides, he's never come by to see how we displayed his donation."

Joanna decided it was just as well. The displays at Hunsford's museum were not exactly known for their artistry.

"Look, enough of this small talk. What will it take to tempt you back, Joanna? Money? An international exhibition or two? Or do you want me to get down and beg? Go on, name your price."

Name your price. First Jacques, now Hunsford. "My decision is final, James. I like being my own boss too much to punch a time clock." Joanna glanced at her watch. "And now I have to go. Time to work."

"Real period weapons again?"

"Of course."

"Joanna, this is sheer madness. Why do you insist on using real pieces in these reenactments?"

"Because history *should* be real. Otherwise you might as well stay home and watch it on television."

Hunsford shook his head. "If Jacques were here, *he'd* talk some sense into you."

Joanna raised her chin. "Good night, James."

The flowers and the jewels and the silk gowns blurred as she made her way down the hill in search of Nigel, an ache growing steadily in her head.

Can't cancel now. Can't disappoint Nigel. Too much money at stake.

At the bottom of the lawn, Joanna sank back against a shadowed wall away from the laughter and the crowds. She massaged her neck, trying to forget everything but the performance.

Crosscut, parry, wait. Two beats, another parry, and then—

A branch rustled at her elbow.

She closed her eyes. "Go away, James. I won't change my mind."

"No, not James." The voice was faintly accented. "I saw you out here in the shadows. All alone, it would appear." A spray of peonies drifted up, caught in powerful hands. Shadows moved against the weathered wall, and Joanna's breath caught.

There could be no mistaking that keen, impatient gaze or the long dark hair held back by a leather thong.

Alexei.

Suddenly the last five years shrank to seconds. Joanna's face burned in the darkness. She felt the stir of the wind along her bare shoulders and a cluster of warm petals above her cheek.

Every sense screamed in primal awareness of the man standing two feet away.

Alexei Turov Cameron, earl of Greywood.

"Hiding out, are you? Care for company?"

"I . . . need to be alone," Joanna rasped.

He moved closer, his face still in shadow. "That would be a pity." He held out a bottle of champagne. "It was a very good year, and I'm prepared to share, you see." His smile was smooth, as flawless as an English lake at dawn.

Joanna swallowed hard. "It's not polite to filch the host's champagne."

"It's allowed in this case." He tugged two perfect crystal flutes from his pockets. "The fact is, it's my party." His voice was silky, confidential, as if he were including her in an intimate secret. "Join me?"

"Not champagne."

"Then I'll get a Château Lafite. Or maybe you'd prefer a Château d'Yquem '55."

"No more wine." Joanna shook her head, fighting to stay calm. He wouldn't know her, not after all this time. She had changed dramatically after all.

His eyes narrowed as he eased the cork with expert skill from the vintage champagne, swirled a small amount into one glass, then held it out. "Go on, try a little. I hate to drink alone."

You don't have to drink alone, she wanted to scream. *Any woman here would kill to drink with you. So why me?*

The cool glass met her hand, but she couldn't seem to pay attention. Her muscles wouldn't grip; her fingers wouldn't close.

The crystal plummeted to the flagstone and shattered into a thousand tiny shards of light.

"Oh, God." Joanna caught a ragged breath and sank down, reaching for the broken Baccarat goblet. Something pricked her skin, and she felt blood on her palm.

"Leave it." Long fingers closed over hers. "There's no need to bother. I have another right here."

"No. N-not for me." Up the hill a clock tolled the first deep stroke of nine and Joanna pushed blindly to her feet. "I have to go." She moved forward and found Alexei blocking her way.

"You've cut yourself," he said sharply.

"I'm fine."

"Then why are you shaking?"

She forced herself to meet his gaze. "I always shake before I work. Shaking is good, in fact. Nerves are part of how I prepare."

"For what, the guillotine?"

"For a performance."

Something crossed his face. Speculation perhaps? Or was it surprise? Joanna wondered.

"You're performing tonight?"

She stiffened. "Is something wrong with that?"

"Not at all." His gaze swept her sensuous silk gown. "I didn't realize you could fight in a dress like that, however."

"I won't be wearing silk. It wouldn't be authentic for the period or the role."

"You pay attention to authenticity. Excellent. In fact, I'm beginning to wonder what I've been missing."

"Hoping to see blood?"

His gaze didn't waver. "Will I?"

"Not if I can help it." Joanna spun around, trying to ignore the pain in her throat. Alexei Cameron was mere inches away from her, yet his eyes had the bland curiosity of a stranger.

He really *didn't* know her. For him the past was long buried. Tonight Joanna was just a face in the shadows, someone he was evaluating for a possible rendezvous.

Something cold and sharp dug at her chest. "I have to go." She turned toward the house.

Alex's fingers caught her wrist. "Not until you stop shaking." His thumb traced her palm, lingering over the callouses created by months of wielding heavy swords. "You have good hands. Strong hands." Again the surprise in his voice was unmistakable. "You work hard, don't you?"

"Hard enough." Joanna had never minded hard work, not when it was for something she loved.

Or for someone.

A white silk tent fluttered in the wind, casting shadows over Alexei's face. Joanna stared at him in shock, unable to believe she was here, unable to believe this was really happening. But the voice was unmistakable and the face was the same, only leaner now, with a polish that had not been there five years ago.

Harder, Joanna thought. *Colder, too. He moves like a shadow now, controlled and observant, never revealing his own secrets.*

She felt him studying her. "Who are you really?" she demanded. He would expect her to be curious, after all.

"Greywood." His fingers brushed the small tortoise-shell clips that held back her hair. Memories stirred, sharp with color and mist and crushed flowers. "Earl of. Your most devoted host." There was a twist to his smile as he said the words. "And for some reason I can't quite name, you take my breath away."

Joanna's heart began to pound. Any moment he would turn her face into the light and stiffen in recognition. *"Don't.* I don't like games."

"It is no game. You are a singularly beautiful woman and you move like a dancer. Ballet?"

Joanna smiled grimly. "Swords."

"Ah, of course. But I keep asking myself why you look so nervous."

"It's late. My partner is waiting."

"Is that an answer?"

The only one you're going to get, Joanna thought.

"He—he'll be worried." She pulled away, only to feel the wall at her back.

Gray eyes probed her face. "I don't think I believe you."

"I don't care what you believe, Mr—Whatever."

"Alex Cameron." The last of the slow chimes died away into silence. "I don't always choose to use my title." His fingers moved lightly over her hand. "You're trembling again."

"Hardly surprising. I didn't exactly expect to perform for the lord of the manor tonight."

His eyes narrowed. "I wonder."

Joanna forced her voice to stay steady. "Don't. There's nothing to wonder about. I'm just a boring person with a boring past who leads a very boring life."

"Boring? You wield antique swords. Your hands are covered by callouses." He laughed softly, studying her palm. "If you're boring, I'm not sure I want to know your definition of *exciting.*"

It isn't this, Joanna thought wildly. *This is horrible.* This left her trembling, sick to her stomach. She hated deception and intrigue, yet most of her life had turned into a lie, she realized. Maybe that happened when you ran away from something long enough.

She pulled free of his fingers. This time he didn't fight her. "And I *don't* care to be mauled, Mr. Cameron."

"Oh, if I were intent on mauling you, you'd know it, Ms. Russell. I wouldn't have let you go just now." The words were silken, their challenge openly sensual. "And I don't think you would have been fighting me."

"How did you know my name?"

"Does that bother you?"

"You didn't answer my question."

His smile was a blur against the darkness. "You're right, I didn't. You should always wear that shade of blue. It's cool, like your voice, but it hints at great depths. I wonder if it matches your eyes."

Joanna stood frozen, awkward and flushed. She felt the cool probe of his eyes and the tension of his shoulders. She had known that one day she would see him again, staring out from the pages of a newspaper or across a crowded auction floor.

But not like this. *Never* like this.

She swallowed hard and tried to move past him. "I told you I don't like games, Mr. Cameron."

He captured her other wrist. "Neither do I." His voice was suddenly hard.

"Then why do you play them so well?"

"Let's see exactly how well I play."

He moved forward, edging her toward the wall. Joanna's pulse began to hammer. "N-nigel is waiting."

Cameron's lips found the pulse racing at her wrist. "Let him wait. We've got more important things to do."

"I'm—not interested."

"I'm interested enough for two."

Joanna stood desperately, engulfed in memories. Moonlight dappled his long hair, and she wondered how the thick strands would feel tangled beneath her fingers, how his mouth would taste under hers, dusky with champagne.

Suddenly there was too much heat, and her head screamed with questions she had no right to ask. "L-let me go. I'll be late," she said raggedly. "You'll disappoint your guests."

"They can wait, too," Alex said harshly. There was a sudden tension in his hands, locked against hers. "Have we met before? In Hong Kong perhaps, at the Mandarin? Or was it Bangkok?"

Joanna felt a sliver of pain at her chest. *Too close,* she thought wildly. *Any minute he will know.*

His fingers tightened. "Well?"

She shrugged. "You collect old swords and I repair them. That's a fairly small world, Mr. Cameron."

"Perhaps." His eyes narrowed. "Perhaps." Slowly, he brushed a moonlit strand of hair from her shoulder, just skimming her cheek. "Still . . ." He frowned. "I'm surprised that Jacques St. Cyr let you come tonight. He's maligning me to anyone who will listen."

"What does that have to do with me?"

"You worked for him, I believe. He's not a man who releases people easily."

"Jacques doesn't dictate my life."

"No?" he said coolly.

Joanna stared at him, anger replacing the fear. "You'd better find a new source for your information, because you're two years out-of-date. I work on my own now. Who I consult for and where I do it are my own business."

He didn't move, as still as the darkness. "Why did you leave him?"

"Why don't you ask Jacques St. Cyr?"

Shadows passed over his face. "I might at that." His jaw hardened. He murmured a word that Joanna didn't understand, then released her hand abruptly. "But as you say, you will be late. My questions will wait."

As she turned, Joanna heard him whisper, "But only until midnight. Then I will certainly find you."

4

ALEXEI CAMERON flexed his hands, feeling electricity race up his spine. With any other woman, he would have said that what he felt was pure sexual attraction.

But not with this one. With her, it was something purer—yet also darker. It was cool and elusive, like moon shadows running beneath swift midnight clouds. Her touch had made his body harden, hungry for much more. And for one instant, he'd tasted something else, keen and fragile, as sharp as a cry in the darkness.

Whether pain or fear, he could not say. Maybe it was both.

Alex cursed softly, watching Joanna Russell disappear into the crowd. Her hair was a heavy fall of cinnamon and honey. Her face was too pale and her shoulders too stiff.

And yet his body ached, heavy with desire.

Insanity, Alexei.

Her name had been familiar once he had asked Hunsford who she was.

Joanna Russell, former chief curator for Jacques St. Cyr. She was an expert at caring for his collection and probably warming his bed. She might even be an "intimate friend" of James Hunsford and several other collectors present tonight. Relationships were casual and nonexclusive among the art set, where anything could be called upon to sweeten a deal.

The knowledge did nothing to dim the hunger Alex

felt. Even now his hands ached to press her to the cold wall and explore the soft curve of her mouth. He wanted to tug her hair free of its clips and make her tremble.

With desire, not fear.

Then you are the blind son of a Ukrainian pig farmer, he thought in disgust. Any woman who worked for a man like St. Cyr would be perfectly trained. She would smile and tease and tantalize. That facade of innocence and vulnerability would be her very best weapon.

All of this Alex knew. And still he wanted her.

He cursed as he turned toward the house. There were too many strangers here, creating too many risks. Greywood did not feel like home tonight. Instead it reminded him of a cold spring night twelve years ago when he had returned with his mother from Estavia. Then, too, he had felt like an outsider, captive in a house full of strangers.

He nodded at two consular officials and noted the security team moving unobtrusively through the crowd. His eyes narrowed as he let his inner vision open, empty and still, waiting for the jab at his spine or the chill at his neck.

Nothing.

No matter. He would let his enemies come to *him.* His gift would make them easy to recognize.

Jacques St. Cyr had managed to hurt him for the very last time. If it was war the man wanted, it was war he would have. But their battle would be man to man, not played out in the bed of a scheming woman trained and tutored by St. Cyr.

Up the hill, the flicker of lights announced the performance was about to begin. Alex watched the crowd assemble, eager to see the reenactment. When Samantha Vail appeared behind him, her full curves poured into a column of silk that showed every detail, he let her slide against his shoulder and pull him toward the lighted stage.

But all the time he was thinking about a woman with cinnamon hair and shadows at the edge of her mind.

* * *

Joanna stood tensely, watching Nigel straighten a
floodlight. She tried not to notice the redhead in the
skimpy chemise who was pouring herself all over Alex
Cameron.

"You OK?" Nigel was already dressed in a heavy
padded shirt. He tugged on a coarse linen vest while he
studied Joanna's face.

Hardly. She was angry and restless and confused. Her
head had begun to throb, and her hands were still
trembling from her encounter with Alex.

"Joanna?"

"I'm *fine*. Don't forget the new ending, Nigel."

"It's burned into my brain. Or maybe I should say
carved with a *very* sharp point."

"No jokes, Nigel. And no improvisation. I don't want
any mistakes tonight." Joanna ducked behind a curtain
that doubled as a makeshift dressing room and tugged
on a homespun blouse and long wool skirt.

"Fine with me. By the way, someone dropped off this
package for you. He said you'd know what it was for."
Nigel fingered a plain manila envelope. "I was rather
hoping it might be our fee. How lovely to get paid on
time for a change."

Joanna slid open the glued flap and pulled out a blank
sheet of paper. "This one's blank." Under the top sheet
was a thicker sheet, the kind of contact sheet a photogra-
pher made before developing single prints from a roll.
Joanna frowned down at the small, blurry shots.

"What is it?"

"Some kind of prints. Whoever took them had a
rotten camera." She made out blurred lights and what
might have been a figure standing in water. She glanced
at the next row of prints.

An arm.

A leg.

White skin feathered in mist. Then a man's back. A
man's hands rising to damp, sleek hair.

The ground swayed. Suddenly the air slammed out of
Joanna's chest.

"Joanna?"

She couldn't breathe. Dear God, someone knew. Someone had seen that night. The knowledge burned through her head as her eyes moved to the next row of pictures. This time her own face registered, dim but visible beside a man's powerful shoulders.

In the next photo, he eased down against her. His hands were opened, peeling back fragile nylon straps.

Alexei Cameron. Kissing her. Touching her. Bringing her to searing passion in the darkness beneath a tropical moon.

Shivering, Joanna crammed the sheets back into the envelope and shoved everything into her leather bag.

"Joanna, what is it?"

Her breath came hot and sharp. Someone had seen. He was here tonight, watching. Waiting.

"Damn it, Joanna—"

"Just jitters. I—I need to warm up." Her hands were not quite steady as she gave an experimental lunge with a perfectly balanced French rapier. Outside, beyond the painted wooden backdrop of oak trees and a Scottish castle, came the first hammer of applause. "You'd better go." Joanna forced herself to smile.

"Are you sure? I could always run the juggling routine first if you need more time."

"Go."

He gave her a thumbs up sign, then strode out beneath the lights. Joanna watched in numb horror, thinking about her face captured in grainy textures of black and white. About her fingers plunged into wet dark hair while her arms pressed over a wet, muscled back.

Alexei Cameron's back.

The contact had not been degrading. The press of their skin had been neither swift nor crude. But the pictures captured their own reality, coldly explicit.

She crossed her hands blindly over her chest, trying to stop the shaking. Dear God, who had sent these? Who knew?

The clapping faded, and Nigel began to speak. Joanna blinked, hearing nothing, blinded by memories of a night of passion five years before.

She had seen him first at a forge. His chest was glistening and bare as he worked on a glowing piece of steel. Beside him stood an older man who murmured advice in a rich, rough language.

The Gypsy swordmaker had not noticed her or anyone else. His focus had been only for the movement of the fire and the blade drawn into shape inch by inch beneath his powerful fingers.

And every stroke as he bent to the hot steel was that of a lover, coaxing and hungry, full of intimate secrets. He murmured and whispered and urged, close to the fire, his whole being riveted to the glowing blade. When his hand touched the flames, he scarcely seemed to notice. Only when the old man whispered tensely did he pull away, looking down in surprise.

Joanna lost her heart to him in those fierce moments of inspiration while his dedication burned clear and absolute and his body strained in the terrible effort of creation.

And she doubted he even knew she existed.

There were too many others thronged around him, collectors and scholars and reporters. A dozen admiring women waited to make his acquaintance.

They, too, were ignored.

Sweat beaded his high cheekbones, matting the long hair brushing his shoulders. His gaze filled with passion as he measured and goaded the glowing steel, never content with anything less than the straightest edge and finest curve.

The blade that Alexei Turov and Constantin Stevanov finished that day was a piece of history, a glinting match of art and cold purpose. The demonstration had been electrifying, for few possessed the old skills that Constantin had passed down to his Gypsy apprentice. Joanna smiled as six-figure bids rained down for the sword, and her smile grew as each was curtly rejected by Alexei. His eyes were hot as the embers when he finished the last edge and threw a towel over one sweaty shoulder.

He rubbed the knotted muscles at his neck. Completely oblivious to his audience, he did a slow stretch, his eyes on the rolling breakers. Joanna could see the restlessness that ate at him, at war with the exhaustion that followed creation. She knew the feeling well, for it gripped her, too, whenever she finished a demanding piece of restoration.

The old man nodded, finally satisfied. The smile that lit Alexei Turov's face had carried Joanna's breath away. Lovingly he wrapped the sword in a length of green velvet tied with black silk bands. Each stroke was slow and caressing, like a lover's touch.

Joanna had stood frozen, watching his hands, wondering how those same strokes would feel slanted over naked skin. Her naked skin, while she trembled beneath him.

Desire rocked her, unexpected and fierce. She who trusted no man wanted to trust this one. She who had tasted no desire in long years wanted to find it in this man's arms.

Their eyes met. He probed her face while her heart raced and heat filled her cheeks. Had he seen the single tear that crept down her cheek, won in admiration of his skill?

Probably not.

He turned without a word, cradling the sword beneath his arm even as a woman in Chanel and black pearls moved toward him, her lips glistening and her eyes on his muscled chest. She whispered a low phrase, one polished nail sliding along his arm.

He shook his head, shrugging, then carefully helped the old man up the twisting path to their bungalow.

The woman frowned, shaking the heavy coin bracelet at her well-tanned wrist.

Alexei Turov didn't look back, his face a mask, his eyes a thousand years old.

It seemed to Joanna then that he had no heart. Or perhaps whatever heart he had was already pledged to the way of the sword and the endless, devouring needs of its steel. No woman could hope to match that heat.

A second tear crawled slowly down her cheek that it should be so . . .

"We are here tonight for one reason, and that is to celebrate a sword."

Nigel Llewelyn's dark gaze bored into his silent audience. The lights dropped, pooling him in a single spotlight. "A weapon forged in a braver age when men still knew how to dream. Legends cling to that sword still, linking its power to Elizabeth I and to the unhappy Queen Mary. I speak of the Cameron claymore."

There was a ripple of sound as he raised his arm. "No, the sword you see in my hands is *not* the Cameron claymore." He swung the heavy blade, parrying as he spoke. "No one knows where that priceless blade lies hidden. But the sword I hold before you is nearly as heavy, and its blade is sharp and true. So you shall now see."

He held up a Celtic cross on a silk ribbon, letting light play over the etched silver. Then in one sharp stroke, he slashed the ribbon neatly in two.

A gasp ripped through the audience, and Nigel bowed deeply. "Now our performance shall begin. But remember, what you see is far *more* than a performance because the swords we use are real. Dangerously real."

Suddenly the night was hushed.

The three hundred guests grew very still, realizing there would be no room for error in the movements they were about to witness.

Alex's hands tensed. What was the bloody fool doing with a *real* blade? The point was obviously razor sharp.

No one had told him that the performance would include *real* weapons!

He felt his hands go cold and clammy. He was too experienced with swords not to know the risks they took.

The risks that *she* took.

One slip. One mistimed turn on a downthrust . . .

Frowning, he started through the hushed crowd, ready to call off the event. But the big Welshman was moving, and the lights had dimmed. Alex's words were drowned out beneath a wave of pounding applause.

The deadly performance had begun.

5

"One person."

Nigel paused for effect, raising the point of his heavy sword. *"One* person knew all the secrets of the Cameron sword." With the point of his sword, he swept an arc before the silent audience. "During her years of captivity Mary Stuart kept the sword with her always. Some say she believed it was her magical talisman, the source of her power. So why did she let it go? Was she convinced to release it as part of a plot to betray her? Did she then call down a curse upon claymore and scabbard to be carried into eternity?"

Nigel's deep voice rolled over the rapt crowd. There were no more whispers, no more clinks of glass. "Or was the sword to be put to her own use, part of a dark political design? Only a few of you will know the significance of this night, which is the anniversary of Mary Stuart's arrival at Greywood House. Two days later she was taken to Draycott Abbey as a prisoner. None among us can know exactly what befell her at the abbey or how the sword came to be taken from her there." Nigel's hand rose dramatically. "But perhaps the story began something like this."

To his left, mist swirled out of the darkness and climbed toward the painted castle. Somewhere a wolf howled, the sound shrill with hunger. As the lonely cry lingered, two men moved out of the shadows. With the same wary care of the wolves that hunted by night, they crept toward the crest of the hill, where a woman tended a brass pot atop a roaring fire.

The woman's features were hidden by her hood. She did not look up as the men inched closer.

"Here's a rich surprise," the taller man growled. "First we'll have food, and then we'll take pleasure in something sweeter." His companion laughed as mist coiled around them.

At that moment their prey spun about, a long claymore in her hand, pulled from the folds of her skirt. The hilt was gold, and a dragon curled over the pommel.

"The Cameron claymore," the men whispered as one. Their eyes narrowed with greed as they watched firelight dance over the great blade.

"Sharp enough to set you to the run," the woman hissed.

"Careful, m'lady. One misstep and ye'll find the blade at yer own throat."

Their laughter faded. The sword's first blow slashed the tall man across the leg and sent him cursing to the ground. Another jab drove his stocky companion back out of reach. Then they separated, circling in different directions.

"Yer cannot protect both sides at once, woman. An' mayhap I have a warmer blade for yer to fondle. Especially since that granite-faced laird of yers will no more return, not from the cold hills of death."

"Nay! My husband still lives."

"Angus Cameron is dead. He fell with the rest of his kind, wearing his woolen cloth around him in death. Now there's none to protect ye, my fine lady. And *none* to protect that sword you're holding."

The great blade quivered in the woman's hands. "Liar."

"The swordmaker is dead. We saw him fall. The cursed Scottish queen he served will never hold the English throne."

The woman's eyes glistened. "Nay! The laird yet lives. His blade would tell me were he gone. Run away and join your coward's pack before he returns."

For a moment it seemed as if her words would send them back into the shadows. Then her hood fell back and her hair spilled free, cinnamon and copper in the moonlight.

"I'll have her, by God. And I'll have the Cameron blade along with her. Our English queen desires it above all things, they say."

The tall man charged, and the claymore drew level. Its keen tip shimmered, then caught the brawny attacker's weight. But the point swung down, deflected by the padded vest of leather covering the man's chest. In an instant his scarred hands circled the woman's neck, driving the air from her throat.

"There will be no more treason plotted here by Camerons, no more messages carried north to filthy traitors. We'll see the Cameron line ended this night," he said savagely.

"I wish you joy of your effort." The woman's laughter was wild. She slid a smaller blade from her sleeve, a narrow thrusting dagger with a damascened hilt that flashed upward just as her captor swung his own sword down in attack.

Suddenly, a shadow fell across the mist. A broad-boned man draped in bright red plaid lunged between the two fighters. His fist flashed out.

Bone cracked on bone, and the big attacker fell with a curse. As his companion retreated, the woman spun about, wreathed in mist. "Angus! Is it truly you?"

"True as life." Her husband's legs were dark with mud, and his face was lined with exhaustion, but he grinned broadly. "You're a sight, Meg, a fair sight indeed. And you have the sword! God's blessings on you for that, my love." His face darkened. "But I canna stay. No matter how I would wish."

"You're off again so soon?"

"I must," he said grimly. "We were betrayed, Meg. First in London, now by someone at the abbey." He slung down a muddied saddlebag. "I must be away before they find I've escaped their net. I'm bound for London to see the English queen and demand an audience. I'll force her to hear my message even if I die to see it done."

His wife swayed, arms upraised. "Nay. She'll have you run down like a dog for your insolence. You canna go, Angus!"

"The choice is not mine." Her husband caught up the great claymore and studied its bright length. "Aye, the secrets are hidden well."

"What riddles are you speaking, my love?"

His face hardened. "Nothing, Meg. I must go. By staying, I only bring you more danger." He studied his wife in agonized silence, then turned away. A moment later only his shadow was left upon the cold mist.

As his wife watched in despair, her attacker roused at her feet. He cursed, then staggered up with a grunt. A moment later, his sword plunged high in search of warm flesh.

But his victim moved quickly, freeing a dagger from its hiding place at her waist. Blade met blade, and the clang of steel filled the night. Lights glinted off the polished blades as the audience watched spellbound. Each movement was swift, beautifully choreographed, and perfectly timed. Back and forth the two figures moved, silhouetted against the bright lights, steel against steel in a battle to the death.

Only someone standing very close would have seen the woman hesitate, swaying slightly before she sent her blade down onto her opponent's wool sleeve.

He staggered, bellowing in shock and anger. And then he fell.

A ripple of surprise ran through the crowd and the lights—a pair of very modern mercury vapor lights—cut into darkness, accompanied by the wild thunder of applause.

As the applause boomed around her, Joanna stood frozen, her hands clenched at her side.

"Damn it, Joanna, you've slashed the hell out of my costume." Nigel groaned as he stood up and rubbed his arm. "Why did you hesitate before that last parry?"

Angus Cameron's "widow" shoved off her hooded

cloak and bent down to examine his hand. "My—my timing was off. Sorry, Nigel. Maybe we'd better go back to using those wooden stage weapons you found in London," she said tightly.

"Joanna, what's wrong? Your timing's *never* off."

"Go and change. I'll pack up here."

"Blast it, Joanna, what is it?"

"I was off, that's all. Just—off. Leave it alone, Nigel."

The Welshman touched her arm. "It's Greywood, isn't it? You were watching him when you should have been watching me. It was just the same for him. Even when Jacques St. Cyr moved beside him, Greywood didn't notice."

"No," Joanna whispered. Panic burned through her chest.

"He couldn't pull his eyes away. His redhead wasn't well pleased either. Be glad she didn't have a sword handy." His eyes narrowed. "What's going on between you?"

"Nothing. I've never met Lord Greywood until tonight." That was true at least. "Now get going, will you?" Joanna forced a smile. "Take care of that hand."

The Welshman rubbed his jaw uncertainly. "But—"

"*Go.*"

"I'm going, I'm going."

Joanna held her smile right up until Nigel disappeared into the darkness where the path rose toward the gatehouse. Then she sank back against a metal stage case. Her face was ashen as she peeled back her woolen sleeve and looked down.

A jagged wound crossed her forearm, and her wrist was dark with blood. She shuddered, closing her eyes and biting back a sob. *You were watching him when you should have been watching me.*

Nigel was right. She had been painfully aware of Alex's presence just beyond the stage. Even against the glare of the lights, she had seen his beautiful companion draped all over him.

Joanna hadn't been able to pull her eyes away. Not

even when tears had pricked at her eyelids. Not even when Nigel's blade had slit her skin.

She clutched her arm, her body braced against the heavy metal case. Alex had been dangerous before, a threat to all she had planned and worked for, but she would not let him threaten her life again. She would be careful this time. Calm and logical the way she hadn't been five years ago.

Alexei had learned how to lock away his heart. Now Joanna would do the same.

She would be long gone before he came back. There would be no sharp questions and no blurted answers to raise his suspicions.

She stood up slowly, wincing as she searched for her bag in the darkness.

Mustn't let him find the pictures. Hide them. Maybe burn them.

As if that would protect her.

Wild laughter pressed at her lips. Whoever had sent the contact sheet would have more, along with the damning negatives.

Pain and shame mocked from the shadows, and she swayed, one hand to her lips. The world seemed to close in around her.

Then she heard angry footsteps hammer over the stage behind her.

6

"You little fool! What possessed you to use *real* weapons?" Alex strode over the stage and caught Joanna's shoulder. "Answer me, damn it!"

Joanna snapped around, fighting back panic at the sight of his angry features. "I—I told you we were authentic, Mr. Cameron."

"That's not authenticity, that's lunacy."

She couldn't take this now. Not from him. "Save the critique." Her jaw clenched with pain. "I was about to dress and I'd like some privacy."

"Forget the privacy. Your timing was off with that last move, and I want to know why."

Dear God, had he seen it, too? She had been so sure only Nigel would notice.

Furtively she slid down her sleeve. "A new stage, different placement of lights." She shrugged. "It happens."

Alex's eyes narrowed. "Don't move."

"Why?"

"Because . . . you're hurt."

"What makes you think . . ."

He ignored her. "Give me your arm."

"Go polish a sword," Joanna said through gritted teeth. She had no more strength for pretense. She fought a wave of pain. *Not now. Can't let Alex see . . .*

He caught her as she swayed, then ran a quick, impersonal hand over her body in the darkness.

"Taking—advantage of me, Mr. Cameron?"

"When I take advantage of you, you'll know it, Ms. Russell. And you damn well won't be fighting me either." He continued his ruthless inspection, then cursed sharply, shoving back her sleeve. A dark stain spread over her forearm. "Damn it, I was right. You *are* hurt."

"N-no."

"Forget trying to hide it." His face was hard. "We're going to the house."

"There's no need." She forced her voice not to break. "It's just a nick."

"Like hell it is." Alex pulled a fine lawn handkerchief from his pocket and pressed it over the welling blood. "Do you always cut your safety margins so damned close?"

Joanna shivered. "That's what the audience wants, Mr. Cameron."

"Alex," he said flatly.

She swallowed, her body tense. "Mr. Cameron," she said tightly.

"You could have been killed."

"Hardly. The scene is designed to look more dangerous than it is."

"Then what happened?"

"I was . . . tired."

Alex found the upper edge of the wound, and Joanna flinched. He muttered darkly, pressing the soft linen tighter. "Is that why you hesitated before your last parry?"

Clever man. *Too* clever. "I don't know what you mean."

"I *saw,* damn it. Something threw you off."

Joanna swallowed. "I have to change. Then the props need to be—"

"I want some answers, Ms. Russell. What happened out there?"

Memories happened. Two dozen stark, grainy photographs happened.

"Bad luck, I guess." Joanna pulled away, thankful for

the darkness that hid her shaking hands. "I was tired and I miscalculated. Now will you go away?"

"Like hell I will. No one is dying of blood loss on *my* property tonight."

"I don't plan on dying, I assure you." Her voice broke. She sank forward, halfway to the ground before she knew it.

Alex lifted her in his arms and began to run. "Can you hear me?"

Her head fell back against his shoulder, her hair spilling over his sleeve. "Want t' go home."

"Not now. You're going into shock." Alex took the shortest route to the house, skirting the stables to avoid curious guests. "Talk to me. How do you feel?"

Joanna frowned. The lanterns were dancing oddly. *Very* oddly. "Don't want to stay. Can't."

"Why? Other plans for the evening?"

Joanna roused herself from the thick, fluffy cotton that was wrapping itself around her head. "None o' your business."

"As of now, I'm making it my business."

Joanna shivered in a blur of pain and dizziness. There was a ringing in her ears. She gasped as he took the steps two at a time.

"Hurting again?" His hands tightened. "Hold me if it helps."

"No. Want to go." The stars were swaying drunkenly above her. "Feel . . . funny."

"Are you going to be sick?"

"D-dizzy." She didn't mention the searing pain in her arm or the cold climbing up her fingers. She turned her hand and discovered her palm was nearly numb.

"Bad, is it?" Again he seemed to pick the image from her mind.

Joanna felt hysteria well through her. After so long, this was *Alex*. She was in his arms, locked against his chest, one hand tangled in his dark hair.

And she was probably bleeding all over his elegant white shirt.

It had to be a nightmare.

As Alex turned the corner, a man with white hair and angry eyes moved to block the path. "Joanna, what are you doing?"

"Jacques?" Joanna blinked at the shadows, but all she could see was the blur of swaying lanterns.

"Has this man hurt you, Joanna?" Jacques St. Cyr's voice was hard with fury.

"Don't know." Joanna looked up at Alex. "Don't think so. Arm hurts." She shook her head. "Don't think he did it."

"What are you doing, Cameron?"

A muscle flashed at Alex's jaw. "What does it look like?"

"Taking advantage of a drunken female. Joanna, what has he done to you? How much did he make you drink?"

Alex's body tensed. "Get out of my way, St. Cyr. Can't you see she's hurt?"

"She's not hurt, she's drunk," St. Cyr said in disgust. "Your doing, no doubt. First you make her drink, then you seduce her. She's never had a stomach for liquor. *Par Dieu,* I should not have let her come here."

Joanna frowned. "Don't take orders from you, Jacques. Not for a long time."

"God, you can't even walk without falling. Look at the dirt all over your arm."

"That's blood. She cut her arm in her last lunge," Alex said savagely.

"Nonsense. Joanna *never* misses."

"She did tonight." Alex moved forward, only to be blocked again by St. Cyr.

"Why?" the Frenchman demanded.

"Ask her. Come back for a chat after the doctor has examined her arm."

"If you're lying about this just to get back at me, Cameron—"

"I don't give a damn about you, St. Cyr. Your trouble is that you see everything one way: how it affects you."

St. Cyr's face was pinched with anger. "You can't stand losing, can you? I've got something you want, and it's eating you up inside."

"Got what?" Joanna asked unsteadily. "Don't understand."

Alex snorted. "What you've *got,* St. Cyr, is a textbook case of paranoia."

"You won't say that next week. Not after you read the interview in *Fine Arts* magazine."

Alex pushed past him grimly. "Good-bye, St. Cyr. Call me when the paranoia's gone. Maybe in around twenty years."

"Joanna, I forbid you to stay here. Cameron knows what I've found, and he'll do anything to get back at me. Don't trust him."

Joanna frowned as the moon dipped and leapfrogged over the dark turrets on Greywood's roof. "No way to draw and quarter 'im. Not feeling so good just now."

"Damn it, Joanna, I *must* speak to you. It's important," Jacques hissed.

"Try tomorrow. Not the morning. Going to Oxford in the morning." Joanna nodded sagely. "X-Ray fluorescence anal'sis on a new blade."

"Devil take the fluorescence report!" Jacques slammed his fist against a serving table full of Baccarat crystal. "I will not permit you to stay here."

Alex laughed coldly. "You heard the lady, St. Cyr. Try her tomorrow. After Oxford—where I'll be taking her personally."

Joanna's head rose. "Need a blade report, too?"

Alex angled her head back down against his chest. "Be quiet."

Joanna frowned. The pain was constant now, and she could feel blood oozing over her hand. She tried not to think of the jagged ridges of skin laid open by Nigel's blade. At least the pain had blotted out the horror of the photos with her grainy face. She swallowed.

"Worse, is it?" His voice hardened. "Hang on."

Somehow he had read the truth, whether through her body or her ragged breath.

Joanna felt an icy prick of warning. How long would it take before he knew everything? "Want down. Want to go."

"Later," Alex said flatly.

"If you think you will use her against me, you are wrong," St. Cyr said.

Alex laughed coldly. "Unlike you, I don't use other people to fight my battles. Especially women."

The flat, emotionless edge to his voice made Joanna shiver. He might have been a stranger now.

A dangerous stranger.

"Vraiment? But I thought women were your specialty."

"You thought wrong."

Joanna tried vainly to see Jacques's face amid the blur of light and shadows. "No need to worry about me, Jacques. I—I'll be fine."

The Frenchman snorted. "How can you be so naive? You are only a small insect he toys with in his web. This man has no interest in you, not for yourself. Believe me, I know too well how he works."

Pain tightened Joanna's throat. Her hands clenched against Alex's neck.

"Steady," he whispered. "Don't put pressure on that arm."

"Let her go, Greywood. I can still stop the article."

Alex told St. Cyr in graphic terms what he could do with his article.

"So you laugh now. You curse with great confidence. But you will look like a fool when *Fine Arts* hits the stands next week."

Alex shrugged. "It won't be the first time. Now get out of my way."

St. Cyr's fists tightened. "Joanna, I *order* you to get down and walk. You are going home with me." He spoke as if he were Moses ordering the Red Sea to part.

Joanna was certain if she tried to walk, she'd end up with her face in one of the potted rose trees. "Sorry, Jacques. Don't think I can."

"It is a very grave mistake. He has lied to you, Joanna. Whatever he tells you are lies."

"Go rattle your saber somewhere else, St. Cyr. Ms. Russell and I have a date."

Joanna blinked at Alex. "We do?"

"Don't get your hopes up. That date's with a doctor."

St. Cyr's fingers clenched and unclenched. "Joanna, I absolutely forbid you to—"

Alex shoved him off the path with one arm. "Time's up, St. Cyr. Have some Krug before you leave. Maybe that will cool you down."

Alex strode toward the house, leaving St. Cyr cursing in the darkness.

Joanna frowned, remembering the triumphs as well as the bitter arguments she had had with Jacques.

"Did you quit because he wanted you to lie, starting with making a fake provenance for that suit of Flemish armor?"

"You *know* about that?"

"It's a small world, Ms. Russell. People talk. Especially about a man like St. Cyr."

"It never went any further. He . . . changed his mind."

"Or you changed it for him."

He was right again, Joanna thought. Jacques had blustered and ranted for a week. Only Joanna's threatened resignation had convinced him to scrap his wild plan to "mislead" a prospective buyer.

Once again, Alex Cameron's information was impeccable. And also unnerving.

"What else have you heard?"

"That you're an expert in eleventh-century metallurgy. Doctorate from Yale, studied with Rowlandson and Fine in London. You did your first paper on the metallurgy of thirteenth-century Japanese hilt weapons while you were still a graduate student. There was quite a stir when you managed to pick up some secrets of lock construction from a twice-incarcerated master thief."

"Nice man. Charles Dickens."

"The author?"

"No, the burglar. Unfortunate name." Joanna shook her head. "Great hands. Charlie showed me how to build a true Greek lock. Used it for a scabbard I had to repair."

Alex's eyes narrowed. "Did he teach you how to pick a lock, too?"

"Couldn't. Illegal."

"That wouldn't stop some people. Like St. Cyr."

Joanna's mouth hardened. "You saying I'm a thief?"

Alex's fingers tightened on her shoulder. "I'm saying that you know some unusual things."

"Don't like being spied on."

"Oh, I'm far from done, Ms. Russell. Next you went to work for Jacques St. Cyr and stayed five years. After that you did conservation and appraisals for James Hunsford. Only six months with him, however. Since then, you've been freelancing. Did I miss anything important?"

Her voice was tight with pain. "Only what I ate for breakfast this morning."

"Give me an hour and I'll tell you that, too."

It was true, Joanna realized blindly. He knew far too much. "How?"

"Standard procedure, Ms. Russell. I run a check on everyone working for me. Your partner teaches elementary chemistry and cricket at St. Adam's Academy. At night he participates in historical reenactments. His group has been in existence for six years but never became successful until he started working with you. You two have quite a reputation. You're good friends and good fighting partners." His voice turned rough. "Are you also lovers?"

"Find out yourself."

"I will." This time it was a sensual promise, all the more disturbing for its silken confidence.

"Am I supp'sed to be impressed?"

"Reassured. It's nothing personal, you see. I can give you the credit profile and sexual history of everyone here tonight."

Joanna shoved at his chest. "Horrible."

"It's a horrible world," Cameron said coldly. "I'm just trying to keep the horrible bits out of my small part of it." Alex shoved open a stained glass door with his boot and swung Joanna inside. "You see, I protect my own,

Ms. Russell. My butler manages the technical data search, and I do the rest. Amazing what you can find with the right program."

"Regular Bruce Wayne, aren't you?"

"Who?"

"Batman." Joanna gave a wild laugh. Her arm was shaking, hot and swollen. " 'To the Bat Cave, Alfred.' Peter would howl."

"Who's Peter?"

Joanna froze. "Nev'r mind. Not—important. Want to go home." She struggled to lift her head, blinking as Alex's features went double and then triple. Panic flared as she realized how fragmented her thoughts had become. She shoved at his chest. "Want to walk."

"After you see the doctor," he said flatly.

"Stop." Fear tightened her throat, tearing at every word. "Can't you *hear* me?"

"I hear." Cursing softly, Alex crossed an alcove of cool pink marble. Lights gleamed from twin sconces above a huge oil portrait.

Joanna caught a glimpse of a man in a kilt brandishing a great sword. Behind him the night sky was cut by jagged lightning.

Her breath caught. "The sword," she whispered. "The Cameron claymore."

"Good eye, Ms. Russell."

Alex continued toward the stairs, but Joanna clutched at his arm. "Want to see. So . . . beautiful."

"Later," Alex growled. "You're in no shape to appreciate it right now."

He was right, of course. Dimly she heard him rap out swift orders. "Get my medicine kit, Metcalfe. Then find Dr. Peterson. He's probably up in the new gallery."

She felt the cushions of a sofa, then a pillow pulled beneath her head. She bit down hard on her lip as Alex moved her arm, tightening the blood-soaked cloth.

He sank down beside her. "Stay with me. Tell me what you hate."

"How I feel." Joanna made a small, broken sound. She

didn't want him near her, touching her, speaking so gently. "Too fragile."

He muttered in that rough language she didn't understand. "Why?"

"Because I'm about to break." She shook her head tensely. "Can't. Not ever again." Joanna closed her eyes, unable to bear the sight of his face so close to hers. Every second brought more memories, more pain. "Then it will happen again. I'll fall and everything will shatter. Oh, God, Peter. I can't let Peter—" Her hands tightened. She twisted in Alex's arms, a low cry breaking in her throat. "I *have* to go."

"You're staying, damn it. I'm going to put a new binding on your arm. The bleeding hasn't stopped, and I can't wait any longer." Alex pulled away the damp cloth and covered her arm with a folded square of white silk. He cursed when he felt her shudder. "Joanna?"

Her fingers dug into his shoulder.

"Go ahead and squeeze."

Her hand tightened and she bit back a moan.

"Harder."

She felt her nails dig into his skin. Even then he didn't pull away. "Almost done. Can you still hear me?"

She moved restlessly, gripped by pain. His words broke over her in strange patterns that she had to struggle to understand. Her face was cold, almost numb.

Like a stranger's face. Like the blurred white features of the woman in those awful photographs. "No more."

"No more what?" The silk at her arm lapped once, then tightened in a knot.

Joanna felt tears burn at her eyes with every movement, but the pain of old memories was far sharper, cutting to her very soul. "No—can't tell."

"You can't tell what?"

Joanna's jaw tightened. She was too dizzy, too close to blurting out secrets that must never be told. She caught a ragged breath and frowned up at the light spilling down from the cut-glass chandelier. "Too much light."

"The light stays. I need to watch you until the doctor comes. You're still losing blood."

The French door swung open. "Here's the doctor, my lord."

"Thank God. She's still conscious, Peterson." Alex's fingers did not leave Joanna's arm. "Have a look over here."

The physician frowned at the blood-stained silk around Joanna's forearm. "Good thing you called me. How are you feeling, my dear?"

"Want t' go home," Joanna rasped.

"Of course you do. But first I'm going to look at your arm if I may." He flipped open a well-worn black bag and pulled out a small plastic case. "Perhaps you could fetch us some hot water, Metcalfe."

Joanna frowned. Their voices seemed to be coming from a great distance. Her body was painfully heavy, sinking lower and lower into the sofa, captured by soft fingers of cotton.

A strong hand gripped her shoulder. "Hang on."

Joanna heard the doctor's voice somewhere above her. "She'll be fine as soon as I stop this bleeding, Greywood. You did the right thing . . ."

The voice drifted away. Alex's fingers were hard at her shoulder, tight and unflinching.

She swallowed, feeling the press of tears, feeling his fingers.

Strong hands. A lover's hands.

His touch was the last thing Joanna felt before her eyes closed.

7

HARRY PETERSON shook his head as he rolled up a length of surgical tape. "I haven't seen a wound like that since I was in training up in London's East End."

"She did it in that damned reenactment." Alex frowned at Joanna. Her face was pale and she was fast asleep, her right arm curled around a pillow. The other arm was covered by a white sling fashioned from a linen towel and surgical tape. "How is she doing?"

"She's lost a good bit of blood, I'm afraid." Peterson closed his bag, clicking his tongue. "I've had to give her quite a few stitches. No swinging swords for a while. No movement at all for a day or two. Dangerous sort of work for a weapon conservator. I didn't realize that conserving the things required wielding them."

"I'm told she's usually very good." Alex's eyes narrowed. "Apparently something threw off her timing tonight." He let his mind empty, trying for a glimpse into Joanna's thoughts. He wanted to know what had disturbed her careful choreography.

He sensed a blur of lights and cold shadows. A stabbing pressure that might have been pain.

Or fear.

"Alex?"

Frowning, Alex narrowed his focus. Images shifted before him, blurred, black on white. Grainy faces. Heat and silence. Hunger–

"Alex."

83

He slammed back to the present, the faint images lost forever. "What?"

Peterson was watching him. "You didn't hear a word I said. Your mother had exactly the same habit. Damned unnerving."

Alex slid a hand through his hair and shrugged. "Just thinking, Peterson. Sorry."

"That's just what *she* used to say," the doctor muttered. "I didn't believe her either." As he finished repacking his bag, the door was swept open by Nigel Llewelyn.

"What have you *done* with her?"

"I've done nothing to her. It was *your* knife that did the damage."

Nigel froze. "Me? But she never said—"

"Be quiet or you'll wake her." Alex nudged the Welshman out into the hall. Once there, he turned to pace restlessly. "If I had known you were going to use real weapons, I would have canceled the performance."

Nigel rubbed his neck. "Joanna's mad for authenticity. We make a point of dulling the blades somewhat, of course."

"Not enough," Alex said grimly.

Nigel looked back into the room at Joanna's pale features. "I'm much in your debt, Greywood. If anything serious happened to her . . ."

"She'll pull through. Peterson says it's a question of rest now. He doesn't think she's likely to lose any movement in her arm."

"Thank God. I don't know what happened. Joanna's damned good with that sword in case you hadn't noticed."

Alex had noticed. Her grace and speed were carved into his mind. His heart had nearly stopped beating during the final sword fight. Little wonder she had the controlled grace of a dancer.

Her performance had left him shaken. He could imagine how she would feel rising beneath him, supple and strong, her body taut in passion. The image tormented him, stunningly real.

He wanted Joanna Russell every way a man could want a woman, aflame with the passion he could sense in every movement of her sword.

"What's going on between you two?" Nigel's eyes were hard with suspicion. "Are you lovers?"

"No." Alex looked at Joanna's hair spilling over the pillow. "Not yet." The words came without conscious thought, but he realized instantly they were true. He wanted her beneath him, wearing nothing but moonlight. He wanted hazy passion in her eyes as soft sounds of pleasure spilled from her lips.

And he would have her that way.

He drew a long, slow breath. *Remember that you have a mind, Cameron. Joanna Russell is off-limits in bed or anywhere else. She's St. Cyr's woman, remember?*

The thought made his hands tighten.

"Alex?"

Alex realized the doctor was waiting at the doorway. "Sorry, Peterson." He drove hard fingers through his hair. "It's been a long night."

"I'll come around tomorrow morning to see her. The pills are here on the side table. One every four hours."

"I'll remember."

The doctor nodded at Nigel. "You two were frighteningly good out there. I enjoyed every minute, I'm ashamed to admit. Now I must be off." He moved away briskly, satchel in hand.

Alex stared at his back. "Where does Joanna live?" he demanded.

The Welshman hesitated.

"I need to know, Llewelyn. She'll need clothes tomorrow. Mail. Phone messages. Whatever."

"She lives about fifteen minutes from here in an old stone cottage across the valley from Draycott Abbey. She rents it from the viscount."

"From Nicholas Draycott?"

Nigel nodded. "She did some restoration work for the

viscount's wife, and afterward they offered to lease her the studio. There's good light and a fine view. It's also isolated. Privacy is very important to Joanna."

Alex knew the old Draycott cottage well. Its beautiful stone walls overlooked a limestone ridge that dropped steeply into a wooded valley. But why the need for isolation?

"Is there someone I should notify?"

Nigel studied him in silence. "If you're asking me if Joanna has a lover, you can bloody well take a jump off that elegant roof, Greywood. The woman's private life is her own, and I'd be no friend of hers if I acted otherwise."

"Then tell me about St. Cyr. Why did she leave him?"

"It wasn't personal if that's what you're thinking. They were never involved, no matter what the press said." Nigel sighed. "I think the real reason she cleared out was because St. Cyr never let her have any privacy. He wanted to control her life the same way he controlled his collections. She couldn't take the hot house environment anymore."

"St. Cyr assumes money can buy anything, even people. *Especially* people." Alex braced one shoulder against the wall. "She mentioned someone named Peter."

Nigel's face hardened. "Do your own spying, Greywood."

"Maybe I already have."

"Then you didn't find out what you wanted. If you had, you wouldn't be wearing that black scowl." Nigel grinned as if the thought pleased him.

"You know her well, it seems."

Nigel's grin grew wider. "Well enough, Greywood. And the thought of that is burning you up, isn't it?"

"Why should it bother me?"

Nigel studied Alex's face. "I don't know. But I do know this. First Joanna can't take her eyes off you, and the air positively crackles when the two of you are even remotely close. Then Joanna makes a mistake in timing that even a beginner would be ashamed of. But she doesn't want me to know and she *certainly* doesn't want *you* to know. You tell me why."

"Who appointed you her watch dog?"

"I did two years ago. Joanna has a way of making people feel protective. She's not as tough as she seems, Greywood."

"Care to elaborate?"

Nigel shook his head. "She'd slice me in two if I did. Just remember I'll be calling to check on her. Be sure you have good news, because I own a very sharp sword."

Alex smiled grimly. "So do I."

She's not as tough as she appears.

The house was quiet as Alex sank into a chintz wing chair near the sofa. He studied Joanna over his steepled fingers while moonlight spilled through the high windows. Her eyelashes were smoky streaks against her cheeks, and her breath was soft and faint.

She can't take her eyes off you.

Alex frowned, feeling the same stab of danger that had bothered him all week. Once again he tried to focus, summoning images from the dark recesses of his mind. Just as before, there were only shadows and something that might have been fear.

He cursed softly, pulling the damask quilt around her. The fabric slid to her shoulder, pooling around the curve of one breast while her hair spilled over his fingers like a bright summer dawn.

Once again desire caught him, as swift and harsh as it had been in the garden.

And by the stage.

And when he'd carried her inside, locked against his chest.

Madness.

Why did he feel this damnable connection with Joanna Russell? It wasn't as if he knew her from some recent art function. A woman like Joanna Russell would not be easily forgotten.

Alex watched the moon rise coldly over the dark lawns, his fingers clenched. He had other things to worry about, starting with the thefts at Greywood. Alex had the feeling St. Cyr was somehow involved, because he had been tracking the lost Cameron sword obsessively for months.

Or was this simply another gambit in his personal feud with Alex? If so, how did Joanna Russell fit into the equation?

Five minutes later, he picked up the telephone in the shadowed study. "Metcalfe, how are you doing with that profile on our guest?"

"Would you like Ms. Russell's credit history, banking references, or phone records, my lord? I also have her SAT scores. Curiously, there are no birth records, but that may take longer."

Alex's face hardened. Getting information was easy when one had the right resources. He scowled out at the darkness, feeling a sudden reluctance to carve so deeply into the life of a stranger, violating her privacy and touching her secrets. "Phone records first. I want to know exactly how often Joanna Russell has spoken with Jacques St. Cyr in the last two weeks. You have his numbers, I believe."

"Two in London. Three for his estate in Surrey."

"Check them. Let me know what you find." Alex put down the phone, feeling dirty.

Jacques St. Cyr studied his unfinished champagne as his Bentley hurtled up the broad drive to his private estate in Surrey. Even when the road straightened, he did not reach for the drink again. Too much alcohol dulled the brain and eroded his control, and he never permitted himself more than three glasses.

Control was everything. Control meant power, and Jacques St. Cyr, illegitimate son of a Marseillais laundress and a very proper minor *conte* from Normandy, wanted power beyond all else.

He was one step closer to achieving that power tonight.

He smiled very slightly as his correct English butler met him without a hair out of place, as if he was perfectly used to holding open the huge oak door at three o'clock in the morning. Which of course he was.

"Any messages, Williams?"

"No, Mr. St. Cyr. But someone is here to see you."

"Here?"

"He was most insistent. He had a letter of reference from your solicitor in London."

Frowning, St. Cyr ran his thumb along a Chinese enamel vase just inside the foyer. Not a trace of dust marred the fine finish. "Who is it?"

"He wouldn't give a name."

"Not that lawyer again, is it?"

The butler shook his head. "I believe he is American, Mr. St. Cyr. He said to tell you his business concerns your newest acquisition."

St. Cyr stiffened. "Where have you put him, Williams?"

"In the Versailles Room."

Jacques thought of the small room lined with mirrors, set off in a separate wing away from the study and offices. He nodded. "Very good. I will see him there. Where is Michel?"

Michel Lebras was six foot four, a three-time world kick-boxing champion, and Jacques St. Cyr's highly paid bodyguard.

"Asleep, I believe."

St. Cyr frowned. "Wake him."

"Right away, sir."

Standing before the huge Regency mirror, Jacques St. Cyr straightened his tie. He smiled at his well-tanned and distinguished face. No one looking at him would imagine that his mother had taken in laundry for a living and his first pair of shoes had come from a street corner refuse bin.

But Jacques had never forgotten.

He touched the fine cabochon emerald cuff links at his wrists. Michel Lebras would see that there were no problems from this insistent stranger. But first Jacques meant to find out exactly how much the man knew about his latest acquisition.

After a final glance in the mirror, the Frenchman moved off to meet his unknown visitor, secure in the knowledge that his two-hundred-pound bodyguard was not far behind him.

Unfortunately, he was wrong. Williams never made it past the end of the corridor.

He was thin with flat, washed-out features. His pale hair was short, almost military in its precise cut.

Jacques disliked him on sight. "What can I do for you?"

The man at the window turned at Jacques's curt question. He moved slowly, as if calculating every movement. His smile was crooked and did not quite reach the end of his mouth. "Actually, I might be the one helping you tonight, Mr. St. Cyr." He patted his pocket. "Mind if I smoke?"

Jacques stiffened. "Certainly I mind. This house has extensive climate controls monitored twenty-four hours a day. I have very rare pieces here, and they must be maintained in perfect condition." St. Cyr's brown eyes narrowed. "But I think you know that already, Mr. . . ."

"Loomis." The man studied the cigarette in his fingers, then put away his lighter. "No smoke then." He did not remove the unlit cigarette from his fingers. "For now at least."

St. Cyr studied him with growing disapproval. "It is very late, Mr. Loomis. I suggest you get right to the point or that you leave."

The American rolled his cigarette twice. "I've got something you need, St. Cyr, and you have something I want very badly. I was hoping we could do a little horse trading tonight."

St. Cyr stiffened. "My offices are in London at Gray's Inn Fields, Mr. Loomis. My solicitor is Sir Gordon Mount. I suggest you contact him there if you have a business matter to propose."

Something fluttered the curtains at the far window. A shadow fell over the Aubusson carpet as another person entered.

St. Cyr stiffened. "You."

His only response was a low laugh.

"Get *out*. Right now before I—"

"You can forget about Michel, Jacques. He won't be going anywhere tonight. You see, your butler had a little accident on the way to the stairway."

"Damn it, you can't—"

"Sit down." Light struck the barrel of a pistol. "While I sample this excellent port of yours, you can open the safe behind your desk."

"I don't know what you're talking about," the Frenchman said coldly.

There was a shrill whine. A bullet cracked a priceless Tang pottery horse, shattering it into a thousand pieces. "Maybe *that* will refresh your memory."

Jacques's jaw hardened. He reached behind him, surreptitiously searching his desk for the buzzer that would summon the police.

The crystal lamp at his shoulder exploded in a fury of glass shards.

"Forget about the alarm, St. Cyr. Otherwise your arm will be next, and I guarantee you a most . . . uncomfortable night. And it will be all so unnecessary."

Sweat covered the Frenchman's forehead as the gun muzzle pointed at his chest. "What—what do you want?"

"Much better. First you will open your safe. Then you will listen very closely while I ask you some questions, beginning with your latest acquisition."

"I don't—"

The mouth of the pistol slid beneath his chin. "Don't even think about lying. You're going to tell me about the scabbard that's hidden in your safe. I want to know where you found it and what other information came with it. Especially about the book."

Jacques swallowed. "Book? I don't have any—"

Cold steel pressed against his throat. "No more lies. Do we understand each other?"

Jacques nodded, feeling the blood rush from his face. He had taken precautions, of course. If he was harmed, new events would be set in motion, and the search for the Cameron claymore would continue without him.

They would pay for their treachery. Jacques would hunt them down and punish them the way it would hurt most. Provided he kept his head and managed to live through the night.

"Well?"

The Frenchman nodded. There was a second alarm button inside the safe itself. If he was very careful—

"And don't try going for the hidden alarm. Open the door, then step away. One false move and my trigger finger becomes very unreliable. First the scabbard, then the book. *Comprenez-vous?*"

The accent was lamentable, but Jacques St. Cyr did not notice. His face was the color of death as he moved around his desk toward the safe.

8

Joanna flinched and sat up, gasping. Darkness pooled around her and through the windows she saw the moon tangled in the branches of a giant oak.

A hand locked over her wrist. "Don't. You shouldn't be moving yet." The voice was peat and wood smoke.

Alexei.

She drew a tight breath. "Where am I?"

"Greywood House."

She frowned as snippets of memory returned. "Where's Nigel?"

"Lie back."

"He wasn't hurt, was he?"

"Lie back, damn it." Alex forced Joanna back against the pillows. "Nigel is fine."

She breathed a prayer of thanks, then pushed forward. "I'm going home." As she sat up, hot slivers of pain worked deep into her arm.

"Not tonight, you aren't. Not until the doctor says it's safe."

Staying put was the last thing on Joanna's mind. She pushed to her feet, wincing at the pain.

Hard fingers gripped her waist, pulling her against a harder chest. "You're following the doctor's orders, damn it."

Leather squeaked as Joanna went down onto a pair of granite thighs. His chest was bare, she realized, feeling the ripple of muscles.

She swallowed angrily. "This is k-kidnapping."

"No, this is being a good Samaritan."

"I—want to go home."

He said something low and savage that was probably Russian. Even Joanna recognized it as a curse. "We can do this the easy way or the hard way, Ms. Russell. The choice is up to you."

"My *choice* is to leave."

"Sorry, that's not on the list."

He pulled her back onto the couch, and his hand slid into her hair.

"Don't touch me."

"I can't help touching you. Maybe I need to know why that is."

His fingers traced the contours of her cheeks and the soft curve of her mouth almost as if he were looking for something. Something lost long ago.

Joanna flinched beneath a wave of memories, clear and bright and burning.

Tell him.

A tiny sound escaped her throat as his lips moved over her forehead.

Tell him now.

"Damn it. What is it about you?" he whispered harshly. "When you tremble like that, making those small, lost sounds in your throat, you make me want to pull you close and—"

He jerked his hands away. "Forget it." He pushed past her and shoved to his feet. "This changes nothing. You're staying."

"Why?"

Alex stood motionless in the shadows, feeling the hard burn of desire at his groin, feeling his blood pump heavy and hot through his veins. Damned good question, one that he was nowhere close to answering. It had nothing to do with medical necessity now. "Because that's the way it's going to be, damn it."

He turned away, angry at his loss of control. He hadn't felt like this since he was a teenager.

Scowling, he strode to the door, shocked by how hard it was to keep from turning around and pulling her to his chest while he ran his fingers through that satin hair.

"Don't worry," he growled. "What just happened won't be repeated. I'm not going to touch you again. That's a promise."

Not unless you want me to, Joanna Russell. And I'm going to do everything I can to see that you do.

Silence followed.

"Joanna?"

He turned. Her head was on the pillow, her eyes closed.

She was asleep.

Alex took a slow, angry breath. "What are you up to now, St. Cyr?" he whispered.

Alex moved through room after room of the beautiful old house, feeling something gnaw at him. Every lock was firm, all the security alarms in order. And still the feeling of wrongness persisted.

He moved to the study and checked the safe hidden behind the painting. Nothing was disturbed there either.

Rubbing his neck, he looked out at the silent lawns, where a single tent of white silk billowed in the wind.

What *was* it about her?

You have a habit of making bad choices with women, that's what it is. Maybe the wrong women are the only ones you'll let close.

He sank into a big leather chair and propped his feet on the mahogany desk littered with correspondence, foreign newspapers, and faxes. He took a small silver dagger between his fingers, rolling it absently while he watched the moon in the trees.

She was an enigma, and Alexei Cameron didn't like enigmas. She was disturbing, and Alexei Cameron wasn't accustomed to being disturbed by women. She also had close connections to one of the most devious collectors in Europe. There was every reason to believe that St. Cyr had set Joanna up to be his spy.

So why couldn't Alex put her out of his mind? Why did the texture of her hair and the curve of her cheek continue to torment him?

How well had St. Cyr prepared her and how much was she prepared to do to gain information? he wondered angrily, imagining her hair flowing over his hand like liquid satin. Her mouth, soft and warm against his jaw, against his chest. Against his—

Desire exploded through him and he cursed.

But desire was easy. Desire was swift and simple, filling the emptiness where he had learned to live. Alex asked himself coldly if primitive desire was *all* he felt for Joanna Russell.

He recognized the stirring of the wild Gypsy soul he had worked so hard to submerge in the years since he had come back to England. Her haunted eyes roused it. Every ragged breath inflamed it.

Fool.

Light played over the tiny Renaissance dagger. Alex looked up, frowning. A beam of light was moving through the darkness, down near the south wing of the house, where the gallery stretched toward the trees.

Cursing flatly, he raced for the door.

Mist crept over the chill lawns, stretching out pale fingers at Alex as he ran noiselessly down darkened paths. He heard a sound to his left, near the swimming pool, and drew back into a flowering hedge.

The clink of gravel sent him down the hill. The white silk tent had fallen, drifting like a great spiderweb tangled in a row of potted rose trees. Behind the silk, he saw the dim movement of a figure.

In seconds, he was beside the drifting silk, tearing away the gossamer trails with savage fingers. But he was too late. Only shadows met him.

And then, beyond the trees, a beam of light and the swirl of a long, dark skirt.

Joanna, he thought savagely.

* * *

His hands clenched as he ran for the house. Now his suspicions were confirmed.

Joanna Russell was St. Cyr's pawn, sent to work her way into his house and probably into his bed. The accident with Nigel had been carefully planned and so had St. Cyr's "outburst" on the flagstone path below the house.

As St. Cyr's victim, she would have Alex's immediate protection; with her inside Greywood, she would have access to every room and every document.

Cursing, Alex threw open the door to his study. And saw Joanna's hair glistening on the pillow. Her arm lay outstretched, just as he had left her.

He drew a harsh breath, wiping beads of sweat from his brow. "What in bloody everlasting hell is going on?"

He had no answer from the woman on the sofa. Her breath moved in and out in soft puffs.

Alex strode to the phone and gave low commands to send the security team out to comb the grounds. But his instincts told him they would find nothing. Whoever had been down by the trees was gone.

And that left him where? With a woman he didn't trust and a hunger he couldn't control.

Frowning, Alex sank down beside the couch. His fingers skimmed her hair, almost to reassure himself she was still there. He felt the warmth of her breath on his neck and stiffened when her fingers slid into the fine hair on his chest. She inched closer, burrowing into his warmth. Damn it, was she working for St. Cyr or not?

Desire grew within him, a shadow companion in the darkness, whispering of dreams forever lost and pleasures never tasted.

Stony-faced, Alex Cameron forced himself to listen to every low, sad whisper while the moon pulled free of the giant Greywood oak and rose in solitary splendor over the silent lawns.

Metcalfe found them together just before dawn. Alex's head was slumped against the back of the couch, and Joanna's hand rested on his shoulder. Standing motionless before that beautiful old room, the butler frowned, reliving a host of memories.

Of Alex at six, sleepy-eyed and frightened as he'd watched his parents argue.

Of Alex at eight, quiet and self-possessed beyond his years, hiding tears as he shook hands without visible emotion and walked in silence to the car that would take him and his mother to the airport, back to visit her relatives behind the Iron Curtain.

What was to have been a short visit had lasted nine years, years of fury and frustration and ceaseless searching by the heartbroken earl.

A different Alexei had returned to Greywood, a grim-faced and pitifully thin youth of seventeen. After years of negotiating, arguing, and bribery by the earl, his wife and son had finally been spirited out from behind the wall of silent hostility that held them captive near the southern border of Russia.

They had come back as wary strangers, Alex most of all.

Metcalfe's eyes glinted with moisture as he remembered the fierce independence of the lad who had walked into Greywood House that day. His face had held no smiles, no curiosity. His icy politeness softened only when he looked at his mother's pale, beautiful face.

The fireworks had come later. Oh yes, what a roller-coaster ride it had been, watching the defiant but self-possessed Gypsy lad grow up to challenge his stern father. Their shouting matches had been monumental.

The butler shook his head, feeling a breeze sweep through the room. He found a wool throw on a nearby chair and spread it carefully over the sleeping woman's shoulders, then touched Alex gently.

He was awake instantly. "Metcalfe, don't tell me I dozed off."

"No doubt it did you good, my lord. Unfortunately, your call to Peking has just been returned. And I have the other . . . information . . . you requested."

Alex peered down at the dial of his watch. "Good Lord, it's five o'clock already?" He eased from the couch, then stood for a moment staring down at Joanna. "Any news from the security team?"

"Nothing, I'm afraid. Whoever was outside had gone. What shall I do about the young lady?"

"Give her whatever she needs, Metcalfe. Fax, computer, telephone. Any books or catalogs that interest her from the library."

"And if she asks to leave?"

Alex's jaw hardened. "Then come and get me."

The butler shook his head. "You really believe she took the replica?"

"I believe St. Cyr was involved," Alex said grimly. "And that means she probably is, too." He moved out into the hall, and Metcalfe followed.

"Forgive me, my lord, but she seems . . ."

Alex laughed tightly. "Too fragile? Too innocent? Maybe that's why he uses her."

"But—"

Alex's voice hardened. "No one wanted that sword as much as St. Cyr, and no one was closer to him than Joanna Russell."

"You think they wanted the real Cameron claymore. But surely the police—"

Alex laughed bitterly. "The police are useless. They believe this was a random burglary and that the sword will turn up eventually at some out of the way auction. But that won't happen." Alex glared out at the darkness. The canopy of silk still floated in the trees, drifting up and down like a great pale butterfly lost on the dark bloom of night. "There will never be another sword like that replica, Metcalfe. I helped Constantin twist and goad and tear it from a slab of molten steel. Now he's dead. That sword was one of the few things I have to remember him by."

He moved to the window, and the breeze ruffled his long hair. In the moonlight, his cheekbones were a slash of shadow, sharp testimony to his Gypsy heritage. "Do you know what it was like in Estavia, Metcalfe? We were shunned, spit upon as American spies. And being Gypsy was even worse than being American. I ran away, and that night fate took me stumbling into Constantin Stevanov's camp. He and his people took me in and accepted me without question. They fed me and protected me and healed my wounds. That tough old man with the magic hands saved my life at thirteen. While we sweated and cursed together beside his blazing fire, he gave me his knowledge and brought back the soul that I had lost. I can *never* repay him for that."

As Alex spoke, hardness filled his eyes, the steel of the swords he loved so well. This house and all its luxury might be torn from him. His title and every possession might be lost. But even with nothing left but his bare hands, Alex would survive.

He had done it once before as a boy. An old Gypsy sword master named Constantin Stevanov had taught him how.

Alex refused to give up hope of recovering his teacher's masterpiece.

"Has the security team left?"

"Not until they have your order."

The restlessness touched his neck, jabbing his shoulders. "Tell them to stay."

Metcalfe frowned. "Do you think someone—"

"I don't know *what* to think, Metcalfe." Alex's finger's twisted on the soft gauze curtains. "But you'd better find Dimitri and send him up."

The neigh of restive horses cut the night.

The laird of Cameron gave a racking cough. With trembling hands, he shoved quill to ink, even as his sight began to fail.

The pounding echoed closer now. Harsh shouts. The slam of boots and armor.

The old laird thought of his wife and the five braw sons sent in safety to Dundee. With God's grace, they would survive. In time his book would find its way in secrecy to the eldest of the five, and from him, it would be passed down to the next and the next of the Cameron line.

These words would be all he could give. As the

shouts came again, the laird knew with icy clarity that he would never see any of his tall, laughing sons again.

He bent again to the page and began to write . . .

The second riddle: He who dies, which is the Key to Today.

My faith is true. There are three signs of it, and each is neither truth nor lie. The key to my faith has no lock and no limit. Like the blade itself, it burns and shimmers.

Oddly sleek.

Coldly silver.

To close the circle, find the words. Holy words, they are. Riddles within a riddle. Heed their message and all gates shall open.

The Cameron treasure will then be yours, with all its pain and joy.

Hear, who would hear.

9

Alex's eyes were dark with exhaustion after he finished his most pressing calls, then sank down before his desk. "What have we got, Metcalfe?"

"Here are the phone records for Ms. Russell that you wanted."

Alex picked up a stack of computer sheets. "How did they match with St. Cyr's?"

"Two calls this month from Ms. Russell's studio matched. One was to his London office. One to his Surrey address."

Alex studied the list of numbers. What did it prove? The two calls could have been merely social. Damn it, he needed answers, not more questions. "Does she have a cellular phone?"

"None listed, my lord."

Alex rubbed the knot of tension at his neck, looking at his watch. "What about St. Cyr?"

"I've tried him for the last four hours, and there is still no answer. Rather peculiar."

"Is Dimitri watching her studio?"

"Since eight o'clock. No visitors and no deliveries. He has the mobile phone if you want to contact him."

"Not yet. She's still asleep, I take it?"

Metcalfe nodded.

Alex looked up at his mother's portrait on the far wall. Her flashing eyes picked up the fire of the rubies at her neck. Behind her stood the earl, dignified in a velvet jacket and bright tartan. There was a hint of softness in his eyes, where the Cameron arrogance had been tempered by love.

They had taught Alex by their example about the value of believing in something greater than themselves. About acting on those principles, even when it involved dangerous risks.

He looked again at his watch. "Any news from Sweden?"

"I'm . . . afraid not, my lord."

"Damn it, we should have heard something about Elena's parents by now."

There was a scuffling outside in the hall, and the door suddenly slammed open. A seven-year-old girl hurtled across the room. Her dress was torn and her shoes were stuffed with Estavian newspapers.

Metcalfe looked distraught. "She will not change, my lord. Here's a fine new dress and shiny shoes, but she refuses to touch them."

"It's not the clothes, Metcalfe. It's all the things they represent to Elena." Alex knew the feeling. He had shared it on his own return to England. Her clothes, old and battered, were all that reminded the girl of her past and the homeland she had left behind. They were her last, desperate grip on sanity.

"Of course. It was foolish of me. But what—"

"Uncle, don't let them take me!" the young Gypsy cried. She threw herself down before Alex and tried to kiss his feet. "I want only to stay here with you. Otherwise the soldiers will come back. They will hurt me, like they hurt my mother in Estavia." Her face was swollen and puffy from crying, and her thin body shook as Alex pulled her up into his arms.

"Hush, little one. You are safe here. Your mother will come soon. We are working on it right now."

The dark eyes were haunted, filled with terror. "I want to stay with you! I will sleep on the floor beside your feet."

Alex brushed her hair gently from her face. "Wouldn't

you rather have your own bed, with a nice soft bear to guard you, my Elena?"

She gnawed at her lip, then shook her head. "No! Only with you!" Her fingers clutched at his shirt, now damp with her tears. "I will trust no one else!"

Alex let her hold him, let the shuddering sobs break through her malnourished body.

And he remembered.

They were all in his memory, the sad, thin faces of the children with hopeless eyes. Trip after trip, forged papers, steamship passage, relocations wherever there were settlements of their Gypsy countrymen. Every face lay engraved on his memory. Dozens, even hundreds of them.

And somehow it never seemed enough.

He smoothed back the girl's hair and smiled. "Come," he said. "Shall I sing you a song, Elena?"

She bit her lip. "What kind of a song?"

"A very nice song. A song about a bear . . . who dances."

She was interested now. "What is the bear's name?"

Alex rubbed his chin. "Hmmm. Ivanushka, of course."

Startled laughter. "Uncle Ivan? But that is my own uncle!"

"Then perhaps he is a *bear*," Alex said, lifting her up onto his desk. "Does he have big teeth?"

"N-no." She giggled.

"A pointed nose?"

"Only a small one."

"Lots of brown fur?"

"Ivanushka is bald," she said triumphantly.

Alex spread one hand, then the other, and his body was transformed into a lumbering, incautious mass of fur. The girl clapped her hands and for a moment the haunting sadness was driven from her eyes as her uncle Alex began to sing an old Gypsy tune.

* * *

Outside the open door, Joanna stood frozen, watching Alex. On the desk sat a little girl in tattered skirts with tears still drying on her cheeks. Joanna felt the deep, abiding ties of blood and language that linked the two.

He began to sing in a deep voice, rich, rolling words that made the little girl laugh as she swayed back and forth. Hesitantly she began to sing along with him.

The breath caught in Joanna's throat. She turned away, feeling like an outsider.

Tell him.

Tell him now.

Blinking, she tried to forget a long-ago night of honey-suckle and madness, a night when she had explored the dark textures of desire with this man who was a stranger. His hands had been sure and swift, and his hard body had brought her to passion again and again in the moonlight.

Now all that remained of that night was a set of blurred photographs, stark remnants of their desire.

What a *fool* she was to have come here! Gritting her teeth, she pushed to her feet and nearly fell as dizziness hit her.

Telling him was as impossible as staying.

Blindly, she turned away.

Joanna could have sworn that someone was following her.

She squinted into the rearview mirror, where a brown car was weaving through traffic. Every time she slowed for a closer look, the car melted back into the crush.

Of course, she could have been mistaken. She wasn't exactly James Bond.

She shoved the gearshift into third, wincing at the tug on her stitches. Her car had been right where she'd left it. Twenty minutes of driving had carried her out of Alex Cameron's reach.

Her gaze returned to the mirror. Once again she saw a blur of brown, three cars back. She saw a break in traffic and shot forward, passing a horse trailer and two BMWs. But when she looked back, the same brown car was cutting through the lanes right behind her, like a dogged shadow.

"Dimitri?" Alex frowned as the connection was interrupted by the crackle of static.

"I am here, Alexei."

"Where are you? That static on your mobile phone sounds like you've set up a base camp on Everest."

"Base camp? What is base—"

"Never mind. Just tell me where you are."

"Not so far, only twenty miles north of Greywood. Is a very nice little town with a duck pond and—"

"Forget the ducks, Dimitri. Where's Ms. Russell?"

"I lose her for a while, but now I have her in sight. She heads north now. A very fast driver, that woman, but I do not miss her again."

"You're wearing your glasses, I hope."

Dimitri gave a guilty look at the expensive new glasses that Alex had insisted on buying for him the week before. At that moment they were resting neatly on the passenger seat. "Of course I wear them," he protested. As he spoke, he scooped up the glasses and shoved them awkwardly in place over his crooked nose. "Very nice they make everything look, too."

"Excellent. Stay close to her, Dimitri, but for heaven's sake, don't let Ms. Russell see you. She's damned clever."

"She has the instincts of a Gypsy, this one! Twice she pulls over and twice I barely avoid to shoot past her. The second time I nearly run into herd of sheep that are crossing road."

"She didn't see you, did she?" Alex didn't sound overly concerned about the sheep.

"Not even for a second." Dimitri smiled. "I am always careful to keep out of sight." As he spoke, Dimitri tugged off the new glasses, which irritated the bridge of his nose. Frowning, he tossed them down beside him. "Do not worry so much, Alexei."

"Just don't *lose* her, Dimitri. I want to know *exactly* where she goes—and with whom."

"I watch her well." Squinting slightly, the big Gypsy watched a blue panel truck turn off at a light. "Better for me to go now." His powerful hands twisted, easing right as a petrol truck tried to lumber past. "She seems to slow down."

"Fine. Call me when you know her destination."

Dimitri hung up and squinted into the sunlight, searching for the dented green Jeep. Two vans. A battered Peugeot. *No Jeep.*

Muttering, he shoved on his new glasses.

But it was no use.

To his horror, he discovered that Joanna Russell's dusty Jeep had vanished.

Not bad, Joanna thought triumphantly.

Only a few people knew that the tiny lane she had just taken crossed the church grounds and then curved back to the highway half a kilometer down the hill.

She smiled as she looked back. The brown car was nowhere in sight. Confident that she was no longer being followed, Joanna turned down a rutted gravel road bordered by elm trees. A hand-lettered sign read SUSSEX ROMAN SITE. TOURS BY APPOINTMENT ONLY.

In no way deterred by the sign, Joanna crept around the deep ruts until she came to a pair of storage sheds. Just beyond, an old truck was parked at the edge of a steep hill. Several dozen students were clustered around the truck's tailgate, where a man with white hair and a green bandanna was holding up a variety of digging tools.

Joanna parked the Jeep and moved quietly through the group, smiling as she heard the familiar oration.

"Of course, on Crete we used a different kind of trowel. Soil variations, you understand. Never forget that all soil is different. Get down on the ground and smell it. Rub it in your fingers and feel the texture. Then choose your tools accordingly."

Joanna headed toward the sectioned earth at the top
of the hill, where a Roman villa was undergoing excava-
tion at the hands of a team of sunburned students. Her
eyes narrowed, searching the assorted faces for one in
particular.

A handful of dirt flew out of the nearest trench.
Joanna heard a loud shriek. "I've found a solidus! A real,
proper gold solidus, perfectly preserved! Just wait until
Grandfather sees *this!*"

A very dirty head popped up out the trench. Red clay
dusted his arms, encrusted both knees, and was ground
over his face. The boy's gray eyes widened when he saw
Joanna. Arms flying, hair wild, he pounded down the
narrow path, clutching his discovery.

It wasn't the rare coin Joanna was looking at, her eyes
misty. It was the boy with the dirty face, the sturdy chin,
and the flushed cheeks.

"Peter!" Her arms opened wide.

"Mom!"

Joanna was laughing as she caught her son hard
against her chest.

10

"It DATES to the time of Publius Hadrianus." Eight-year-old Peter Russell brushed dirt from his cheek while he beamed at his grandfather. "He ruled—for nineteen years?"

"Absolutely right," Harrison McTiernan boomed. "Closer than your mother guessed at your age."

Peter squeezed his mother's fingers. "She was probably just testing to see if *you* knew, Gran. She does that sometimes. Maybe she was distracted. She does that, too, especially when she's been rubbing her eyes a lot."

Joanna ignored her father's probing look. "Well, I'm not distracted now," she said. "I'm very impressed by both of you."

"I told you he had huge potential," Harrison said mildly. "The boy is definitely going to be an archaeologist when he grows up." He beamed triumphantly at the boy on his knee.

Joanna smiled, wisely remaining silent.

"It's a real one, too, Grandfather. See the letters? Magnus Maximus. That's the usurper," he said gravely.

"Absolutely right, my boy. And what period was that, do you think?"

Peter Russell stared intently at a shelf of broken pottery. "Fourth century A.D." He looked up uncertainly. "More or less."

"Close enough." Harrison McTiernan III, Harvard professor and Nobel Prize-winning archaeologist, ruffled his grandson's dark hair. "Now tell your mother what you found yesterday."

"It was *awesome,* Mom! A piece of a real Roman breastplate. Grandfather says it belonged to a centurion who fought from the hill fort right over there." The boy's clear gray eyes glinted with excitement. "And *my* name is going to appear as the discoverer."

Joanna touched her son's cheek. "I'm so proud of you."

"Proud enough for double fudge sundaes in town?" he said promptly.

Joanna brushed a bit of dust off his jaw. "A real Roman breastplate is probably worth a fudge sundae."

"Double fudge with chocolate sprinkles?"

Joanna winced but nodded.

Peter shot to his feet. "Hooray for chocolate sundaes!" Abruptly, he went still. His clear gray eyes turned serious. "But Grandfather helped me. He saw the section of wooden beam first. It's really half *his* find."

"Nonsense, my boy. Take all the credit you can get." Joanna's father tugged off his pith helmet and fanned his face. *"You* did the spade work. Any fool can open a map and wave his fingers, but it's the one who squats in the dirt who gets to claim the find. Remember that." Harrison studied his daughter thoughtfully. "Your mother found her first solidus when she was about your age. North Africa, wasn't it, Joanna?"

"Carthage," Joanna said. "Renamed Hadrianapolis if I recall correctly." Memories of hot wind and sand against a blinding blue ocean swept over Joanna. "I had the worst case of sunburn in my life in spite of that horrid hat you and Mother insisted I wear. I was just about to pitch my trowel into the sea when I saw something gleaming in the sand."

"A solidus?" her son asked eagerly.

Joanna nodded. "Much more worn than yours. I think I found an amber drinking cup that day, too."

Peter sighed in delight. "Bloody marvelous."

Joanna looked at her father, who shrugged. "It's these

graduate students, I'm afraid. Say the first thing that pops into their heads. Still, you can't keep the boy insulated forever."

Peter turned to look at his mother. "What does in—insulated mean?"

"Protected."

"Oh." His gray eyes were thoughtful. "Did I say something wrong? They all talk like that, you know." He frowned. "They say lots of other things that I don't understand."

Joanna had a fairly good idea what those other things might be. "You might ask Gran or me before you try out a new word."

"Mad?" he said softly.

"Mad? At the boy genius who found the solidus? How could I be mad?"

Peter danced over the ground, language questions temporarily forgotten. "Then could Gran come with us? Gramma too? Pleeease?"

"It might be arranged." Joanna eyed her father. "But only if they agree to tell us how they first met in Crete."

Peter giggled. "You mean the time they both fell into the same trench?"

The dignified white-haired archaeologist made a half-hearted protest. "You can't want to hear *that* boring old story again, my dears." His words were drowned out by the protests of his daughter and grandson. The three were still arguing when they piled into Joanna's Jeep. The sweater she had thrown on before leaving the cottage snagged against the gearshift, revealing the edge of her bandage.

Peter's eyes widened. "What happened to your arm, Mom?"

"It's a long story. Let's go and find Gramma, and then I need to change."

Harrison's keen eyes narrowed. "Later, Dad," Joanna murmured. "I need to get Peter away before he steals all your best tricks."

"Not quite all of them, one hopes," her father said

softly. "I believe Rachel is in the cooking shed. She was going to try out an early Roman recipe for fried cakes with honey. We're experimenting with a reconstruction of a clay oven."

"How interesting," Joanna said.

"Yes, isn't it," her father replied blandly.

Joanna knew he was *not* referring to old Roman recipes. As she reached for the gearshift, she winced. She sat staring at the wheel, keys in hand.

"Does it hurt?" Peter blurted. "You're all white."

"I had a little misunderstanding with a sword. Nothing to worry about."

"Last night's reenactment, was it?" Harrison's voice was tight. "Joanna, are you—"

"It's nothing to *worry* about, H.R." It was an old and well-used code Joanna always adopted when her father was being overprotective.

Peter looked at his mother, then at his grandfather. "There's something wrong, isn't there? Something you're not telling me."

Joanna eased open her door and passed the keys to her father. "Everything's fine, my love. But we'll let H.R. drive today, shall we?"

"You lost her?" Alex looked across the big desk at Dimitri.

"She was going north. Past duck pond, just as I tell you."

"Yes, I know all about the duck pond. *Then* where did she go?"

Dimitri Stevanov pulled out a handkerchief and rubbed his forehead. He looked at his cuff, rubbed his neck, and sighed. "She was very good, that one. All the tricks of a Rom. A thousand of apologies, Alexei Andrei-ivitch. I am old and stupid fool who should be kicked by mule."

Alex shoved his hands through his hair. "You're only two years older than I am, Dimitri. And as for the mule, we might both be entitled." He drummed his fingers on the desk, staring out at Greywood's neat beds of peonies, lavender, and camellias. "I've been underestimating Ms. Russell."

Dimitri pushed to his feet. "I give you my resignation. No use you keep me. Better you find smart man. English man," he said softly.

Alex was around the desk in a second. He gripped Dimitri's shoulder tightly. *"You* are the help I choose, Dimitri Stevanov. Not from pity, not from convenience. Because you are honest and as stubborn as a dog with pups, and I can't think of anyone I'd rather have beside me in a fight. So forget this talk of resigning."

Dimitri's eyes widened. "Is *true?"*

"Of course it's true."

Dimitri touched his shoulder. "Is news from Sweden? Elena's mother and father are safe with our people yet?"

Alex's jaw hardened. "No word. They're five hours behind schedule. If only I had *been* there."

Dimitri's fingers closed with surprising force on Alex's arm. "Is foolish, this talk. Cannot *always* be you driving truck and bribing guards. You do ten, twenty, fifty already, no? Now your face is known. No more is safe. Better you stay here to direct the others."

Alex's eyes were blank as he looked at the man and woman in the portrait on the wall. "When is it enough, Dimitri? My father never gave up. After he brought out me and my mother, he helped many others by legal and illegal means. He did whatever it took to rescue people who had no other hope. There are always more children, Dimitri. I can't forget their tired, sad eyes in Estavia and a dozen other countries."

"You do what is possible, Alexei. We all do this." Dimitri frowned, holding out a brown envelope. "Metcalfe tells me to give this to you. He finds it beneath sofa. Perhaps belongs to you, he thinks."

Alex opened the stiff paper and pulled out a sheet of photographs.

Grainy black and white photographs taken on a night he had never been able to forget. A night of wind and stars. He muttered a curse, his face hardening.

"I should go and find Miss Russell?"

Alex's face was grim. "Not you, Dimitri. This time I'll handle Ms. Russell."

Peter looked wanly at his grandfather. "Where is Mom?"

"Resting. I think her arm hurts." Harrison looked thoughtfully at the stone house.

"Is she sick?"

"In pain, I suspect. But I don't think she wants us to know that." H.R. McTiernan cleared his throat. "It's rather a . . . woman kind of thing."

"Oh, one of those." Peter dug at the dirt with one toe. "Women," he muttered.

His grandfather hid a smile. "Women," he agreed sagely.

As the sun shone over the green hills where Roman legions once fought against ragged bands of Britons, Joanna stood on her parents' porch, teacup in hand.

Her father was loping up the crooked path with the easy gait of a man who spent most of his hours outdoors. "Feeling better?"

"Wonderful," Joanna said. It was almost true. The pain in her arm was only a dull ache now.

"You're too pale."

"I just woke up, H.R."

"Hmmph."

Joanna planted a kiss on his ruddy cheek. "I don't know how to thank you. Peter has been talking about this two-week vacation for months. He's loved every minute of it, but I know how hard it is for you and Mom to—"

"Rubbish," her father said fiercely. "It's been a pure joy having Peter here. And don't try to imply anything else or you'll make me angry." His voice fell. "Now tell me what's really going on. How did you hurt your arm?"

"It's a long story."

The archaeologist settled back against the stone porch and crossed his arms comfortably. "Good. That's my favorite kind."

Joanna sighed. "Why are things never simple? When we look for answers, all we come up with are more questions."

"You're not making a great deal of sense, my dear."

She swirled the last of her tea. "No, maybe I'm not."

"It's not Peter's father, is it? If that scoundrel has come back, I swear I'll—"

"No." Joanna touched his arm. She felt the comforting strength in those old muscles and smiled. "Peter is safe. He will never know the truth about his father, and his father will never find us."

"I hope you're right. Now tell me what really happened to your arm. I see how you wince whenever you think we're not looking."

"My timing was off, that's all."

"Why?"

"Things. Things that won't stay simple."

Her father started to speak, then sighed. "You're a grown woman, Joanna. I won't try to tell you what to do. But I'm your father, and that gives me full privilege to worry."

"What would you do if someone said I'd done something wrong, H.R.? Really wrong?"

"I'd probably knock out his front teeth," her father said harshly.

"It didn't feel wrong." Joanna watched the dark tea dregs spin and shift. "But sometimes people see what they want to see."

"Go on," her father said quietly.

Joanna frowned, searching for words. "It was . . . a man. Just a few days and then . . ." She shrugged. "Then it was over. There was no other choice."

"Is he bothering you now?" Harrison frowned. "It's been a long time since Normandy, but these fists can still put a bully in his place."

"I know. I saw you in action when that reporter came sniffing around the dig site last month." Joanna laughed softly. "Trapped overnight in a muddy trench during a rainstorm. *Really,* Father."

"The scalawag deserved every minute of misery. I

won't have people bothering my daughter and grandson and asking questions about your relationship with Jacques St. Cyr. I know he helped you when you were starting out, but I don't really like that man."

"This isn't about Jacques." She looked out at the fiery curve of the setting sun. "If things get sticky, I'd like to know that Peter would be safe here."

"He will be safe, I'll see to that. But this man—what happened to him? You're not the kind of woman to take a physical relationship lightly."

"It happened, and then it was over," Joanna said flatly. "I don't have room in my life for complications."

"Did you love him?"

Joanna's fingers tensed. She did not answer.

"My dear child, not *all* men are complications. Not all men are suspicious, control-mad brutes."

"It doesn't matter. I've got Peter to think about now. I'm not going to have any more complications in my life."

"Are you willing to give up a chance at love in exchange for this organized life you're plotting?" her father asked softly.

"You don't miss what you've never had," Joanna said firmly. "Not the kind of love you and Mother have."

Her father's gray eyes narrowed. "This has something to do with that trip you took with Jacques to the Caribbean, doesn't it? You were never the same afterward. You lost weight, took up yoga, began the sword demonstrations. Then you let your hair grow back to its natural color. But you never told us why."

Joanna's face went very pale. "Please, H.R."

"If a man was involved, a man who is bothering you, I want the truth, my girl."

"I'll tell you someday," Joanna promised. "But now I want to hear about Peter." Some of the shadows lifted from her eyes. "He was so excited about finding his first coin."

"The boy has a real talent. He's more patient than the best of my students, and he misses nothing. I feel guilty that you've let him spend his vacation here with us. We ought to be paying him."

Joanna put an arm around her father's shoulders. "If Peter is good, it's because he has such wonderful teachers. You two bring history alive when you work. I think it's because you love what you do."

Her father studied her thoughtfully. "Sometimes I feel guilty that your mother and I did just as we liked, traipsing from Asia Minor to Crete to North Africa without a second thought. There was so much you missed—a settled home, friends." He laughed uncertainly. "The American dream, complete with two-car garage and prom night. I hope we didn't cheat you."

Joanna's eyes softened. "Do you think I would give up those memories for a few hours of bad music and wilted flowers in the company of a boy with sweaty palms?"

"Archaeological sites weren't the best places to meet eligible males," he said slowly.

"I'm not *interested* in meeting any males, eligible or otherwise. And if you start matchmaking again, I think I'll push you off the top of that scaffolding."

"No, I learned my lesson last time. He seemed such a nice young man, though. Ph.D. from Harvard, too." Harrison shook his head. "Who would have thought he'd turn out to be such an—"

"An unprincipled, egotistical stud?"

Her father chuckled. "I'm afraid so. Just the same, I wonder if we didn't give you unrealistic expectations. Maybe all that moving when you were young left you feeling that something was missing."

"Missing?" Joanna gave a sly smile. "Who else got to grovel in the dirt, be burned to cinders by a savage sun, and turn out her shoes for scorpions every night?"

Her father chuckled. "When you put it that way, I suppose you should be thanking *us.*"

Joanna's eyes darkened as she watched the sun slide over the horizon. "Do you think he misses not having a father? I feel dreadfully guilty sometimes . . ."

"No regrets, my girl." Harrison McTiernan frowned

at his daughter. "You did what you thought best. Peter has a family who loves him. Someday you'll tell him the rest but not until he's old enough to understand. Then he can make his own judgment about what happened."

Joanna sighed. "But what if . . ."

"What-if is no way to live, Joanna. There is always the chance Peter will resent the decisions you made, and that's his right. But I believe in the end he will come to understand. Meanwhile, what about you? I'll wager it was one of those blasted Viking swords that mangled your arm." He snorted. "Never could stand the Vikings. A great, unruly lot, with no respect for civilization. Nothing like the Romans. Now *they* were a people who knew the value of building for the future. Their roads and aqueducts are *still* in use in France and Spain."

"Don't forget the plumbing and indoor heating," Joanna said, encouraging her father's particular passion.

"Absolutely right. What did the Vikings leave behind but terror and death, I want to know?"

Joanna chuckled. "There are those who hold that your savage Vikings were the first Europeans to discover the New World."

"A bunch of poppycock! Prove it, that's what I say."

Smiling, Joanna tucked her arm through her father's as the sun burned bloodred above the green hills. Just as she had hoped, Harrison was soon too absorbed to pursue his questions about his headstrong daughter.

An hour later, Peter tugged Joanna off for a personally guided tour of what everyone was now calling "Peter's trench."

Joanna watched him with a mixture of pride and sadness. Already he seemed perched on the edge of boyhood. His gray eyes held a maturity beyond his age and occasionally a glint of sadness.

But only occasionally.

Clearly, he thrived in the excitement of a working dig. Joanna was proud of her son, but the specter of the past was always at her shoulder. Surviving had meant making hard choices, and now she was faced with hard choices once again.

Joanna looked down at the old silver scars crisscrossing the top of her right wrist. She barely noticed the marks now.

But another person would notice. Another person would wonder what had left the tiny silver lines across the tender skin. As she moved down the passage lit by torches, something tightened at her throat. She stared at the old scars and wondered if they could have been avoided. Or had her only sin been her naïveté?

"Here's the spot!" Peter tugged her through the darkness past the ghostly outline of metal scaffolding. "What's wrong, Mom?" His head cocked. "Not afraid of the dark, are you?"

"I never want you to go beyond this point, Peter. These old tunnels aren't stable anymore."

"I know all about that. Gran tells me about them probably a million times a day. I may be a kid, but I'm *not* stupid."

Joanna hid a smile.

"But sometimes I'm . . . afraid," he said softly. "Mainly when the wind slams the trees and rattles the windows, like it's trying to get in." He frowned. "Gran told me about the wind, how it comes from hot air and cold air when they run into each other. But sometimes knowing *why* a thing happens doesn't change how you feel." His fingers tensed. "You know what I mean?"

"I know." For a blinding instant Joanna felt the terror of darkness and cold air. The narrow tunnel walls loomed close, pressing down over her. In that second, knowing that she was only reliving the past didn't make what she felt any less frightening.

Yes, Joanna could certainly understand her son's nightmares.

"Mom?" Peter was studying her intently. "We're here. We're at the best part of the tunnel now, where I found all the good things."

Joanna shoved her feelings deep into the place where

she kept the past and all its pain. She summoned a smile. "Yes, we *are* at the best part, aren't we?"

Not back with the fear.

Not back in the darkness. She would never allow anyone to threaten Peter or her again.

Gradually her smile widened. "So what are you waiting for, Einstein? Show me everything."

Two hours later, Joanna was at the base of the hill, walking to her car in search of a set of soldering tools for Peter. Light glinted off a pair of silver fenders as a dented Land Rover pulled to a stop beside her. Alexei Cameron's hands were curled around the wheel. "Get in."

Joanna felt her heart slam against her chest. "Go away."

"Get in," Alex said flatly. "Unless you want to hold this particular conversation in front of three dozen witnesses."

Joanna saw the white outlines of his knuckles, gripping the wheel.

She got in.

11

"How did you find me?"

"It doesn't matter," Alex said grimly.

"It matters to me."

He looked straight ahead, almost as if he were afraid to look at her. His hands were still wrapped around the wheel. "Metcalfe tells me a woman came to the house today. She said you had forgotten your shoes and sent her to fetch them."

Joanna frowned. "I didn't send anyone to Greywood. I didn't leave any shoes either."

"I didn't think so." Alex didn't move, his eyes locked on a puzzle only he could see.

Joanna felt the blood rush from her face. "Who was she? What did she want?"

For long seconds, Alex did not speak. The sun was nearly above the trees now. A flock of geese sailed east, their long necks a precise silhouette against the sky. "Maybe it had to do with these." Something hit the seat between them.

Something long and flat inside an envelope.

Joanna didn't move. She felt her heart skip crazily. And then came the *wham*—pain at her chest like a fist.

The photos. Alex had seen them.

"Metcalfe found them under the sofa," he said grimly. "He thought they were mine. But they fell out of your bag, didn't they?"

Joanna stared blindly at the black and white frames, pressure billowing against her chest.

"No tearful apologies? No breathless, inventive explanations?"

Joanna drew a shuddering breath. "Alex, don't."

"Don't *what?*" he said savagely. "Don't feel like a horse just kicked me in the chest? Don't feel so damned angry that I'm afraid to take my hands off this steering wheel for fear of what I might do?" Then for the first time his head turned, and he looked at her.

The sight of his drawn face made Joanna's breath catch. His eyes were hard, furious. "Don't bother trying to lie, Joanna—or whatever your real name is. You really don't have the face for it. Just answer one question. It was you, wasn't it?"

"Alex, I—"

"Just answer."

The wind threw up dirt in little spirals across the old Roman site. Joanna's fingernails dug into the soft leather seat as the brown clouds spun past.

She swallowed. "Yes, it was."

His hands twisted involuntarily. "Then God help us both," he said, jamming the gear forward and spinning off over the rutted earth.

"What are you doing?" Joanna whispered.

"Taking you to the studio you rent at Draycott Abbey," Alex said curtly. "I know about that, too, you see. And when we get there, you're going to tell me exactly why you gave your body to me five years ago."

Dusk veiled the road as Alex roared south. Joanna didn't ask how he knew the route. Clearly his sources of information were excellent.

Her hands locked in her lap as the peaceful hills flashed past in a blur. After all the years, she found she was no more prepared with answers now than she had been then.

She stole a look at Alex's face. His cheekbones were etched against the twilight, and his eyes were locked on the road. Joanna felt her hands begin to tremble.

Answers? What answers were there that wouldn't hurt them both?

Alex pulled around the drive, slammed the car to a halt, and strode toward the beautiful cottage, its windows purple with approaching night.

"Give me the key," he ordered.

"I—I don't lock it."

He turned around and laughed grimly. "With the old pieces you handle? Are you *mad?*"

Joanna shrugged. "It's never been a problem."

"It is now." He pushed open the door and disappeared inside. The last rays of sunlight filtered through the floor-to-ceiling windows, filling the room with purple shadows. A pair of Italian rapiers glowed where they lay side by side on Joanna's worktable.

Alex turned slowly, his fingers curved around the edge of the table. "Why, Joanna?"

"It . . . just happened, Alex. Maybe it was your passion when you worked. It touched something deep inside me. I won't apologize and I won't explain any more than that."

His fist slammed against the wall. "Damn it, you *will* explain. I was there, too. It was my body wrapped around you, my fingers that made you cry out with passion, remember?"

Joanna's voice shook. "Don't."

"Don't remind you of the truth? Are you afraid of how the truth feels? God knows I've stayed up enough nights asking myself what I did wrong, how I drove you away. And when I did, I thought about you with another man, with your hands buried in his hair while you made those low, wild sounds against his lips."

Joanna froze, stunned by his admission.

"What were you hiding, a wealthy husband? Or was it Jacques all along? Were you afraid he'd wash his hands of you if he found out you were sleeping with a common Gypsy?"

"I'm not ashamed of who you are or what we did. But there were reasons, Alex. Reasons why it could *never* go farther."

"None that count."

He meant it, Joanna realized. Nothing would deter this man once he set a course of action. Arguments would not touch him. How right she had been to vanish, leaving no trace.

"I don't have to explain."

"Wrong," he said softly, striding through the twilight, his eyes like a hunter's. "You do have to explain, starting now." His hands rose slowly, almost as if he was trying to change his mind. They anchored her cheeks and slanted her face upward. "Your hair was black as night then. You had glasses, too. But, God, I should have known you sooner. I should have *felt* you." His hands tightened. "Lie to me, Joanna," he whispered. "Tell me that you forgot what this feels like. Tell me that the memory of our locked bodies hasn't teased your dreams a thousand times."

Joanna put up her hands, desperate to shove him away. Desperate to tell him that everything he said was true.

"Go on," he whispered. "Lie to me like you did five years ago. Tell me you've forgotten how I taste, how I feel inside you." His voice hardened. "And then tell me you don't want this just as much as I do."

He kissed her eyelids slowly, then her cheek and her jaw. His fingers eased into her hair, meeting at her neck.

Joanna fought to keep back a moan of shock and pleasure. "I don't remember," she said brokenly. "None of those things."

His mouth covered her trembling lips. "I'm listening," he whispered. Then he opened her mouth with his.

She thought the touch would be angry, punishing, but he tasted her gently, his control absolute. His hands framed her face, and Joanna felt the brush of his cuff links. She caught the scent of lemon and sandalwood drifting from his skin.

The memories rushed back, just as he had sworn they would. She wanted, oh, God, how much she wanted in that moment.

But her hands closed, shoving at his chest. "No, Alex."

He kissed the line of her cheekbone, then caught her lower lip against his teeth. "You're trembling, Joanna. I can feel it where our bodies touch. You remember, don't you?"

She bit back a ragged sound of pleasure. Desire rocked her, making her fingers open over the hard muscles of his chest. She shoved away, wincing as pain burned through her arm.

"No matter. Because I remember, Joanna. Maybe I remember enough for both of us. And someone else remembers, too." He tossed the grainy photographs onto the table. "How long have you had these?"

Joanna shoved her hair from her face and drew a deep breath. "Since yesterday."

"Before the performance." Alex cursed softly. "So that's what threw you off."

Joanna didn't deny it. Lying to him now would be useless.

"Is that the first time you were contacted?"

She nodded, afraid to trust her voice.

"Are they after money?"

"I doubt I have enough to make it worth their while."

Alex slanted a quick glance over the room, assessing the colorful pillows, framed prints, and bright chintz furniture. His frown implied that what he saw was tasteful but not necessarily expensive. "So if it's not money, what *are* they after?" He might have been talking to himself, moving through a list of possibilities. "Revenge? Or maybe they want the access that could only be gained through you. Access to Jacques perhaps." His eyes narrowed. "Or maybe access to me."

"You—you can't believe that, Alex. I didn't plan this. I didn't come looking for you."

"That's only too obvious. You've done everything possible to hide from me. But like it or not, we're bound now. Whoever sent those photographs did it for a reason."

"What reason?" Joanna whispered.

"I don't know yet." He reached for the grainy prints, and Joanna stiffened. "I need them, Joanna. It's the only way I can track these people down." His eyes darkened. "Besides, I've seen everything there already, remember?"

She remembered. God help her, she remembered far too clearly. And it was tearing her up inside.

Alex didn't move, photos in hand. His eyes narrowed, almost as if he were trying to read her thoughts.

"Don't, Alex."

"Don't what?"

"Look at me like that, as if you can see right into my head."

"Maybe I can, Joanna."

"Gypsy mind reading?" She laughed grimly.

"You might be surprised," he said tightly. "And I'm warning you now, it's not over for *me,* Joanna. Not nearly over."

She stood very still. "When?"

His eyes moved along her flushed cheeks, across her full, high breasts. "When you lie beneath me, Joanna. When you feel me inside you and then say that you don't want me," he said hoarsely.

He turned. The sound of his footsteps was harsh against the quiet of the gathering night.

Like a sleepwalker, Joanna moved to the corner closet. With trembling hands she removed a small cedar chest containing a silk dress, a fragile pressed camellia, and a sheet of paper.

She held the yellowed page tightly, oblivious to the moonlight that gradually filled the studio. The silence was complete, without beginning or end as she sat motionless, remembering her betrayal, knowing even now that it had been her only choice.

She did not need to look down to see the words on the sheet of paper. A number was written there, the phone number where Alexei Turov had promised she could reach him at any time and for any reason.

Joanna moved to the telephone. Holding the fragile sheet, she dialed the number that Constantin Stevanov's apprentice had left her so long ago.

She counted twenty rings before she had an answer.

"Greywood Foundation," a cultured female voice announced. "May I help you?"

There had been no Greywood Foundation then, Joanna knew. Through all the change, all the growth, Alex had kept that old number.

So you could call him. So you could contact him if you needed him.

The pain that had been pressing at her heart threatened to crush her.

"May I help you?" the woman repeated.

Joanna's fingers tightened. She stared at the telephone through a blur of tears, unable to speak.

"Is anyone there?"

Slowly, she slid the phone back in its cradle. He had kept the number unchanged all these years just as he had promised. She hadn't even known.

Joanna sank to the floor, her face buried in her hands, trying to forget the pain in Alex's eyes.

Instead she remembered.

Just like all the other times . . .

Midnight.

A tropical sky like velvet sprinkled with phosphorous stars.

The sound of rustling palm trees rose above the distant crash of the surf. Joanna barely heard, nursing the bruise on her cheek.

A tree shook behind her. Gasping, she sank back into the darkness as a shadowed figure loomed closer.

The palm fronds whispered, and the footsteps came to an abrupt halt.

"Are you well?" His voice was low and heavily accented. "I know you are there. I hear first you quarreling out here, then a cry. Like pain."

Joanna winced as a palm frond touched her

bruised face. What he said was true. Jacques's senior art consultant had pursued her out to the beach and trapped her inside a deserted boathouse. In seconds, his attentions had gone from insistent to frightening. When Joanna had confronted him with irregularities in pricing and purchases, his crude desire had exploded into fury.

His fist had landed one blow before she managed to hit him with a fallen oar. Cursing brokenly, Simon Loring had vowed to pay her back by passing those same financial "irregularities" off as hers.

Now Joanna sat in the darkness, thinking about what would follow.

Simon Loring was part of the old-boy network. He had impeccable credentials and powerful friends. He would see to it that Joanna was fired from a job that she desperately needed to support herself and her young son.

"Come out. If not, I will go to find St. Cyr myself."

Her long black hair curled about her shoulders as she stepped out onto the deserted beach. The quarter moon was veiled by clouds.

"He hurt you, this pig?" Joanna recognized the swordmaker's rough voice. "I watch him come after you."

"You saw him?"

Alexei Turov shrugged. "After sword is done, I am restless. I drink, which is bad. Then I see you go toward beach." He moved closer. "He hurt you, no?"

"It's . . . nothing."

He brushed her throbbing cheek, and Joanna knew her glasses wouldn't hide the dark circle of bruised skin. When she winced, he cursed harshly. "With Constantin's sword I hack this Loring in two. That will please you, no?"

"No." Joanna caught back a broken sound of pain. "Then he'll come after you and Mr. Stevanov. You don't know what Simon Loring can be like."

"I know," he said grimly. "Such men growl at

the moon but run at their own shadow." His gentle, strong fingers moved along her swollen jaw. "Let me see. Come here into light."

"No." It wasn't just the embarrassment of having him see her bruised face that kept Joanna where she was. It was the sudden, desperate yearning for warmth, for the strength of the arms that had bent so lovingly above his sword.

He muttered in that dark, rich tongue he used with Constantin. "So, we will sit together in shadows, I think. Just you and me." He sat down at the edge of the sand, bowed formally, and held out his hand. "I am Alexei Turov."

Joanna took the hard, calloused fingers, remembering their power at the forge. "I know."

"Your name?" he prompted.

"Annie. Annie Smith," she lied, glad for the darkness that concealed her flush.

"Sit, Annie Smith." He swayed, and Joanna wondered if he wasn't a little drunk.

Warily, she sank onto the sand.

He pressed a pale bloom into her hands, a camellia he had pulled from a nearby shrub.

Joanna touched the soft petals. Maybe all life was just this fragile, fate hinging on the tiny details of an unexpected encounter.

"Drink."

A bottle touched her hand. Frowning, Joanna took a swallow. The expensive brandy slid like fire down her throat. After a moment, she took another sip.

"So he hits you and you conceal this. Very stupid, I think. Such a man will always find a dark path where he can hit you again."

The wind blew up cool and fragrant from the sea as Joanna stared out at the darkness. He was right, unfortunately. She had finally faced that fact tonight. Simon was now her relentless enemy, one she would always have to avoid.

Or she would have to leave.

*She took another slow drink, then passed the
bottle back.*

"So. Do you stay or do you go?"

*Joanna made her decision. "I go. As soon as I can
find another place. I won't allow Simon to frighten
me off without the recommendations I've earned."*

*"He will try, that one. He will think of many lies
to stop you."*

*"Let him try. I know too much for that." Now that
the choice was made, Joanna felt light-headed,
exuberant, more alive than she had for weeks. At
that moment she realized exactly how painful it had
been to work under Loring's tyranny.*

*She tilted her head and studied the lacy clouds
shadowing the quarter moon. "No more about
him."*

"About the pig, you mean."

*"Yes, the pig." Joanna smiled crookedly. "I want
another drink, Alexei Turov. I want to be very drunk
tonight."*

*He laughed. The sound was music, soft and husky
and rueful. "You drink enough already, I think."*

*"Not nearly enough," Joanna said firmly, reach-
ing for the bottle cradled in the sand at his side.*

*Her fingers grazed his chest, and she went very
still. Her breath came slow and ragged in the
darkness as Joanna realized what she was doing was
dangerously reckless.*

*One more drink, she told herself. Just one hour
and perhaps a kiss to blot out the weeks of Simon's
crude threats. She would never see this quiet, fierce
man again, so what harm could there be for either of
them?*

"You are trembling, Annie Smith."

*Joanna touched the mat of dark hair on his chest.
"So are you," she whispered.*

*"You are right," he muttered harshly. "It is
better for you to go back up the beach now.
Alone." He forced her fingers to stop their slow*

movement. "You see I am very, very drunk tonight."

"You don't sound drunk."

"Is second bottle. First was vodka. Good Russian vodka."

Joanna gnawed at her lip. "I don't want to go back." It might almost have been a stranger who spoke those fateful words. "I think I want to be drunk, too. On brandy." Her voice fell. "And on you, Alexei Turov."

The bottle slid onto its side against the sand, forgotten. The man with the poet's voice and artist's hands turned slowly. "You want me to make you forget, Miss Annie Smith. Maybe Alexei Turov is good enough for that. Maybe I, too, have things to forget."

Joanna's heart hammered as he moved closer. She felt hot, dizzy. Stop him, she told herself. The idea was crazy, even dangerous. After all, what did she know about this man?

That he had the hands of a poet as he slid a fresh camellia behind her ear. That he would not hurt her, her heart whispered.

He would make her feel very beautiful, even if it was only for one night.

"Is bad idea. I am very drunk to think of it." His palms brushed her bare shoulders and covered her cheeks. "But you are very beautiful woman," he said hoarsely.

"You can't be that drunk."

Up the hill, palm fronds cracked in the silence, and then Loring's voice rose in a shout. "Of course she's out here. The black-haired bitch nearly pulled off my pants, I tell you. Now I know why she was so hot to get me alone." Loring laughed crudely. "Believe me, Jacques, that sweet young thing just stole two of your finest dueling pistols, and she didn't want me up at the house taking any last-minute inventories."

Joanna's hand tensed. She barely felt Alexei tug her back into the shadows as the smell of Jacques's *distinctive pipe tobacco drifted on the still air.* "He can't say *that!*" Joanna hissed.

Alexei pressed a hand to her mouth. "Be quiet for now. Is better to listen."

"So you think she's been stealing from me, Simon? I confess I've had some doubts about her." St. Cyr took a thoughtful puff on his pipe. "When did you first suspect something was wrong?"

"About a month ago. It was right after that last shipment came in from Paris. She told me everything was received, but when I checked the bill of lading, one scabbard was missing."

"I see. A pity. I was coming to like your assistant."

"I know you were. That's why I waited to be sure before I came to you," Simon said coolly. "I know how you trusted her with extra responsibilities."

"You have no idea how much it pains me," Jacques said slowly. "Let's go back to the house, shall we? Then you can tell me all the rest, and I'll decide what must be done."

Tears burned in Joanna's eyes as she heard the two men move back over the sand. Her hands twisted, clenched into angry fists. In minutes, Simon Loring had reduced her world to ashes.

Slowly, Alex released her. "Is clever of him," he said harshly. "But St. Cyr is a great fool if he believes such a story." Alexei brushed a strand of hair from her shoulder. "You are crying, I think, Annie Smith."

"What if I am?" Joanna thought about starting over, faced with applications, interviews, and endless questions. Word of her dismissal would travel swiftly. Simon would see to that. And because the art world was still very much a man's world, Simon's story would be believed, not hers.

There would be curt rejections with no concrete reasons given. She would be dealt with summarily, discreetly, and crushingly.

Starting over would not be easy. It might even be impossible.

Calloused hands opened over her waist. Strong hands.

An artist's hands.

"Let him talk. Tomorrow I tell St. Cyr what happened and why you ran—that it was not as this pig told him."

"Jacques won't believe you. I don't think he likes you very much," Joanna said bleakly, staring out at the pale line of the crashing surf.

"Is true. But tomorrow I will be most persuasive. I can when it suits me, you understand." He tilted her head slowly. "You believe this?"

"You make steel sing, Alexei Turov. How could you not move people just as easily?" A tear crept down her cheek.

"No, you are persuasive. I think so today while you watch me with the sword. Your eyes are different from the others. They watch my face, my body, but you watch only my hands."

"Because they are beautiful. Always with great control."

"No, you are the beautiful one tonight."

"Me?" Joanna laughed shortly. "I am ordinary. Less than ordinary."

He lifted her hands slowly and kissed each finger. "A woman who can touch so carefully, so gently, is never ordinary. There is magic in these hands, only you do not see this." He brought her palms to his chest, and Joanna felt the race of his heart. "You see?" he whispered. "This power you have is very great." He touched the fragile blossom tucked behind her ear. "You should always wear this one. How do you call it?"

Her breath was a mere hint of air. "Camellia."

"Camellia," he repeated. "Is good word. Now close your eyes, Annie Smith."

"But I—"

"You trust me?"

Joanna thought of his hands above the blade and the coaxing timbre of his voice. "I trust you."

"Is good. Now close your eyes." When she obeyed, he gently kissed her eyelids. "If you do not see, instead you feel. Is this way I first learned about fire. Without eyes, you can truly feel with deeper eyes and real heart. This, Constantin taught me. Blind is only way to see."

Joanna shivered as his lips trailed over her jaw, down her throat. "But if I can't see . . ." The words fell away. His hands moved gently over her cheek, each stroke taking more of the pain from the bruise Loring had left. "How do you do that?"

"Old Gypsy secret. Now you can feel, because you do not spend so much time looking." He pulled her to her feet. "Come." His laughter was reckless as he tugged her through the palm fronds and down toward the beach. At the curve of the cove he stopped, one arm at her waist. "You see? Really see now?"

Joanna blinked at the restless darkness. Then she noticed streaks of pale foam that rose along the ridge of crashing waves. Beneath the sliver of the moon, she saw that the sea itself was alive, a network of subtle, shifting light that stretched all the way to the horizon. "Moonlight and something else," she breathed. "What is it?"

"This light is from sea creatures, tiny things. Millions of them."

"They're beautiful."

He nodded. "Not at all ordinary, you see?" Their hands slid together and linked gently as they stood before nature's splendor. "Yet one minute you see only darkness."

Joanna's throat tightened. "Now I can see what was there all along, something that I nearly missed."

"Very beautiful. Just like you." He raised their linked fingers and pointed to a serpentine trail of luminescence. "They make their own fire, these *creatures of sea. But only special eyes can see and only on darkest nights." Slowly he brought her palm to his mouth. "Now you see, too. Is good."*

The wind danced through Joanna's hair. She closed her eyes, feeling the warmth of his mouth at her palm. "Thank you."

"No." His fingers tightened. "Is for me to thank you. And now I go."

"Go where?"

He shrugged. "For a walk up the beach. All alone." He planted a slow kiss on her lips, then turned unsteadily. "Before all this brandy makes me change my mind."

"No, wait. I haven't had a chance to—"

And then everything happened at once. A dark figure came crashing through the camellia shrubs. She heard cursing and the slap of fists.

"I knew you were here, you little bitch. Bloody clever of you to document the purchasing discrepancies you found. Jacques saw them, and now you've cost me my job along with the very tidy sum that I was making from his competitors." Simon Loring lunged at her, cursing. "That entitles me to some compensation."

Abruptly, he went sailing onto his face in the sand.

"Damn you, I'll make you sorry for—"

There was another blur of movement. This time Loring tumbled toward the water. Cursing, he staggered to his feet and circled the tall figure who had appeared from the shadows behind him.

"Nice bodyguard. I didn't know you liked slumming with illiterates. But maybe it takes inbred Gypsies to make a prim curator like you excited." Loring swung wildly and missed. "Hitler should have finished your lot off when he had the chance, Turov. In fact, we should have paid him to do the job."

A fist exploded against his jaw. Loring swayed sideways, then was jerked back onto his feet.

"Now you take back what you say to her."

"Like hell I will."

Alexei laughed coldly. "Then we stay here and I break your jaw. After this, I move your nose to other part of face."

"I'd like to see you try, you damned inbred—"

A powerful fist slammed into Loring's cheek. He swayed forward, then tottered toward the sand. "Watch—your back, Gypsy. I'll be—coming," he grated. "For you, too, Joa—"

And then he pitched facedown onto the sand.

"You see, his kind do not give up. And your St. Cyr is not so stupid."

Joanna took a ragged breath. "I don't understand. Jacques said he believed Simon."

"Only to get more information. Is very clever of him."

Joanna couldn't pull her gaze from Simon's motionless body. "I thought I knew him. Oh, he was unpleasant, but I never really thought . . ." Suddenly, she couldn't stop shaking. "If you hadn't been here—"

His hands ran over her hair. "This one will do no more harm. There will be other men for you. Better men with gentle hands."

"Your hands are gentle."

"Men with good English and fine names."

"I like your English just fine. I like your name, too."

"Annie, is better I go," he said harshly.

"I can still hear his threats. They make me feel . . . dirty."

Alexei cursed. "This I have an answer for." He pulled her over the sand.

"What are you doing?"

"Seeing is good, Annie Smith. Now you learn about feeling."

* * *

"A swimming pool?" Joanna blinked down at the glowing water, where stream rose in slow gray trails. "Now?"

"We swim. Here. Then you feel clean again."

"But I don't have a suit."

He fingered the strap at her shoulder. "You wear that. A very pretty dress. Silk, no? It will wash?"

Joanna laughed unsteadily. "Yes, it will wash, but I still don't think—"

His watch dropped with a clatter, followed by his shoes. Then he dove cleanly into the water, pants and all. When he broke the surface, he slung back his long hair with a noisy sputter. "Drunk." He shook his head. "A curse on all brandy. Even more, a curse on Russian vodka."

Through the steam rising from the heated pool, Joanna saw him mutter, then swim toward the far edge. After a moment's hesitation, she tugged off her glasses and dove in after him.

In an instant, she was immersed in blurred aqua light and drifting veils of steam. Water lapped gently around her as she did a lazy backstroke toward the opposite end.

She stood up slowly, and the thin silk clung to her body like a lover's touch.

Alexei's eyes slid downward. "I am very, very drunk to think what I think."

Joanna stopped him with one hand on his shoulder. Her lips came down, tracing the curve of his spine. "Tell me what you think."

His powerful muscles tensed at her touch. He swung about, gripping her face between calloused palms. "About touching you. About taking more and more. Is very dangerous."

Warm currents brushed Joanna's skin beneath the clinging silk. "Touching you would never be dangerous." Her mouth opened over his hard palm.

"Better for us to stop, Annie. Now. Before we . . ."

Her lips blocked his words. Cursing, he gripped her hips through the thin wet silk.

Joanna shivered with a rush of desire as the mist rose around them, making her feel separate from all she was and would be.

She swallowed slowly. "Kiss me, Alexei. Touch me. Dangerous or not, I want this . . ."

Dreams, sweet and reckless.

Alex's hands—

The shrill ring of the phone startled Joanna from lingering dreams.

The clock beside her bed showed 2:14 A.M. as she searched blindly for the receiver.

"Hello?"

"Is this Ms. Joanna Russell?"

"Yes. Who are—"

"This is Sir Gordon Mount, Ms. Russell. I am Jacques St. Cyr's solicitor."

Joanna sat up slowly. There was a clipped formality to the English voice that made her frown. "I've heard Jacques speak of you."

"I'm afraid I have bad news, Ms. Russell. Jacques St. Cyr has been . . . hurt."

"Hurt? I don't understand."

"I'll answer all your questions at the hospital." He gave an address in London, and then there was a silence. "I suggest you hurry."

12

JACQUES WAS in a private hospital room surrounded by banks of machinery that whirled and blinked and beeped. His face was pale and gaunt, his breathing barely visible beneath an oxygen mask. There had been a surprising amount of security to pass before Joanna finally found herself standing beside him. It was only later that she realized the significance of that fact.

"Oh, Jacques," she whispered, stunned to see his pallor and the signs of age.

A thin man with receding white hair rose soundlessly from one of the room's two chairs. "Ms. Russell?" he asked.

Joanna nodded.

"I'm so glad you could come. I'm Sir Gordon Mount."

Joanna couldn't look away from Jacques's face. "What happened?"

The Englishman moved to the door, looked outside, then moved back. "I'm afraid it's rather complicated. There are still a great many questions to be answered."

"What kind of questions?"

"Last night Mr. St. Cyr was found on the drive of his Surrey estate. It would seem that he had fallen from an upper window."

"You're not certain?"

The solicitor frowned. "The window was open, and the body was in the proper position."

"Are you saying Jacques tried to kill himself?"

139

"I am saying that Mr. St. Cyr fell. The blood tests show he had been drinking."

Joanna swallowed. "Wasn't anyone else there at the time?"

"His bodyguard spent the evening in his private apartment. When he heard noises and went to the house to investigate, he found the butler unconscious. The man knew nothing except that he had been hit from behind."

"And Jacques?"

"They found him on the drive. There were signs of a struggle in the house—broken lamps and that sort of thing."

"Then he was the victim of a robbery?"

The Englishman sighed. "Sit down, Ms. Russell, and let me explain." He waited until she was sitting, then turned to pace the narrow room. "Jacques left me instructions about people to contact should he—come to some kind of harm. You were at the top of the list. The police are working around the clock on finding answers." He held out a sealed envelope. "But Jacques said this should be delivered to you immediately. It was almost as if he expected something like this."

Joanna sat frozen with shock. Behind her, the soft beep and hiss of the machines continued.

"I'll be outside if you need me," Sir Gordon said quietly, moving to the door.

Joanna opened the envelope and stared blindly at the bold letters, so distinctively Jacques's. Blinking back tears, she began to read.

It pains me to write these words, Joanna. It pains me even more to know that you may soon be reading them. The only way you will be holding this letter is if I am badly hurt, possibly dying. Maybe even dead already. But I am a methodical man, and I have always faced life practically.

What I cannot prepare for is how my death will affect others, you most of all.

Recently, I added a fine piece to my collection. I hoped to discuss it with you before I wrote these lines, but it was not possible. So now I will tell you what I would have said then. It is only what you must know, only enough to keep you safe. Many others wanted this piece, and I paid greatly for it.

If I am dead, they will come after you next.

Joanna stared at the words in confusion, then looked at Jacques's motionless body, feeling icy fingers of panic. She was next?

You must assume they know everything, Joanna. They know your skill and how I have relied on you in the past. They know, too, that I have found the three clues after years of searching. These are in my hands now, so simple.

So impossible.

Now you must find the answers I could not. Find the key and you will know who did this to me. Be certain that no accident brought me here, no matter what they tell you.

And remember, trust no one.

Joanna stared at the paper in confusion. Who would kill for a piece of art? And why would they threaten her next?

Her hands tightened as she immediately thought of Peter. No matter what happened, she could not allow him to be endangered. If Jacques was right and she was a target . . .

She sank into the chair by Jacques's bed, the paper crumpled in her fingers. She thought about the anger and the arguments, about Jacques's brilliant instinct for authenticity fueled by his obsessive drive to possess and control.

He had never been an easy man to understand. Possession was everything to him, and they had quarreled often over acquisitions and the necessity of documentation. It had been one of those arguments that had driven Joanna out into the warm tropical night five years before, into the arms of Alexei Turov Cameron.

No, she wouldn't think about that. Not now.

Around her lights flashed. Sterile tubes opened and closed over Jacques's face, keeping him alive.

Joanna looked down at the letter clenched within her trembling fingers.

"You have read it, Ms. Russell?" St. Cyr's solicitor stood looking at her from the doorway.

"Yes," she said softly. "I've read it."

The Englishman came inside and closed the door behind him. "He is a hard man, Ms. Russell. A careful man. I have handled business matters for many men over the last twenty-five years, but none were as complex as his. And I still cannot say that I know him, not well." He sighed. "And now this." His eyes flickered to the motionless figure lying against the white sheets. "If there is anything I can do, you must feel free to call me. Jacques set aside certain funds for your use, should it become necessary."

"But I don't understand. In this letter he said . . ."

The solicitor's eyes narrowed. "Yes?"

Joanna swallowed. Was he watching her too intently? *Trust no one.* "I don't understand what happened to him," she finished.

"As of this moment, the police report is unclear. How or when he fell is still open to dispute." His eyes slanted to the paper in her hands. "Perhaps his letter says something to explain."

"No," Joanna said tightly. "It's personal." She shrugged. "As you say, he was a hard man at times. Tell me, did he leave any other letters for me?"

The solicitor ran thin fingers over his silk tie, smoothing it carefully. "There are many more papers to examine. But I will stay in close contact, you may be assured of that."

Joanna stayed at the hospital for the next six hours, pacing blindly, hoping Jacques would regain consciousness. After falling asleep twice, she reluctantly gave her phone number to an attendant and left orders to call her if there was any change.

On the drive back home, her eyes kept flickering to the road behind her while Jacques's words echoed through her mind.

Be certain that no accident brought me here.

Light flashed behind her. Headlights flared briefly, cutting through the night.

They will come after you next.

Only a dairy truck turning off the road, she saw.

Joanna's fingers tightened on the wheel, but she could not shake the feeling that she was being followed.

Alex paced the quiet nursery beneath the eaves of Greywood House. Old stuffed animals filled the walls next to a pair of stuffed owls. Broken fishing nets lay atop stringless tennis rackets.

The relics of a boyhood of shadows.

"I spoke to someone in the hospital," Metcalfe said gravely. "There is no doubt about it."

"So it's true." Alex shook his head. "I never liked St. Cyr as a man or as a collector, but I did not want this. Is his condition still the same?"

Metcalfe nodded. "Still on life support and his prognosis is guarded. The staff is being very closed mouthed."

Alex rubbed his jaw, bothered by images he couldn't quite see. "Who do we know in the Surrey Police Department, Metcalfe?"

The butler frowned. "There is a deputy chief inspector who's very fond of us."

"There is?"

"Yes, my lord. He has a cousin in Greece whom we helped immigrate here last year. There was a bit of unpleasantness about his political background."

Alex laughed tightly. "I can bloody well imagine. So what has this deputy chief inspector told us about the police report on St. Cyr's accident?" His voice hardened. "If it really *was* an accident."

"Not very much so far, I'm afraid. There seems to be an unusual wall of secrecy in this case."

Alex frowned at the electronic equipment spread out

over his old nursery. The room had been temporarily
turned over to Metcalfe while a new area was finished
for him on the ground floor, complete with the
industrial-grade wiring to support Metcalfe's interest in
high-tech instruments. "I don't suppose there is anything you can do about that secrecy."

Metcalfe's eyes took on a glint of excitement. "The
codes they use are five years outdated. A proper disgrace
actually." He rolled up his shirt sleeves, frowning at his
computer screen. "I've been longing for a chance to
crack that particular mainframe."

"Wicked, Metcalfe."

"All in the interest of scientific progress, of course,"
the butler murmured.

Alex picked up an old stuffed rabbit from a Cameron
tartan blanket. He held it gently for a moment, replaced
a dangling eye, then tucked the fragile figure back into its
spot next to a row of turtle shells. "Jacques mentioned
Fine Arts magazine. Any contacts there?"

"One. A nice young woman with a very good hand for
soufflés. Shall I give her a try?"

Alex nodded. "It might be important. St. Cyr seemed
very full of himself about an announcement he was to
make there."

Metcalfe turned away and began tapping at the keys
on his computer, losing himself immediately in arcane
codes. Computers were Metcalfe's second love after
cooking, which was fine with Alex. All he had to do was
look at the things, and they developed sudden, irrepara-
ble malfunctions.

As Metcalfe went about his electronic wizardry, Alex
prowled restlessly, straightening books and touching the
forgotten old toys that had belonged to his childhood.
The news about Jacques had disturbed him deeply.
Despite their hostility, Alex knew he would not be able
to relax until Metcalfe came up with some answers.

A Tiffany lamp cast jewellike pools of pink and violet
over a battered old rocking horse. Alex touched the
threadbare bridle, remembering angry rides taken as a

boy, lost in a world of imaginary speed as he escaped from a stern father and a mother who was trying to adjust to a new country.

The horse's eyes were distant now, and they held no answers for the man Alex had become. Even the old key hanging from a frayed cord around the horse's neck was rusted and tarnished.

Alex turned away, feeling old shadows creep out from his unsettled past. His father's death had come suddenly. Alex had barely reached his bedside in time to touch his frail hand. There had been no time for explanations or answers, and the years had ended without either man saying the words of love and forgiveness that would have given absolution.

Alex touched the chipped and painted horse, wishing the end could have been different. If only there were a way to go back just for an hour to say good-bye.

Suddenly, the muscles at his neck tightened. He watched the floor move sharply. "What the hell?"

He felt waves of burning color pour over him in mad, restless patterns.

Voices.

Terror.

"My lord?"

Alex bent over the old horse, gasping for breath, struggling to speak. He was spinning in a world of shadows and screaming heat, feeling each color slide against his skin, hard and metallic.

He was in the dark place where his visions burned unimpeded. They had come sharply to him before, some frightening in their clarity but never like this, choking and oppressive.

His legs gave way. Dimly he felt his elbow slam against the floor. He tried to choke out a word, any sound at all.

Joanna.

". . . can't hear you . . ."

Joanna. Danger.

He felt Metcalfe's hands loosening his collar. A pillow was shoved beneath his head.

"Find—Dimitri," Alex finally gasped, "—to the cottage. To Joanna."

Dawn. Slow light filtering through lace curtains.

Alex opened his eyes dizzily and saw a stuffed owl staring at him morosely. Metcalfe's worried face was the next thing he saw. He gave a crooked smile. "Hell of a mess, isn't it?"

Metcalfe didn't smile back.

"That bad?" Alex muttered.

"You scared ten years off my life. What in earth happened?"

Alex struggled forward, propping his back against an old leather wing chair with a ragged seat. "Visions, Metcalfe."

"I've seen you have those Gypsy flashes of yours. You've never looked like *that* before."

"No," Alex said slowly, "this was different. Choking. Almost like fear." He drew a slow breath, wincing as pain shot through his elbow. "Took a pounding, did I?"

"You bloody well did. I've brought you some scotch."

Alex sipped slowly, trying to make sense of the chaotic visions. "Joanna?" he asked tightly.

"Dimitri's at her cottage, parked just down the hill. No one has been in or out for an hour. She got back from London and went straight inside. Her lights went out ten minutes ago."

Alex felt some of the tension drain from his shoulders. But the primitive fear was still there, triggered by a blood vision he could not ignore.

Someone was in danger. Great danger.

Metcalfe cleared his throat. "I was able to find an editor at *Fine Arts* magazine. She told me they had arranged an interview with St. Cyr last week, but because they couldn't verify a number of claims he had made, they pulled the piece."

Alex frowned. "What sort of claims?"

"That's all I could find out. But someone else was interested in that article. The magazine staff received another inquiry two hours ago."

Alex pushed to his feet, half afraid the floor would start pitching again. "Better," he said. "I think I might even be able to walk."

Metcalfe sniffed. "You should be resting, you young fool."

"Can't. Work to do." Carefully Alex made his way to Metcalfe's table. "Now tell me what you've found."

13

LATE THAT afternoon Alex Cameron stood on the third floor of St. Adam's Academy and watched sunlight spill through a pair of stained glass windows. St. Adam's was the most exclusive school in Kent and had been for two centuries, dominating fifty wooded acres just outside Hastings.

According to Dimitri's latest report, Joanna Russell was inside the door directly in front of him.

Alex frowned, moving closer.

"Like that." The female voice was low and muffled. "Try again."

A pair of giggling nine-year-olds in crisp navy blazers and polished shoes shot past as Alex stood listening.

"More to the left. Harder."

Alex heard the swish of clothing and a body moving hard over wood.

"Like that. You're *incredible,* Nigel."

Alex glared at the closed doors, imaging a dozen scenarios for what was taking place. Fury shook him as he reached a conclusion.

Two people having gritty, vocal sex.

A girl with pigtails headed for the door, and Alex cut her off. "Come back later."

"Why?" Blue eyes zeroed in on him with the force of radar. "I left my gym shoes."

"You can't go in now. They're . . . busy."

"Busy doing what?"

"Mopping." Alex scowled. "Mopping the floor."

"Is that what those funny noises are?"

"Just come back later. I'm sure your shoes will still be there."

After a moment, the girl shrugged and headed back down the hall.

Alex glared at the closed door, his expression grim. Joanna Russell was inside, Nigel was with her, and Alex was having a bloody hard time keeping his anger in check. When he had discovered the sheet of photographs half hidden beneath the sofa, memories of that tropical night five years before had come slamming over him.

He had tried to forget.

He had tried to close his mind to her softness. But the sight of her face had brought it all rushing back.

Her stubborn pride.

Her desire, like a soft satin rain.

His fingers tightened. Had she heard about St. Cyr?

He glared at the door and moved closer.

"No, it's not fitting. Try again, Nigel. Harder this time."

Something slid across the floor.

"Nigel. I'm almost there. Any second now—"

Scowling, Alex jerked open the door.

Joanna turned, her hair a copper glow in the sunlight. She was holding a coil of wire between her lips, tugging at what appeared to be a chain mail gauntlet attached to a life-sized figure of a knight from roughly the First Crusade.

So much for his suspicions, Alex thought darkly. But he wasn't prepared for the jealousy that shook him at the sight of Nigel's hand bracing Joanna's shoulder. He took a slow, hard breath and tried not to curse as he saw Nigel's fingers tighten.

Joanna looked too pale, and there were lines of strain at her brow. Obviously, she had heard the news about St. Cyr.

The copper coil wavered in her hands when she saw him. "What do you want?"

"To help. I know about Jacques. I'm—sorry."

The copper coil slid free. Gauntlet and sword fell back with a clang. Joanna frowned at the case. "I don't need your help."

Alex said something short and crude in Russian.

Joanna turned away, her back stiff. "Nigel, help me with this wire, will you? We're going to have to start again."

Alex watched in fascination as she reached down the plastic tube over the warrior's arm and searched for the fallen gauntlet. Beneath the plastic sleeve she had attached a twelfth-century double-edged sword that would move freely by copper wire. The result was a museum-quality display that would give children the sense of handling a real sword without any danger of contact with the blade.

Damned clever, Alex thought. No wonder she was in such demand.

"It's not going to work," he snapped. "You've got the angle wrong."

Cool blue eyes surveyed him carefully. "I beg your pardon?"

"Your wire has to be tilted lower." Alex gestured at the plastic sleeve. "Otherwise the sword will keep falling off. Give me the pliers and I'll show you."

Nigel stalked closer, cutting him off. "I don't think we need your help, Greywood."

"Down, boy," Alex muttered.

Joanna looked from one man to the other, her body rigid. Finally, her breath hissed free, and she nodded at Nigel. "I can manage things now, Nigel."

His brow rose. "Are you certain? When you're around this man, things seem to happen. Bad things."

"I'll be fine."

"You're the boss." The door closed noiselessly behind Nigel. Without a word, Alex tugged the pliers from Joanna's fingers, setting to work with the display case. By the time the sword was securely wrapped and the gauntlet connected, Alex was sweating. He gave the wire an experimental tug and smiled as the sword swiveled, sliding perfectly through the clear tube.

"Nice work," Joanna said reluctantly. She looked wary, Alex thought. Vulnerable and aching from the news of Jacques.

"We need to talk."

"Impossible. When this is done, I have a jousting figure to set up, complete with a tournament sword and a brigandine." She coughed. "That's a—"

"I know what a bloody brigandine is," Alex said tautly. "It's a form of armor constructed of small plates inside a cloth cover. A layer of pauldrons would be hinged over that to cover the shoulders."

The wariness in her eyes grew. "Of course, you would know. Forgive me."

"How's your arm?" Alex snapped.

"Fine."

Alex realized this was all he would get out of her. Considering that she showed no stiffness, he decided to accept the answer.

"How did you hear about Jacques?" Her voice was tight.

"I have my ways." He leaned against the heavy case, one brow rising. "You think I did it?"

"I don't know what to think. One day he's angry and shouting, the next day he's—" Her hands closed convulsively over a coil of wire.

"Bad?"

She nodded.

"Respirator and a dozen other machines?"

"It was terrible. He . . . he didn't seem like a real person anymore."

"It's not over for him, Joanna. He could come around any second."

"I keep trying to tell myself that."

Alex pushed away from the case. "We need to talk."

"Not now. All I can think about is Jacques."

Alex drove a hand through his hair, tugging the leather throng free and slapping it impatiently on his thigh.

"You tried to bury the past once, Joanna. It didn't work. Someone found out, and whoever it is will be back."

She turned away, kneading a hauberk of quilted linen made to be worn by a knight beneath his armor. "If they do, I'll deal with it."

Alex stopped behind her and caught her shoulders. "No, *we'll* deal with it."

She spun around, her eyes ablaze. Alex realized that when she was angry, the blue outweighed the green.

There was a whole lot of blue in her eyes right now.

"I don't need your help."

"Too bad," he said, pulling the hauberk from her fingers. "You've got it anyway. In case you haven't put two and two together yet, you're drifting in shark-infested waters. Whatever predator sent you those pictures will be back with his price, and he'll have no qualms about collecting. You're a fool if you think you can handle that by yourself."

"I'll manage," she said flatly.

It was the tremor in her fingers that made Alex play his trump card. "What are you going to say to your family when they open up the Sunday tabloids and find glorious, full-color photos of us spread across the centerfold?"

Joanna's fingers tightened. Grimly, Alex drove home his advantage. "And Jacques St. Cyr can't help you now. I checked twenty minutes ago, and his condition was unchanged. Damn it, Joanna, has it ever struck you that this might be connected? Maybe they wanted something from Jacques, something that he couldn't or wouldn't give them. In that case, you might very well be the next target. After all, you worked with him longer than anyone. No other curator has ever lasted more than six months with him, Simon Loring included."

Joanna swayed slightly, sinking back against the table. With a curse, Alex tugged her against his chest. "You need help, Joanna. Damn it, let me give it to you."

"No," she whispered. "I *can't.*"

A muscle flashed at his jaw. "Is it all people you don't trust or just me?"

She didn't move, not by a single muscle. "This has nothing to do with trust. It's about being weak or being strong." She drew a slow breath. "A long time ago, I swore I would not be weak. Not ever again."

There was pain in her eyes before she fought it down. "Even strong people ask for help, Joanna."

She looked away, her body rigid. "Not me. Not ever."

"Damn it, Joanna, I—"

Her hands tightened to fists. "Don't, Alex. Just go. Please."

"I'll go," he said grimly. "But first I want you to look at me. I want you to know what I'm offering. *Help*, Joanna. With no strings attached."

"Appreciated. But rejected."

Before she could move away, he brought his palms to her face. *"This* has no strings attached either."

He watched her eyes darken. He felt her breath catch. Damn it, he felt her with every raw nerve in his body.

And then Alex felt nothing but the warm silk of her mouth, sweet with tea and strawberries. The taste left him reeling. His fingers opened, anchoring her face while his lips brushed across hers. Her scent was wild flowers on a warm afternoon.

He wanted more. He needed to drink in all that sweetness.

Her hair filled his fingers, heavy and thick. Alex groaned when he felt her mouth soften, opening beneath his. Had he been thinking clearly, he would have stopped then.

But her scent was addictive, and the brush of her mouth was muddling all his senses. His hand slid to the soft curve of one hip as he molded her to his rapidly hardening body. And first he was going to deal with one question that had been tormenting him.

"Who's Peter?"

She hesitated, and he eased his fingers over her cheek. "Tell me, Joanna."

"He's . . . someone I like very much."

Alex frowned. There was fear in her thoughts. He could read it clearly. "Have you told him about us?"

She gave a dry, brittle laugh. "Told him what? That you're a man I met five years ago? That we spent a few pleasant hours on a lonely tropical beach?"

"Damn it, it was more than that and you know it." Frowning, Alex palmed the perfect curve of her breast through her sweater. Gentle, relentless, he smiled darkly at the sight of her nipple pressing against the soft cotton. "And you haven't forgotten, Joanna. Any more than I have. You're trembling against me but not with fear. Your eyes are hazy, dark with desire. God, I remember how you tasted against my mouth. The same way you would taste right now."

"No, Alex."

He felt her shudder. He heard the sudden catch of desire that stole her breath. The sound was like being slammed in the chest by a solid bar of steel.

And then she stiffened. Her hands shoved wildly at his chest.

It took Alex several seconds to focus. He frowned at her white face and darkened eyes and slowly brushed a curl from her cheek. "I meant it about no strings, Joanna." His voice was still hoarse with desire.

Her shoulders could have been carved from stone. "Just go."

He pressed a card into her hand and released her slowly. The fear was in her face now, too clear to ignore. Not for her, but for someone else, and Alex was bloody well going to find out who. "There's my number. Keep it with you while you think about me. About us."

"I won't be—"

"Yes, you will. And someday you'll tell me who left you twisted up inside and frightened like this."

Joanna watched him stride to the door, her heart still pounding. His hair was a dark wave to his shoulders, and his face was a study in shadows.

Five years had vanished in the space of a heartbeat. He left her shuddering, mindless, her thoughts in chaos.

Just as he had on that tropical beach.

"No." Her fingers closed over the cold metal gauntlet,

and she blinked back tears. Five centuries ago Alexei Cameron would have worn that hard gauntlet, fearless in the din of battle. Fearless in his conquest of the woman he loved.

With a soft cry Joanna dropped the heavy glove. Looking down, she saw that a piece of steel had snagged her palm, drawing blood. One dark drop covered the card Alex had shoved into her hand.

This time she was ready. This time she would keep him out of her heart.

Her arm stung as she sank back against the table crowded with wire and armor parts. Heat still shimmered from the slow, liquid brush of Alex's lips. She closed her eyes, fighting the sweet memory of his hand molded to her hip while he drew her against the hard line of his desire.

For a moment she had wanted.

God forgive her, how much she had wanted.

For a moment it had been a tropical night rich with flowers and warm wind. Blindly, Joanna touched her mouth, shivering.

Remembering . . .

The world was banked in gray, cocooned in fingers of mist. All was silent except for the gentle hiss of the water lapping at their skin.

Clouds rushed before the moon, and Alexei's hands were not quite steady as he raised her face. His mouth moved over hers, liquid and searching.

Joanna made a ragged sound of surprise.

"Good?"

"Is—very good," she breathed.

Alex laughed softly as her head fell back, her hair trailing down her back. Then the silk parted and fell away.

He froze, staring at the lush curves veiled by drifting mist. "You are more dangerous than brandy," he said harshly. "You make me forget I am a stranger."

"*Make me forget, too.*"

His voice hardened. "*You ask for me to betray you. What honor is in this?*"

Joanna opened her hands. Only the tips of her fingers met his chest. "*I don't want honor. Not tonight. All I want is you, without apologies or regrets.*"

"*You are clever with words,*" he said harshly. "*Too clever, I think.*"

Her fingers moved, tracing his tense muscles. "*Then don't use words, Alexei. Don't speak at all. You have the hands of a poet.*" She drew one palm to her mouth and bit it gently. "*So use them now. On me.*"

He swore harshly, a complex blend of anger, desire, and confusion. "*You want a poem. I do not think I have this in me.*"

"*I want . . . whatever you have to give me.*"

"*So clever.*" His lips closed over her, as primal as the drift of mist and sea wind. "*How can I not want this?*" Joanna felt herself melt, changed by his touch, a creature shaped of mist and foam.

Beautiful.

As beautiful as the low, broken words he poured over her skin.

Heat speared upward from his mouth, his flicking tongue, the hands that snared her hips. Through the haze he watched her face as he swept the damp dress away.

She shivered, uncertain and suddenly wary, remembering angry words and dark threats that she had tried hard to forget.

Behind her came the click of metal, and the underwater light winked out. In the sudden darkness, their touch seemed infinitely more intimate.

And Alexei gave her no quarter. His hands eased along her thighs and trapped the silken folds nestled in dusky curls. Slowly, slowly he eased within a fragile barrier of lace.

Joanna shuddered. She wanted—forever.

She needed—always.

His touch gave her both, teaching her to want, forcing her to reach out with every sense to find the pleasure he kindled so expertly.

Something trapped his hands. Muttering, he stripped away her last garment, a wisp of lace. Then she wore his hands as intimately as the water.

Joanna gasped as he moved within her, triggering waves of sweetness. Her back arched, and she sank her teeth into his shoulder, clenching fiercely around his fingers.

"Please—oh, God, Alexei—"

Too late. Again she felt the blinding rush, the hot sweet burn.

His mouth sealed hers, muffling the wild cry of passion upon her lips. Then his tongue filled her fiercely. "Open," he whispered. "Share your fire with me."

Her hands shoved at the restricting denim. Cursing, he stopped her, his calloused hands hard on her wrists.

Joanna laid her face against his naked back. She felt his indecision. The angry play of his muscles told her the price it cost him. "Alexei, why?"

"It is also I who try to forget. But even drunk, my head tells me a woman like you does not meet men in the darkness. She does not share her body with strangers."

"All I have is tonight," Joanna whispered. "And for tonight, we are not strangers." Overhead, the sky was full of stars, and the wind carried the sweetness of jasmine and orchids. She smiled crookedly. "After all, you taught me to see."

His fierce silence stretched out. "You deserve more." He cursed softly. "And I cannot give it."

The anger in his voice seduced her as no brandy could. Gently, she kissed the base of his neck while she combed through the soft hair at his chest. "Tonight the water is like silk. All I want to wear is water." She touched his shoulder. "And you."

He turned, pressing deep until his fingers were sheathed in sleekest heat. "Now you wear me. What man could not want to see you like this?" There was anger in his voice as he pressed deeper. "But since I cannot see, I will feel you." His fingers stroked, making patterns of light as they found a haven in her velvet heat.

"Alex—" Joanna shuddered, feeling the fire uncoil again, arching her back beneath each powerful, thrusting stroke. "But you—"

"Yes," he said tightly. "Now, while I feel you wearing only me."

Light exploded through her. Colors filled the night. Her nails dug into his powerful shoulders, and she gasped in fierce pleasure.

He pressed her face to his chest, catching her telltale cries of passion. Cries that Joanna had never made before. He watched her with narrowed eyes. "You cry. Is first time like this, no?"

"I—yes." She swallowed. "I never knew—"

"Now you cry again, for only me."

"Alexei, I—"

Her breath was still ragged when he drew her up to the heights again. She stiffened, struggling against him, planting hot kisses on his naked chest. "Please, Alex. Now. Be with me."

He lifted her above the water. "You are certain?"

She nodded, her cheeks filled with heat.

His hands were at his belt when a match flared in the darkness beyond the pool. For a moment the irritated face of one of Jacques's uniformed security guards was lit by flame as he spoke into a *cellular phone. "Hell, no. Nobody's out here." A cigarette flared red, and the match hissed out in the pool. "I don't give a damn what Loring told you, it's deserted."*

He listened, the tip of his cigarette glowing red. "The Gypsy? No sight of him. Yeah, right. If you ask me, Loring had too much to drink at dinner. He does a lot of that. There's not a damned sign of anyone out here, believe me."

Dimly, Joanna heard the words while Alex pulled her back beneath the rim of the pool.

"What? The swordmaker? No kidding. OK, I'll get the doctor. Sure, sure, whatever St. Cyr wants. Tell him I'll be right up."

Muttering, the guard holstered his small radio receiver and headed toward the lighted heart of the compound. "Who listens to me anyway?" he growled. "Man has some kind of attack and falls down. Sure, I'll go get the doctor. I got nothing better to do." Smoke drifting, he strode back into the night.

Joanna didn't move. "It's Constantin, isn't it? You have to go."

"Is his heart, I think." Alexei's voice was harsh. "I must go and do what I can. We leave tomorrow."

Joanna swallowed. "But—" She sighed, her hand opening on his chest, trembling with the fires that still licked at her skin. "I only wish . . ."

"Do not say it." His lips found her mouth, rough and angry. Then he pulled away. "To wish is sometimes a curse. I will not forget you, I think."

He pulled himself from the water. Joanna heard the hiss of a match and then a soft foreign phrase.

"What did you just say?"

"Words for the fire. We must always say thanks to the fire for sharing its light." The match went

out, and something landed in a pale blur near the edge of the pool. "Is towel for you there. I do not see your dress."

"I—I'll find it."

"You will be safe? Is far to your room?"

She shook her head, her throat burning. Why was the sense of loss so keen? "Not far," she said, glad of the darkness. Glad of the shadows that hid her trembling. "Go on."

"Then—good-bye." His voice hardened. He whispered the same soft phrase as he had before. "Thank you for sharing your fire with me, Annie Smith."

Joanna turned her back. Her body was cold in the wind now. She swallowed, very careful not to watch him go.

The same moisture was cold on Joanna's face now as she stood in the silent room with afternoon sunlight spilling around her.

She cupped her cheeks, remembering, searching for some trace of warmth lingering from Alex's kiss. There was none, of course.

Only in her imagination.

When Joanna opened the door of her studio two hours later, the memories were shoved deep and she was exhausted with the effort. She thought longingly of a hot bath. She had already phoned Peter from the school, promising him she would be with him for story time.

They were doing the Scots versus the Vikings tonight. H.R. would no doubt find an excuse to put his head in and rail against the "uncivilized marauders from the north."

Joanna was smiling as she flipped on the light. Then her smile froze.

Drawers hung crazily atop the slashed arms of the sofa. Her worktable stood upended, swords and armor scattered over the flagstone floor. Her tools were dumped at the foot of the massive stone fireplace.

She looked around her in stunned disbelief. Her hands began to tremble as she was gripped with a sense of raw violation.

She groped for the telephone on its side near the far wall. Without conscious thought, she began to dial.

Her eyes were leaden, and there was a dull ache between her shoulders when she heard the familiar voice with its hint of foreign cadences.

"Yes?"

"A-Alexei?"

"Joanna, is that you? Where are you?"

"Here. At my studio." Her voice was thick. It could have been a stranger's. "C-can you come?"

And then the receiver slid from her fingers.

14

ALEX DROVE too fast, his thoughts on the fear he had heard in Joanna's voice. He knew the way to the cottage across the valley from Draycott Abbey. He and Nicholas Draycott had once been ordered to repair the steep slate roof after Nicholas's father had caught them sneaking out for a midnight swim.

His back had been sore for a month, Alex remembered. The forbidden swim had still been worth it.

He stabbed at his cellular phone. "Dimitri, are you there?"

Static filled his ear.

Cursing, Alex glared out at the wooded hillside where Dimitri was supposed to be parked, keeping an eye on Joanna's studio. Once again, he felt a tight stab of warning.

He took the curve in a cloud of dust, and just beyond the old oak, he slammed left. The powerful wheels dug in and churned up the narrow drive past fields of wild flowers and ended in a circle before the two-hundred-year-old stone cottage with mullioned windows and slate roof.

Alex was out of the car before the gravel had settled. "Joanna?" he thundered, running to shove open the door.

The alcove was quiet. Sunlight spilled over a pair of polished benches covered with an array of straw boaters and sun hats. Alex hammered down the hall toward a broad sunroom just off the kitchen.

"Damn it, Joanna, where are you?"

He heard the rustle of paper on stone and pushed open a door painted with trompe l'oeil rose hedges.

Afternoon sunlight pooled through floor-to-ceiling windows overlooking Draycott's sweeping valley. Inside was a scene of wanton chaos. Alex blinked as he took in the overturned shelves, upended desks, and scattered books. "Joanna, answer me!"

Then he saw her, sitting motionless by the fireplace, her face like marble. "I . . . shouldn't have called." Her fingers twisted restlessly. "It has nothing to do with you, Alex." She rubbed her cheek, looking blankly around her. Slowly she pulled papers from the floor and lifted a cracked computer disk from beneath a pile of tools. "Why?" she said brokenly.

Alex pulled her against his chest. "Are you all right? They didn't hurt you, did they?"

She blinked. "No, not me. Just my work. My files. Oh, God, all my tools and new materials . . ."

Alex heaved a sigh of relief. Joanna was safe. The rest were just things, and things could be replaced. "Was there a note? Any sign of who did this?"

She shook her head.

"What about your period swords? Were any of those stolen?"

"I . . . I don't think so." She took a shaky breath. "Most are locked in my safe. I never wanted one, but Jacques kept insisting . . ." Her voice trailed away for a moment. Then she straightened her shoulders. "You can let me go now. I'll be fine."

Alex's face was grim as he watched her walk to the far wall and pull a stone from the fireplace. With a low hiss, a metal door sprang open. Joanna dialed a four-stage combination, then slid open an inner door.

"Everything is here."

"Good. I'll take a look outside and see what I can find. Stay here." He left before she could object, the prickle at his shoulders like tiny claws as he made his way through the field toward Dimitri's old brown car.

His friend was lying across the front seat, a nasty gash across his left temple.

Alex cursed softly. "Dimitri?"

The big Gypsy groaned and sat up.

"Did you see who did this?"

"No. They come from behind, out of valley. I do not think to watch there." He drew a labored breath. "I am backside of a blind horse."

"Come on, you big bear." Alex started to help him out of the car, but Dimitri shoved away his hands. "Miss Russell, she is well?"

"Fine. But her studio has seen better days."

Dimitri slapped a broad palm against his forehead. "My fault. You go inside. Take care of Miss Russell. I call my cousin to come for me. Giorgio." Dimitri reached for the mobile phone.

Alex thought of the six-foot four-inch Gypsy with the hands like trash compactors. "He is nearby?"

"In the village. And he drives very fast."

"God help you. But you're sure?"

"Go on," Dimitri snapped. "Take care of lady."

"Go to an emergency room, understand? Not back to Martina for some recipe made of bird's feet and clover."

Dimitri barked out a laugh. "I tell her this, Alexei. I tell her this, and she curses your sleep, your love life. You feel everything shrivel up, never able to have woman again."

"Promises, promises," Alex muttered.

Joanna, with a stack of papers on her lap, sat unmoving on the single upright chair.

Alex looked around, frowning. "Next time you might not be so lucky. If you intend to keep your studio here, you'll need a better security system."

"I'm *not* leaving."

"Then I'll have someone put in a fiber-optic alarm. Any professional could have opened that safe in seconds."

"Then why *didn't* they?"

"Because they didn't know the safe was there. Next time they'll be looking."

"How do you know there will *be* a next time?"

Alex frowned. There were instincts he couldn't explain, suspicions even he couldn't see clearly yet, but he knew enough not to doubt them. "Because there is always a next time." He looked at the scattered papers and the chaos of Joanna's desk. His eyes narrowed as he saw the metal blade of a sword glinting by one window. "What period commissions were you working on?"

Joanna bent to the floor. "Two fencing foils, eighteenth century. An Italian rapier. They're over here. At least they *were*." Her hand shook slightly as she lifted a broken hilt from a pile of books.

Alex saw the tremor in her hands and bit back a curse. Touching her would come later, after he had answers. "The swords were here when you came in? Just the way they are now?"

Joanna nodded. "I thought it was odd to find them all together."

Alex fingered the hilt of an old claymore. "Not odd."

"I don't understand."

"Look at the room, Joanna. Really look at it."

Her eyes swept the room. Papers were scattered over the floor. All along the fireplace lay a tangle of upended books and tools. "You mean that this was done at the end, don't you?" She picked up a book shoved beneath a set of pliers. "Everything else is scattered, but the swords were put aside together very carefully. And that isn't the act of a casual burglar."

"Exactly," Alex said grimly. "Those swords should have been over at the wall by your table."

Joanna locked her hands over her waist. "What did they want?"

"Something they didn't find." Cursing softly, Alex strode to the telephone and punched out a number, then gave low, precise information to the police officer who answered. After he put down the phone, he stood staring at the empty fireplace. "A police car will be here in ten minutes."

Joanna sank back down on the chair, her eyes bleak. "This couldn't have anything to do with . . . the photographs, could it?"

"I wish I could tell you no, but I can't."

"Will I have to tell the police? About the photos, I mean?"

Alex heard the weariness in her voice and clenched his fists in impotent rage. "Not yet. Let me handle that."

"No." She straightened her shoulders. "It's my problem."

"Damn it, there were *two* of us there in the water, two of us caught in those pictures, remember?"

She turned the broken hilt over and over in her fingers, then finally nodded.

"Fine," Alex said tightly, desperate to pull her against him, to burn away the fear with his hands and mouth. But he was afraid that once he touched Joanna Russell he would not be able to stop. "Were you expecting anything special in the post? New swords, for example?"

"No. I . . . I haven't taken any new assignments because I'm so behind with these." She took a steadying breath, then lifted a pile of papers from the floor. "They don't seem to have taken anything. My computer disks have all been cracked, so they weren't interested in my notes."

Alex stood motionless, opening his inner vision, trying to reconstruct the scene.

They were anxious. They knew they didn't have much time, but they didn't know where to search first.

"Maybe they had someone watching you," he said.

"I've felt that way," Joanna said. "Someone in a brown car."

"That's *my* man," Alex said tightly.

"Since when do you have the right to follow me?"

"He was down the hill, laid out cold, Joanna. He has a two-inch-long gash in his forehead. Now will you believe these people aren't playing around?"

"Will he live?"

"Dimitri has the hide of an ox. Don't worry, he'll be fine."

"Could this somehow be involved with Jacques?" she asked slowly.

"It's a damned good possibility." Alex picked up a fallen lamp and set it on the sofa. Then he stood up a nearby bookshelf and began stacking books.

"What are you doing?"

"Helping you clean up." He set Joanna's worktable back on its legs, centered it before the broad windows, then bent down to a pile of tools.

"Don't," Joanna said tightly. "I'll manage by myself."

"You don't have to manage by yourself. Not this time."

Joanna looked at the scattered papers, at the slashed pillows, anywhere but at Alex's face. "I should never have called you."

"What is that supposed to mean?"

"Do I have to make it any clearer? It's over, Alex. It was over before it ever began," she said raggedly. "What will it take to make you see that?"

Slowly Alex came to his feet. "It will take emptiness. Here." He pointed to the center of his chest. "Emptiness instead of heat and memories."

Joanna stood tensely, all too aware of the gray eyes narrowed on her face. All too aware of the broad shoulders only inches from hers.

Alex slowly traced her cheek. "You have some dirt on your skin. God help me, it only makes you look more beautiful." His fingers opened. "Joanna, let me touch you."

"Don't, Alexei." She swallowed, achingly aware of the warmth of his hand, the leashed power of his body. He was holding back his hunger but at great cost, she realized. And maybe his control was the only thing protecting them both. "Touching only makes it harder. There are too many reasons why what you want can never happen."

"Not a single one matters." His gaze locked on her soft mouth. "Let me prove it to you."

She hesitated for a heartbeat. And hated herself for that hesitation. "No."

Slowly his thumb circled her mouth, then dipped within.

He traced the liquid recess and used her own moistness to brush her lips with his thumb. Joanna closed her eyes at the erotic friction, at the wet slide of his fingers.

She knew exactly what he was making her remember. A deeper penetration, a tighter fit, until he was sheathed deep inside her.

"Alex, I—"

His eyes were stormy gray. "Say yes, Joanna."

Her pulse gave a dizzying lurch. "No." It was the word she had to say.

"How long has it been since you were with a man?" His voice was rough with desire. "Intimately."

Her face flamed. "None of your business."

Gently, with aching care, he traced the heat staining her cheeks. "I think you just gave me my answer. God help us both." A muscle worked at his jaw.

He stared at her, motionless. With a shaky breath, he reached to feather the sensitive skin at the corner of her mouth.

Joanna felt something lurch inside her. She bit back a moan as he touched her lower lip. This time the moisture was his own.

"Damn it, you're not going to run from me again, Joanna. And you're not going to forget *this*. Together, Joanna. Hot and slow. Forever, the way we couldn't last time. No one prying, no one watching. Just my hands, my mouth giving you anything you want. Everywhere you want."

His fingers moved as he whispered, an exquisite seduction on her heated skin.

And somehow Joanna's lips softened, opened to his touch.

He murmured a low phrase of approval, then caught her moan beneath his mouth. "Your hair reminds me of cinnamon. I wonder if you'll taste like cinnamon, too." His control still unbroken, Alex pulled her against his chest while his tongue played over her with expert skill. "That's it, love. Hold me. Like wet satin. Until I think I'm going to die."

God help her, she did, her mouth closing around him, her hands clinging, searching for some point of safety in the restless, shifting chaos around her.

And Alex was that safety, his shoulders unyielding as he gave her only what she could accept, only what her body so desperately wanted.

She fell, lost in a thousand textures of pleasure, in warm arms that steadied her beneath her restless fingers. His mouth distracted her, infinitely inventive while he eased her between his rigid thighs.

Joanna shuddered when she felt the awesome heat of his desire. Her eyes flashed open.

"That's five years of fantasies you're feeling," Alex said hoarsely. "Five years of memories. I've waited too long to skip seeing something else."

Warm air touched her heated skin. Joanna made a desperate, lost sound as Alex freed the buttons on her vest and nudged aside the soft linen of her shirt.

One breast spilled into his calloused hand, the other captive of his searching lips. Pleasure made her blind, her fingers tugging at the heavy softness of his hair until the leather thong went flying.

She claimed him as he claimed her in that moment. Her skin burned, and her body melted around him. She blotted out the chaos, the destruction, and the fear. Time fell away, and the world receded until there was only hungry skin, only exquisite waves of silken discovery beneath Alex's fingers.

Blindly, she tugged at his hair, bracing her body against his chest.

"God, you're small. Incredibly tight." He eased past copper curls to find the sleek petals. "First this way, Joanna. While I remember."

She stretched to take him, and the silken movement of his hands made her stiffen, arching in his arms. Then pleasure shattered through her like a night full of tropical stars.

"Sweet God, yes. Just like that." Again he moved, easing deeper. "Remember how it felt. How it's going to feel again."

"Alex, I—" Her nails dug into his shoulders. Satin tremors rocked her.

His forehead fell, resting against her neck. "I can't wait, Joanna. I've wanted this too long." He eased her back, staring into her flushed face, her dazed eyes. "Tell me now to stop if that's what you want," he said hoarsely.

She didn't answer. Her breath was raw, and her pulse thundered in her head. This was Alex's body, Alex's voice, and she wanted him more than breath itself.

"I—it's been so long. There was no one else. That's why I feel, why when you touch me, I can't help—"

A vein throbbed at his forehead, and he took a ragged breath. "Don't talk. If you talk like that, I'm going to lose control. God help me, that's the last thing I want to do." His face was hard, his eyes probing. "This time I won't stand for running, Joanna. No more lies. That's part of the bargain. I want more than a few minutes of hot sex this time, damn it." His voice was raw as she caught his words with her mouth.

"We can't go back, Alex."

"I don't want to go back. I want to go forward. Starting now."

Her eyes closed as his hands sent the golden tremors spinning once again. "Alex, I—"

"Yes, love. Hold on. There's more. All the pleasure I can give you." His fingers tightened. His lips coaxed.

And she fell away, gasping, into waves of silver and sunlight. Into gray eyes that saw forever.

He caught her when she swayed, cradling her between his thighs. Their rigid heat made Joanna blink, recognizing the price of his control.

"Alex, I don't—you haven't—"

He smiled, a slow, hot curve of his lips that was achingly beautiful. "No, I haven't. Not yet. But waiting five years made me very, very patient." Heat filled his eyes. "Remember how we fit, Joanna. Remember how you felt against me when I tasted you."

She swayed, remembering all too clearly, her pulse a thunder in her head. He was too good, her body too disobedient. She felt herself slipping under his spell, losing the independence she had struggled so long to possess. Caring did that.

"What's wrong, Joanna? Tell me."

"There are others involved, Alex. People I love. People I can't allow to be hurt."

His eyes hardened. "Not a husband. Don't tell me that, damn it, because I don't believe it."

"No." She gave a short laugh. "Not a husband."

"Then there's no problem. I'll be sure they're all invited to the wedding. I like big families and lots of friends. Hell, I'm a Gypsy, remember. We'll have two hundred before I even start counting. Thankfully, Greywood's got a big lawn."

Joanna stiffened, dazed by his calm assumptions and his immediate need to control her life. The commitment was too great, too soon. She had left Jacques because he had made the same kind of assumptions.

And what about her family? What about Peter?

She shivered, suddenly cold. "Us, together like this. It solves nothing."

"It's a damned good start," Alex said darkly. "At least our bodies never disagree. There is no way it could feel any better and not be illegal. Come to think of it, maybe touching you *is* illegal."

"Don't make me laugh."

"Why not? Laughing is good. It extends your life. Increases your potency. Not that I have too much anxiety in that particular area."

"Alex, I mean it. This is *serious.*"

"No," he said softly. "It's wonderful. It's worth dying for. But it's only another part of life, Joanna. This is only a small part of what I feel for you."

She shuddered, outgunned and outmaneuvered. How did this man come to be so wise?

"It's the Gypsy blood," he said with a crooked grin.

Gravel hissed outside on the drive. Feet crunched around to the back window.

Cursing softly, Alex shoved down Joanna's shirt. With hands that weren't quite steady, he tugged down her soft, flowing skirt. "Joanna, it's the police."

She swallowed, her face filling with heat. She was unbearably conscious of where his hands had been and the tiny, ragged sounds she had been making against his neck.

Then she saw the marks of her teeth on his shoulder. Had she lost every shred of sanity and control?

"Not again," she whispered hoarsely.

Someone banged twice. "Police. Open the door."

15

ONE OFFICER dusted for fingerprints while the other questioned Joanna. Neither showed haste or any marked interest.

"Let me check this again, Ms. Russell. You came back from an afternoon appointment and you found this."

Joanna nodded.

"Everything was just as it is now? And you say nothing is stolen?" The police officer stared at the room, scanned Alex, then turned back to Joanna. "Nothing at all?"

"Nothing that I can see."

"Ms. Russell, have you ever had a break-in before?"

"No."

He looked around the room, his eyes narrowed. "Exactly what kind of work do you do?"

"I restore period swords and armor."

His finger tapped at his badge. "Period. That means old things, right? And you use specialized materials?"

Joanna frowned. "Authenticity is crucial. I use only what the craftsman of the period would have had available."

"I see." The officer studied the room. "So with more expensive pieces, you would use gold, silver. Maybe even some jewels."

Joanna nodded. "In certain cases."

"I see." He slapped his notebook closed.

"What the hell do you see?" Alex said.

"I don't believe I got your name."

173

"Alexei Cameron."

"You and Ms. Russell are . . . involved?"

"Yes," Alex snapped.

"No," Joanna said simultaneously, flushing.

"Interesting." The officer's eyes hardened. "As to the rest, I'll spell it out. Obviously someone knew of Ms. Russell's profession. The lure of precious metals and jewels would be hard to resist."

"But they didn't take the swords," Alex said furiously.

"Maybe they didn't have time, Mr. Cameron. Or maybe they didn't know what to look for."

"That's a bloody lot of maybes," Alex said grimly.

"Do you have anything better?"

"Not yet." Alex braced a shoulder against the wall. "What news do you have on Jacques St. Cyr?"

The officer's face was a mask. "You'll have to speak with HQ about that."

Alex frowned. There was something hovering, something he should have been able to put his finger on. He'd have to remember to contact the chief inspector in Surrey tomorrow.

"We'll be in touch when we turn up something, Ms. Russell."

"Like hell you will," Alex muttered as the policeman left.

Joanna sank into a chair. "What happens now?"

"Nothing," Alex said flatly. "Not a bloody thing. They'll file their report in triplicate, and there the matter will rest." As he stared at the trees, there was a knock at the front door. "Not another police officer."

It was Dimitri, shaky but calm. "I apologize for intruding."

Alex strode to the door and took his friend's arm. "Why the hell aren't you in a hospital?" Then Alex saw the Gypsy's face. Anger and strain hardened his jaw. "What is it, Dimitri?"

"I'm afraid it's news from Sweden." His voice fell. "Elena's parents didn't made the ship. This morning they were taken into captivity in Estavia."

Alex's hands opened and closed in helpless fury. "Does Elena know?"

"Not yet," Dimitri said. "Marston just phoned. He thought you would know what was best to tell her. She is waiting at the window. Always waiting . . ."

For travelers who might never come.

"Alex?" There was a question in Joanna's eyes.

"I have to go."

"Is someone hurt?"

"Just some problems with a shipment from Europe," Alex said curtly.

In a way it was true. In the ebb and flow of desperate humanity, there were nations and governments that regarded people as no more than commodities whose only value was measured in the blood and fear and labor that could be squeezed out of them. For centuries, Gypsies had been a target for ignorant, frightened minds in a dozen countries. They were different, and all too often anything different was to be feared. Alex had experienced that kind of government firsthand and still had nightmares about it.

"I'll be back," he said. "You can't run away from me, Joanna. Not this time. There's too much left unfinished."

Joanna's face was like a mask. "I meant what I said, Alex. I'm not going back."

"Neither am I."

After an hour of work aided by Dimitri's two-hundred-forty-pound cousin named Giorgio, Joanna felt as if the shadows had finally been driven from her studio.

The books were stacked in neat piles. Sunlight spilled over the now spotless floor. Joanna thought about the lavender growing in purple spikes at the kitchen door and smiled. A few fragrant stems would dispel the last of the bad memories.

As she bent for her basket, she saw something propped against the back window.

A brown envelope.

Just like the one Nigel had handed her at Greywood.

Joanna felt her life rush away beneath her, like sand torn away before a gale. Suddenly, there was nothing to trust in or hold on to.

They're watching. There's something they want, and they won't stop until they have it. They don't care who gets hurt in the process.

"I clean the desk and all the bookcases, Ms. Russell." Dimitri's cousin studied the room. "Now I start on books?"

Joanna swallowed. "Fine. I . . . I think I'm going to sit outside for a few minutes."

"Is good," he said. "But not far. Is not safe, you understand. Alexei, he tells me to stay close."

Joanna barely heard. She moved into the sunlight like a sleepwalker, her hands on the envelope. The paper seemed almost heavier than she could bear.

It was the same set of photos but enlarged this time. Every detail was glaring, captured in harsh realism.

But that wasn't what made Joanna sit down in her chair while tremors shot up her body.

It was the dozen snapshots of a boy's smiling face taken with a telephoto lens. Shiny brown hair, sharp gray eyes. A reckless smile as he held up a digging trowel.

Oh yes, their message was crystal clear. They were watching Peter now. He was their key to Joanna. And he would be the next one to pay if Joanna didn't do everything they wanted.

Fear closed over her. Helpless fear.

Not Peter.

She dialed slowly, as if every movement was part of an arcane magic ritual. If she did any part of it wrong, the world might come to an end.

Or maybe the world had already ended.

"Greywood House."

"Alex, please. Lord Greywood, I mean."

"One moment." There was a click, a brief wait, then another click of a line being transferred.

"Joanna? Is that you?"

"Don't say anything, Alex. Let me speak. It's . . . going to be hard enough as it is."

"Damn it, Joanna, are you all right?"

"I'm fine." She looked down, feeling her body sway in the grip of forces beyond her understanding. She almost expected to see the floor melt into sandbars flung away before churning seas. But of course it was just the floor, just the room as it had always been, Winston chewing on a carrot in a bright pool of sunlight.

While her world came wrenching to a halt.

"Don't call me, Alex. Don't come see me. Not anymore."

"Damn it, Joanna—"

"I can't, Alex. Not again. I don't want to feel this way. Helpless. Fragile." Tears slid down her cheeks, and she shoved them away impatiently. "If you come after me, I'll hide. I won't hesitate. There are places I can go, places where even you can't find me. I don't want to do it, but I will." There was cold desperation in her voice. The danger was not just for her now. Every second with Alex made her weaker, far too vulnerable.

Alex gave a muffled curse. "You're wrong, Joanna. *This* is wrong."

She didn't speak. She could almost feel the sandbars sliding, twisting beneath her feet. *Be strong.* "Good-bye, Alex," she whispered, and then she hung up.

Sunlight pierced the towering trees like bars of gold. Joanna stood stiffly, feeling the wind move over her shoulders.

Softly.

Just the way Alex's hands had been.

Something pressed at her chest. Lost chances . . .

"Excuse me, miss." Giorgio stood at the back door. Winston wriggled in his hands. "Is someone to see you."

Alex.

Joanna didn't look up. "Tell him to go away." She couldn't bear to see Alex now.

"I do not think I can. He is very determined." Giorgio

moved uncertainly from one foot to the other. "He says to tell you he comes about Jacques."

Joanna swallowed hard. *Jacques?*

St. Cyr's dignified chauffeur stood in the foyer, weary and uncertain. Standing behind him was Michel Lebras, the bodyguard Jacques had hired several weeks before Joanna's resignation.

The chauffeur handed her a letter. "This comes from Mr. St. Cyr's solicitor, Ms. Russell."

"From Sir Gordon Mount?"

The chauffeur nodded. "He wants you to come to Beau Rivage. It's very urgent. Sir Gordon said his letter would explain."

Frowning, Joanna slit open the envelope and read the terse words.

> *I have found papers with important matters that*
> *Jacques wanted you to know about. Please come im-*
> *mediately. The car is at your disposal.*

"Nothing's happened to him? You're sure?"

The chauffeur nodded. "Sir Gordon seemed most anxious to discuss something with you."

Joanna rubbed the knot of tension at her neck and sighed. "Very well."

"You're sure everything is fine?" H.R. McTiernan's voice was sharp with suspicion. "You sound tired, Joanna."

"I am tired, Father. It's Jacques. I'll be back as soon as I can."

"Don't worry about us. Everything's fine here. Peter is with his grandmother, mapping the stone circle, or I'd fetch him to the phone."

"Tell him I'll be there later," Joanna said. "And . . . keep a close eye on him, Father."

"Is something wrong, Joanna? Something you're not telling me?"

Joanna swallowed. "Just . . . keep him close."

The drive to Beau Rivage passed in a blur. Joanna sat stiffly, seeing nothing of the road she had traveled so many times during her years working for Jacques.

The sun was a ball of crimson in the west when they drove up the broad avenue leading to Beau Rivage's stone steps.

Sir Gordon was waiting, his face grim. "I am sorry to summon you at such short notice."

"Jacques? Is he—"

"Exactly the same," the solicitor said tightly. "But I found a message he left for you. He seemed most anxious that certain information be brought to you in the event that he had an . . . accident."

Joanna frowned. "What information?"

"I do not know. Jacques's orders were that the material be given to you unread. He was most insistent about that."

Down the drive came the distant growl of a motor. Sir Gordon tugged at his cuffs, smoothing his jacket.

Joanna stiffened as a dusty Land Rover hurtled up the drive.

"Excellent," Sir Gordon said. "Lord Greywood has arrived. Now we can begin."

Plum blossoms and fresh peonies in crystal bowls perfumed Beau Rivage's beautiful study, but an air of death hung about the house. Joanna felt the anger that Alex was barely keeping in check.

It was best this way. All her emotion and weakness had to be shoved deep and forgotten. Joanna had almost convinced herself she'd succeeded when she looked in Alex's eyes and saw the barely banked flames that shimmered there.

She looked at Jacques's solicitor. "May we begin?" she said tightly.

"Of course." Sir Gordon opened his briefcase and removed a thick document case sealed with red wax.

Michel Lebras stood at one side and a stranger at the other.

The solicitor cleared his throat. "This is Terrance North, of Lloyd's. It was Jacques's wish that Mr. North be present to witness that his instructions were correctly carried out. Nothing was to begin until both of you were present."

Alex tapped irritably at the gleaming mahogany table. "Get on with it, Mount. I don't trust you or Jacques, and I can't imagine why I'm supposed to be here. Jacques and I aren't exactly the best of friends."

"I shall attempt to be as swift as possible," Sir Gordon said. "You may not know that Mr. St. Cyr was transferred this morning to a private hospital."

Joanna went very still. "Why? Is there fear of another attack?"

Sir Gordon shrugged. "It seemed prudent in view of the continuing questions about his accident." The solicitor carefully broke the seal on the document case. "As you can see, the materials in here have not been read since Mr. St. Cyr sealed them with his own hand. The two of you are to read the contents of this document together. Tomorrow you are to be given another document, and on the following day, a third. No one else is to see any of these. Is that understood?"

"Why all the dramatics?" Alex demanded.

"Because it was Mr. St. Cyr's wish." Sir Gordon's eyes narrowed. "It was also his wish that you work together. If you find the conditions onerous, you are free to leave. In that case the documents will be left unread and shipped to his personal vault in London. Well?"

Alex drummed on the table. "Go ahead."

Sir Gordon looked at Joanna. "And you, Ms. Russell?"

She nodded tightly.

"Very good." He eased out one envelope and slid it across to Joanna. "Mr. Lebras will be outside the door if you need him." He closed his briefcase and stood up.

Frowning, Joanna touched the envelope. "But I don't

understand why we were to be given only one envelope at a time."

Alex laughed grimly. "Because Jacques didn't want us to have all the information at once. This way, if either one of us is kidnapped, his information will still be safe. *We're* expendable, you see. But his clever little scheme is not. Isn't that right, Sir Gordon?"

The solicitor looked down at the document case. "He has always been a very careful man, Lord Greywood. I can say nothing more than that."

The door closed softly behind all three men.

Joanna's face was pale as she looked at Alex.

"This changes nothing, Joanna. In a month or a year, I'll still feel the way I do right now, like a truck ran over me. And I'll still do everything I can to convince you that we're meant to be together."

Joanna stared down at her hands. They were shaking slightly. "I can't look into the future, Alex."

"Can't? Or won't? Maybe you've lived too long in shadows, denying your own desires."

It was too close to the truth. Joanna closed her eyes. "Let's just get on with it, shall we?"

"My pleasure. Open the envelope and tell me what it says."

The paper tore beneath Joanna's fingers, a creamy sheet like the others she had received from Jacques. She frowned, studying the page. "It's a code of some sort. Or a puzzle. I can't make any sense out of it."

"Let me have a look." Alex took the paper. "'With words of warning for the seeker. Only those who are pure may understand the three keys, which are both truths and lies.' What the bloody hell is *that* supposed to mean?" Abruptly his eyes narrowed.

Joanna watched a muscle flash at his jaw.

"Listen to this. 'If you are pure in heart and seek the sword, read on.' The sword," he whispered. "My God, could St. Cyr have finally discovered the truth about the claymore?"

Joanna hesitated, then reached into her bag. She

shoved a sheet toward Alex. "He left this for me at the hospital. It . . . it mentioned something about three clues he had found."

"Damn it, why didn't you tell me?"

"Because he told me not to trust anyone."

Alex said nothing. After reading the sheet, his face hardened. "It's a warning, Joanna. He was frightened. He knew he was in danger. It's possible that he knew the people who pushed him from that window. But why did he want *me* here? He doesn't trust me. He hates me in fact. So why was I summoned?"

Joanna was asking herself the same question. What information had Jacques found? What could frighten him so much that he would trust Alex, whom he considered his enemy?

Joanna looked down at the sheet Sir Gordon had given her moments before. "He's talking about some kind of test."

Alex nodded. "Read it."

"'Here begins the test. The first riddle of the three: The Sword, which is the Key to Yesterday.'" Joanna went very still. "It has to be the Cameron sword. That's why he wanted you here. And these look like some kind of notes."

"I don't put much faith in legends about the sword. They always lead to dead ends," Alex said.

"Why do legends about your own family bother you so?"

Alex crumpled the paper. "Because they're not *my* legends, damn it. And if they were in the Cameron family, they bloody well skipped me. My father said nothing about the sword's existence. I guess that makes a clear statement about his feelings for me, doesn't it?"

Joanna sat back slowly, only now beginning to understand the vast gulf between father and son. The pain of that separation still gripped Alex years after his father's death, and this talk of an ancient Cameron legacy only made that pain worse by exposing the lack of trust between the two men.

Joanna knew there was nothing she could say to heal that gulf.

She took a breath and read the last lines of Jacques's latest letter. "'Three are the times, and three are the keys.'" She frowned as the handwriting grew less legible. "'Grasp all three and the metal will stir beneath your fingers.'"

She sat back slowly. It had to be the sword.

Jacques had to have come very close to finding it when he was thrown from that window. "Do you have any idea what it means?"

"It could be a riddle describing how the sword is separated from the scabbard. Not that it helps much, because we still don't have the sword or the scabbard." Alex frowned. *"If* they even exist. We could be misreading this whole business. These could be nothing more than random notes with no connection at all with the Cameron claymore."

Joanna sat very still. "But you don't believe that."

Alex's hands tightened. "I'm not sure what I believe, Joanna. If there was a set of clues and my father *didn't* tell me . . ."

At that moment Sir Gordon Mount eased open the door. "Have you finished?"

Joanna stacked the sheets of paper and slid them back into one envelope. She was slipping it into her bag when Michel Lebras carried in a large box.

The solicitor's eyes flickered around the room.

"More dramatic revelations?" Alex said dryly.

"This is Jacques's next request. He was most specific that you should be here before it was opened, Lord Greywood." Sir Gordon nodded to the bodyguard, who slipped open the cardboard carton and pulled out a case of rare Chinese rosewood. The wood was intricately carved and polished to a glasslike sheen.

Joanna sat forward, excitement welling through her.

"Mr. St. Cyr's directions were that the case was to be opened in the presence of us all." He motioned the gentleman from Lloyd's closer. "If you would do the honors, Mr. Lebras."

The bodyguard slid open a solid silver fastening at the front of the carved box. The room was silent except for the sound of his fingers on the exquisite wood.

Joanna turned to Alex, shocked to see him standing tensely, his hands flat against the table. Did he see something that she could not?

The clasp sprang free. The box hissed open.

Joanna gasped. Sunlight kissed the long blade of a sword. Excitement gripped her. She longed to run her hands over the cool metal face and across the sinuous grip of etched gold.

She was bending forward when Alex gripped her arm and pulled her backward.

"Don't touch it."

16

Sir Gordon Mount stood tensely, his jaw hard. "What do you mean, Greywood?"

"Just what I said. Don't *touch* it. That means you too, Lebras. Unless you want an appointment with a casket."

Sir Gordon's florid face flushed a deep red. "Damn it, Greywood—"

"There's something on the blade." Alex didn't move, his eyes fixed on the sword. At the same time he seemed to look beyond it to images visible only to him.

Joanna stared at the beautiful old sword with its heavy curved grip. "But it's the Cameron claymore. I saw the portrait at Greywood. There couldn't be two swords as extraordinary as this." She saw the tension that gripped Alex's shoulders beneath his gray wool turtleneck.

"Don't touch it," he said sharply. "Not any of you."

Sir Gordon's pale eyes narrowed. "So it's true, isn't it."

"What's true?" Joanna said. "I don't understand."

"Lord Greywood has a rather strange ability to see the unseeable," the solicitor said. "Jacques knew, but I didn't believe him. Not until now."

"Don't make more of it than you should," Alex said tightly. "Sometimes I'm totally off." He frowned. "But not this time. Excuse us for a moment."

He strode out into the hall, with Joanna following. He guided her into a quiet alcove.

"There was poison on that blade," he said flatly.

"But I didn't see anything. What did Sir Gordon mean? Surely, it can't be true, the things he said."

Alex shrugged. "Sometimes I feel things. Things that other people don't feel. I'm seeing all kinds of things around that bloody sword. There are shadows all over it, especially on the blade."

"Shadows?"

"Usually I feel them. When they're strong enough, I can see them."

"Alex, are you trying to tell me you're—you're some kind of . . ."

"Go on, say it, Joanna." His voice was harsh.

"Well, psychic. I suppose that's the word."

"Yes."

"That's it? *Yes*. Just one word?"

"You asked. I answered."

"God." Joanna ran a hand through her hair. "How did Jacques know?"

"There seems to be very little that he *doesn't* know."

"And because of this skill, you think the blade is tainted?"

"I *know* it. The feeling is too clear to be a mistake."

Joanna sank back against the wall. "Even if it were true, why would Jacques set such a terrible trap?"

"That's what I keep asking myself. You noticed the left hilt, of course."

Joanna frowned. There had been something odd about its shape. "The curve is slightly different from the portrait at Greywood. More graceful. With finer detail."

"Doesn't that tell you something?"

Joanna's hands locked at her waist. "Later workmanship," she breathed. "It's not the Cameron claymore at all, but a copy. An exquisite and absolutely impressive copy. How did you know?"

Something came and went in Alex's eyes. "Because I designed it. That's the replica of the claymore I made with Constantin Stevanov's help. It was stolen from Greywood recently," he added grimly.

"You don't think Jacques took it?"

"I don't know what to think. One thing is certain. Jacques had to know it was a copy. His eye for authenticity is unmatched."

"I don't like this," Joanna whispered.

"Neither do I." Alex caught her hand and moved toward the door. "Let me do the talking when we get back inside. Whatever I say, go along with it. Jacques might have been paranoid, but he was no fool. If he wanted this information kept secret, it was for a reason. We're going to have to find out why."

Sir Gordon watched them return, his eyes narrowed. Alex sat down opposite him and steepled his fingers. "I've got three questions. If you don't have answers, this charade is over."

The solicitor spread his hands. "I'll tell you whatever I can."

"Where did Jacques get that sword? *My* sword?"

Sir Gordon shrugged. "Jacques left me instructions in a document that was to be opened in the event he was hurt or killed. I was to remove a box from his safe, but I would know nothing about the contents. St. Cyr was most precise in his instructions."

"What happens to the sword now?"

Sir Gordon frowned. "In view of your concerns about the danger it presents, it will be handled very carefully. The ultimate destination will be a vault in Kent under the supervision of two Lloyd's guards. Jacques indicated that the sword was to be held there until you find whatever it is he set you to find."

"For now, I'll entrust it to Lloyd's for safety. But the sword is *mine,* and I'm damned well going to have it back!"

"St. Cyr specified one more thing," the solicitor added calmly. "Mr. Lebras is to act as Ms. Russell's bodyguard until this matter is finished."

"Like hell he is," Alex growled. "I'll be taking care of Ms. Russell." His neck was tight with the stab of emotions overlaid on the weapon. "Meanwhile, I suggest you have the blade analyzed."

"You don't actually believe—"

"Do it. Otherwise this game is over."

Sir Gordon bit back an angry answer. "Where should I send the results?"

"I'll check back with you." The two men's eyes met. Alex saw something flash over the solicitor's face before it was carefully hidden. "When do we get the next envelope from St. Cyr?"

"Tomorrow. I'll deliver it personally to Greywood."

Alex frowned, not liking this detail any more than the rest. "I'll be in touch," he said, taking Joanna's arm and steering her into the hall.

He felt the solicitor's eyes follow them all the way to the door.

Outside, sunlight gleamed off the fountain at the front of Beau Rivage's broad drive. "Where's your car?"

Joanna eyed Alex warily. "I don't have one. Sir Gordon sent a car for me."

"Fine. I'll drive." Alex looked at Joanna, seeing the tension in her shoulders. "It's a bloody mess, and the sooner we get it over, the sooner we can start arguing about the things that really matter, things like family and future and trust."

Joanna's fingers laced at her chest.

Alex felt her confusion. He knew she was struggling hard to keep from coming apart. Frowning, he held open the door to his Land Rover. "Why didn't you tell Jacques's solicitor about the contents of that first letter?"

Joanna rubbed at her neck. "Jacques told me I should trust no one."

"But you told me. You trusted *me,* Joanna."

She looked out over the darkening lawns. "Jacques trusted you. Otherwise he wouldn't have specified we were to work together."

"When did it get so hard for you to trust? Who did that to you?"

Joanna's hands slid over the sleeves of her sweater,

restlessly moving across her wrists. "A long, long time ago," she whispered.

Twilight slid over the hills, over the wooded valleys and winding silver streams. As he drove, something ate at Alex. Possibly it was anger at being manipulated so completely by Jacques.

Or possibly it was something deeper and more malevolent.

Muttering angrily, he roared around a curve, nearly hitting a branch that had fallen across the drive. As the miles grew, he and Joanna sat in moody silence. Not even the calm of the English countryside worked its quiet magic, and Alex's hands were tense as he expertly maneuvered the narrow, twisting roads.

Suddenly, a pale shape lumbered into the road. Alex slammed on the brakes, cursing at the large, frightened sheep caught in the glare of the headlights.

A sharp blast on the horn sent the bleating animal back through a gap in the hedgerow, and Alex eased into gear, gradually becoming aware of a faint humming behind them.

Light streaked over the hill, blinding him in the mirror. He inched left, giving the impatient driver room to pass.

No good. The headlights loomed larger, swung right. The car, a large black Citroën, slowed and drew alongside him.

Metal cracked against metal. Alex cursed, clutching at the wheel as a second impact slammed him to the left. "Bloody fools!"

He jammed on the brakes and skidded to a halt. The other car shot forward and disappeared around a curve. Minutes later it was gone, the road empty and still, the hedgerows giving away to sparse woods on both sides.

They weren't far from Greywood now. Ten more miles and then—

The black car roared out of a hidden lane, its lights blinding. The first blow shuddered through the Rover and sent them skidding wildly. Alex fought to hold the wheel as the Citroën made another direct hit.

Swerving wildly, Alex pitched over the road. They bumped down a grassy slope, hit a rock, and then slid into a dark pool.

Water sucked and gurgled. Steam hissed on hot metal.

"Joanna?"

"I—I'm fine."

Abruptly, the car tilted backward. Alex cursed, searching for the door handle as water surged up over the window. Alex shoved savagely at the door, working it open inch by inch. Suddenly cold water rushed over their feet, and the car gave another lurch.

The instant the door slid free, Alex gripped Joanna's shoulders and pulled her out into the icy water.

It seemed an eternity until he felt the silty bottom and shoved upward, fighting a stiff current. Behind them the car creaked and shuddered as Alex pulled Joanna closer, kicking powerfully. The car's metal mass swung past, then toppled downward in a churning fury of mud. A moment later they broke the surface, gasping.

The dark outline of a tree hung out over the water. Alex swam forward, one arm anchoring Joanna's shoulders. "Hang on. We're almost there," he muttered, feeling the reassuring bulk of a trunk beneath his feet.

Then tires swished along the top of the bank behind them. A car slipped past, its lights off. Moonlight glinted off the metal hood.

A black Citroën.

Alex jerked Joanna back into the network of roots and leaves, his hand to her lips.

A door clicked open. Flashlight beams crisscrossed in the night. Two figures moved back and forth along the bank, sweeping the darkness.

Shoes squished just above them.

Alex's hand tightened on Joanna's shoulder, part warning and part reassurance. Time stretched out in a dark, cold blur.

The boots slapped away over the mud, and a car door slammed shut. Seconds later, an engine coughed to life.

Not a single word of speech had been uttered. Nothing that could identify their pursuers.

That mark of icy professionalism frightened Alex more than anything else had. What kind of men had Jacques become entangled with? How had they followed the trail to Alex and Joanna so quickly?

"Come out," a voice hissed just up the bank.

Mud trickled down into their faces.

"You have nothing to fear." The voice was rough, accented. "They have gone." More mud slid down the bank. "I said, come out."

A hand snaked through the network of roots and branches.

"Be careful with her," Alex ordered as broad hands tugged Joanna into the air and dropped her squirming on the bank. Her teeth were chattering as she stood up, sputtered, then landed in a tangle of wet cloth.

"We must go, Alexei." A broad figure loomed out of the darkness. "I see them follow you and push you from road. But we have no time for chat. They will soon come back. You take my car. Here are keys."

Somewhere in the darkness a horse whinnied softly.

"You feel up to riding back to camp, Dimitri?"

"A horse is more comfortable than a car any day."

"And what about your head?"

The big Gypsy shrugged. "Eight stitches. The nurse was very nice. I tell her fortune, especially about the tall dark man who is coming into her life. Someone who needs her gentle touch."

Alex shook his head. "You could talk your way past a firing squad, Dimitri."

His friend was quiet for a moment. "Maybe I have, my friend. Maybe we both have."

Alex took Joanna's arm and pulled her up the bank. Dizzy and cold, Joanna sloshed along beside him. "Dimitri is well enough to ride?"

"I told you it would take more than a crack on the head to stop him." Alex tugged her up onto the road. "He's an expert rider. He'll be at the Gypsy camp in less than five minutes. I wish I could say the same for us."

Alex frowned as the dark outline of Dimitri's car loomed up before them. "From now on, you stay with me. If I have to go away, Dimitri takes my place. These men aren't looking for tea and conversation, Joanna. In their eyes, whatever Jacques found is worth killing for. Now, shall I take you back to the cottage or do you want to go somewhere else?"

Joanna's face was pale in the moonlight. "The cottage."

"Fine."

"What about you?"

"I'm staying with you. Tonight and every other night until this bloody business is done, Joanna."

"But—"

"Don't argue." His eyes were dark as he tossed a jacket around her shoulders.

Joanna stiffened. "What about the envelope from Jacques? It was in the car when—"

He shoved something into her hands. "Your purse, wet but intact. I took it before we left the car."

Joanna tugged out one of Winston's half-eaten carrots, a tangle of copper wire, and a sodden comic book.

Alex studied the last item. "Spiderman?" His eyes narrowed.

"It's my father's. He confiscated it from one of his students," she explained hastily. "Here's the envelope." She eased the damp sheets open, then looked up slowly. "It's gone. All that's left is blurred ink."

Alex cursed softly. "We'll have to reconstruct it from memory." He stared down the dark, silent road. "At least those bastards in the Citroën didn't get it."

High above the steep valley, the moon hung between the gray stone parapets of Draycott Abbey. All was silent. Even the wind was still as somewhere a bell began to chime—twelve times and then once more, the sound dim and very sad.

As the trembling peal hung on the air, a shadow darkened the high granite roof. Head low, hands locked behind his back, the solitary figure paced the gloom. His features were hard in the moonlight, nearly as weathered as the abbey itself.

Only when soft gray fur pressed against one booted foot did the sensual lips curve into the faintest of smiles. Yet that simple movement changed the face, lifted ages from the lined features.

"So you are restless too, Gideon?" Adrian Draycott looked down into the amber eyes of his friend and companion through the centuries.

The great cat's tail arched, then flicked sharply.

White lace fluttered over an immaculate black satin sleeve as the ghostly figure slid one hand over the cat's powerful back. In life, pride had been only one of Adrian Draycott's manifold vices. In death, pride was the only vice left.

"You feel it, too?" The abbey ghost looked thoughtfully over the dark patchwork of trees beyond the lawns.

The cat uttered a low cry.

"Yes, the danger returns tonight. Perhaps it was always here in spite of my efforts."

The keen amber eyes blinked.

Adrian Draycott walked to the edge of the roof. The cat glided over the ancient stones and settled against his leg, purring softly.

"The portrait? No, that is safe. I would know if any harm were done to my resting place," Adrian said grimly.

The cat's tail arched.

"The abbey beneath us? Every inch untouched, down to this ancient capstone." White lace fluttered briskly though there was no wind. "No, it is out there at the edge of the valley. Something to do with the woman and those around her." A bird cried from the darkness. The ghost stiffened. "An intrusion. I feel it again."

The cat's head cocked.

"You felt it before? Why did you not tell me?" Adrian frowned at the cat's low hiss. "Because I did not ask? You know how dangerous the sword can be! Its secrets must be protected at any cost."

The cat waited, his keen eyes unblinking.

"You don't know the story even now?" Adrian rubbed his jaw. "I was afraid to involve you, knowing how reckless you are when our abbey is threatened. A grave mistake, I acknowledge it freely. I hope you will forgive me, Gideon."

The cat settled back on the cold, weathered stone.

"Begin?" Adrian sighed. "But where? For centuries the Cameron sword has been a curse to all who possess it." He turned, his features hard against the rising moon. "And now, despite all my skill, its secrets have been broached. I will need your help, Gideon. The sword is beautiful, but one glimpse of its beauty and all else is forgotten. It should never have been left here."

The cat moved, pressing gently against Adrian's hardened fingers.

"You are right, of course. We cannot control history. Not even our small part of it." As Adrian touched the cat's warm fur, the moon struggled free of the trees, casting its chill light over moat and field.

Far below at the rim of the valley, lights flashed on in the little stone cottage. Adrian studied the light thoughtfully, his hands moving over Gideon's back. "Now I shall tell you a story, Gideon, a story of beauty and great greed, made worse because the Camerons have always been a proud and unpredictable lot. Listen well, my friend, and pray you are never faced with a choice such as Angus Cameron faced."

17

MOONLIGHT SPILLED through the high studio windows as Joanna shoved a faded camellia back into a dusty old box. Memories clung to that faded flower.

There was no escaping the truth any longer. Alexei Cameron had charged back into her life, kindling dangerous emotions. She remembered his hands, warm and effortlessly powerful. She remembered the texture of his mouth on hers.

Her heart slammed as she shoved the box back behind a row of books. As she did, moonlight played over her arms and wrists.

Silver skin. Silver light. Faint silver scars.

Shivering, she kicked off her sandals and padded through the tiny bedroom set high under the eaves. Clothing fell as she went. By the time Joanna reached her closet, she was wearing only sheer underwear. Frowning, she stopped and looked at herself in the cheval glass.

Moonlight dusted her shoulders and pooled over her cheeks. Were the scars visible too? Joanna wondered. Did the old pain lay clear for anyone to read?

She tugged open a drawer, angry when she saw her hands shake as she reached for her swimsuit. Cool lapping water would wash away the memory of Alex's lips. Hard exercise would tire her so she could sleep.

She tugged on the suit and padded silently down the back steps, then flipped on the lights to the lovely old pool set in flagstones down the hill. With a sigh, she eased into the cool depths and began to swim. With each stroke, the tug of the water lulled her to relax. She did not notice the figure that moved past the windows of the studio. Only at the pool's far edge did she see Alex cutting through the water toward her.

She frowned, trying not to watch the beads of water glide down his sculpted chest or the moonlight that painted streaks of silver against his long, wet hair. "What do you want, Alex?"

"We have some unfinished business."

She turned, her body rigid.

His eyes were sleek with flecks of moonlight. "You're running again, Joanna. It's time to tell me why you wanted me out of this." Around them the water lapped, soft and cool. "Tell me what you're afraid of."

Of you. Of myself, she wanted to scream. *Of the things you make me feel and a past I've tried so damned hard to forget.*

. "Nothing."

"You're lying."

"What gives *you* the bloody right to—"

His wet hands covered her cheeks. His eyes turned to silver. "This."

His mouth covered hers before Joanna had a chance to pull away. She froze, expecting him to punish and demand and possess.

But what he did was far more dangerous. His mouth softened, finessed, seduced. He drew fire, painted sweetness, coaxed a slow sigh.

"No, Alex."

He cradled her face. Waiting. Letting her see his need. "It's finished. It *has* to be finished."

His hands were infinitely gentle. "It's just beginning."

Joanna shivered as he eased closer. She felt the slam of his heart. "I—I can't." She looked down at the fine lines at one wrist and swallowed, trying to turn away. "Just go."

"Not until you tell me what you're so damned *afraid* of."

"Of *you*." Her breath caught. "Of wanting like this." Her voice broke. "There, are you satisfied?"

Alex breathed a soft curse.

He wasn't satisfied. He hated the pain in her eyes and the tension in her voice. But the time had finally come for truths. "No, I'm not satisfied. Not at hearing you're afraid of wanting me. And you can feel that my body is far from satisfied." A current drove her against him into the jutting evidence of his desire. "If all I wanted were simple sex, I wouldn't be here."

She raised one hand as if to ward off a blow. Alex cursed at the pain that simple, telling gesture brought him.

Who had caused her to have so little trust?

He pulled away, scowling. Damn it, why did her suit have to cling to her breasts, perfectly outlining every lithe curve? And that damned skimpy bottom, hinting at silken curls, was enough to drive a sanc man mad. Not that Alex had felt sane for days now, he admitted grimly.

He edged her toward the side of the pool. "Who left you like this, Joanna?" The wall was at her back. "Tell me the bastard's name."

"You're imagining things again."

"Am I?" Water hissed and swirled around them. "Then why are you trembling, Joanna? Why are your hands like ice?"

"I—I'm not trembling."

He found the line of her shoulder and planted slow kisses along its ridge. "Here." His lips brushed her neck. "And here," he whispered, tracing the edge of her suit.

She shivered. "Go away, Alex."

His tongue found wet skin and eased lower. "Not yet."

She was a fish in moonlight tides, he thought. Untamable, untrappable, she would slip between a man's fingers, leaving him wild and hungry.

But he wasn't going to make running easy for her. When she opened her lips to protest, he slid his tongue to hers, groaning.

Her breath caught. He felt a tremor sweep through her. And then a breathless sob spilled from her mouth.

The sound made him curse. He wanted to explore every inch of her silver body. He wanted to hear her laugh. Then he wanted to fill her and make her cry out in her passion.

He caught her wrist. Slowly he raised it to his lips.

And then Alex saw the fine silver lines that crossed the delicate skin.

One. Four. A dozen.

He cursed, the sight like a fist to his kidney.

"No, Alex. Let me go."

Ignoring her trembling fingers, he swept her into his arms and carried her to the light at the pool's edge.

More lines. Faint but noticeable, these scars marched brokenly across her stomach.

Alex felt fury rise in his throat. "How, Joanna? When?"

She pulled wildly to be free. "You've seen, Alex. Now you can go. I didn't *ask* you to come here. To see—*this*."

Alex swallowed the bitter anger. Although he yearned for answers, he forced himself to wait. The pain in Joanna's eyes had to come first. "A man did this?"

She made a broken sound and turned, her body stiff.

"He hurt you like this?"

"Who doesn't matter." She shook her head blindly. "Go. Just go, Alex."

"It doesn't have to be that way, Joanna. It can be slow and hungry, so sweet you want to cry out with the wonder of it. Believe me, Joanna." His mouth brushed her cheek, her hair. "Or don't believe me. Let me show you instead."

"No." It was a choked sound, half muffled against his chest. "Last time—I never could forget you. And then the pain . . ." She pulled free. "I wish things could be different, Alex. I wish that the past had never happened. But touching you, loving you now would only bring more pain. You're an honest man. A very decent man. You deserve far better."

He cursed, aching to kiss her, aching to make her moan as she found all the sweetness he could bring her.

Knowing he could not. Not when her heart was so full of fear.

"All I want is you. And a chance."

"There are no more chances, Alex. I used to wake up crying, wondering who I was and why *these* happened to me." She held out her wrists. "Too fragile, that was the reason. Too hopeful. But not again. Not with you or any other man. No more scars, Alex. The pleasure simply isn't worth it."

Alex felt her pain overflow, breaking in her voice. He had never felt more angry or helpless than he did at that moment.

He watched in rigid silence as she struggled up the steps.

A movement at the lower slope caught his eye, and he saw Dimitri's bulky shape outlined in the moonlight. "All is well? I try the phone and then I look inside. When you do not answer, I begin to worry you are not safe."

Alex strode from the pool and yanked on his trousers.

The big man frowned, watching Joanna move tensely up the hill. "She is fine?"

"She's fine. But I'm not so sure that I am. How can I fight with shadows, Dimitri? With ghosts I can't even see?"

Comprehension filled Dimitri's eyes. "Ah, like that, is it?" He made a soft, sympathetic sound.

Savagely, Alex swung his sweater over his shoulder.

The big Gypsy's eyes narrowed, and he shook his head as he watched his friend stride off toward the cottage.

An hour later, Alex stood at the broad windows overlooking the valley, feeling the old ache throb at his neck. He had phoned in a report to the police. Soon after that Joanna had gone upstairs, pale and tense.

Alex had ached to follow her, to hold her until she eased into sleep.

But not without trust. He had tried that once before, and the results had hurt them both.

Frowning, he slid open the door and moved silently

out into the darkness. Across the valley, the abbey's gray towers rose black against the night sky. Something called to him there, deep in his blood. For a moment it felt almost like a memory.

And as he studied the distant roofs Alex felt a loss such as he had never known. But what had he lost? And when?

There were no answers in his restless blood, no answers in the darkness. The low cry of a bird drifted over the wooded slope.

Then came another, half a mile up the hill.

A third call echoed from the meadow on the far side of the house, followed by another and another.

In the end, there were twelve, all from men of granite hearts, men that Alex would trust with his life, brothers of blood and country. He cupped his hands and answered with a similar cry that lingered in the lonely silence.

It was his own message that all was well.

When he went inside, Alex saw a white blur against the floor and bent to nuzzle Joanna's rabbit. "Sorry, fella, but it looks like the couch is mine tonight. You'll have to bivouac on the floor."

Winston's nose twitched. He nibbled delicately at Alex's finger, then hopped off to explore the kitchen.

Alex sank back against the chintz couch, too keyed up to sleep. He thought again about Joanna's face in the moonlight. He thought about the faint silver scars. She had been hiding many things from him. He had felt their touch like the press of small, soft fingers.

Even now they fought his search, denying the probe of his mind.

Cursing, he sat watching the moon rise higher over the steep hill, knowing that sleep would not come that night.

"Did you get it?"

Sir Gordon Mount spun around, nearly knocking the priceless antique lamp from his desk. "What are *you* doing here?"

The woman was tall and exquisite. Her wavy black

hair was held back by two diamond clips. "I thought you would be happy to see me, my dearest."

Jacques St. Cyr's solicitor looked anxiously at the open door, toying with his collar. "Of course I am. But—but not here. Anyone could walk in."

Her crimson lips eased into a smile. "With the door open, no one will suspect anything, will they? Now where have you put it?"

The solicitor lifted a cardboard carton from the floor and slid it across his desk. "It was damn hard to talk the Lloyd's man into letting me keep it overnight. I had to convince him the blade needed to be analyzed. I'm taking it in first thing in the morning."

She frowned. "Analyzed?"

"According to Cameron, the thing's covered with poison. He froze up the minute he caught sight of the blade. Seems that the rumors of his strange vision are absolutely true."

The woman's eyes flashed. "How very inventive of Jacques," she whispered. "But not clever enough. Open the box."

"But the poison—"

Laughing coldly, the woman pulled a pair of heavy latex work gloves from her elegant Vuitton bag. The contrast would have been humorous in any other setting. "I'm protected." She eased her fingers into the gloves and slid open the box. "Bring the light closer."

Sir Gordon set the heavy antique Chinese lamp on the desk beside her. His eyes were eager as she lifted the sword from its elegant case. "Aren't you going to see if it fits the scabbard?" he asked.

Light spilled over the polished steel.

"Nathalie?"

The woman did not answer. She pulled a velvet satchel out of her case and laid it gently on the table. Lamplight played off the glinting jewels and beautifully hammered gold of a priceless old scabbard. "Let's see if Jacques was right." She carefully slid the scabbard over the blade.

Metal touched, fit sleekly, then came to a sudden halt.

"It doesn't fit." The woman shoved harder, first right, then left. No matter how she twisted the jeweled scabbard, the blade would not move. Cursing, she pulled the blade free and held it to the light. "Damn him!" Furious, she dropped the sword back into the case.

"What are you doing?"

"It's a *fake,* you fool."

"That's impossible, Nathalie! It came from Jacques himself."

"Then he was even smarter than I thought."

"I don't understand why we don't steal the clues. I have them all now."

Natalie frowned. One long red nail traced her full lips. "Not yet. If we did, Alex would know of your involvement. No, we'll let the two of them do our work for us, answering the clues until they track down the real Cameron sword. Then we will reveal ourselves. It will be a pleasure to see Alex Cameron's face when I relieve him of his precious heirloom. Almost as pleasant as seeing my father's face."

Sir Gordon paled. "What did you say?"

Nathalie smiled faintly. "My father, of course. Jacques St. Cyr."

"My God, you're his *daughter?*" Sir Gordon stiffened. "You never told me that."

"You didn't need to know, my love. Now you do need to know, because we are going to be partners. Such *close* partners." With her fingers still encased in the latex gloves, Nathalie caressed the replica slowly.

"He's your father, and yet you ordered that he be—"

Nathalie St. Cyr's eyes darkened. "I told you, Gordon, I am a very dangerous woman. And, as we both know, my dear father is brilliant at the game of deception. Who else do you think taught me all my tricks?"

"I don't understand."

"That's rather your problem, isn't it, my love?" Nathalie St. Cyr's full lips curved in a sensual smile. "Listen and I will explain. There are few people who would recognize that this is *not* the authentic Cameron claymore. No doubt Alex saw at once. Presumably, the American woman saw, too. They are very clever if they concealed their surprise from you. A bad sign."

"You think they suspect?"

"Perhaps. We will have to be careful. No doubt Jacques hoped to confuse us into doubting the clues we already have. He knew that our scabbard would never fit, because this replica lacks the secret mechanisms of the true sword." She studied the beautifully made hilt, one finger tapping on the mahogany table.

"What are we going to do now?"

"We are going to be very, very clever, my love." Something shimmered in her eyes as she turned to Sir Gordon. Her fingers played over his collar and slid down to his belt.

The solicitor licked suddenly dry lips. "Nathalie, I don't think we should—"

Her hands were slow, searching. "We shouldn't do what, my dear?"

His breath caught. "Nathalie, you can't. Not *here*. Anyone might walk in."

She eased against him, her smile coaxing. "Which will make it all the more exciting, don't you think?" She shoved him back until his thighs were against the desk. Her hands were swift and skillful.

Sweat beaded Sir Gordon's brow. His fingers shook on the table. "My God," he said hoarsely.

"I told you I was good." A zipper hissed open, and she laughed huskily.

His back was to the door, his body tight with arousal when he heard his secretary's firm knock. "Get out," he rasped. "Close the door behind you."

And then he heard no more, desire spasming through him as Nathalie St. Cyr's cool, clever fingers closed around him only seconds before her lips.

The last riddle: The Heart, which is the Key to Forever.

Only when given does the heart prosper. Only when shared does love take wing. When man and woman stand together, hearts entwined, the riddle will be solved. Like scabbard and sword, their power will rise beyond all evil.

Love is the magic and the key. Find the still, sweet yearning in the heart and cherish it well, you of Cameron blood. This is the hardest secret and the greatest power.

Let the heart lead the way. Then and only then will the real treasure be yours.

Hear who would hear.

18

JOANNA DREAMED in slow motion that night. Like a tired swimmer, she eased through castles of sand, along corridors of polished pearl. Water swirled around her, straining in cold currents. She was pushed relentlessly forward, captive of forces she could neither see nor understand. With every movement, her fear grew greater, pressing at her chest, blocking out all logic and finally all hope.

Far away in the distance, through the shadowed sea halls she saw a faint figure outlined in phosphorous trails of light. He turned, a gold coin clasped in his fingers as he moved to meet her. Then a wave rose, sweeping him into the darkness while she churned futilely, caught against a countercurrent.

Peter.

She screamed, but there was no sound. A perfect, deadly silence trapped her and everything around her. Sand shifted around her feet, clutching at her ankles while she watched the most precious part of her heart being dragged away before her, inch by terrifying inch.

When Joanna awoke, her throat was raw from crying.

The whisper of silk woke Alex just before dawn.

He sat up swiftly, studying the flagstone terrace. Against the first pale streaks of sunlight, a slender figure moved with elegant grace in a series of slow stretching movements.

He sank back, savoring the sight of Joanna in a pale aqua leotard and a flowing silk tunic. Every movement was smooth and practiced.

He did not interrupt, sensing that this was her way of finding balance and peace amid the chaos Jacques had thrust them into. Alex understood the strain she was feeling. There had been a time when his own life had been turned upside down and he had struggled with bouts of despair and cold fury.

Because of a woman who had intoxicated him with her exotic beauty and her insatiable appetite for novelty—in bed and everywhere else.

His wife.

His *ex*-wife, Alex corrected himself sharply. Only with the passage of time had he seen that her energy was no more than restlessness and her unquenchable appetites were only a desperate effort to camouflage a gaping flaw in her personality.

There had been no love in her reckless coupling, no love in her effervescent laughter. But it had taken Alex months to understand—and to forgive himself for his monumental stupidity in thinking there was anything real between them.

Wrong choices. Wasted time.

As Alex watched Joanna move in the dawn, he thought about Greywood's neat borders of lavender and roses. He thought about the knot garden and the new greenhouses. After five years of careful work, Greywood was now fully restored, the roofs repaired, the carpets spotless. Years of grime and tallow smoke had been removed from the mellow old walls, and the house was finally ready to become a home, ringing with laughter, warmed by a woman's touch.

As long as the woman was Joanna.

Fool.

Muttering, he turned away and picked up the phone. A smile eased across his high-boned face as a familiar voice answered. "So, Mikhail, you have forgotten your old Gypsy friend?"

Michael Burke, ex–Royal Marine Commando and

Marquess of Sefton, laughed deeply. "I only wish."
There was a rustle of fabric. "Do you know what time it is?"

"Oh, we Gypsies have no use for clocks. The sun is up.
That's enough for us."

"That and the fine Rolex you keep on the back of your
dresser," Michael said dryly.

"Baiting me is useless. No doubt you are trying to
back out of tonight's misbegotten dinner with the visiting trade delegation from Estavia."

Michael chuckled. "I must admit, the thought had
crossed my mind. Drinking vodka with a dozen sour-faced Estavian bureaucrats is not exactly my *favorite* way
to spend an evening."

"I quite understand." Alex knew that his old friend
was enjoying the first year of a very happy marriage to an
American archaeologist whom he had met at Draycott
Abbey under trying circumstances. Alex was still trying
to worm the details out of his old friend. "Admit it,
you'd rather be at home with Kelly, poring over old
books."

"Quiet evenings have their attraction, Alexei. You
should try one sometime."

"Stop changing the subject. If you and Kelly back out,
I'll never speak to you again."

There was a long silence. "The idea holds a certain
appeal."

Alex mumbled something in Russian.

Michael, who had learned the language at the knee of
his Russian mother, responded in kind, then laughed.
"Eight o'clock as I recall. Let's hope the ambassador and
his entourage are on time. I understand they kept a
cabinet minister waiting for nearly an hour last week in
London."

"Politics, my friend. You can see why I've never liked
it." His voice fell. "My apologies, Mikhail, but are you
alone?"

"Yes. Why?"

Alex toyed with a stem of dried lavender next to

Joanna's telephone. "You spoke to Nicholas Draycott before he left for France last month, didn't you?"

"I did. Not looking to buy more land for Greywood, are you? Nicholas will never sell. Very stubborn, these Draycotts."

"I'm interested in answers, not land," Alex said grimly. "Did Nicholas mention the woman renting the old stone cottage overlooking the valley?

"You mean Ms. Russell, the weapons expert."

Alex's eyes narrowed. "Exactly."

"My wife knows Joanna rather well. They worked together on a Scottish restoration project several months ago." Burke seemed to hesitate. "Is there something specific you wanted to know?"

"There are a hell of a lot of things I'd like to know, but I'll start with this: Do you know much about her past?"

There was a moment of hesitation. "Perhaps."

"Do you or don't you, Mikhail?"

"I might have heard something. She lives very quietly, and I haven't met her often."

"You haven't heard anything about a husband, I suppose?"

There was a low chuckle. "Does this mean that the footloose and antimatrimonial Lord Greywood has finally been corralled and branded?"

"It does not."

"Touchy, aren't you?"

"You would be, too, if a woman nearly died on *your* terrace."

"Ah, yes, the reenactment."

"What is that supposed to mean?"

"Calm down, Alex. There was some talk, that's all."

"What *kind* of talk?"

"I believe that the museum director said something about Ms. Russell looking very pale before she literally fell into your arms. I believe there was some mention of that fatal Cameron charm of yours."

"Is there anything that *doesn't* get gossiped about in this county?"

"Not where you are concerned, Alex." Michael

Burke's voice was very serious. "You are famous. Even better, you are a figure of mystery. Exotic Gypsy heritage, years of absence on the desolate edge of Russia, then a stunning reunion with one of the most respected peers in Britain, who happened to be your father. How could you *not* be a figure of endless gossip?"

"It never bothered me before."

"So it's serious this time."

"I don't know what you mean," Alex said tightly.

"You know *exactly* what I mean. I saw you the day you came back to Greywood, remember? You swore you would never care about anything but work again. No emotions, no attachments, just work with those devilish swords of yours. Now you're agonizing over a little piece of gossip."

"What's agonizing is Jacques St. Cyr. It seems that he discovered clues describing the location of the Cameron claymore."

Burke whistled softly. "Are you certain?"

"No. But we have the notes in his own hand. We also have reason to believe someone tried to kill him to steal those clues." Alex's voice hardened. "He's comatose, I'm afraid."

"What do the police say?"

"Precious little. My house has been robbed, and Joanna and I were run off the road last night." Alex stared out at the mist curling over the terrace. "And she's hiding something from me. Something bloody important. I need to *know,* Mikhail. It might keep us both alive."

"Kelly might know. I understand that Joanna has had some difficult years," Burke said slowly. "She doesn't open to people quickly."

The understatement of the century, Alex thought. "Fine. Why don't you two come over to Greywood early tonight? We'll have drinks before that blasted delegation arrives."

"So you can pump my wife for gossip?"

"If Kelly is willing to talk, I'll be only too happy to listen. Joanna is in danger."

"If these people are after the Cameron claymore, then you're in danger, too."

"I can take care of myself," Alex said grimly. "It's Joanna I'm worried about."

"Do you think this is connected with the theft of your replica sword?"

"Without a doubt. And St. Cyr was definitely involved in that, because the replica was in his possession. He left instructions with his solicitor to see that the piece was turned over to Joanna and myself if something happened to him."

"Why would he steal the thing, then return it?"

"Maybe something frightened him off." Alex frowned. "Or maybe he was trying to tell us something."

Burke sighed. "I'll see what I can find out through official channels, Alex, but don't hold your breath. I'm not in active service anymore, and my resignation left a bitter taste in certain people's mouths. Years of expensive training gone down the drain, that sort of thing. Mind you, if you say a word about this to Kelly, I'll—"

"I won't, you can count on that. Come to think of it, any time you want to talk about a job with Greywood Enterprises—"

Burke laughed. "Generous of you, but I'm building my own little business now. Private security, museum thefts, that sort of thing. I'm also enjoying some time off. Kelly's time is getting close, you know."

Alex stiffened. "There's nothing wrong, is there? She isn't—"

"No, Kelly's fine."

"What about the baby? There's no problem with—"

"Kelly's fine and the baby is fine," Burke said firmly. "I'm just staying close. Otherwise, Kelly would still be on her feet, inspecting artifacts ten hours a day."

"Maybe she shouldn't come tonight . . ."

"She's looking forward to the evening. She can't understand what could be so unpleasant about one small trade delegation."

"I hope she need never find out." When there was no answer, Alex frowned. "Mikhail, are you still there or have you gone off to contemplate early American arrow-heads?"

"I'm still here. I'm just trying to decide how much trouble you're going to get me into this time."

"Me? When have I ever caused you a single problem?" Burke snorted. "How about last summer in Cannes?"

"That was different. That was business, pure and simple."

"The owner of the gallery didn't see it that way."

Alex snorted. "The bloody Frenchman had cheated tourists out of a fortune. Every one of those 'antique' medieval swords was a fake!"

"Alex, we have government agencies to deal with these things. Whole bureaucracies in fact. But *you* had to throw the man headfirst through his plate-glass window."

"Bureaucracies take too long."

"It's a good thing Kelly and I will be there tonight. If we leave you alone, there's no telling what disasters you'll cause."

Alex smiled. "Thank you, my friend. Whatever else I do, I shall try not to throw *you* through a plate-glass window. But only," he added wickedly, "because Kelly would murder me if I tried."

Michael Burke was smiling when he hung up the telephone. There was a light tap, and his door was opened by a woman with sparkling eyes and dark auburn hair.

"I hope I'm not intruding, my love."

Michael came around the desk. "Not at all." Gently he touched his wife's very pregnant stomach. "You shouldn't be up. The doctor said you should rest every day now."

"What do doctors know?" his wife said crossly. "If I stopped to rest every day, I'd be wild with boredom long before our baby is due."

Burke gently touched his wife's cheek. "You're not worrying again, are you?"

His wife sighed. "No. Just being cranky and generally

impossible. I seem to be doing far too much of that lately."

"If you rest, we'll go out early. Alex insists we come for drinks before the trade delegation arrives."

"Wonderful. I can't wait to see his new acquisitions. He has a wonderful eye for line and authenticity."

"Humph."

"Michael, what is it? Alex isn't in some kind of trouble, is he?"

"To hear him tell it, he's *never* in trouble."

"He hasn't done anything since Cannes," Kelly said loyally. She tried to hide a smile and failed.

Michael shrugged.

"Tell me, my love. It can't be as bad as all that."

"Blast it, what is it about Alexei Cameron that makes all you women fall in love with him?"

Kelly Burke tilted her head and pretended to consider. "Do you mean, other than his exotic good looks, his smoldering gray eyes, or the air of palpable sexuality that clings to him?"

"I see," Burke said tightly.

"No, you don't, you great idiot." Kelly caught her husband's face and kissed him fiercely. "Alex's attraction is his air of untouchability. Beneath all that charm, a woman senses that his heart has been badly broken in the past. No woman can resist a challenge to mend a broken heart."

Michael sniffed.

His wife's hands inched inside his sweater. His muttering turned to a groan as she found his belt. "And I suppose you find that kind of challenge irresistible, too?"

Kelly hid a smile. "Not at all. It makes me a traitor to my sex, I suppose. My obsession is with tough, stubborn men who wear their hearts on their sleeves. Men who fret about their wives over a tiny little thing like a baby on the way." She opened her lips over his and sighed as she pulled his belt free.

Her kiss was hot, demanding. His response was equally fierce.

Abruptly Burke froze. "Kelly, are you sure we should be—"

His sweater went flying over his head and landed on the floor. "The doctor recommended rest, not celibacy, my love." Kelly's lips curved in an inviting smile. "After all, there *are* ways . . ."

Her husband's groan of pleasure a moment later proved that he was in complete and utter agreement.

19

THE SUN was just burning away the morning mist when Alex moved silently out onto the terrace.

Joanna stopped instantly. Her face was flushed, and a tendril of cinnamon hair drifted above her cheek.

"No need to run. I come bearing gifts." He held up a steaming cup of tea.

"Is that Darjeeling I smell? I think I could grow used to this service."

Alex bent closer, the cup held just out of reach. "That's the general idea."

She stiffened instantly.

Alex cursed, angry at her response. Angry at himself for pushing too fast, too soon. He held out the tea. "Truce."

"I doubt you know the meaning of the word."

"Try me." He crossed his arms, his eyes lazy. "You're very good at those movements. Tell me why."

"I've had lots of practice. *Tai-ji,* rapier. And of course basic garden-variety yoga." She did a deep move that brought her nearly to the ground while her hands rose smoothly in front of her.

Calm strength filled her eyes. Alex knew that she had not always been like this. Somewhere in her past lay a jagged puzzle piece that explained the defenses built so thoroughly around her heart.

Were they to protect herself or someone else?

Joanna ran a towel across her face and studied the

valley. Mist crept up the dark slopes, and in the distance the gray towers of Draycott Abbey could be seen above the trees. "I love this place. There's a magic to it, a sense of timelessness." She shrugged. "That probably makes me certifiable."

"Not at all," Alex said. "I've felt it, too. Nicholas Draycott is one damn lucky fellow. Of course, I couldn't think of a better person to be responsible for that magnificent old house and its heavy heritage."

Joanna looked at him, her head cocked. "Surely you're not jealous? Greywood is lovely, filled with its own kind of magic."

"But it's not gold-plated enchantment like Draycott Abbey." He smiled crookedly, jamming long fingers through his black hair. "I don't imagine anything could match up to this valley, but I don't envy Nicholas. Draycott Abbey is in his blood, just the way Greywood House is in mine."

"And the Cameron claymore?" Joanna asked softly.

Alex's eyes hardened. "It's in my blood, too."

"You . . . can feel it? The way you knew about the poison on that replica?"

Alex nodded. "There's no more avoiding it. Almost as if—" He broke off.

"As if what, Alexei?"

"As if I was meant to be here. As if *you* were meant to be here with me. You mentioned certifiable, and maybe you just got it. The sooner we get out of this bloody mess of Jacques's the better." Frowning, Alex studied the mist trailing along the hillside. "I'd feel a lot better if you weren't involved. There are too many questions." He looked at Joanna, and heat filled his eyes. "I'm not going to lie. I want you right now. Maybe more than I've ever wanted you. But when I take you to bed, it won't be with secrets, and it won't be without trust. We did that before, and we've both regretted it."

Joanna took a slow breath. "You don't ask for much, do you, Alexei Turov?"

"From you," he whispered, "I will ask for everything. That's exactly what I will give you back in return."

"It sounds as if the truce is over," she whispered.

Inside the phone began to ring. For long seconds neither moved, the air shimmering.

A line of birds cut across the morning sky, their cries dim over the misty hillside. As before in the night, Alex felt as if he had been here long ago. Or maybe in some way he had never left.

The ringing continued. With a curse, he strode inside and swept up the phone. "Yes?"

"Metcalfe here, my lord. I have the reports on that blade analysis. Sir Gordon just called from London."

"What did they find?"

"It was poison all right. The report mentions something called aconitine, a poison present in the monkshood plant. It appears to have been applied in a liquid form mixed with some sort of common household varnish, which was painted over the blade and the sword grip, where it would be absorbed by the skin."

"So whoever picks up the sword gets a nasty surprise."

"Not entirely. This is where the analysis seems odd. The poison was present in a diluted form, probably not enough to do much more than initiate numbness in the face along with some nausea and dizziness."

Alex looked out over the wooded hillside. "What were you playing at, St. Cyr? What were you trying to tell us?"

"He wasn't trying to kill, is that what you mean? Forgive me, my lord, but if so, it seems that Mr. St. Cyr went to a great deal of trouble for nothing."

"Maybe. Or he was simply trying to buy time."

"For whom?" Metcalfe asked.

"I wish I knew." Alex felt Joanna behind him, her perfume a light mixture of moss and roses. There were dark circles under her eyes, and her face was pale. "Thanks, Metcalfe. I'll ring you later."

Joanna frowned. "Who was that?"

"Metcalfe with the report on the sword's blade. There was definitely poison present." Alex saw her stiffen.

"You still believe that Jacques would do such a thing?"

"It's a fair assumption, Joanna. The sword was in his

possession. It certainly had no poison present a month ago when it was stolen from Greywood."

"I can't believe it. I *won't* believe it. Jacques is arrogant and possessive, but he's not a killer."

"Maybe he didn't want to kill. The poison was present in a very dilute form. He might have been trying to leave me a message." Alex frowned. "Something he knew only I could read. After all, he did specify that I was to be present before the sword case was opened."

Joanna's fingers moved restlessly over the towel. "So we're back to this ability of yours." She shook her head. "That kind of thing only happens in movies. Bad movies."

"Does it?" Alex caught a handful of her shining hair. He watched it spill through his fingers, his eyes narrowed in concentration. "Right now you're frightened. Last night you slept very little, and your dreams were full of dark shapes and cold water. You feel lost." He opened his mind, letting the images flow through him. "You feel as if someone kicked your feet out from under you. And you hate feeling that vulnerable."

Joanna shoved away his hand. "Any sidewalk psychologist could come up with that."

"There's more. I can feel the barriers you put up, Joanna. Everything you love is hidden behind them. I can feel the light, the laughter, and the warmth. But no one is allowed to cross that line or get close to that part of you. And I have a damn good idea that you're worrying about those pictures because of how they'll affect someone else."

He saw her swallow. "Very clever. But as I told you once before, I'm not keen on games."

"It's no game, Joanna. My gift is very real. It's only a matter of time until I see everything."

"Damn it, Alex, you have no *right* to pry into my life."

"Until I find the sword, I have every right. This gift of mine might be the only thing that will keep us alive. We've been run off the road and nearly drowned. Yesterday we could have been poisoned. Your studio has been ransacked and my home robbed. Oh yes, I have the right to interfere, and I'll keep interfering until I have all the answers I need."

He jammed his hands into his pockets, fighting to keep them away from her stiff shoulders, away from her pale cheeks and haunted face. Her leotard was damp with sweat, molded to every sleek inch of her body, leaving little to his heated imagination.

Not that Alex needed to imagine. Five years ago, he had tasted those heated curves and velvet hollows. He knew the innocent abandon of her desire and the soft, broken sounds she made in her passion.

The memory made him harden painfully. He cursed softly. "Get dressed. We have an appointment in thirty minutes. Sir Gordon is waiting at Greywood to give us the next clue."

"Why don't you like him?"

"Because he's a frightened man as well as a very greedy one. A dangerous combination."

"Frightened? But how do you know—?" Joanna swallowed. "You can feel that?"

Alex nodded, daring her to protest, daring her to do anything more that would give him an excuse to sweep her into his arms.

She took a slow breath. "This is not going to be easy for either of us, Alex. Working together. Sleeping here . . ."

The woman was a master of understatement. "And?"

"And I think we need some ground rules."

Ground rules. Does she think it's a bloody rugby match? "What kind of ground rules?"

"I won't do anything . . . obvious. Provocative, I mean. Disturbing."

Like breathe? Like move with all that sleek, powerful elegance? Like look at me with those haunted, changeable eyes?

Alex sighed. "I'm listening."

"It's work now. Just business. Finding that lost sword is all that matters. We've got to be partners. Just . . . business partners. We both have to understand that."

"Go get dressed, Joanna."

"You didn't answer me."

"Because it will never work. If you're anywhere within two counties, I'll feel you. I'll smell that faint hint of your perfume and I'll remember the heat of your skin." His voice fell. "And you'll be thinking of me, too."

"You're wrong."

His eyes narrowed on her face. "Just the way you're thinking about me now."

"Adrian?" The voice drifted above the moat and along the weathered abbey walls. "Adrian, we must help them."

The moat rippled. Bees hummed among the crimson roses.

Her eyes came first, huge and luminous. Her cheeks were pale with concentration as the rest of her slender body shimmered into solid form. "There is danger in waiting. You must feel that."

"Of course I feel it." His voice was deep, irritated. It climbed over the weathered walls and brushed the shadows at the corners of the abbey's towering roof. "A curse on all of them for disturbing our peace."

Black velvet gave way to white lace and the brooding features of the eighth viscount Draycott.

"You must release the binding spell you put upon the sword."

"And why is that, my dearest heart?"

Gray Mackenzie, Adrian's kindred spirit, moved closer. "You must free them to make their own choices, Adrian."

"I? A man who has been dead for centuries. No one pays any attention to me. I am the butt of endless jokes, a source of humor for impudent news commentators and lazy tour guides."

"You are most magnificent as always, my love."

His frown softened slightly. "You lie to flatter me."

"It is the truth," Gray said, her eyes shining.

"Then why in the name of all that's holy have you been avoiding me?" His voice was gruff.

"Because I hoped you would make the decision on

your own. It is your abbey after all, and I do not like to interfere."

He made a sound of disbelief. "It is your home now. I assumed you were offended because of all these malicious tales about the Evil Viscount."

"Have you so little faith in me? After all we have experienced, all we have shared?" Her golden sleeve brushed his shoulder, and the air shimmered between them. Her smile was slow and filled with infinite tenderness. "Yes, there is darkness in you, but there is far more light. It pours from you even now, my heart. It is *you* the tourists come to see. The paintings and the tapestries are very fine, but you are the heart of this wonderful old house."

"We," he corrected. "You and I, our love bound here, entwined as it has been for centuries."

The glow of their bodies grew, merging slowly. Leaves whirled up in a soft eddy of unseen currents, as roses swayed drowsily in the sun.

He sighed. "You're right, of course. The time has come. Mary has walked here far too long, caught in her anger and her pain. Both are emotions I know all too well."

"Then you'll do it?" she whispered. "You'll take away your binding spell that has shielded the sword from discovery? You'll let them find their own destiny at last?"

"There *is* danger, you know. The spell can backfire when it is removed." The abbey's guardian ghost was silent for long minutes, staring at his beloved roses. Finally, he nodded. "I will. Not because it is time or because it is right. Only because you ask it of me, Gray, for you are more to me than time or hope or even these beautiful stone walls."

Her lips brushed his palm. A tear traced her cheek. She moved against him, her eyes holding the shimmer of the moat and her scent the sweet perfume of a thousand centifolia roses.

Her heart opened with love as it always had before. As it always would.

A thrush called from the willow tree beside the moat.

Suddenly Adrian's voice was hard. "I tire of being a buffoon, an afternoon's diversion for a tourist's entertainment."

"Never," she breathed. "You bring them things they cannot have. You help them touch truths that cannot be seen. Visitors leave here as different people from when they came, my love."

"Perhaps." Yet his voice was lighter and his jaw was not so tense. "It will be dangerous for me to remove the spell. Dangerous for them as well. Much will be set in motion, for great anger touches the sword," he said slowly. "The past can be a dangerous place to visit."

"It was dangerous for us, too. But the chance was worth taking, was it not?"

"Can you doubt it?"

Her eyes were chiding. "Then let them take their chances, too. Let them find the true measure of their hearts. Because the heart remembers. Isn't that what you say?"

Adrian sighed. "So it will be done." His eyes darkened. "But not now. Right now I have more important work." His hands trailed along her slender waist.

"And what kind of work is that?"

"This. The most important of all mysteries." His hand traced the soft line of her hip. "My exploits were much exaggerated, you know. But touching you like this, I find the most inventive notions coming to mind."

She smiled. Her lips found the hard line of his jaw. "Such as?"

He murmured softly and laughed when heat filled her cheeks.

"Not here, Adrian. It's broad daylight."

"And who is there to see? No one will be shocked by our exploits. It is one of the great advantages of the state we occupy now."

Gold shimmered in the drowsy sunlight, and her garment fell away.

"As beautiful as the first day I saw you," Adrian said hoarsely. Light seemed to fill the banks of the moat, shimmering off the clear water. "For you, Gray. For all you have brought me. An end to pain and a light to ease my sorrow." For a moment, a high ringing seemed to fill the air. Then their beings spilled together, glowing, merging.

Light beyond light.

Joy beyond joy.

Soon a shining mantle was spun out of their love, glinting golden over hill and glade and crimson rose, covering every corner of their drowsy, beloved abbey. And their laughter blended with the gentle murmur of the silver moat.

20

M ETCALFE MET them at Greywood's broad steps, looking somber. "Sir Gordon is in your study. He has been rather . . . impatient. I'm not sure I quite trust the man if you'll forgive my saying so."

Alex saw Joanna's sharp, questioning look and shrugged. "I don't trust the man either, solicitor or not."

Sir Gordon's eyes were hard with impatience as they entered Alex's study.

"Sorry we're late. Unexpected business."

Sir Gordon nodded gravely. "I heard about the problem last night with your car."

"Good news travels fast, doesn't it?"

"There have been no other problems, I trust?"

"No one firebombed the road as we drove up if that's what you mean," Alex said grimly. "If you don't mind, can we get right to business?"

"Of course." Sir Gordon pulled another wax-sealed envelope from his attaché case and shoved the heavy vellum across the table to Alex, making a point to keep the intricate red seal upright. "Still intact, as you can see. Jacques was most insistent about that."

"Bravo for him." Alex studied the envelope, not reaching for it immediately.

Sir Gordon's eyebrow rose. "Something wrong? No more poison, I trust."

Alex shook his head. For a moment, he had touched

something unexpected, something bright and sharp. St. Cyr, he decided, had been very agitated when he wrote this. "Thank you, Sir Gordon. You can leave us now."

"You *didn't* have to rub it in his face," Joanna said after the door had closed. "Now he knows you don't trust him."

"He knows something he's not telling us. If I push him a little, he'll reveal what it is."

Joanna shook her head. "You're wrong, Alex. You're seeing enemies where none exists."

"Am I? Twenty-four hours ago I might have agreed with you," he said harshly. "Not now." His fingers closed over the envelope, and he held it out slowly. "Go on. Read the damned thing."

Joanna slipped open the red wax seal and pulled out a single sheet of paper, then began to read. "The second riddle: 'He who dies, which is the Key to Today.'" Joanna frowned and read the next line. "'The key to my faith has no lock and no limit. Like the blade itself, it burns and shimmers.'"

Alex watched Joanna's face. He saw the searching, the frown of recognition.

"Faith. Could that be religious faith?" Her brow creased. "Something like a statue. Or maybe a biblical painting?"

"Reasonable enough." Alex shook his head. "But there's nothing of that sort at Greywood. Read the rest."

"'To close the circle, find the words. Holy words, they are. Riddles within a riddle. Heed their message and all gates shall open.'" Joanna looked up. "Holy words. That would be a Bible." Her breath caught. "Oh, God, Alex. Listen to this. It sounds as if Jacques copied this from a very old source." *The great blade of Cameron burns and shimmers, heavy with old magic that tests men's souls, as mine was tested. Beside it lies the jeweled sheath. When these two are one, together paired, the enchantment will begin, bound by oath, linked for all eternity. God protect you if your heart is not true when that day comes and their power is linked. The Cameron treasure will be yours then, with all its pain and joy.* Her fingers gripped the paper. "Linked. Alex, the sword and scabbard are a *pair*. There must be some mechanism that is triggered when the two are attached. It was fairly common in walking sticks with concealed pistols."

Alex sat back slowly. His jaw hardened. "My father told me nothing of this."

"Maybe even *he* didn't know. Maybe the source Jacques found has been hidden for centuries."

"Now all we have to do is find the sword and its scabbard, then figure out how the two fit together. About as easy as finding a needle in the middle of Piccadilly Circus."

"At least we know what we're looking for now."

"Tampering with the sword, even if we do find it, is not something to be done lightly, Joanna. The warning is clear."

"But you're a Cameron. It's your privilege, your *responsibility,* to see the sword and scabbard joined."

Alex rubbed the knot forming at the back of his neck. "Maybe there's a bloody good reason why the sword and scabbard were separated."

"Magic swords that sing and curses that can't be broken? Alex, this is the twentieth century, not the Middle Ages."

"I am a Gypsy, Joanna. It's in my blood to believe far stranger things than that." Alex tapped restlessly on the table. "As I recall, my father left some of his books at Draycott Abbey. He said they were to repay an old debt. I suppose I'll finally have to face them . . ."

Sir Gordon was pacing in the hall when Alex and Joanna went outside. "Well?" he said.

"You can go," Alex said curtly. "We'll see you tomorrow."

"But—"

Alex strode past, guiding Joanna down the hall to the front door. A shiny red Alfa Romeo gleamed beside the fountain, delivered by Dimitri.

"I don't mean to be run off any roads today," Alex said grimly. "They won't be looking for us in this."

"In this car, the whole *world* will be looking at us."

Alex studied her face. "Do you mind being looked at? With me?"

Joanna took a tense breath. "No," she said finally.

Alex felt a smile work through him. "Good."

"But the rest of what you want . . ."

"Will wait," Alex said flatly. "I've got my whole life, Joanna. As I said, I've learned to be a very patient man. Now let's start digging up the past."

In the silent gallery on Draycott Abbey's highest floor, sunlight filtered through high mullioned windows. An unseen gust of wind toyed with the lace curtains, making shadows stir in the beautiful old room. Beyond the Whistler canvases, beyond the priceless Chinese porcelains, sunlight outlined a vast oak armoire. As the curtains fluttered, the carved figures seemed to move against the polished wood.

Somewhere in the shadows a voice whispered urgently. "Adrian?"

"Nearly done."

"They're coming." The curtains fluttered again. "Nearly at the drive now."

"Yes, I know. But these damned spells are harder to remove than to place, Gray." His hands shimmered for a moment, and a high ringing seemed to split the air. *"Done."* He sank back, his features merged into the shadows beneath the great armoire. "For all the good it will do them."

"It will." Gray caught his hand. "I can feel the change around this room already." She frowned. "There will be danger. Choosing is àlways dangerous."

"What's done is done. There will be no going back now, my love."

She gave him a gentle smile. "But we may watch. And perhaps assist . . . just a little?"

The abbey ghost laughed dryly. "More than a little if I know you." His hand eased over her cheek. "Very well. But the choice must be theirs, Gray. I will allow the sword to be found and released, but its discovery may bring them into grave danger unless their trust in each other is strong."

Slowly the two voices faded, moving through the stone walls and out over the bank of the moat, where a great gray cat lay curled drowsily in the sun.

Beautiful, Joanna thought. *A vision from a dream.*

Before her, the moat shimmered silver, winding beneath weathered walls splashed by climbing red roses. Draycott Abbey was more beautiful today than it had ever been before. More *alive.*

And also more dangerous?

A shiver played through Joanna's shoulders as Alex took the last curve. A sudden wind rose, casting twigs and dead leaves against the car windows. She looked at Alex, feeling a sudden urgency. "Maybe we shouldn't go in." Joanna shook her head. "The abbey feels different today. In all my visits, it's never felt so overpowering." She swallowed. "So alive."

"Gold-plated enchantment, is that what you mean?" Alex studied the high towers. "I thought you didn't believe in magic."

"I don't." Her hands shook slightly. Then there was heat and hard callouses where his fingers covered hers.

She turned her head, and images rippled like quicksilver, swift and changeable. Passion hid in those images, mingled with the pain of old betrayal. Joanna saw the same images playing through Alex's eyes. "Do you feel it, too?"

He nodded, his hands tightening. He looked up at the windows ablaze with midday sun. "I've always half expected a horde of mounted knights to come charging down over the hill from Lyon's Leap. The place is said to be haunted by a ghostly rider, did you know that?"

"Whatever you do, don't mention it during one of my tours. I have enough trouble keeping them in line as it is. All they want to see is the Evil Viscount's bedroom."

Alex chuckled, and suddenly the spell was broken. They were in front of the abbey's old gate house, bright with roses. "Maybe looking at their beautiful tour guide gives the men lustful thoughts."

Joanna's brow arched. "I hate to think what the dear ladies would make of *you,* my Gypsy lord."

Jacques St. Cyr awoke with a wrenching shudder. He stared around him, his eyes fixed and dilated.

White sheets. White walls. Humming machinery. Tubes and wires everywhere.

Slowly, his hands crept over the crisp linens, tracing the plaster that covered both his legs. He blinked once.

His mind was a blank.

Then memory returned. Betrayal was bitter in his mouth as he struggled to reach the call button dangling inches from his left hand.

But he was too late. A woman entered, tall and striking. There was a gentle smile on her full lips as she moved toward him. Though she wore a white uniform, Jacques knew she was no nurse.

"So," she said softly. "You are finally awake, *mon père.*"

It was too late for him to close his eyes and feign unconsciousness. He stared at her with revulsion.

She stroked a long crimson nail along his gaunt cheek. "Such a pity it had to come to this. Had you been reasonable when we came to see you that night at Beau Rivage, everything would have been different. But you left us no choice. Now we have both the scabbard and your notebook, and all you have is two broken legs." She tapped a finger against the cast, which rang hollowly. "What, no comment? For once my arrogant father is caught speechless?"

Jacques simply stared, his eyes unblinking.

"Sir Gordon has been most helpful by the way." She gave a secret smile. "His needs are so uncomplicated. Most men's are. He has handled everything just as you liked. Alex and Joanna are now diligently tracing your clever clues. Soon the sword shall be mine."

Only with a desperate effort of will did Jacques keep his hands steady as her cold, flat words flowed over him.

"The last clue is yet to come. The Key to Forever."
She laughed softly. "You see, I even know about that.
Still no protest or nasty questions?" She clicked her
tongue. "How clever of you to leave poison on the blade
of the replica. You hoped that would frighten us off so we
would not notice it was only a copy. Dear Sir Gordon,
you fooled him perfectly. But not me. After all, I had the
very best of teachers, didn't I?" Her eyes narrowed.
"You taught me for years, didn't you, *mon père?*
Through hard words and impatient glances. You never
had time for a mere girl, the daughter you never wanted.
Never a word of encouragement when all your love went
to those dead pieces in dead rooms in your dead
collection. You always had to have one more treasure,
didn't you? There was always one more auction, one
more collector to harass." She laughed coldly. "Yes, I
learned well from you how to be clever and hard."

She reached for her elegant Chanel bag. "Did I tell you
that I have a buyer for the sword? Cash on delivery, of
course. You taught me that, too." As she spoke, she
opened her bag and removed a tiny glass vial and a
syringe, which she filled slowly.

Jacques opened his mouth, desperately fighting to
form words, but only a dry rattle emerged.

Then it was too late. There was a crushing pressure in
his head. Suddenly he was heavy, endlessly heavy, and it
was too painful to keep his eyes open.

The last thing he heard was the sound of his daughter's
cold laughter.

21

Alex stood in the abbey's sunny study, feeling the weight of old dreams play about him. "You received my phone message, Marston?"

"Yes. You said you were looking for something." Nicholas Draycott's dignified retainer smiled, well used to all kinds of requests from all kinds of people, including the maharaja of an Indian principality who had brought a pair of tigers into the abbey and insisted that they sleep in his bedroom. "And what are you looking for, my lord?"

"We're not quite sure." Alex gave a crooked grin.

"I see. And do you know where you are supposed to look for this thing that you do not know?"

"Only that my father brought some papers somewhere here to the abbey. He said they were to repay an old debt."

Marston's keen eyes narrowed. "I seem to recall that he brought a trunk over from Greywood. I believe it was stored in one of the attics. If you'll follow me, we can have a look. It might take quite some time, because few of the pieces up there are in any kind of order."

Alex didn't turn. He felt a force, a sudden resistance at his chest. There was a deep silence around him, almost as if the great house was waiting for him to make the next move in a chess game with unseen players and invisible pieces.

Fragments of color and clarity struck him as they had

with the poisoned blade. Just as then, Alex knew what the images represented.

This time he didn't have to reach, only to lower barriers of mental blocking that he hadn't even known existed. It had been years before he had fully understood his gift, and Alex realized that some of those years had been spent trying to ignore the powerful impressions racing up his spine right now.

"It's here," he said softly. "My God, the fire of it. The sweeping, restless power." His voice hardened. "The old blood."

"The sword—you can actually feel it?"

"Now. Maybe always, though I didn't realize it before. For a Cameron, the link would always be great." He grimaced. Light seemed to hiss between his temples. There was color and movement all around him. Anger and whispers . . .

He took a deep breath, feeling the danger that coiled around this beautiful old house, dark entwined with light. Swaying, he reached for the sun-dappled wall.

He realized Joanna was staring at him. "The visions can come like this sometimes. Just . . . give me a moment."

Her hand touched his shoulder. "What exactly are we looking for?"

"A box. A drawer. Maybe a secret compartment. If the dimensions on the portrait are true, that sword was nearly five feet long."

Two hours later, kneeling in an attic surrounded by bolts of old silk, wicker hampers, and dusty china, they were still no closer to solving the sword's mystery. Alex was stiff with tension, stiff with unmet expectations, angry at waiting for clues that never appeared.

He slammed a hamper shut with a curse. "It's not here."

"But I thought you said—"

"Oh, it's here at the abbey, just not here in the attic." He shoved to his feet and paced restlessly between the pictureless frames and yellowed papers documenting generations of Draycotts. "Something is resisting me, almost as if it doesn't want us here."

"Alex, you're not making much sense."

"You're right, I'm not. That doesn't mean it's not true. And I'm not going to be frightened off." He shook his hand at a tarnished old mirror. "The sword is too important, do you hear me?"

A pile of books stacked on a nearby end table toppled with a crack. "Something *definitely* doesn't want us here." He cursed softly. "How much do you know about Mary's days of captivity here at Draycott?"

"Not much. She was kept here for a matter of months while Elizabeth's advisors decided on a course of action. Some accounts hint that there was a plot to free her with the help of one of her Scot retainers."

"Angus Cameron," Alex said tightly. "My ancestor was a passionate man, a world traveler, and an expert in locks and metalwork. He had the utmost loyalty for his Scottish sovereign."

"The plot was betrayed," Joanna reminded him.

"Not by Angus," Alex said savagely. "Never. I've seen letters in his own hand, and he was a loyal supporter of Mary's cause."

Without warning, an old wooden croquet ball eased free of a stack of wickets and rumbled down a wooden incline. Gathering speed, it flew free and cracked down onto the floor.

Inches from Alex's foot.

"It's *true,* damn it." He jammed a hand through his long hair. "I can't believe I'm talking to a wooden croquet ball."

Joanna didn't smile. She felt her own senses stretched tight with unnamed dread. The attic seemed to close in, reminding her of old terrors buried deep. Cold shadows never quite forgotten.

Dangerous . . .

She stumbled to her feet.

"Joanna?"

Alex's voice was distant. There were other voices now. Closer voices, harsh with anger.

How dare you come back, they hissed. *How dare you dare you?*

Her arm slammed against a cabinet behind her. A box of baby toys spilled over the dusty wood.

The enmity was tangible now, the shadows pulling closer.

Joanna looked up and saw Alex as if from a great distance. A single ray of sunlight slanted through a high window, illuminating his face. And then she froze.

His hair was fair now, his eyes a slashing blue. A bright wool tartan hung over one shoulder, but it was not half as bright as the blade he cradled tightly in one arm.

From some distant place she heard the neigh of horses and the cry of angry soldiers.

English soldiers. With English guns and swords.

"Angus," she whispered.

His eyes hardened. He raised a slow, sad hand in farewell, already looking exhausted, already regretting the lonely task before him.

His great sword glinted. Oddly sleek. Coldly silver.

"Don't go!" she cried, the words belonging to a stranger. "There will be no coming back, not from where you're bound. You're Mary's man, and they'll hang you in the south."

"Too late for regrets," he said sadly. "Too late to touch you and tell you all the ways I'm sorry. We've missed too much, you and I, while I followed empty dreams and cold mist. A curse on this sword that has made me its slave too long."

The blade seemed to shimmer. Burning. Feeding on the force of his anger.

"But I'll find you," he whispered. "This I vow. Some- where and sometime. When the duty to my sovereign is finally done, I'll find you, love of my heart."

Darkness pressed at Joanna's mind. So close, and now she would lose him again.

"Don't go!"

Her words were swallowed by the shadows.

How dare you come back, either of you? How dareyou dareyou dareyou? the house whispered.

Joanna awoke anchored against warm muscle. Alex's hands were buried in her hair. "Damn it, Joanna, what happened to you?"

She frowned, her head splitting. "I lost you. I *lost* you, Alex. Just like before!" Her face was wet with tears she couldn't remember shedding. Tears that might have been four centuries old. "Damn it, I don't believe in magic."

"Maybe magic is everything else, and *this* is what's real," Alex said tightly.

"Why? What's happening to us, Alex?"

"I think," he said slowly, "that the past has found us. I can feel the sword somewhere in this mysterious old house, very close. That would explain your vision of Angus Cameron, which sounds as if it might have been a vision of *me*. Or the man I once was."

Light played off his hair, warm with flecks of blue and gold and copper. This time he was no Highland chief, only a desperate man lost in love. "Maybe that's why I've felt linked to you so closely."

His lips brushed her upturned face, the sensitive skin at her neck. Joanna stiffened in the shocking rush of desire.

For a heartbeat, her fingers opened over his chest, searching for warmth. Then she pulled free. "No, Alex. This frightens me. I don't believe in ghosts or memories of other lives. I *don't*." Her face was pale. There could be nothing permanent with this man. Trusting only brought pain and betrayal.

As it had for the wife of Angus Cameron.

"Stop running, Joanna. You're running from yourself now, don't you see?"

She closed her eyes, feeling his hands slip into her hair.

"Maybe we had to remember." His fingers curved over her neck, sliding along the warm skin. Slowly, he made her turn.

Joanna was mesmerized by the heat in his eyes, the hunger written in every hard line of his face. His fingers found the base of her spine and eased upward. Joanna shivered, her body softening. When he pulled her into his awesome heat, she moved to fit him, hungering to feel more.

The realization hit her like a wall of moving earth. Cheeks flaming, she struggled to turn away.

Alex cradled her face, holding her still. "No more running, Joanna. This *is* about sex, yes. I want you, *drushka,* as I have not wanted a woman for years." Darkness filled his eyes. "But what I want is the sight of you trembling and hungry, helpless with need, just as I am made helpless now." His voice hardened. "The sex would be very good right now. But that is only the start of what I want. And you would hate me the instant your tremors stilled. As I would hate myself."

She shivered as his fingers found the swell of one breast.

Don't remember, she told herself. *Memories are too dangerous.* Then she thought of his features as she had seen them moments before: filled with the sorrow and exhaustion of a warrior already regretting his commitment to honor.

Maybe it *was* time to remember. Maybe they had both fought the past long enough.

Joanna slowly turned. She rose against him. Lips parted, she brushed his mouth lightly.

Alex cursed. "Joanna, I—"

She tugged the leather thong from his long hair and let her mouth sink against his. It was *her* choice, *her* control. The power freed her, driving away the old fear.

Alex didn't move. He didn't have to. The slow slide of his lips was enough to summon fire. To seduce and compel.

"How do you do this to me?" His words came harshly. He was huge against her, and memories pounded through her, hot and fine.

She wanted more. She wanted a magical night by a tropical sea. "Alex, please," she whispered.

"Please touch you? Please kiss you and tug off this stupid sweater so I can feel you against my mouth? Tell me, Joanna." His voice was raw with desire. Caution and logic were only memories now.

Joanna couldn't find any words. Her body was a stranger's, shocking her with each new revelation. Now she knew exactly how to touch him in turn, as old memories were revived. She slid her hands into his hair and let the memories guide her.

Alex muttered harshly. "How do you do what no one else has ever done?" He bent to the tender skin beneath her ear, where her pulse raced. He cupped her breasts, already aching for his touch. "How do you make me feel like one person cut in half, looking for the part that's gone?"

"Because you do the same to me," she whispered, realizing what her body had known and remembered all these years. She had given her heart to Alexei Turov that long-ago night by the quiet sea. Passion was the prelude but far from the conclusion.

"Love me, Alex. Don't let me lose you again."

Alex cursed. His hands found the wispy lace that held her breasts. In one movement, sweater and lace fell away. "No more lies, Joanna. No more running. Today there will be only the truth." He groaned as she filled his hands. A muscle flashed at his jaw. He stood frozen, looking, just looking. Like a drowning man before a pool of water.

Her breasts were high and full, capped with coral buds. A single tiny beauty mark lay atop one lush curve.

"God help us," he said harshly. "I can't stop wanting you."

He bent his head, and his lips closed over her. Joanna gasped as desire raced from that searing point of contact. She yielded. She burned. She wanted . . . beyond safety or reason.

Her hands dug at his shoulders.

Alex cursed and found her skirt. His hands were not quite steady as he pushed at the soft wool. A vein pulsed at his forehead as he followed the curve of her thigh and brought a calloused palm to nuzzle her velvet heat.

Joanna pushed against him, dazed, blind with desire.

"God, so sweet. I can feel your wanting, Joanna." His voice was savage. "Only it won't be a few stolen moments in an attic when you shudder for me."

Joanna didn't hear. Her body moved against him, restless, trapped by a desire that she had forced herself to forget.

Cursing, Alex pulled her sweater down, then took her face gently in his palms.

She blinked, studying his face, studying her twisted skirt.

"Don't run from me, *drushka*," Alex said harshly. "Don't run from what we are."

He saw her take a deep breath. Her hands rose as if shoving away shadows. Or painful memories.

What had she seen in her moment of dreaming? Was it the same shreds of a past that haunted him, dark with regret and anger and betrayal? Or was it just this beautiful old abbey playing its clever tricks, wrapping them both in its dark spell?

Alex swore. He wanted all night with her, time to coax her laughter and erase the bitter memories.

Not sprawled on a pile of dusty silk in a dim attic, by God.

"You . . . stopped." Her eyes were intent on his face.

"I stopped." His eyes closed. "I want it to be right this time," he said. "I want it to be forever. Nicholas Draycott says this abbey has too much history and too many memories, and he might be right. Forgetting can be a kind of protection, don't you see?"

Joanna didn't, not entirely. She was awash in emotions that felt dredged up from a stranger's mind, possibly from events that had taken place centuries before.

"I feel anger here, Joanna, even evil. If I wanted you less, I would take you here and now, fast and blinding. But I want a lifetime. Can you understand that?"

She understood that honor had brought them here. In an angry age centuries before, honor to clan had taken precedent over honor of the heart.

And the heart remembers.

"When, Alex?" Joanna whispered, with a perspective of time and linked destiny that would have been more frightening if Alex's arms had not been firm around her.

"Tonight. Tonight the waiting stops," he said fiercely. "I've made my share of mistakes, Joanna. Some were worse than others. But mistakes are how we learn, how we are pushed to grow. When the hurting stops, we're different—usually stronger, thank God." He looked out at the abbey's restless moat, choosing his next words carefully. "I was married, Joanna. Convinced it would be forever. Hoping for a house full of impish children and dogs underfoot. But they were *my* plans, not hers. She wanted to own the world and was busy running, always running."

"To what?" Joanna asked softly.

"I'm not sure. To a life full of material possessions and men and things that don't count, perhaps. I doubt that she'll ever stop running. But what matters is that I came through. Now I know exactly what I want, Joanna, and who I want it with. *You.*" His voice was rough. "People always make mistakes. It's essential that we learn from them." He gave her a crooked grin. "Now my preaching is done and I want you to rest. No more attic treasure hunts."

"What about you?"

"There is someone I have to see, someone who just might be able to help us. But I'm afraid my questions aren't the kind that can be asked over the phone."

Geordie Hamilton had once been brawny and ramrod straight. Now he leaned on a well-used cane, but a fire still burned in his light blue eyes, and there was a lift to his lips. When he saw Alex, he immediately enfolded him in his arms. "It's been a long time, young man," he said gruffly.

Alex swallowed, feeling like the awkward seventeen-year-old boy he had been when he first met his father's oldest retainer, who had been secretary, confidant, and majordomo. "Too long, Geordie."

The servant picked up his cane and swung open the door to a pin-neat cottage. "You'll take a glass of Glenfiddich, I trust."

"Nothing better."

After they sat down, Alex toyed with his tumbler. "I trust you're comfortable here, Geordie. It was always my wish for you to stay on at Greywood, you know."

"Nonsense. I'm too old to be helpful there. This cottage suits me and my wife perfectly. If you don't stop sending us things, we're going to have to protest."

"It's small enough thanks after all the years you gave at Greywood." Alex frowned, clearing his throat. "I'll come right to the point, Geordie. There's been some trouble, and I need to ask some questions about my father. Particularly about those last two weeks before I came back from Asia."

"You never wanted to talk about it before, lad."

"I couldn't. But I've lived with the guilt long enough."

The man made a rough sound in his throat. "Guilt. Now that would be a sad word to use. The two of you carried too much guilt for too long. It seems to be a genetic trait with you stiff-lipped Camerons. But guilt was never what your father wanted from you, Alex. What he wanted was your love."

Alex felt a burning in his throat. "Did he leave anything for me that might have been overlooked, Geordie? Legal documents or something more . . ."

"Personal, you mean?" The Scotsman pushed awkwardly to his feet and moved across the room to a bookshelf with heavy glass doors. "He left this book, so he did. I tried to give it to you twice, but the pain in your eyes told me to keep my distance."

Alex's hands closed tightly over the worn leather that covered a scrapbook of some sort. He thought of his father touching these same pages. "I wish I could go back, Geordie. But it's not possible."

"He wouldn't want you to go back. Andrew was proud

beyond words of all you had done. He kept these newspaper clippings locked in his desk. Every award you won is there, every sword you made and sold."

Alex turned page after page of yellowed clippings. His first finished sword. His first auction. His graduation from Oxford.

"I never knew."

"I only found out by mistake. He was damn stubborn, that father of yours. Almost as stubborn as his son," Hamilton said dryly. "And he loved you with all his heart, the same way he did your mother. How else do you think he could have brought you home from that godforsaken place where they kept you?"

"It's *myself* I blame," Alex said softly. "Not him."

Hamilton's fingers closed on his shoulder. "Put the past away, lad. Keep the best part of him and yourself. Do you remember that old rocking horse up in the attic, the eyes wild and strained as if he was flying over the turf at Newmarket?"

"I remember," Alex said softly.

"After he finished making it, your father told me he wanted you to have something to remember him by, something that would last forever. He left his love in every line of that polished horse, hoping it would say all the things that he never could. He even hammered the key around its neck. He said it could never match the work you did, of course."

Alex stared down at the album. Why hadn't his father told him? Why had they both hidden so much until it was too late?

"Take the album. He meant for you to have it. The Cameron Bible, that's meant to be yours, too."

Alex looked up, shocked. "What Bible? I never saw it."

"You wouldn't have, would you? Andrew had it placed inside an old Chinese chest at Draycott Abbey."

Alex had a hard time breathing. "Why didn't he tell me?"

"I think your father was frightened sometimes, lad.

Almost as if he had made some kind of bargain with the devil. Don't ask me more, because I can tell you naught beyond what I felt. He never spoke of it to me, you understand. When the black moods were upon him, nothing anyone said or did could reach him. It was in one of those moods that he had the Chinese chest carted down from the attic and sealed. He took it over to his friend, the old viscount Draycott. Andrew said the Bible would be safer at the abbey. I think he meant to tell you about it and many other things, Alexei, but there wasn't time."

Alex felt a quickening along his spine, a stab of excitement that could not be restrained. "Thank you, Geordie. Thank you more than you can know."

The old man rubbed his jaw. "Oh, I've a fair idea of the dark place where you've been. I saw the old laird wandering in that same place far too often." He pushed awkwardly to his feet. "Strange how I'm becoming popular in my old age."

"Popular?"

"Aye, lad. You aren't the only one to come knocking this week. There was a woman here just yesterday asking to interview me for a history book she was writing. All about you Camerons, she said."

Tension clawed at Alex's neck. There was no historical research volume planned on the Camerons, not to his knowledge. "If someone comes by again, better send them around to me, Geordie."

The old man's eyes narrowed. "Some bit of trouble, is there?"

"I'm afraid so. I don't want you involved."

The Scotsman nodded slowly. "Aye, I'll be careful."

Alex squeezed his gnarled fingers. "Thank you, Geordie. For the things you've said and for all the things you haven't."

"Take yourself off now," the old man replied, emotion tightening his voice. "And God's blessing be upon you, young laird," he whispered as the door closed.

* * *

As the sun burned into the west, Joanna stood in the abbey's sunny study, surrounded by bright chintz furniture and roses in crystal bowls. The house seemed still now, almost as if it were sleeping.

Or waiting.

Frowning, she looked down at the moat's shining circle, still reeling from her odd visions in the attic. Had her memories truly gone further than she realized, back to some shadow memory of an earlier time? Or was this simply more of Draycott Abbey's elusive magic?

Joanna watched a robin fly over the granite bridge and thought about the son she had put first in her life. Now that she was faced with the possibility of her own happiness, the thought was so alien that it terrified her. Alex had turned her expectations upside down, demanding her honesty and her trust, insisting that she shape a future that took into account her own needs.

Joanna touched her cheek where the imprint of his lips still burned.

Her own needs? She wasn't sure she knew what they were. She did not consider herself weak or easily frightened, yet Joanna saw that there was comfort in self-denial.

She was looking south over the valley toward the cottage when Marston tapped on the door. "Telephone for you, Ms. Russell."

Alex, she thought, unable to keep a crooked grin from her face. With unsteady hands she took the phone. "Alex, did you—"

"No, it's not your handsome Gypsy."

Joanna frowned. "Who—"

"Just listen. Don't interrupt."

"Who *is* this?"

"This is your first warning, Ms. Russell. When you hit three, something bad happens, so keep quiet and let me do the talking. You have beautiful breasts, did you know that? I'm looking at them right now in the pictures."

The room swayed. Joanna's heart began to hammer.

"I especially like the one of you and Alex Cameron

near the edge of the pool. He's touching you. You know the one I mean."

Joanna felt the blood rush from her face. "*Damn* you," she hissed. "Where did you get the pictures?"

"This is your second warning. Next time, the little boy gets a nasty bump on the head. Oh yes, he's your son. How could I forget?"

Joanna's hands tightened. *Peter,* she thought desperately. *No, not Peter.* "He—he's not my son. You must mean someone else."

"Don't bother trying to lie. We know everything about you. Yes, an accident to the boy would be so easy to manage. A graduate student asks him to come along to another part of the site or maybe a visitor wants Peter to point out where he found that nice Roman coin." He clicked his tongue. "No challenge at all."

"What do you *want* from me?"

His laughter was swift and hard. "The sword, of course."

"I don't *have* it."

"You think we don't know that? You think we don't know every step you take, you bloody little fool? When you find the sword, it will be up to you to get it away from Cameron. Given the sight of his face in these wonderful pictures, I'm sure you'll come up with something very persuasive."

Joanna felt her heart pounding, pounding. "And if I don't?"

"Then those nice parents of yours get a set of photographs hand delivered. After that, your precious young Peter goes missing. Maybe permanently."

Joanna's hands clenched against the receiver. "How do I get in touch with you?"

"All you have to do is find the bloody sword, then wait until you're contacted."

"But—"

The line went dead in her hands.

She didn't move, frozen with fear. Then she dialed wildly.

"H.R.—"

"Father, where's *Peter?*"

"Joanna, is that you?"

"Yes. Just tell me where Peter is!"

"Calm down, love. He's on his way to help your mother at the old stone circle. One of the new graduate students came by just a few minutes ago, offering to drive him over."

Dear God, not Peter. "Go get him, Father. He—he's in danger. You all could be."

"But—"

"Go now! There's no time for questions. I'm coming as fast as I can!" Joanna flung down the phone and ran.

22

Joanna's hands were trembling as her car jolted up the pitted drive and skidded to a halt before the dig site entrance. Her heart pounded as she searched for keen gray eyes and brown hair. *Peter, be here. Be fine. Oh, God, let him be safe.*

She gave a broken cry of thanks when she saw her father standing by a wall of scaffolding with Peter beside him, pith helmet in hand. Harrison was trying to hide his worry as he showed the boy a set of arrowheads.

Joanna flung her arms around Peter. *They won't get you, love. No matter what, I swear.*

"Joanna?" Her father's voice was quiet but determined.

"Why did Gran come get me?" Peter asked, looking from one to the other. "Is something wrong?"

"I . . . don't want you going with anyone but family, Peter. Only Gramma or Gran. Or Uncle Michael and Aunt Kelly."

The boy's keen eyes widened. "Is this some kind of game?"

"No. No, it's not. I can't always be here, and I'll count on you to remember, OK?"

Her son nodded. "Should I take care of Gramma, too?"

Joanna nodded blindly, blinking back tears. "That would be grand of you, my love."

"Anything else? We were just about to finish up our sketches of the old stone circle, Mom."

"You can go. Just stay in sight for now."

Peter opened his mouth to protest, caught his grandfather's look and shrugged, then trotted away down a dusty trail that led to the bottom of the hill.

"What the devil is going on?" her father demanded.

Joanna looked at the little eddies of dust playing over the hillside. A faint gray curtain of rain cut the sky far to the south. She almost imagined she could see the English Channel beyond that, bright and shining in the sunlight.

She took a deep breath and told her father everything, about the meeting with Alex, the pictures, and finally about Jacques's fall at Beau Rivage and the search for the long-hidden Cameron claymore.

"Sweet, sweet heaven," the archaeologist said when she had finished. "You should have told us before."

"I wanted to." Joanna's voice wavered. "But I didn't want you to be ashamed of me," she finished flatly.

"Ashamed that you met a man and found him attractive? Lord, Joanna, it's been years since you threw that miserable fool, Peter's father, out of your life. We want you to be happy, not some kind of saint!"

Joanna reached out without looking and gripped his fingers.

They sat that way for a long time while currents of air lifted dust along the path and the wind played over the green fields.

"I take it that this Alexei Cameron doesn't know you have a son."

"No, he doesn't."

"Don't you think it's time you told him?"

"But what about Peter? How will he feel? I can't let a complete stranger barge into his life."

Her father shook his head. "Maybe, my dearest daughter, having a stranger in his life would make it that much richer." He touched her cheek. "Be careful, Joanna. Don't let being alone become a habit."

"England in 1200 had only twenty-five residents to the square mile. Look south over heath and fen, and you can still see the faint outlines of huge forests of ash and beech and elm that once stretched for miles. After the arrival of the Normans in 1066, many of those large tracts came under Forest Law, with its harsh penalties for trespass and poaching."

Arms waving, Harrison McTiernan led a group of visitors up the slope while Joanna watched from the sunny hillside. On her lap lay a sketch pad where she was tracing boundary lines for the old Saxon estates that had followed the Roman settlement here, marked by ditches and deep sunken lanes.

But Joanna couldn't concentrate on scale markers and vertical grids. With a muttered oath, she slammed her sketch pad shut and looked over the bustling site. Peter was talking to a pair of admiring French tourists, pointing out where he had found his Roman breastplate. Pocketing her sketchbook, Joanna picked her way down the hill, frowning. The dig site had become so popular that some of the work areas were in danger of being overrun, compromising scientific data. As a protective measure, Harrison had ordered new fences set up to protect the vulnerable trenches as well as unstable areas near the old tunnels.

But the flood of visitors would make it nearly impossible to protect Peter.

Joanna was considering the problem when she looked down at the bottom of the hill and saw her parents deep in conversation with a man in jeans and a black turtleneck.

Her hands tightened. She felt a choking pressure at her chest. "Joanna, my dear, look who has come to see you." Harrison smiled broadly. "It's your friend, Mr. Cameron. He was telling us how memorable your performance was the other night."

Joanna didn't move. "So I see."

Alex studied her impassively. "If I didn't know better, I'd say you weren't happy to see me."

"I'm *not.*"

"Joanna," her mother said in a horrified voice. "And Mr. Cameron was just telling us how interested he is in our archaeological work. In fact, he's been planning to offer you a commission, because you are clearly the finest restorer of period armor he has seen to date."

Joanna glanced down the hill. Peter was flat on his stomach in the bottom of a trench.

"Mr. Cameron says he's read my recent article on Roman hill-fort communications," Joanna's father said. "He's also interested in the effect of Forest Law on the native Saxon population under the Normans."

"Call me Alex please, Dr. McTiernan."

The tall archaeologist smiled. "Very well. Do you know, Joanna, Alex has offered to come back tomorrow and help us work on our new trench measurements."

"He can't. He's busy tomorrow."

"Oh?" Her father looked at their guest with disappointment. "Then perhaps Wednesday?"

"He's busy Wednesday, too," Joanna said flatly.

"I see." Comprehension filled her father's face. "In that case, there's nothing to be done. Not many people want to rummage around in four inches of mud at the bottom of a wet trench. That's why I was so glad when Joanna let her s—"

Joanna cut him off sharply. "I'm sure we'll be able to find another time convenient for Mr. Cameron. Assuming he is still interested, of course."

Alex braced one shoulder against a row of wooden scaffolding. "Oh, I'll be interested. Archaeology has always been one of my obsessions," he said. "Joanna knows most of my others."

"Darling, are you well?" Joanna's mother peered at her thoughtfully. "You look pale."

"I'm fine, Mother."

"Perhaps I should get you some of my buckwheat cakes. They are very nourishing with honey."

Harrison nodded. "A good idea, Rachel. Some seaweed, too. A little raw oyster might also be beneficial."

"I'm *fine*, you two."

"She is not fine," Alex said harshly. "She doesn't sleep well."

As Joanna glared at him, Rachel McTiernan looked

from Alex to her daughter. "I used to have headaches." Her eyes took on a slight gleam. "Until I married Harrison."

Joanna frowned. "Mother, I really don't think—"

"You're right, Harrison. She is pale." The white-haired woman turned slowly. "Are you two sleeping together?"

"Mother!"

"A good question." Harrison crossed his arms and waited for an answer.

"No," Joanna said explosively.

All eyes swung to Alex, who smiled faintly. "She's right, Mrs. McTiernan. Though if I had my way, we would be."

Joanna made a choking sound.

Her father patted her on the back. "Calm down, my love. In Sumerian times, lovers had to prove their faith by a series of tests of courage and strength. In fact—"

"Hush, Harrison." Rachel looked at her daughter. "Is something bothering you, Joanna? Something serious?"

"*Yes,*" Alex snapped.

"I'm fine," Joanna hissed at Alex. "Why don't you just leave?"

"Not until we've talked." Alex crossed his arms and stared back at her.

"Drive carefully when you go back to Draycott, Joanna." A slight smile curved Rachel's lips. "Remember how you tend to speed when you're angry." She turned serenely and caught her husband's arm. "Come along, Harrison. Let's give Joanna and her friend some privacy, shall we?"

"But I—"

The eminent archaeologist was hauled off by his gently implacable wife.

"What happened, Joanna?" Alex put out a hand, trapping her beside the scaffolding. "Tell me the truth for once."

She didn't move, her shoulders stiff. "It . . . was a man. He called about the pictures."

Alex cursed. "What did he want?"

"They want the sword. They know everything, even about the clues Jacques left us. And if I don't get them the sword, they'll hurt someone."

Alex's hands caught her face. "Tell me who and where. I'll see that they're protected, Joanna."

Her eyes were leaden. "You can't protect the whole world, Alex. Your friends can't be everywhere. What happens then?" she said raggedly. "How many will be hurt before this stops?"

"No one," Alex said grimly.

A group of students filed up the hill, laughing and joking, crowded together on the narrow path. High in their hands, carried in triumph with a pith helmet perched rakishly on his head, sat Peter.

Joanna froze. There was no place to move in the narrow path, not with the students surging closer.

Peter raised his hand and waved. "We're going to the trench," he called, squinting through a cloud of dust. "See you later." His face was streaked with dirt.

Joanna waved back, her heart slamming.

"Cute boy," Alex said. "One of the students' kids?" Then his eyes narrowed. Even without looking, Joanna felt his body tense. "My God," he whispered.

And then Peter's voice drifted above the good-natured laughter. "Bring your friend along, Mom. Aunt Kelly and Uncle Michael are coming later."

Mom.

There was no mistaking the word. The boy's voice had been clear, ringing out above the jokes and teasing of the older students.

Mom.

Alex felt his hands tighten. He turned slowly. Joanna's shoulders were rigid, her face pale.

"Why didn't you tell me?"

She tensed as if he had struck her.

"We're going to talk, Joanna. I want answers."

"Find them yourself." She spun away, her eyes very blue.

"Is he your son?" Alex had few doubts. He had seen

the boy's clear, curious eyes and the full brow, so like his mother's. But he wanted the words. She owed him that much honesty. "*Is* he, Joanna?"

Pain filled her eyes. "Yes, he is, damn it. And they said they'll take him. They'll *hurt* him, Alex, unless I do exactly what they want."

"My God, do you think I would let that happen?"

She shook her head. "They know too much. I can't risk my son's life."

Alex caught her hands and pulled them to his chest. "Giving up now would risk his life even more. I have people to help, Joanna. They'll be here whenever—"

"*No.* You can't know what it's like unless you have children of your own." Her eyes were dark, haunted. "The answer is no, Alex."

"I don't have children, that's true." He reached into his chest pocket and pulled out a thick wallet. His jaw was very hard as he slid out a packet of photos. "But this is Sergei. This is Marta. This is Yussef." One by one, he fanned the pictures open. "I can give you the month, day, and year that they were lost. Every picture will be in my mind until the day I die," he said hoarsely.

Joanna stared at the thin faces, the haunted eyes. "I don't understand."

"Dimitri and his people help me. We . . . work to bring people at risk out of harm. These are the ones we didn't get to in time. They're all gone now, dead of malnutrition or sickness or the thousand cold political decisions of an uncaring government. Many, though not all of them, are Gypsies."

"You smuggle children?"

"They're not children. They're not even people in the places we take them from. They're commodities, carefully weighed and inspected for the amount of blood and sweat that can be squeezed out of them. No, they're not children until they can be free to laugh and hope. Our success rate has been good, and we've found caring homes for most of them. But we haven't always won." He looked at the faces as if he had seen them too many times. "They stay here, next to my heart, so I won't be tempted to forget where my mother came from—and how many children still suffer there."

Joanna's throat burned. "I'm sorry."

"You must never speak of it, because many people would be put in danger. We work within legal bounds whenever possible, but in desperate cases, we place a child's needs above those of governments. You must begin to trust me, Joanna. If you trust me, we can win. If you cannot trust, then our enemies have *already* won."

She looked out over the green patchwork of fields, a lazy landscape of peace and abundance, while her mind beat like a tiny bird against the iron bars of a cage. Finally, she drew a shuddering breath. "I'll try."

Alex drew her palm to his lips and kissed it fiercely. "Peter will be watched in teams. Every minute, every hour. We'll have men all around the dig site." He spoke quickly into a cellular phone, using the low, hard syllables of Romany. "Dimitri will be here soon, and he will stay with Peter at all times. They are strong, these men. They have good reason to be strong. I would trust them with my life."

After long moments, Joanna nodded.

"Mom?"

Peter had come up the path and was staring at her expectantly. She smiled crookedly, ruffling his hair. "I'd like you to meet someone," she said softly, trying to keep her voice steady. "This is Lord Greywood, Peter. He makes swords, beautiful swords."

"Like the ones you repair?"

"Yes, that's right."

"Will he let you use them in your performances?"

Joanna looked at Alex.

"Anytime she likes."

"Good." Peter held out a hand. "It is nice to meet you, Lord Greywood."

Alex took the small dusty fingers and shook them gravely. "It's a pleasure to meet the youngest archaeological expert in the county."

Peter's face flushed. "I've had lots of help. Gramm and Granpa are capital teachers."

Alex knelt beside Peter. "I have a favor to ask of you, Peter."

The boy looked at his mother, who nodded. "I'll do what I can."

"I have a friend named Dimitri who wants to learn all about digging. Do you think you could show him around and teach him what you know?"

Peter brightened when he realized the favor wouldn't involve extra school lessons. "I'll try. When is he coming?"

Alex looked down the hill, where a broad-shouldered figure was just leaving a brown car. "In about three minutes."

Peter's expression turned suspicious. "Is something wrong? Granpa was very upset this morning, but he didn't want me to know. Is this man Dimitri here to protect me?"

Alex sighed. "Yes, he is, Peter. But it's important that you tell no one. Everyone except for your grandparents and your mother must believe that Dimitri is here as a student trainee. Can you do that?"

The boy nodded gravely, then reached for his mother's hand. "If I'm in danger, my mother is, too. Who's going to take care of her?"

Alex looked at Joanna, a fire glinting in his eyes. *"I will."*

Dimitri trudged up the hill, looking a little confused. "I am here, ready to learn everything, Alexei."

"Excellent. This is Peter Russell. He'll be showing you the ropes."

"Ropes? You do not tell me there is climbing to be done, Alexei."

Peter laughed. "No climbing, Mr. Dimitri. Not by ropes at least."

As the two shook hands, a smile curled Dimitri's lips. "I am pleased to have you teach me. I will be a slow student I fear."

"That doesn't matter," the boy said. "There's plenty to see. We'll have fun."

As they walked away, Alex called out, "Be careful, Peter. Dimitri cheats at cards."

The boy's eyes widened. "Really? Do you think you could teach me, Mr. Dimitri?"

The big Gypsy laughed. "I think there is very little I *couldn't* teach you, my friend."

Alex took Joanna's hand, and she pulled her eyes from her son, who was chatting eagerly with his bodyguard. The only sign of her tension was her hand moving restlessly over one wrist.

Alex turned the tender skin to his mouth and kissed the ragged silver scars. "He'll be safe, Joanna. I promise you that."

Her eyes closed. His fingers moved to her palm. She had to swallow before she could speak. "What happens now?"

"We go exploring. I've found the answer to the second clue."

The sun was setting when they crossed the stone bridge over the abbey's moat. Marston hovered anxiously as they made their way to the Long Gallery high above Draycott's green lawns.

"This is the only antique Chinese chest I know of," the butler explained. "I'm quite certain all it contains is a set of seashells brought back from Tahiti by the late viscount."

Alex bent over the panels of polished rosewood, testing every corner. "There must be a false bottom in one of the shelves."

Marston frowned. "The viscount never spoke of it."

"He might not have known," Alex said. As he spoke, he probed the brass hinge on the lower shelf.

With a low hiss, an inner mechanism opened and a panel slid free, giving access to the bottom of the chest.

Something was hidden there, encased in a leather box laid diagonally across the base. Alex eased the heavy box out into the sunlight.

Around them, the room seemed suddenly full, rich with forgotten voices and gentle laughter. Perhaps what they felt was the ghosts of happy Draycotts who had lived and loved in this beautiful old house, Alex thought, watching sunlight cast copper sparks off Joanna's hair and bounce off the exquisite figures engraved in the massive oak armoire that stood behind her.

Or maybe it was generations of Camerons.

Dim voices swelled around Alex. His skin prickled as if they were being watched.

"What's wrong? Not more poison, I hope."

"No, not poison. But there could be different dangers." Carefully, he eased open the case.

Gold filigree and a huge emerald winked back at him, ineffably beautiful.

"The Cameron Bible," Joanna breathed. "And you never knew it was here?"

Alex shook his head, unable to speak. He traced the exquisite filigree hinges and the jewels set into the cover, his Gypsy blood burning.

There was a pressure behind his eyes and an almost painful sensitivity in the tips of his fingers as he eased open the heavy cover. He skimmed the yellowed pages with elegant entries recording the births and marriages and deaths of generation after generation of Camerons. At the last two entries, he stopped.

The earlier of the two was the day he and his mother had left for Estavia. The last entry was the date of their return, nine years later.

In that moment the legacy of the Camerons burned within Alex, and his thirst to touch the sword was like a sickness. He knew if the clue existed, it would be somewhere in this old Bible.

"There's a loose sheet in the back," Joanna said softly.

Alex lifted the blank sheet and scanned the printed page it marked. At the top, an exquisite illuminated square showed a dove soaring above a tree heavy with fruit. The green branches hung down, merging perfectly into the first letter of the verse that followed.

Raw sensation tore through Alex.

Too close. Too deep.

"Alex, what's wrong?" Joanna said sharply.

"The contact is very strong. God only knows what happened to make my father hide this book." He closed his eyes, fighting the colors that stabbed at his mind. For a moment, he could have sworn he heard the drumming of hoofbeats, the roar of angry voices. Then, impossibly, the faint, high drone of a single set of bagpipes.

He looked down at the old Bible, feeling the reverence of generations of Cameron hands.

"I've seen that illuminated design somewhere else." Joanna frowned. "On the armoire, I think." She pointed to a vast piece of carved oak that covered the gallery's far wall. "There, do you see it?"

Alex bent down, studying the square of a dove above a tree. Beneath it was a fleur-de-lis carved beside a dragon. "France alongside Scotland. That would be Mary's sign, all right. Can we open this, Marston?"

"I'm afraid the armoire has been locked for as long as I can recall. The viscount never could find the key. We might be able to pry the door open, of course, but I would hesitate to ruin the armoire without the viscount's permission."

Alex muttered softly, rubbing his neck.

"I beg your pardon, my lord, but I was asked to remind you that your dinner tonight is set for seven."

"Good Lord, I nearly forgot." Scowling, Alex gave the armoire a last look. "I suppose this will have to wait."

After Marston left, Alex lifted Joanna's hand to his lips. "Giorgio is waiting to drive you home. He'll stay until I can get away, probably around midnight. I wish I could send you away until this is over, but they've been watching every step we make. If you leave, they'll know it."

"Is it someone close to us?"

Alex's jaw hardened.

"You have an idea who it is, don't you?" Joanna whispered.

"I only wish I didn't."

23

Water glistened on Alex's naked chest as he strode into the kitchen in search of Metcalfe. His shower had been brief and had brought him no relaxation.

The butler looked up. "The Estavian mission will be arriving in twenty minutes. I trust you don't mean to meet them that way."

"My diplomatic skills may be weak, but they're not *that* weak." Alex ran a towel over his hair. "How was Elena today?"

"After she returned from the Gypsy camp, she didn't move from the front hall. She simply stared down the drive, waiting for a car that never came. Even Dimitri couldn't make her laugh."

Alex cursed. "Giorgio will take her back tonight. I can't be much company until this business with the sword is resolved."

"What about her parents?" Metcalfe asked.

"No further information. It could be a simple matter of improper processing fees," Alex said grimly.

"Bribes, you mean."

"Possibly." Alex looked at the gleaming crystal arrayed in readiness for the coming dinner. "The Estavian ambassador will be here tonight, and I intend to squeeze as much information out of him as possible."

But something else had been bothering Alex. Since early in the morning, he had been unable to gain any information about St. Cyr's condition. This time when he tried, he was put through to Sir Gordon Mount.

The solicitor's voice contained the appropriate element of surprise. "Is something wrong?"

"Just checking on St. Cyr. How is he?"

"No sign of returning consciousness. In addition, he had a minor stroke about an hour ago, which isn't helping matters."

Alex cursed softly. "How serious was it?"

"No way to tell yet." There was a pause. "Any progress on your end?"

"Jacques was definitely onto something. I don't suppose we could get a look at that next clue right now."

"It would violate his express wishes. Unless you have a reason for urgency . . ." The sentence lingered delicately.

"I'm afraid not. Is St. Cyr's attending physician there?"

"He's already been by. Did you have a question for him?"

"Nothing important. We'll meet you tomorrow for that clue."

After Alex hung up, he stood looking at the pale camellias, nearly silver in the gathering twilight. "Metcalfe, maybe you'd better do some checking with the hospital by phone."

"Is something wrong, my lord?"

"I'm not sure." Alex rubbed his neck, feeling a growing sense of uneasiness. "Apparently, Jacques has had a stroke, and I want to know if there is any evidence of foul play. Don't give your name. Just say you're a distant relative. And don't speak with Sir Gordon Mount, even if they put you through to him."

"Understood."

Alex frowned. "These hospitals are usually on computer networks, aren't they?"

Metcalfe nodded.

"Can you break in?"

The butler smiled faintly. "It would be a pleasure."

"Excellent. Try a computer search of current patient

records. Maybe you can find more detailed information about what caused St. Cyr's stroke. If there was anything out of the ordinary, anything at all, I want to know about it."

Twenty minutes later, starkly handsome in evening dress, Alex Cameron handed a glass of spring water with a slice of lime to Lady Sefton. "Anytime you come to your senses and want to leave this clumsy oaf, just let me know."

Michael Burke gave a snort as he sat down beside his wife near the open French door.

"Not just yet, Alex, though I thank you for the thought." Kelly Burke winced. "As I'm beginning to feel like the Goodyear blimp, I doubt I'll be running anywhere with you or anyone else." She sighed as her husband expertly massaged her back. "Ah, Michael, you truly can perform miracles."

"Wait until we get home, and I'll show you some more," her husband murmured.

Alex watched the two kiss lingeringly. When he had decided enough time had passed, he cleared his throat. Loudly.

Kelly pulled away, red faced. "How rude of us, Michael."

"It would take a good deal more than that to embarrass Alex, I assure you, my love." Smiling calmly, Michael Burke pushed to his feet. "Well, aren't you at least going to offer me something decent to drink before you start your interrogation, Alexei?"

"Interrogation?" Kelly was instantly alert.

"Alex has some questions to ask you, my love. They involve our neighbor who's renting Nicholas Draycott's old cottage."

"You mean Joanna?" Kelly's face took on a certain wariness. "Why are you interested in her, Alex?"

"That's the same question I've been asking," Michael said. "Well?"

"I'm not sure where to start." Alex turned his glass slowly. "She's in some kind of trouble. We both are."

Kelly was frowning. "What kind of trouble?"

"Someone tried to run us off the road yesterday. Dimitri tells me he saw the same black Citroën earlier today near the abbey."

Michael's eyes narrowed. "Did he get a plate number?"

"Afraid not. He's too vain to wear the new glasses I bought for him." Alex's shoulders were stiff beneath his beautifully fitted evening jacket. "This whole business with Jacques—it's a bloody mess. And today he suffered a stroke. Unexpected, according to hospital records."

"Alex, perhaps I should go." Kelly made a move to stand up, but Alex stopped her with a wave of his hand.

"Stay. I have no secrets from you, Kelly. Besides, I'm sure Michael has already told you about . . . About my ex-wife," he said savagely.

"Michael told me a little." Kelly's eyes darkened. "I haven't words enough to tell you how sorry we are."

"Nathalie St. Cyr." Alex traced a line in the condensation on his glass, his face very hard. "It's been six years since she left, did you know?" His fingers tightened. "She had gone off to look at a place for rent in the hills above Nice that summer. It was very run down, and she wanted something much grander, but there simply wasn't enough money. It was the last straw. She walked out of my life that day without an explanation or a farewell and ran crying to Jacques about how I had been mistreating her." His hand gripped the glass. "How could I have been *such* a bloody fool? There was not a single honest thing about her."

Kelly gave Michael a helpless look, but her husband shook his head. "Go on, Alexei. It is long past time that you spoke of this."

"I wanted a child, you know. Nathalie told me she was . . . that a child was on the way." He laughed coldly. "God, I was so happy that day. It changed everything. Suddenly, all the anger and the arguments over money seemed irrelevant." He shook his head. "But it was just another one of her lies."

"No," Kelly breathed, horrified.

"It was her way of holding me until she decided if I

was worth her time. When she saw there wouldn't be as much money as she wanted, she left. I never heard from her again after that day. I sometimes wonder how much trouble her mercenary, scheming mind has caused her—and anyone else associated with her. But this was to be *my* interrogation, not yours."

Michael put a hand on his friend's shoulders. "You aren't the only one who can ask questions. Nor are you the only one who can listen. Remember that."

"I will." Alex's eyes were dark, full of shadows he was not yet ready to share. Nathalie St. Cyr had been fiercely intelligent and had had a vast knowledge of art when they'd met at a Paris gallery opening. It was her insatiable curiosity that had first attracted Alex. They had roamed Paris's galleries and museums, talking about art and artists until the early hours of the night. By the time Alex had glimpsed Nathalie's recklessness, he was already ensnared in her sensual web.

She had taken great care to keep him there while she decided how much money he could bring her. She had hungered for his title and the social standing it conferred. When she realized Alex was estranged from his father, her interest waned. Her tricks grew less subtle and her craving for excitement more blatant. Alex suspected that all along she had only wanted him as a weapon to get back at her father.

In the end, he was glad that there had been no child.

"I don't yet understand his game, but Jacques left us these clues to the location of the Cameron sword." Alex held out a sheet of vellum. "They're not very much help, I warn you."

Kelly frowned. " 'To close the circle, find the words.' "

"It's a line from the old Cameron records about the sword. Jacques must have found them recently. Family legend always said there was a treasure hidden in the sword." He frowned at the rapidly darkening lawns. "Unfortunately, without more answers we won't be able to find anything. And now someone is threatening Joanna and her son."

Kelly looked surprised. "She told you about Peter?"

"Not willingly. I happened to see him at the dig site today." Alex smiled. "He's very like her, changing from fiery to formal in seconds. She's terrified that he will be hurt. Her past has left her very wary of men."

Kelly's fingers traced the paper slowly. As she did, her eyes seemed to focus on a point just above the old, elegant carpet.

Her husband stiffened. "Kelly, you don't know what you'll find. These men could be violent."

"Hush, Michael." Her slender fingers moved back and forth. Her eyes narrowed, then closed. "Shadows. Weight." She frowned. "Stone perhaps. Or something very old." Again her hands moved, circling slowly. "Something shadowed coming into light. Bound once but now freed. Death all around. Dead—but not dead." Her breath caught. "Right now. Right here." A shudder went through her. "All around us."

Michael caught her shoulders and pulled her to his chest. "Kelly, *break* it. Let it go."

"Close. I can almost see—" Her face paled.

"*Stop,* Kelly." Michael cradled her face between his palms. "Now, damn it!"

With a gasp, she sat forward, blinking. She looked from her husband to Alex. "You two look as if you've just seen a ghost."

"Damn it, Kelly, you scared the hell out of me. You agreed—no more of that until after the baby comes."

Kelly touched his face softly. "It was only a little test. I'm fine, see?"

"But I've just experienced cardiac arrest. A good thing Alex knows about your particular skill or he'd think we were lunatics."

"Amazing." Alex shook his head, plunging his fingers through his long hair.

"And she doesn't make mistakes," her husband said grimly. "So pay attention to what she just said. She's *not* going to be trying that again anytime in the near future."

Kelly frowned. "From what I could pick up in the note, something old is involved, something that's very well hidden. And there's danger all around it."

At that moment, a knock came at the door. Metcalfe appeared bearing a silver tray laden with dishes. "I've brought the rabbit pâté and Gruyère tarts, my lord." His eyes twinkled.

"Dearest Metcalfe." Kelly eyed the colorful array of dishes. "My brutish husband has been starving me for the last month under the guise of maintaining my health."

"A quart of ice cream for breakfast hardly seems like starvation, my love," Michael said calmly. "She'll have one tart, Metcalfe." His lips curved as he saw his wife's mutinous look. "Perhaps two. I know a way for her to burn off some extra calories later."

Kelly's face flamed. *"Michael."*

"Weeding your rose beds, of course," her husband said blandly.

Metcalfe turned to Alex. "Your dinner guests are expected in five minutes, my lord. You asked that I notify you."

Alex rolled his eyes. "I was hoping they had canceled."

"I'm afraid not."

Michael gave him a resigned look and raised his sherry glass. "We who are about to die salute you."

"I don't know what could be so awful about a simple dinner with a few foreign businessmen," Kelly said impatiently.

Alex looked at Michael. "You'll find out."

Joanna stood by the tall windows looking out at the wooded valley. The high towers of Draycott Abbey were silhouetted against the distant moon. Was the old sword there at the abbey right now while Adrian's ghost laughed at their clumsy efforts to discover it?

Beside her the phone began to ring.

"Hello?"

Silence stretched out.

"Who is this?"

With a click the line went dead.

Joanna stood frozen, cold fingers of fear playing over

her neck. When the phone rang again, she swept it to her ear. "Hello," she snapped.

"He didn't tell you, did he?" It was the same flat voice she had heard before, calling about the photos. "Jacques sent your Gypsy a separate letter. In it, Jacques promised Alex Cameron ten thousand pounds per day to protect that lovely body of yours."

Joanna's fingers tightened on the receiver. "You're lying."

"Am I?"

"Why would Jacques do that?"

"You must be very important to him, Ms. Russell. Or something that you *know* is important to him. And that's not all Jacques St. Cyr took care of. You see, he paid us to keep those pretty pictures of you out of circulation. He paid very lavishly in fact."

Jacques had known about the pictures all these years, and he had never told her? "I don't believe you."

Cold laughter. "Of course, now that poor Jacques can't pay, *you'll* have to. The price is the sword. Find it tomorrow or the boy gets hurt. *Very* hurt."

A click, then a silence that felt like death.

Tomorrow.

Joanna stared out at the darkness. *Tomorrow or the boy gets hurt.*

Suddenly, she couldn't keep her hands from shaking.

"Did you call her?"

"Sure."

In the darkness of the lonely hillside a match flared, lighting the faces of two men standing beside a black Citroën. "And?"

"She bought it all right. Every single word. She'll get the sword for us. She'll do anything to save that kid of hers."

Cigarette smoke drifted over the quiet hill. "She'd better. Time's running out in case you hadn't noticed."

"But St. Cyr—"

"He'll soon be out of the picture." The tip of a

cigarette glowed red for a moment. "Nathalie got to him."

"But what about our money? You know what will happen when they find the sword."

"Nothing will happen." A dry laugh. "Not if we get to it first."

Down the hill, a car door slammed. Two figures materialized from the darkness. The man with the cigarette stiffened. "Shut up. They're coming back."

A woman moved out of the shadows. "I called you before, Simon. Why didn't you answer?"

Simon Loring dropped his cigarette and ground it out calmly. "Didn't hear you, I guess."

"So I gather. But *why* didn't you hear, I wonder?"

Loring met her gaze with cool arrogance. "If you really want to know, Nathalie, it was due to a call of nature."

"Lying to me would be very unhealthy, Simon, dear. Double-crossing me would be even *more* unhealthy."

Loring laughed. "Now why would I hurt the sweet bird laying the golden egg?"

Nathalie St. Cyr's eyes were remarkably like her father's, only colder and far more arrogant. "That is exactly what I ask myself, Simon. Perhaps you should remember that what happened to my father can happen to anyone. Even *you*."

24

THE ESTAVIAN ambassador was an hour late. The lead car had had a flat tire just outside of Kensington.

The young interpreter was tongue-tied with embarrassment when the group finally arrived in a fleet of shining black Mercedes sedans. "My name is Gavra. Please to accept my deep apologies, Lord Greywood." The small man patted his forehead with a clean white handkerchief. "The ambassador . . . Punctuality is difficult, you understand."

"My sympathies," Alex said, feeling sorry for the man, who seemed genuinely uncomfortable.

"I will introduce our group," the interpreter said. "But perhaps my service as translator is not required. You are Estavian, no?"

Alex's eyes narrowed. "England is my home now, Mr. Gavra. Considering we have other guests, it would be polite to speak in English."

"Of course, Lord Greywood." He turned to a stocky man with hard eyes. "This is Mr. Uland, ambassador of Estavia."

Alex shook hands, aware of the ambassador's pale, keen eyes probing his face. "Welcome to Greywood," he said, watching for a flicker of comprehension. But the ambassador was either genuinely ignorant of English or a superb actor.

Alex regretted saying yes to this dinner but reminded himself that good diplomatic relations were essential for the projects he had planned in Estavia. With that thought in mind, he put on a smile, ushered the group inside, and saw to it that Metcalfe kept every glass filled. When he turned to introduce his other guests, he saw that Michael was already deep in conversation with a thin, intense man with a receding hairline.

"The cultural attaché," Kelly whispered. "They met several years ago when Michael was working in Germany. Something terribly dangerous, no doubt. Thank heavens he's given up that life."

Alex squeezed her hand. "Why would he need danger and adventure? Now he has all that right in his own home."

"I'm not sure that was a compliment, Alex."

Before he could answer, Mr. Gavra was back with the ambassador in tow. "Ambassador Uland asks to make the introduction of the beautiful lady."

"This is the Marchioness of Sefton," Alex said coolly. "Her husband is speaking with one of your cultural attachés."

"Lady Sefton," the translator said. His anxiety seemed to grow. "Ambassador Uland says for me to tell you—" He hesitated and the ambassador spoke sharply. "He says that your eyes . . ." Fresh sweat touched his brow.

"Something is wrong with them?"

"Not at all. I mean—he says your eyes remind him of the Adriatic at dawn."

"Thank you," Kelly said smoothly. "The ambassador is very kind."

Gavra pointed to her stomach. "He asks if this is your first child."

Kelly nodded, smiling.

"And you have been married long?"

"Three years."

Mr. Gavra listened, then translated. "It is a long time for no children, the ambassador says."

Kelly's smile faded a little. She moved toward the sofa. "I'm afraid you must excuse me if I sit."

"But of course," Mr. Gavra said quickly.

Kelly cleared her throat. "Perhaps you can tell me about this new archaeological site in your country."

The small man beamed. "A very fine discovery, yes. Dating back at least one thousand years, our scientists say." He rubbed his hands. "Yes, very fine. Much gold."

The ambassador shot off another quick question to Gavra. "The ambassador says it is his honor to extend you an invitation to visit the site. With your husband, of course." His eyes slid downward. "After the birth of your child."

"How very kind." Kelly gratefully accepted a drink of mineral water and lime from Metcalfe, who also handed her a small pillow to slide behind her back. "Thank you, Metcalfe. You are a lifesaver."

The translator frowned as the ambassador spoke sharply. "A grown man should not do such domestic work."

Kelly stiffened. "I beg your pardon."

"The ambassador says the English system of class privilege is demeaning and insulting, and it exterminates free thought."

"I assure you that Metcalfe performs his job with great skill and flair," Kelly said tensely. "His work is hardly insulting, and his thought is probably far freer than mine."

"But the ambassador says—"

"I don't care what the ambassador says." Kelly's eyes glittered. She was on the verge of another angry reply when her husband appeared.

"Feeling poorly, my love?"

"A little." Her eyes said, *Please take me away from these people.*

Her husband's eyes answered, *I told you so.* "Perhaps you'd like some air?"

The ambassador fired off a phrase, and Gavra mopped his brow. "But surely Lady Sefton will be better to sit," the translator said quickly. "The ambassador was just beginning to enjoy a deeper discussion of your social system and its iniquities."

"Unfortunately, the discussion will have to wait,"

Michael interrupted, helping Kelly to her feet. "After a walk in the fresh air, my wife will no doubt feel strengthened to resume this, er . . . fascinating discussion."

Kelly frowned. Her eyes promised him serious punishment if he brought her back anywhere *near* these people.

On the far side of the room, Alex was fielding his own questions from Pavel Orlov, a sharp-eyed trade representative, and his assistant. Now that the three of them were present, Alex switched to Russian.

"We have examined your mining proposal and find it interesting," the trade representative replied. "Wholly unacceptable, of course. I believe that the total international revenues of Cameron Industries exceed twelve million pounds, do they not?"

Is there nothing these people didn't know? Alex wondered. "I couldn't say, not off the top of my head," Alex hedged, snagging a glass of champagne from Metcalfe and emptying it. "Will you have something, Mr. Orlov?"

The taller man shook his head. "I do not drink. Drinking is a vice that makes a strong man weak."

Alex frowned. His temper was not at its best after watching Kelly's hasty exit from the ambassador. On the heels of that, he had had to rescue Metcalfe from an Estavian official lecturing him on the primitive working conditions in England.

"Is that so? I wonder what drinking does to a weak man?"

Orlov frowned. "It makes him think that he is strong. Especially when it is expensive French champagne such as the kind *you* are drinking."

Their eyes locked. Alex felt an urge to fling his champagne in the man's face. "I'm sorry you feel that way, Mr. Orlov. Now perhaps we could focus on some of your questions about our proposal. We will conduct the preliminary surveys and work with your government to set a reasonable production schedule. In addition, we plan to plow back twenty percent of our profits into humanitarian programs: schools, orphanages, hospitals, and—"

Orlov waved his hand curtly. "When I wish to know

business details, I will send low-level staff to find them. Tonight I wish only to be a guest." His eyes surveyed the room, missing nothing. "To enjoy your English hospitality."

And to find out every bloody detail about my life that you possibly can, Alex thought. *And you won't hesitate to use them against me.*

"Lady Sefton is a respected archaeologist. We have heard of her studies of Norman weapons. The fame of your sword collection, too, has spread to our country."

Alex said nothing, waiting.

"I believe the ambassador would enjoy a tour of your collection."

Mr. Uland, well into his fifth glass of champagne, would enjoy nothing less, Alex thought. "It will be my pleasure. But the tour will have to wait until after dinner. We are nearly ready to sit down."

Something flickered in the man's black eyes. *So you don't like to be countered, do you, my nasty friend?*

"Very well." Orlov crossed his arms coolly. "You must know many archaeologists. People interested in culture."

"Many." Alex returned his hard stare. "Why?" He was tired of playing cat and mouse. Better to see an enemy out in the open than worry about shadows, he thought grimly.

Orlov's dark eyes filled with anger. "Because, Alexei Andreiivitch Turov Cameron, Estavia has many cultural relics of great importance to the world."

And by using my whole name, you show that you know my family background. Every bloody detail of it. What other secrets do you possess?

"I'm interested in business, Mr. Orlov," Alex replied, "and in the ways business can benefit your people. Not in trinkets or cultural relics."

The black eyes flickered. "You miss my point. We want the whole world to know of our great achievements. That is why we wish to invite distinguished visitors to share our discoveries."

Tourism, Alex translated cynically. *Big money, all of it in hard-to-acquire foreign currency that could be used to purchase all sorts of bright, shiny new Western technology.*

From legitimate sources or otherwise.

"You're asking me for a list of cultural contacts?" There was patent amusement in Alex's voice.

The trade representative—if that was indeed his real job—stiffened. "I am asking you for *nothing*." Orlov's fingers opened and closed. Behind him, the other man moved nervously from foot to foot. "For a man said to be intelligent, you resemble a pig farmer."

"Pig farmers do honest work, Mr. Orlov. Their labor helps feed the world. I wonder if the work you do is even half as useful."

A hiss escaped Orlov's lips. His hand went to his pocket.

"I wouldn't suggest it," Alex said coldly. "Not while you are a guest in my house. Definitely not on English soil. You'd be behind bars before you could spell Marxism–Leninism."

"And you, Lord Greywood, would be wise to remember that our government has *many* sources of information. We know, for example, that two of the Russian swords in your collection were taken from protected cultural sites without appropriate government permits."

"The swords were bought at public auction in Paris," Alex said coolly. "The museums in question had all the required documents."

Orlov muttered a curse. "Those swords were stolen during World War II, and we both know it."

Alex smiled thinly.

Orlov bent close, his face hard. "Weakness can become a habit, Alexei Andreiivitch. I think you must confront that weakness now." With icy arrogance, the Estavian snapped his fingers, and his subordinate pulled an envelope from the case beneath his arm. "Read this carefully, and you will begin to understand."

Alex stared at the document. Double columns of text ran side by side, first in Estavian, then in stilted English.

As Alex read, he finally did begin to understand. Ten years ago, his father had made a desperate bargain.

The document was a legal contract stipulating that in

exchange for exit visas for Cameron's wife and child, which would allow them to leave Estavia, the Cameron claymore would be turned over to a representative of the Estavian government upon request. Next to his father's signature were the names of two members of the Estavian ruling council. Both men still held key positions even today, Alex noted.

His fists clenched. Now he understood his father's constant tension and the years of silent guilt. The Cameron sword had been the price of their freedom all those years before. But clearly the sword had never been delivered. Perhaps because his father couldn't bear to part with it. Or perhaps even he didn't know where it was.

"Why do you bring this document to me now?" Alex asked.

"There is no time limit set on its duration," Orlov said sharply.

"I knew nothing about any such agreement."

"But you know your father's signature, and it rests there on the last line. Or do men like you care nothing about family honor?"

Alex fought back his fury. "I'll have to have the signature verified. That could take quite some time."

"You have *two* days, Lord Greywood." An icy smile curled Orlov's lips. "We have tried to contact you about this before, but with no success."

"Why do you want the sword, Orlov? What good is a family heirloom to you?"

The Estavian's eyes glittered. "That is our concern. I warn you: Our government is ready to take action to ensure your compliance."

Alex didn't move. "Such as?"

"Perhaps you know of a family of Gypsies who were recently caught smuggling illegal documents into our country? It was most unfortunate that they had to be arrested. I understand that their only daughter, Elena, managed to escape."

Orlov's message was unmistakable: Give up the sword or Elena's parents would die.

Alex was blinded by a wave of fury. His hand was clenched and rising when he felt Michael grip his shoulder. "Still discussing trade figures, you two?" Calmly Burke moved so that he stood between the men. "It is bad for the digestion, you know. Besides, Metcalfe tells me dinner is served."

Alex glared at Orlov. "One more word. Say it."

His guest gave a cold laugh. "I do not know what you mean, Lord Greywood. A contract is a contract after all. This is your English law."

"Law has nothing to do with holding human beings for ransom, you bloody bastard."

"Alex." Michael's hand tightened.

Alex stepped back. "I'll be along in a moment. I have a phone call to make."

Orlov smiled faintly and turned away.

"Alex?" Michael was staring at him. "What did he mean about a contract?"

"I'll tell you later. Go on. I'm fine," Alex said tightly.

"Then why are you tearing that gardenia into tiny shreds?"

Alex looked down at the torn petals in his fingers. "Thank you for stopping me from doing something I would one day regret. But now perhaps you should go eat." His voice hardened. "I need to be alone."

Michael was the last of his guests to disappear into the dining room. Alex watched the door close, then shoved his hands into his pockets and drew a long, harsh breath.

So this was the bargain that had haunted his father for so many years. Perhaps he had meant to tell Alex the truth someday, or in the end he may have decided it would be better to keep Alex in the dark, because his son could not surrender a sword he did not have.

Thinking about Orlov's icy smile made anger burn through Alex all over again. The man knew more than he was saying, that much was certain. Now Elena's parents would pay the price if Alex did not do exactly as Orlov demanded.

Bloody, bloody hell.

* * *

Dinner crept on for two more hours of veiled innuendos and blunt questions. As the last of the black cars finally glided back down the driveway, Alex yanked off his tie and breathed a sigh of relief.

Beside him, Michael frowned. "I thought the ambassador was going to strangle Orlov during dessert."

"You mean when Orlov said champagne was for old women and spoiled children?" Alexei laughed harshly. "A bad diplomat, that one. But less stupid then he looks."

Michael muttered darkly. "I should have strangled the ambassador myself for what he said to Kelly."

"I'm sorry, Mikhail. I had no idea the evening would be so unpleasant."

Kelly was sitting with her feet up. Despite her determined smile, she looked pale and exhausted. "Now I understand your dread of the evening."

"You were a wonder, my dear. Without your charm and conversation, there would be at least three dead bodies in that room now, mine among them." Alex frowned. "Take her home, Michael. And take good care of her. I do not want my godchild to be angry with me for being remiss in my duties as godfather."

Kelly's eyebrows rose. "The child isn't even born yet."

"For a Gypsy, family responsibility begins very early." Alex took Kelly's palm in his hand and studied it intently, tracing a line here and there. A smile tugged at his lips.

"What?" Kelly demanded.

"What?" her husband echoed, staring over Alex's shoulder.

"Great joy and laughter for you both." He planted a light kiss in Kelly's palm, then waved his hand. "Off with her, Mikhail. She needs to rest. I think we all do. I only pray that Metcalfe hasn't resigned in utter disgust after this night."

"Call me tomorrow. I want to know what that man Orlov meant about a contract."

"Tomorrow." Alex watched his friends walk to their car. As Michael helped his wife into her seat, Alex felt a pang of envy at the love displayed so clearly between them.

A wife and now a child on the way. A son, Alex had seen in Kelly's palm. A boy with a demanding cry and dark, intelligent eyes who would make his mother laugh and his father's heart swell with pride. Perhaps even more than one child.

Michael and Kelly deserve their happiness, Alexei thought. But in the wake of their departure, Greywood House seemed a cold and quiet place.

"I will *kill* the man," Michael said flatly.

"It was nothing, my love."

"Nothing? The bloody man asked how much you weigh, what you eat, if you feel sick. I thought he would ask how recently we had been to bed together. Then I was going to knock every tooth out of his mouth."

Kelly gave a tired laugh. "They were very blunt, weren't they? Alexei didn't look happy at all, and he barely ate anything."

Michael frowned, wondering at the exchange he had overheard between Alex and Orlov. "What else is bothering you?"

"Nothing," his wife said quickly.

Michael searched her face and saw the shadow of fear that lingered there. "Tell me. I'll have it out of you one way or another."

"It's absolute nonsense really." Kelly watched the dark countryside slip past. It was not cold, but she was glad for the warmth of her husband's arm at her waist.

"Then tell me about this nothing that is *not* bothering you."

Kelly sighed. "It was the ambassador. He said I was . . . too big. That it would be unhealthy for our child," she whispered.

Michael mouthed a harsh curse and caught her tightly in his arms. "I'll break every bone in his body. But first I'll have him apologize to you."

Kelly gave a little shiver. "I don't want to talk to him ever again." She gave an unsteady laugh. "I'm being impossible." She rested her head on Michael's shoulder.

"Better?"

"Much."

"Good. Now what else did you see that you couldn't tell Alexei?"

Kelly sighed. "How well you know me. What I felt was that they were lovers."

"That's what I was wondering. But why didn't Joanna tell him about Peter?"

"She's very protective, and now the danger is close to them both."

"Alex will take care of her," Burke said confidently.

His wife's hands touched his cheek. "I was in danger once. Without your help at Draycott Abbey, I would have died."

Michael cursed softly. "Don't, love."

Kelly brushed a strand of dark hair from his cheek. "I just wanted to thank you."

"Every hour we spend together is thanks. Every minute you bring me new happiness," he said gravely.

"And you, Lord Sefton, with all that scandalous talk about ways for me to burn off calories. You are absolutely impossible, do you know that?"

Her husband eased open the interior window. "Let's drive around for a bit, shall we, Gardner? It's a lovely night."

"Very good, my lord."

After the window hissed closed, Michael gathered his wife into his arms. "Now, Lady Sefton, we were talking about exercise. I believe I know a new method." His lips brushed Kelly's forehead. One hand slid to her hip.

"Michael, you can't—" His wife's breath caught. "I don't . . ." Fabric rustled.

"Oh, Michael." Her laugh was low, breathless. "Maybe you're not *entirely* impossible . . ."

25

Standing just outside her cottage after arriving home, Joanna looked out at the abbey's dense woods across the valley. She thought about Alex and Peter and the ways her life would soon have to change. The only sound around her was the wind whispering through the trees. The only light was the moon, caught on the dense forest canopy. Growing up on dig sites in desolate areas of the world, she had become accustomed to silence and isolation.

So why did silence bother her now?

Peter was safe with Dimitri. The burly Giorgio was somewhere in the woods, watching the cottage. And yet . . .

She inched closer to the side of the house.

Enough, you idiot. No one is waiting for you in the shadows.

Silently, she unlocked the oak door and shoved it open, then peered into the darkness.

There was no sound as she moved through the studio, flipping on lights. None of her tools showed any sign of having been touched, and her papers were neatly stacked as usual.

Absently, she picked up a set of blunt-nosed pliers and set them on top of a case with gold wire for fine inlay work. Fighting uneasiness, she finished polishing the hilt of a priceless Italian rapier and repaired its grip of braided silver.

Abruptly, Joanna turned, staring out at the moonlit valley. Tonight, Alex had said. She felt her hands tremble.

Tonight.

So close, after all these years. Would he be as she remembered?

Suddenly, the sandpaper fell from her hands, and she was engulfed in memories . . .

It was nearly dawn when the doctors finally left the small bungalow on the edge of Jacques St. Cyr's rented compound. Joanna saw them go as she watched from a beach chair in the darkness.

The lights went off, and a man came outside. Joanna heard him mutter softly, then slam one fist against his palm.

She moved toward him, stopping by a small fountain where night-blooming jasmine spilled over a cedar wall running up to the house.

Alex did not even look up. "Better you go away," he said flatly.

"How did you know I was here?"

He shrugged. "That smell. Like oranges and gardenia. Now you go. This is very dangerous time to be clever."

"I don't want to be clever." The cotton dress Joanna had changed into fluttered in the wind, brushing his thigh. "I want to help."

"Can you bring strength back to an old man's tired heart? Can you make his crooked fingers straight again?" Alexei asked bitterly.

"Constantin?"

"So."

"I'm sorry," Joanna said softly. "How bad is it?"

He sighed. One shoulder sank against the wall. "Doctors are too clever to say. Maybe two weeks, maybe ten years. But every day he grows weaker, and the magic hands do less of what he tells them." He kicked the edge of the stone steps savagely. "Is not fair."

"But he has given you his skill."

"Me?" He laughed harshly. "I am nothing next to that brave, stubborn old man. In twenty years I cannot learn half of what he knows."

"Then you'll have to work harder."

He looked down at his hands. "You go now," he said curtly. "I must pack for him, make arrangements. The plane will be here in four hours."

Four hours. Joanna felt a tightness in her throat. So soon?

The words gave her sudden resolve. She touched his hand, her fingers sliding through his.

"Do not do this," he said hoarsely.

"I think that's supposed to be my line," she said gently, lifting his hand to her mouth and kissing the calloused ridges earned from hours at a forge.

"Do not be clever, Annie Smith. Clever is very dangerous tonight."

She brought his palm to her breast, pressing against soft cotton. A shudder went through him.

"This is what I want, what I can give you. Not because I am clever, but because I . . . care for you." She stepped closer, heat to his heat. "Let me, Alexei."

His fingers opened. With a raw sound, he filled his hands with her soft curves, not careful. Ruthless now. Angry. His mouth shaped hers, and he shoved her back against the warm cedar wall screened by pale white jasmine.

He was trying to frighten her, Joanna realized, and some part of her was frightened. But the rest reached out to him with mute sadness, sharing the loss of a master whose skills could never be replaced. She would stay with Constantin's apprentice this night, honoring his sorrow. Offering him whatever he might choose to take from her.

Without regrets or apologies. Not because she was clever, but because he had opened a long-locked door deep inside her.

"Go," he ordered flatly. His mouth was a slash of darkness. "Before it is too late."

"I'll stay."

"Mother of fires, are you weak in brain? I am angry. It has been very long time for me. I will hurt you." He kneed apart her legs so that she felt the unmistakable jut of his manhood. "Not slow. Not as a woman should be taken. Only for myself."

Joanna knew him better than he did. There would always be part of this man held in check. She raised herself on her toes and slid her hands into his hair. "Then so it will be. Only for yourself."

"Damn you for fool. And me for bigger fool." He found her thigh and slid his hand higher. When he felt no interference, only warm, dewy skin, he muttered softly. "You do not—"

"No. Because I was waiting for you," she said huskily. Then she pulled his face to hers. "To give you this." Her tongue pleasured his, slow and sweet.

"Mother of God," he whispered. His hands caught her hips, and he lifted her against him. "I do not have . . ."

Joanna nibbled at his chin, his throat, his lower lip. "Already taken care of."

"Damn it, we—"

She opened his shirt, smelling the clean citrus scent of his skin. When he did not move, Joanna took a desperate breath. "Maybe I should find Simon. He will not turn me away, leaving me to wonder what is wrong with me."

"Is lie," he said angrily, hands in her hair. "You will not go to him."

After a moment her breath slid free. "Yes, it is a

lie. I never would have gone to Simon. Though he wanted—he threatened that if I didn't—"

"He is fool, that one. But now you forget about him," Alex said grimly. "Yes?"

"Yes," she whispered against his chest.

She felt him rise against her, smooth and hot. Shuddering, she moved closer, seeking blindly.

"Not easy. Hard and deep. So you do not forget about me."

She shivered, planting soft kisses over his skin.

"Like this. Until you know nothing else, only a great hunger for how the fire binds us together."

It was already true. She whimpered beneath his searching hands. He made wonder fill her and pleasure blossom in heavy flowers.

Abruptly, Joanna stiffened. With a stunned cry, she sank her teeth into his shoulder as his hands kindled a wave of pleasure.

"Only for me," he grated.

"Alex—" *Light crested, exploded.*

He lifted her against the bungalow wall. "Now." *With a low groan, he spread her and impaled her, inch by aching inch, her back to the still warm wood.*

She shivered, shoving at his chest, twisting blindly.

He did not hurry. Legs planted, head thrown back, he tasted the increments of his own pleasure. And he taught Joanna her own.

"Like this," *he said harshly.* "Slow. So you do not forget the man with poor English. The man who made your body sing."

"I won't forget," *Joanna whispered.* "Nor will you."

"No," *he agreed, higher now, half-seated. Still without hurry.*

"Dear God, please—" *Her voice broke as she tensed around him, captured by pleasure yet again.*

"Holy God." *Groaning, Alexei braced his arms against the storm-worn wood, then drove inside her, thrust following velvet thrust until both were panting, blind with need.*

Joanna cried out, rent by passion. At the same instant, his hands tightened on her hips, and he sent his hot seed spilling inside her, deep and potent.

And then the world was torn away from both of them.

Like this. So you do not forget the man who made your body sing.

Joanna stood trembling, her body flushed, stirred by sweet, hot memories.

Tonight there would be no more waiting. Tonight Alex would claim her honesty and her passion. Was she strong enough to give him both?

As she climbed up to her bedroom, the stairs behind her creaked. A shadow crept over the wall.

"Well, well."

Joanna took a step back. A man moved toward her in the darkness. "Who are you?"

His soft laugh had a chilling edge. "You don't remember me, Joanna?" Moonlight fell over hard lips and eyes that missed nothing.

"Simon?" Joanna's breath caught. "Simon Loring?"

Smiling, he moved closer. "So you haven't forgotten. How very flattering."

"What do you want?" Somehow she kept her voice steady as she inched backward toward her room.

"I want many things, Joanna." There was a cold twist to his lips. "As you'll find out. But I'll ask the questions now."

"I'm not interested in talking, Simon. It's late. Call me in the morning, and we'll set a time to meet."

"I think not." His eyes moved over her pale face, then traced the curve of her breast through her linen dress. "I've come a very long way to see you, Joanna. You've been a hard girl to find." His fingers caught her wrist, and he turned her hand, studying the delicate skin. "Still here, I see. I often wondered how you got all these ugly scars."

"Let me *go*."

Loring's hands twisted, and he jerked Joanna savagely against him. "I'll do the talking. Now shut your mouth and listen." He pushed Joanna against the bedpost. *"Where is the sword?"*

Joanna swallowed. Dear God, Simon knew about the sword. Had he been part of the attack on Jacques? If so, she was in very grave danger. "I have half a dozen swords downstairs, Simon. Which one do you mean? The Venetian rapier or the pair of French—"

Loring's hands tightened. "The Cameron claymore, damn you! What have you and Cameron come up with so far?"

Joanna raised her chin, fighting her fear. "I suppose that was you on the telephone. And that was you in the black Citroën, too."

Simon's eyes narrowed, and he smiled. "Of course. We wanted the clues, but Cameron was too clever, damn him."

"Why do you want the sword, Simon? What makes it so valuable to you?"

Loring's fingers dug into her shoulders. "There's a treasure hidden inside that sword."

Joanna managed to laugh. "That's just a legend."

"Hardly. Jacques discovered the truth in an old notebook he bought at auction in France last month. The Scots traitors went there after their plot to free Mary failed."

"Angus Cameron was *no* traitor!"

Loring smiled. "And how would you know that?"

Joanna swallowed, shoving at his chest. "I just know. But you're lying. Jacques would have told me if he had found anything so important."

Loring laughed. "Wrong, my dear. Jacques didn't trust you, not after your passionate encounter with the Gypsy. Beats me why he agreed to pay to keep those nice pictures of you secret." He laughed at the expression on

Joanna's face. "Yeah, I took them. Jacques was furious when he found out. But he still paid up. Now it's your turn to pay."

Loring's eyes were hard and flat, like shark eyes. "Enough history. Tell me where you put the sword, damn it! I know you and Alex were looking for it at Draycott today."

Joanna forced herself to stay calm. "The sword is hidden, of course. We would hardly leave it lying about in plain sight."

Simon smiled, and the curve of his lips was extraordinarily ugly. "At least you're not wasting your breath trying to deny you have the sword. I'm in rather a hurry, you see."

Joanna frowned. "There are others involved. They don't know you've come, do they?"

"Shut up and stop delaying." He eased one finger beneath her collar. "You wouldn't like it if I became angry, Joanna. This time I'd do a lot more than hit you," he whispered.

She managed a shrug. "You've won, Simon. There's nothing for me to do but give in gracefully."

Simon studied her face. "Give in. I like the sound of that." He twisted his hands in her hair. "Take off my belt," he ordered hoarsely. "Let's see if you're as good as in those pictures."

Joanna's heart slammed wildly against her chest. "I thought you wanted the sword. Why complicate matters when you're in a hurry?"

"I have time for a small digression. I want a taste of what the Gypsy got. After that, you're going to show me where you've hidden the sword."

Joanna's eyes swept the nearby chest. Lamp, books, papers. Dear God, what was she going to do? What could she use against him?

"I'm waiting, Joanna."

"If you want the sword, you're going to have to move, Simon. I don't exactly keep it on me."

The brown eyes narrowed on Joanna's body. "Try anything clever, and I'll make you sorry."

"It's too late for anything clever." Joanna moved past him toward the dresser. "How did you find out I had the sword, by the way?"

"You took too long in that gallery at the abbey. Greywood was carrying a box when you left. It had to be the sword."

Loring had seen them carrying the chest containing the Cameron Bible, Joanna realized. "You were nearby?"

"We've been watching your every step."

"But it wasn't you on the telephone. I would have recognized your voice."

"That was my brother. Dumb but loyal."

"You're more clever than I thought, Simon." With her back turned, Joanna searched the drawer. Perfume bottles. Two combs. What could help her? "And though it breaks my heart to do this—" She spun about and tossed a box of bath powder directly into Loring's eyes. Cursing in pain, he bent double, scrubbing at his face.

Joanna ran for the stairs. She winced as she hit the edge of the landing, then plunged down the corridor toward her studio. Behind her, she heard Simon shouting.

Blindly, she grabbed up the old rapier and ran to the door. He was moving now, his feet pounding closer.

"Bad move, bitch. I told you what would happen if you tried anything clever."

Joanna ran out into the night, over the flagstone path.

Then Simon was behind her, his hand grabbing her wrist. Gasping, Joanna brought the rapier down across his chest. He bellowed with pain, jerking her savagely backward and clawing the rapier from her grasp.

He smiled as his hand circled her neck and closed painfully. Joanna felt a burning sensation in her chest and throat. Darkness filled her eyes as she fought desperately to breathe.

"Now you pay, Joanna. Here in the dirt while your Gypsy entertains his Estavian friends."

Suddenly, Loring's body stiffened. As if from a great distance, Joanna heard the dull thud of a fist. His fingers opened and closed convulsively while his big body swayed forward.

A figure moved through the darkness.

Something long and bright glittered in the moonlight. Joanna blinked as she saw her rapier hefted from the ground and raised flashing overhead. Loring cursed as the blade hissed down across his arm.

"Damn it, Cameron, you're fighting the wrong person. *She* has your blade. She took it today. She was trying to sell it to me."

The rapier hissed again, and Loring stumbled backward. Blood rose in a dark trail across his chest. "She *has* it, I tell you!"

"Not interested, Loring. But I know someone who will be." Down the hill, car engines whined in the darkness. Two police cruisers pitched up the gravel drive, their lights ablaze.

An officer leaped out, weapon leveled to fire. "Police! Stay where you are."

Cursing, Loring threw himself at Joanna, knocking her sideways. He gave her a vicious shove, then plunged around the corner of the cottage and disappeared.

Joanna heard the snap of twigs as he crashed blindly into the steep ravine. "Alex, he's—"

"I know." Alex pulled off his suede coat and covered Joanna's trembling shoulders. "Did he hurt you?"

She shook her head. "He—he wanted the sword. He was waiting for me. After all these years, it was *him,* Alex. Simon."

Alex touched her pale cheeks. "Go inside, Joanna. We'll find Loring, don't worry."

Then Alex, too, vanished into the darkness.

26

JOANNA DIDN'T move.

Her hands were shaking and her body was numb. She sank blindly onto the damp moss, clutching her arm where Loring had shoved her.

Simon. After all these years.

With her arms around her chest, she tugged Alex's coat closer. Down the hill she heard shouts, then the crack of a gun.

Dear God, not Alex.

She pushed to her feet and ran to the back of the cottage. The swimming pool lights cast a phantom glow around a figure moving up the narrow path. Joanna's fingers clenched. "Alex?"

"He'll be along shortly, miss." The police officer pushed back his hat. "But I'm afraid your intruder got away."

Joanna's legs began to shake. Alex was safe. That was all that mattered.

"Are you all right, miss?"

Joanna nodded, feeling tears burn down her cheeks. "Alex—he came just in time. Otherwise, Simon—he would have—"

The young officer nodded. "So I understand. We found someone named Giorgio locked in the pool shed down the hill. You'd better go inside now. I'm sure your man will be back any minute."

Your man.

Was he after all these years? Could Joanna finally accept that fact?

She straightened her shoulders. "I'll wait here, Officer."

The bushes down the hill shook, and Alex stepped onto the path. "He went over the edge of the ravine. I don't know if he could have survived the fall without the devil's own luck." He turned to the officer. "Do you have search lights with you?"

"Only the cruiser. Nothing else is big enough to work at that distance. I'll radio for assistance, but I doubt anyone will be here for several hours. We've had a nasty pileup on the A21 just outside of Tunbridge, and every available officer has been sent up to help." He pointed to Joanna. "You'll keep an eye on the young lady?"

"You can bloody well count on that."

"Good. We'll need a formal report from her tomorrow. Better look after that arm of yours, too," the officer said.

"What's wrong with your arm?" Joanna demanded. "Alex, did Simon—"

"It's nothing." Alex slid his hands into her hair. "I love how my jacket looks on you, but I think you'd be more comfortable in something a bit more substantial."

With a small broken sound, Joanna turned her face to his chest. "It was Simon, Alex. He was the one who took the pictures. He said Jacques found some sort of notebook in France last month."

"And that's where he found those clues. Amazing, after all these years."

Joanna nodded. "Loring said there was a treasure hidden inside the sword. Jacques knew about it, too. Oh, God, Alex, they've been watching us every step of the way."

"I'm afraid so." Alex pulled her close and guided her up the path to the cottage.

"How is Giorgio?"

"Angry more than anything else. Loring sent someone dressed in a pool cleaner's uniform. The disguise bought him enough time to knock Giorgio out."

Joanna pulled Alex to a halt. "I have something to tell you, Alex. Now, before I lose my nerve."

"Whatever it is can wait."

"No, it can't." Joanna turned slowly, her face in dim profile as she looked out at the darkness of the valley. "I learned tonight how swiftly life can change. And I want you to know this, Alex. All of it. Now—in case something happens." She took an unsteady breath. "About Peter's father—it was swift and irrational. It happened when I was very young."

Alex cursed softly. "Joanna, you don't have to tell me this."

"I do have to tell you. Even Kelly doesn't know the whole story." She looked down at the silver scars that marked her wrists. "I realized it was a mistake, but by then I was pregnant with Peter. I was young and foolish enough to think a child would change everything."

Alex drew her against him. "Joanna, you've said enough for now."

She shook her head. "Not yet. I have to say it all. You see, even now it's hard for me to face those memories. His name was Jason Harris, and he was an archaeology student just as I was. He was also the son of a very powerful man. Beneath all his confidence and enthusiasm was another person, someone who had to control everything around him." She gave a shaky laugh. "Including me."

"What happened, Joanna?"

"We argued. He left." She shook her head. "How simple it sounds, put that way. But of course, it wasn't simple at all. It happened slowly over gray days and lonely weeks. And then . . ." Her body stiffened. "There was a spot for a seasoned archaeologist on a dig at Hadrian's Wall, and Jason told me to have my father arrange it. I wouldn't. After all the arguments and lies, I couldn't take any more."

"What happened when you told him?"

Joanna didn't move, didn't speak.

Alex held her very gently, knowing what she was going to say even before she said it.

"He was . . . very angry." She worked the folds of

Alex's shirt beneath her fingers, pleating and unpleating the fine cotton. "He said he had to teach me how life works. Really works. He . . . locked me in a gardening shed behind our flat. It was midwinter, freezing. There were rats."

Alex's hands tightened, but he forced himself not to interrupt her.

"I broke through the only window with my hands. That's how I got the scars. Other scars, too. Later—well, Peter was born that night."

"Sweet God above," Alex said savagely. "You were about to have his child and he left you out there?"

Joanna shivered. "I never went back, never saw him again. From the hospital, I went straight to Greece, where my parents were on a dig. He swore he would take Peter just to hurt me. Over the years, I periodically received letters from him asking about Peter, warning me I could never be free of him. Finally, I changed my name, hoping I could cut him out of my life. I wanted to be able to live without looking over my shoulder."

The tears came then. Alex held her while she shook with tight sobs. The soft words he murmured were in no language Joanna understood. And yet they meant everything, because they offered a comfort and reassurance far beyond words.

When Joanna's tears stopped, she looked up at Alex. Her face glistened in the moonlight, silver and wet. Beautiful.

"There's more, Alex. Other things I need to tell you."

"Later," he said harshly.

"There are other scars. You won't find them attractive. I would understand if you didn't want to—"

With a curse, Alex tightened his embrace, locking her close. "Then you would be a fool, *drushka*. Ten thousand times a fool to think that. If I wanted you any more than I do . . ." He moved, knowing that she could feel the rock-hard evidence of his desire.

"But later . . ."

"Now, later, forever. *Nothing* changes this. Your body was perfect."

"But you don't know. You haven't seen—"

"No more explanations." He cradled her cheeks and frowned. "You're shivering. Why didn't you tell me?"

"Not . . . with cold." Joanna's voice was husky. "Because you said . . ." She swallowed. "Tonight. I've never forgotten. Not really, Alex. Your face, your hands—they were always with me."

Alex felt desire burn away the fury he had been nursing against the monster who had hurt Joanna so badly. "The police could be back any moment."

"Yes."

"You're upset. You'll be thinking of Simon."

"I'll be thinking *only* of you." Her lips nudged the warm skin at his neck.

"Damn it, Joanna, you're not *listening* to me. I want you. I want your legs wrapped around me and the moss beneath us. I want you until I can't be careful or calm or sane." He touched her scarred wrist. "I can't understand or accept what Peter's father did. All I can do is try to make you forget. That means taking time, Joanna. Going slowly." His fingertips touched her face. "But if we stay out here, going slowly is going to be the *last* thing on my mind. Do you understand?" he said harshly.

"I understand."

"How you make me feel—it scares the hell out of me. I feel as if this is our last chance, as if I've stood here before, wanting and waiting, only to find my dreams turned to mist. I've looked for you, Joanna. Maybe longer than I know."

She looked up at the hard, handsome face locked in lines of uncertainty. She found his shirt. Tugged it free. Started on the first button.

"Joanna—"

Two more buttons slid free.

"Not here. Not in the shadows. This time I want a soft bed. I want *all* night."

"Here." The cotton slid down his powerful shoulders. Joanna eased against him, seeking his heat, offering all her secrets. *"Now,* Alex." His belt hissed free and landed askew on a rose bush. "With nothing but shadows." She caught the beautiful old rapier and with exquisite skill lopped off the button at his waistband.

Cursing softly, Alex tugged the priceless weapon from her hands.

With the cool grace of a master swordsman he found the narrow strap of her dress. His hand tightened.

Her gaze burned on his. "I'm not running, Alex. Not tonight. I've run long enough."

Moonlight silvered Joanna's body. The rapier moved, shearing the fragile lace.

Alex's breath caught. With a ragged oath, he planted the blade in the ground. The hiss of swaying steel was the only sound above the whisper of the wind. He brought his hands to her shoulders, her neck, her face. His fingers trembled against her skin, his control shredding. His need made Joanna's heart lurch. He was implacably honest, even now.

"Joanna?"

She touched his jaw, feeling his muscles tense beneath her fingers. "You saved my life, Alex."

"Damn it, this isn't about owing. I want a hell of a lot more than gratitude from you tonight. But I told you before, there are no strings attached. Come to me because you want to be part of my life—or don't come at all."

She gave a lopsided grin. "You don't ask for much, do you?"

"Only everything," he said softly, eyes hungry, heart bared so she could see exactly how much his honesty was costing him.

The look in his eyes took her breath away.

Without a word, she tugged the shirt from his shoulders. It fell to the ground, a pale stain against the dark moss. With a low, breathless sound of wonder and need, she brought her body to meet his.

It was as perfect as he'd promised. She felt every hard band of muscle. She felt the stark power of the man.

For a moment, she tensed, remembering the past.

"Tell me, Joanna. Everything you want. I'll make it happen tonight." Alex found her wrist and brought it to his lips, tracing every silver scar. "I'd take them away if I could. One by one, I'd make them mine. I swear it."

Joanna closed her eyes. Something twisted and stirred, opening inside her like a fragile flower. Alex freed the buttons on her dress, then shoved aside the fine linen. Slowly, he bent to trace the faint scars he found at her neck.

His face was hard as he covered each mark with his mouth. Slow. Searching. Patient in his hunger.

"Alex?"

"I'm right here. And not quite believing it."

Joanna laughed, a breathless sound. "I just wanted to say your name. To be touching you, feeling your heartbeat when I said it." She slid higher, linking her hands behind his neck.

"God, Joanna." The words were a little unsteady. "Tell me what you want."

She closed her eyes, feeling Alex warm and heavy against her. Her naked breasts grazed his chest, sending shock waves of pleasure to her toes. "Want?" She smiled when she heard him groan. "I want to see all of you. And I want to touch you slowly, exquisitely, until you swear at me. Then I want to close my eyes and feel you make us one." She made a low, ragged sound, twisting his hair, thick and warm against her fingers.

Then the moss and his coat were beneath her and only his body above. He snagged the last scrap of lace and pulled it free while his mouth burned across her jaw, her neck, and down to the thrusting tip of one breast.

His fingers moved where the lace had been, covering her, teasing her, stroking and parting until Joanna moaned, remembering another night in the sultry Caribbean darkness. The pleasure came without warning, sweet and swift and shocking.

"Alex."

"I couldn't want you more than this, Joanna. Somehow I'll make you forget everything that came before."

His hand nuzzled her soft curls.

Joanna felt the soft folds open, easing to meet him. The silence was suddenly loud against the hammering of her heart when pleasure broke, racing through her in silver waves. She strained against him as fire bloomed inside her in heavy liquid waves. "Dear God, Alex, now. I can't—"

With a hoarse curse, he nudged the hot cleft of her womanhood. Joanna dug her nails into his back, terrified he would leave her, that this was simply another dark memory come to haunt her.

Then his hard, straining length opened her, filled her.

And in the same instant, a wave of blinding pleasure broke inside her, sending her up, up against the soft moss, against the cool suede of his jacket, into the rigid line of his body.

She cried out his name, shuddering while her toes dug into the cool earth. Even then she felt his hands against her, powerful, anchoring, infinitely controlled.

When her eyes opened, they were dark with passion, calling to him as only a woman in love could call.

"Joanna." Alex's hands closed. He pinned her to the moss, his eyes savage, tormented.

"Fill me, Alex. Make us one."

He closed his eyes. When he sank against her, his body was a shuddering blade moving in a primitive choreography of power and heat. Again and again he slid deep, teasing, always giving less than her straining body demanded.

"Alex, please." Joanna took and took, her hands twisting in his hair, wanting his hot, impaling length captured inside her, a reality now, no longer only in dreams.

He arched his back, driving her over the soft moss with each velvet thrust. She shuddered, flowing into him as if their souls had melted together like fine metal at a flame.

Pleasure raked her as she opened to him, body and soul. When she thought there was no more, he showed her she was wrong, pleasure spinning out, then pulled tight as she trembled on the very edge of forever. Blindly, she wrapped her legs around him, her hands urgent.

Then Alex gripped her hands tightly and cried her

name, pouring himself inside her, hot and potent in his release.

The low, hoarse words he said then were only for Joanna, only for the darkness.

Only for the forever they had forged between them.

A bird cried far away over the hillside. Alex eased a curve of hair from Joanna's cheek.

One eye blinked open. Very blue. "If this isn't real, I don't want to know."

"It's no dream." Smiling lazily, Alex rose on one elbow and kissed the faint bruise on her elbow where Simon had seized her. "But it's time to go inside."

Joanna came fully awake. "You're dressed?"

"Yes. The police were just here."

"I didn't even hear." She sat up sharply. "Simon?"

"No trace. Of course they won't know for certain until daylight."

"You mean he could be down there, somewhere in the ravine."

Alex nodded grimly, then took her face in his hands. "It's no use remembering. He's gone, no longer part of your life." He traced her lips, studying her face in the moonlight. "I wish I'd known you when you were eight, all blue eyes and chatter. Or maybe when you were twelve, all skinny knees and tangled hair beneath one of your father's pith helmets."

He wasn't far wrong, Joanna thought. "And you would have been silent and strong, already breaking girls' hearts."

"I was too busy for that." For a moment, something darkened his eyes.

"Alex?" When he didn't answer, Joanna touched his cheek.

His breath hissed free. He pulled her up into his arms.

"But my clothes—"

"Leave them." He kicked open the door with his foot, then made for the stairs.

"Where are we going?"

"To bed. Moss is nice, but linen and down are even

better. It will be dawn in two hours." His face was hard with shadows. "Inside I can keep you safe. I don't want to think about how close Loring came to hurting you tonight."

In Joanna's bedroom, the air was rich with the tang of lavender and verbena growing in pots on the window seat. The curtains fluttered as Alex set her on her feet, then found a candle and lit it, muttering the old Romany phrase of thanks for the fire.

He turned. His body was sculpted with shadows, brushed with candlelight, intensely beautiful. The night seemed hushed, breathless, expectant.

He rubbed his forehead, frowning. "It's too soon. You should sleep. We shouldn't—"

She blocked his words with a kiss, with a hunger of her own. There was desperation in Alex's face when he pulled her down against him on the bed. Her soft breasts filled his fingers.

"Not so soon," he said. "I don't want to hurt you."

She closed her eyes, shivering at the sweep of his caressing hands. A broken sound escaped her throat, and her hips twisted restlessly.

With a groan, Alex found the sleek petals of her desire. Slow and sweet, his fingers eased into her liquid heat.

Joanna cried out in shock, in wonder, certain there could be no more.

Alex's eyes were bottomless as he watched her. "I shouldn't touch you again, even like this. I swore to wait, to seduce you slowly, to drive you mad."

"You already have," Joanna whispered, smiling crookedly. "Five years ago."

Behind Joanna the candle danced. The quilt toppled to the floor. The pillows followed. Blindly they twisted and sprawled and fought their way over the bed, legs tangled, fingers entwined.

Joanna caught him beneath her. She fought his honor and challenged his control, exploring the beautiful planes of his rigid body.

"Damn it, Joanna—"

She circled his hard length slowly, entranced by his need, by the fire playing through his eyes. "Is something wrong?" she asked.

"You know bloody well there is. I wanted to wait—"

"We'll wait tomorrow. We'll be cautious and safe and logical tomorrow. Tonight . . ." Smiling darkly, she brushed the velvet tip of him. "Tonight we'll be a little mad."

Alex cursed as her lips brought him fire. "I've been mad, *drushka,* ever since I first saw you."

Her lips tightened. Alex's fingers slid into her hair as it cascaded over his chest while he died of an exquisite agony that he never wanted to end.

"No more." His body tensed, and he swept her sideways, bringing her mouth to his. He pinned her beneath him, taking resolute pleasure in her high, full breasts, in the pale hollow of her belly, and finally in the dusky curls below.

Her body arched. Her fingers dug at his shoulders. "Alex, now. I want you with me when—" She gasped as the tremors began, then twisted sideways and wrapped her legs around him, easing onto his rigid blade.

"Sweet God, Joanna."

Her eyes were bright, hazy with desire. "Come with me, Alex." Smiling, she tugged the leather thong from his hair and slid it around his neck, pulling him closer. Desire burned through her blood as she traced his granite length captured against her thighs. "Very impressive, Lord Greywood."

Alex bit back a groan. "Joanna, I took you fast and hard before. This time I want to be slow, to watch your face when I fill you and take you over the edge."

But Joanna had her own ideas. Her head fell as she caught his lip between her teeth. Gently. Then not so gently.

She smiled when he groaned. Her toes dug into the bed. Gasping, she moved against him, driving him deeper inside her, dizzy with her woman's power.

Dizzy with her love for this man with a warrior's eyes and an artist's hands.

Sweat beaded Alex's chest. With a groan, he thrust down into velvet heat. But even then Joanna could not hold him. Again and again he shaped her to his blade, then retreated slowly until her pleasure shimmered, stretched fierce and taut like a bowstring.

"This time forever, Joanna. The sword can sing and time can stop, but I'll always want you like this."

Joanna gasped as he slid his hand low, nuzzling her hidden heat until she cried out blindly, rising against him. "Alex, I don't—I can't—"

Then he taught her a wilder, fiercer pleasure. His eyes were dark as he pinned her against the soft sheets, driving deeper, shaping heat and fire until her blood sang. He gripped her hips to meet him, plunging her that last inch across the cool cotton into bliss. He watched her as her body tightened, as she cried out and convulsed against him.

Blindly, Joanna arched and sank her teeth into his shoulder, feeling his control even then. "Alex?"

"It begins now, Joanna." Alex's fingers tightened, laced through hers. "No shadows and no regrets."

Their eyes locked.

"Now," she whispered, welcoming his body with her silken tremors and soft cries. And then there was no ending between them, no words left.

Only beginnings. A thousand new beginnings that burned in Alex's eyes as he groaned her name and carried her down with him into the shifting silver heart of oblivion.

27

ALEX'S HAND was thrown across her chest, his leg against her hip. Even in sleep his hand made gentle patterns on her skin.

Joanna smiled, replete. Dizzy with love.

The sky was still dark as he slept, his long hair warm against her shoulders. There was no tension in him now, no doubting.

Joanna eased from the bed, inch by inch, so she would not wake him. Silently, she caught up a silk robe and moved to the door.

The box was exactly where she had left it, shoved to the back of her bookcase. Her heart was pounding as she lifted the lid and saw the old dress. Its silk seemed brittle now, and there was a mustiness to the dried bloom lying beside it.

There was a creak at the doorway. "Joanna?"

She stiffened. Alex's shadow fell across her.

His body brushed hers as he sank down beside her. "What is it?"

"I kept it." She swallowed audibly. "I remembered, Alex. I remembered everything about that night. But there were too many reasons why I had to leave, shutting you out of my life."

The silk rustled through his fingers. "Maybe waiting was better for both of us. Time taught us well."

Joanna couldn't breathe. Her body felt brittle, as

fragile as the moonlight dusting the wooden floor. "Do you hate me for running away?"

His hands locked over hers. He said nothing as he pulled her to his chest. She felt the wild, angry race of his heart.

"At least now I understand *why,*" he said harshly. "But I have to know that you trust me. I'm *not* going to take your son, and I'm not going to lock you inside any shed."

"I know, Alex." Joanna's breath slid out on a sob. "I was never frightened of you. Only of wanting too much and being vulnerable again."

Alex's hands opened and closed. "So many years lost for both of us." Tears streaked down Joanna's cheeks as Alex rocked her against him. "Don't run from me, Joanna. Never again."

"It was for Peter. I was terrified of what they might do. I couldn't trust anyone."

"Peter will be safe, Joanna. This is for us. For all the nights we lost."

Alex crushed her mouth beneath his, and Joanna met him with equal desperation. Beneath them on the floor, tangled and forgotten, lay the old dress and the single musty flower.

Joanna woke to sunlight, warm and golden. She stretched slowly, burrowed into the covers, then gasped as she felt warm fingers trailing up her thigh.

"Alex!"

"You were expecting someone else?" His smile was very lazy.

Joanna pulled him closer and ran her fingers over his chest. His instant tension made her smile. "Perhaps *you* were expecting someone else."

"Never. I've been waiting for you forever." He sank against her, his lips hard and searching as desire flared. "I even kept my same phone number all these years, hoping that you . . ."

"I know. Believe me, Alex, I didn't want to hurt you."

"But you did." His eyes were very dark for a moment. "You hurt both of us when you ran away." Slowly his lips curved in a sensual smile. "And I'm going to see that you pay for every lost minute."

Joanna eased against his aroused body. "Starting now, I hope?"

Alex leaned forward and ran his hand over the pouting nipple peeking beneath the quilt. "That's the general idea."

Abruptly, he pulled away, cursing softly. "Marston just called. I intercepted the call at first ring because you clearly needed your sleep. It seems that your tour group is waiting at the abbey."

Joanna blinked, then shot from the bed with a gasp. "The abbey tour! How could I have forgotten?"

"You *were* rather distracted last night. And at dawn. And three times since then."

Joanna grabbed for her purse and shoes. "I have to go."

"It *might* be better if you put on some clothes first, my love."

Joanna looked down and flushed at her utter nakedness.

Alex laughed softly. "Catch." Satin lingerie hit her fingers followed by a dress of clinging crimson velvet. "I picked them to please myself," he warned her.

Joanna barely heard, struggling with straps that wouldn't stay in place and fasteners that wouldn't close.

Sighing, Alex strode toward her and shoved away her fingers. "Let me. The sight of you is doing bad things to my physical system. The sooner you get away, the sooner you'll be back." The hook slid home, and then Alex's fingers trailed lovingly over her breast. "A curse on all abbeys and all tour groups." His mouth swept down on hers and tightened savagely.

For a moment there was only fire, only the blindness of his touch. Then with a hoarse curse, Alex pulled away.

Something cool and smooth eased around Joanna's throat. Her breath caught as she looked down to find a necklace of gold worked with links of three exquisite ravens. "I made it for my mother a long time ago. I want you to have it."

Joanna touched the smooth figures reverently. "It's lovely, Alex. But I can't—"

He cut her off, pressing a small, rectangular object into her fingers. "Here's something else for you. Keep this with you at all times."

She frowned down at the gleaming square of silver. "A cigarette lighter? But I don't understand. Why do I need to—"

"It only *looks* like a cigarette lighter." Alex fingered a small button, and a red light began to blink. "It's really a transmitter, sound enhanced. With that we can always be in touch. Don't forget it." His jaw hardened. "And don't hesitate to use it."

Joanna paled. "Do you think Simon will be back?"

"If he does, we're going to be ready." Alex smoothed a curl from Joanna's cheek, then gave her a little shove. "Go on. Dimitri's waiting to drive you. And no arguments this time."

"You're not coming?"

Alex gave a crooked smile. "Later. *After* I've had a long and very icy shower to put me out of my misery."

Joanna flushed. "I . . . I'd like you to see Peter. He'll be at the abbey later. He's bound to notice that I—that we—" Her flush deepened.

Alex released the breath that he hadn't even known he was holding. "It would be a very great honor." His voice fell. He knew how much it cost her to open her small circle to someone new. "Thank you, Joanna."

Outside a car horn honked.

"You'd better go."

Joanna touched his lips with her fingers. "I love you, you arrogant Gypsy."

Alex pressed her palm to his mouth, his eyes closed. "*Go.* Before I change my mind and drag you back down onto this bed, tour or no bloody tour."

Ten minutes later, Alex padded down to Joanna's studio and lifted the phone. Water glistened in his dark hair and beaded his chest as he punched out a number. "Mikhail?"

His friend's voice was grim. "Yes, Alex. You've got Dimitri with Joanna, I trust?"

"They just left for the abbey, and I'll be leaving shortly. I got your message from Metcalfe, but Joanna doesn't know you called. Let's have it."

"The police have found Loring. His body was dumped at the bottom of a road construction project near Norwich."

Alex cursed softly. "There's no question about identification?"

"I'm afraid not. The body was battered, but the features were quite recognizable and he still had his wallet. The man had a great many aliases, it seems."

"I'll just bet he did. Any sign of how he got there?"

"Nothing yet. The police are checking into a report from one of the construction workers who saw a van pull up briefly last night. I'll let you know if anything concrete comes to light."

"I'd appreciate it." Alex frowned down at the Italian rapier Joanna had used on Loring. "I'd also appreciate it if you could help keep an eye on Peter."

There was a taut silence. "You think these people would harm the boy?"

"Loring threatened Joanna with that once. We have to assume there are others and that they'll do anything to get the sword. Anyone close to Joanna could be a target."

"I understand. I'll ring up Joanna's parents and arrange a riding lesson for today instead of next week."

"Thank you, Mikhail. For an arrogant snob you can be very nice."

"Don't count on it. Now tell me what you were growling about with Mr. Orlov before dinner last night."

"The sword. It seems that my father signed it over to the Estavian government to 'defray the costs' of releasing my mother and me."

"Good God," Burke said. "What will you do?"

Alex frowned. "I have to find the thing first."

"Your tour is waiting for you in the ballroom, Ms. Russell. I took the liberty of offering them tea and blueberry scones."

Joanna took a shaky breath and shoved down her wind-blown hair. "You're a prize, Marston." She planted a kiss on the cheek of Draycott Abbey's unflappable butler. "How late am I?"

"Fifty-one minutes, I believe."

Joanna made a strangled sound. "They'll be furious. Rightly so."

Marston cleared his throat. "I think your tour will be in very good spirits today. You see, I bent the truth."

"Bent the truth?"

"Just a little. I intimated that you were busy."

Joanna's head cocked. "And what exactly was I busy doing, Marston?"

The butler smiled faintly. "It seems that you were having tea. A very *private* tea. You couldn't be disturbed, of course."

"I couldn't? Just where was I having this very private tea?"

"Er, at the palace, miss."

"At *Windsor* Palace?"

Marston nodded. "It seemed like a good idea at the time."

"But I didn't—I haven't any idea what—"

"A suggestion, if I may? Say nothing. Answer no questions directly. It's an old politician's trick. Just smile and look very secretive. They'll be eating out of your hand in minutes."

Joanna sighed. "Marston, you were made for a life of high intrigue."

"I have had my moments, miss." The butler's lips twitched.

"I'm afraid that I was made for a life of rusty armor and broken rivets."

"I doubt Lord Greywood would agree with that." The butler's eyes glittered.

As so often before, Joanna was left wondering if there was anything Draycott Abbey's meticulous and efficient butler did not know. She flushed slightly, avoiding his gaze. "They're in the ballroom, you say? I suppose I'd better get on with it then." At the door Joanna halted. "By the way, has someone been opening a window in the Long Gallery?"

The butler looked shocked. "Absolutely not. Lady Draycott has instituted very specific regulations about temperature and humidity for the conservation of the paintings in that room."

"I see. On my last tour, I could have sworn I felt a draft."

"I'll check on it immediately."

Joanna sighed. "It's probably nothing. Just my imagination."

"This abbey seems to work on the imagination. By the way, may I say how radiant you look today?"

Not radiant, Joanna thought. The glow was strictly from beard burn. She smiled, remembering how that faint, erotic scrub had made its way all over her body while her sheets fell in a tangle on the floor. Then she and Alex had found their way down atop those sheets not long after.

She felt her cheeks burn.

"*Very* radiant."

Joanna cleared her throat. "Windsor Palace. A private tea."

Marston smiled conspiratorially. "*Very* private."

Joanna shook her head as she closed the door behind her.

28

"DO THEY really eat on solid-gold plates?" Two dozen curious faces studied Joanna avidly. "Does the queen have the little corgis sit around her on their own chairs?"

Joanna sighed. "If so, I didn't see it." Trying not to lie was taking its toll. So was the strange sensation of being treated like a celebrity by two dozen strangers. "Now, as I was saying, this is one of the finest of the abbey's many suits of period armor. As you can see—"

"Did you see the Other Woman?"

Joanna shook her head.

A man interrupted, very dapper in a hunting jacket with enough pockets to accommodate a deer hunters' convention. "Is it true that they have the Princess of Wales's phone tapped?"

"I have no idea. Now, if you will turn your attention to this gauntlet, you can see how—"

"Did you see the Heir and the Spare?"

Joanna counted silently to twenty, then squared her shoulders. *"Armor. Fifteenth century,"* she said tightly. She glared as a woman with very big hair started to speak. "Don't even think about asking."

She marched toward the gleaming suit of armor near the wall of the Long Gallery. The history of armor might not be as sensational as the intrigues of the royal palace, but Joanna was determined to do her duty by the abbey tour. "If you will look closely, you can see several small designs here—flowers, crowns, and letters. These are what we call proof marks, indicating that the armor was tested against musket shot, arrows, and swords. Think of it as a kind of early inspection sticker. Over here is a crowned A, which happens to be the mark of the Armourers' Company of London. This gives us a very reliable way to date this particular—"

The man in the hunting jacket cleared his throat. "Is it true that the queen refuses to receive the Princess of Wales?"

Joanna made a strangled sound. How was *she* supposed to know?

A woman in a large red hat leaned close and squeezed her arm amiably. "Never mind them, love. Go on and tell us all about these lovely metal things. There's those of us what wants to 'ear all about the abbey." She glared pointedly at the man in the hunting jacket. "Take that great armoire thing over there." She gestured at the vast structure of carved wood on the gallery's other wall. "Why 'as it got those carvings on it?"

Joanna gave her a grateful look. "Actually, that's one of the abbey's finest pieces of furniture. It contains the insignia of every king and queen of England and Scotland."

The woman whistled, bending over one particularly ornate row of figures. "What's this one then?"

"That one belongs to Mary, Queen of Scots. The fleur de-lis represents France and the dragon represents Scotland."

"Now *there* was a female what knew 'ow to manipulate a man." The woman gave a knowing laugh. "'Ad 'em at 'er beck and call, she did."

"Right up until the day they lopped off her head," the man in the hunting vest said curtly.

Joanna shivered, aware of a heaviness in the air around her, almost like a presence at her shoulder.

Sunlight hit the polished old wood. Joanna felt the tiny hairs rise at the back of her neck.

The two dozen faces studied her curiously.

"Shouldn't ought to talk about Mary like that," the woman in the hat said crisply. "Walks, she does."

"Walks?" The man in the hunting jacket sniffed. "Not bloody likely."

"It's God's truth, she does. Probably walks this place, too, seeing as 'ow she was prisoner 'ere once. I'n't that right, Ms. Russell?"

"For less than a year. The English felt that she had become too friendly with the current viscount and so she was moved."

"That's when the armoire thing was carved, was it?"

"Possibly." Joanna made a mental note to ask Nicholas Draycott when he returned from France the following week.

"My, my. Very nice all this carving is." The woman in the hat traced the old wood, her red lips pursed. "Reminds me of an old coffee table what I used to 'ave."

"Er—the pieces are not to be touched, I'm afraid."

The woman clucked her tongue. "Sorry, love. Can't 'elp myself sometimes." Her head cocked. "'Ere now, am I bloomin' mad or is that dragon crooked?"

Joanna blinked. "Dragon?"

"Right there, love. Don't tell me as 'ow you never noticed it before."

Joanna frowned, following the woman's red-tipped finger.

The dragon on the top of the armoire was indeed crooked, one shoulder slightly higher than the other. Only in certain direct light would the slant be noticeable. "It's probably nothing more than the carver having a bad day."

"Bad 'air day, you mean? I get *them* all the time, love."

Amid loud laughter, the group set off for their last stop at the abbey roof. As Joanna stayed behind to switch off the lights, some instinct drew her to the magnificent armoire framed in a beam of sunlight. Gently, she traced the old wood, touching the top of the rampant dragon.

Instantly, pain slammed through her forehead. For a moment, she heard distant voices and the clang of metal, followed by something that could have been bagpipes.

With a gasp, she pulled away.

"You awright, love?" The woman in the red hat was staring at her in concern.

"What?"

"Gone all pale like. Touchin' that bloomin' dragon, you were."

"It's nothing. I thought I saw a crack in the wood." Joanna took a last look, then frowned. "I guess I was wrong."

"Did you ever notice the dragon on the armoire, Marston?"

"Dragon, miss?"

Joanna stood in the abbey's sunny kitchen, savoring a cup of perfect jasmine tea. The tour had left minutes before, their shrill voices resounding through the abbey's forecourt. Joanna breathed a sigh of relief as she kicked off her shoes. "Beneath the insignia of Mary Stuart. It looked crooked."

"Indeed? I'm afraid I never noticed." Marston gave a faint cough. "Of course, it might have been a shadow. This old house often plays tricks that way."

Joanna swirled her cup thoughtfully. "Do you know much about her?"

Marston frowned. "I've heard the viscount mention that the Scottish queen was housed here briefly under Elizabeth's order. Over the years, historians have combed through the abbey's family records, hoping to find more information, but I believe that very little new has come to light. Was there something specific you wanted to know? I could phone the viscount in France."

Joanna remembered that strange moment when she had touched the dragon and heard the sound of clashing metal. There *had* been something in the room, she could swear it. A presence . . .

"Tell me about the abbey ghost, Marston. And don't deny he exists. It's the only subject the tour visitors ever want to talk about, and if anyone has seen him, it would be you."

The butler made a great business of arranging freshly cut roses in a silver vase.

"Don't clam up on me, Marston."

The butler frowned. "It has always been believed that there is a . . . presence about the abbey, glimpsed often on the high roofs, dressed in starkest black. The viscount himself has seen this figure several times since he was a boy. I believe that Lady Draycott has also had that questionable privilege."

"Questionable? Is he as notorious as the legends say?"

"Perhaps notorious is not the word. Rather, he was an individualist. A man stubborn and very unpredictable. Draycott legend holds that he is the spirit of the eighth viscount, a man who answered to no one in life. One might suppose he is the same in death. Nevertheless, in times of danger to the abbey, the figure has made himself felt."

"Have *you* seen him, Marston?"

"What is seeing, Ms. Russell? What is hearing?" The butler looked out over the sunny moat, crisscrossed by a trio of swans. "When a shadow passes at the corner of our vision, is it real or an illusion? When footsteps seem to echo long after a room is empty, is it a trick of our hearing or something very different?"

"You *have* seen him!"

Marston gave Joanna an exasperated smile. "I will say no more, my dear Ms. Russell. And you had better be off to the stables. There is a sturdy young fellow with brown hair down there looking about for his mother."

Joanna turned in a whirl of velvet skirts. "Peter?"

"Lord Sefton and his wife phoned to say they were coming by to pick him up later." Joanna was at the door when the butler's final words stopped her. "And tell Lord Greywood to let you get some rest tonight. You're looking tired." His lips curved. "Radiant but rather tired."

Joanna made a strangled sound as the butler's soft laughter followed her to the door.

Arms flying, Peter Russell raced down the hill, across the grass, and headlong into his mother's arms. "Grandpa's down in the village, but he dropped me and Mr.

Dimitri off." Abruptly, the boy's eyes narrowed. "You look different, Mom."

Joanna felt her breath catch. "Different good or different bad?"

"I'm not sure." Keen gray eyes scrutinized her face. "Good, I think. But different. Did you get a sunburn somewhere?"

"Um, I suppose I might have."

"Your face looks all red. And there's a funny kind of light in your eyes."

Joanna buried her face in Peter's hair, laughing unsteadily. "It sounds fatal."

"Only because I didn't say it right. You look nice, Mom. Really." Peter began to wiggle. "Guess what? Gran says I may have turned up a boundary marker from one of the old Saxon estates."

"Well done, my love!" Joanna gave her son a hug. "You must be putting the other workers to shame."

The boy frowned. "A few of them have been grumbling that it was just beginner's luck. Or something worse."

Joanna bit down a stab of anger. "That's just plain stupid."

"Gran told them to mind their own business." Peter's dusty sneaker dug at the ground. "Do you think Gran hid those things in the dirt? You know, just so I could find them?"

"Harrison Ryan McTiernan tamper with a dig?" Joanna was aghast. "Never in a million years. And he'd have the head of anyone who'd try, I can tell you that."

Peter shook his head uncertainly. "I don't know . . ."

"Whatever you found was put down centuries ago, Peter. Never be afraid of your skill, and never deny it because of what jealous people say."

The boy brightened. "Just like Tommy Hammersmith at school."

"Tommy who?"

"He doesn't have a father. At least none that anyone knows about. Then one day his mother came home and brought him a new father. He's a famous soccer star, a ripping player. When Tommy Hammersmith told the others, they went green with jealousy. They said it was all a hum, that Tommy had just made it up." Peter frowned. "After a while Tommy shut up about his father. If anyone asked, he said it was just a story."

Joanna saw the tension in his face. This anecdote obviously had a special significance for Peter, who had no father of his own. "Do you think that was right of him?"

The boy's sneaker scored tight lines in the earth. "No. But it's hard when all the fellows go at you from dawn to dusk."

Joanna felt her throat tighten painfully. "Is there anything I can do to help? To help Tommy Hammersmith, I mean."

Peter sighed. "I guess not. He's got to learn for himself what's important." He looked up suddenly and squeezed his mother's hand. "Thanks for letting me go to the dig with Gran and Gram."

Joanna feigned a frown. "I suppose this new discovery means another trip for ice cream."

Peter shook his head. "Not today. Uncle Michael and Aunt Kelly are taking me for a riding lesson later on."

Hearing a low gurgle of laughter, Joanna turned to see Kelly walking slowly over the grass. "But Uncle Michael will do the actual riding. Aunt Kelly will probably be mistaken for the horse."

As Lady Sefton was looking absolutely beautiful, Joanna simply snorted. "No sympathy for you here, Kelly. I've just had to fend off two dozen prurient tourists who were convinced I'd come straight from tea at Windsor Palace. A very *private* tea."

"Marston again." Kelly smiled knowingly. "He did the same to me last year when I had to fill in on one of the tours. Thank God you've agreed to take the job."

"It's little enough. Nicholas refuses to take half what he deserves for rent."

"Don't be too sure about that. Nicholas would probably pay *you* to live in the cottage as long as you'd manage the abbey tours. Believe me, he is too impatient to manage one, and if Kacey did it, the group would be milling around the place all day, since she's far too good-hearted to make them leave." She looked down and rubbed Peter's hair. "Hullo there, handsome. Looking forward to your ride?"

"Am I ever!"

"Good. Only promise to keep an eye on Uncle Michael, will you? He goes too fast over the jumps and that makes me worry."

"You want me to hold back so he has to go slow, Aunt Kelly?"

"That's the general idea. But nothing obvious, you understand." The two shared a conspiratorial look. "There *might* be chocolate cake afterward."

"A cinch," Peter said excitedly. Abruptly he went still. "Who's that?"

"Who is who?" Joanna turned. And her heart lurched into her throat.

Alex was walking over the lawn. His flowing white shirt opened above well-worn denims. His hair was unbound over his shoulders, and his eyes were locked on Joanna.

"I think," Kelly Burke said carefully, "that what you're looking at is a man who will not take no for an answer."

"He doesn't have to take no for an answer," Joanna said softly. "Not anymore."

Kelly went very still. "Joanna, what aren't you telling me?"

Joanna took Peter's hand and started toward the moat. "I'll talk to you later, Kelly."

"Call me."

Joanna kept walking.

"No, I'll call you," Kelly said. "And I'll want answers."

Joanna kept right on walking.

"Traitor," her friend muttered. Then she smiled, thinking about the bet she was going to collect from her husband.

* * *

Alex was holding a dueling sword of damascened silver. The pommel was perfectly balanced. Alex knew because he had made it himself.

His eyes sought Joanna's. "And how was the tour, Ms. Russell?"

Her lips curved. "Quite tolerable, Lord Greywood."

Alex smiled at Peter. "How are you today? Any more exciting finds?"

"A few. Maybe even a boundary marker for one of the old Saxon estates." Peter's eyes glinted. "That sword of yours is capital."

Alex smiled and made a quick experimental thrust. The blade hissed through the air. "I hope you don't mind. I brought it in case there were any tourists left wandering about."

Joanna laughed. "They've all gone." She studied the blade admiringly. "Remind me to spar with you soon. You're very good with that."

"It's rather a passion of mine. That and several other things." For a moment, heat filled his eyes. Then he looked at Peter and cleared his throat. "Is it really safe?" he asked Peter. "Have the noisy tourists finally gone?"

"Ten minutes ago. Marston was muttering when they got on their bus."

"Marston mutters a lot," Alex agreed.

The boy hesitated. "Is that *really* your sword?"

Alex nodded.

"It's very fine."

"Do you think so?" Alex studied the gleaming steel critically, then stood back and gave another thrust. "You're right. I wasn't so sure when I finished it though."

The boy's eyes widened. "You *made* it?"

"Hilt, grip, and pommel. It was this piece here that gave me the most trouble. The ricasso." He pointed to a small plate beneath the hilt that was pierced by the blade. "You know what a ricasso is?"

"That's the flat piece between the grip and blade, isn't it?"

"Very good."

"Not every sword has a ricasso though. Only the very fine ones."

"True enough. Your mother knows a great deal about swords. I can see you do, too."

Peter gnawed at his lip. "I know more about Roman things. Still . . ." He studied the glistening hilt. "That's an Italian shape. A dueling sword, I think."

"Right again."

Peter frowned, looked at his mother, then slowly smiled. "She likes you."

"Oh? What makes you think that?"

"Because of her eyes. See how they go all crinkly when she looks at you?"

Alex gave a lazy grin. "Thank you for pointing that out, Peter. I like her, too."

Alex did not miss how the color skimmed over her cheeks. Nor, he expected, did Peter.

"Are you two going to get married or something?"

Joanna coughed.

"I think it's very possible. Would you mind?"

Peter frowned. "Would I have to go and live at school like Tommy Hammersmith?"

Alex looked at Joanna, whose eyes were gleaming.

"No, you won't have to stay at school," she said. "We'll be together. The three of us."

Peter smiled a little, then a lot. "See, look at her eyes. They're doing it again."

"So I see," Alex said gravely. "I rather think I like it."

Peter's head cocked. "So when is the wedding?"

"Er, we haven't decided."

"Do you guys have a license?"

Alex blinked. "License?"

"Sure. That's a piece of paper that says you can get married and sleep in the same bed."

Alex cleared his throat. "Not yet, I'm afraid."

Peter considered this for several moments. "So, where do we go on our honeymoon?"

We.

Alex smiled. "How about white-water rafting on the Colorado River?"

"Cool."

"Or maybe horseback riding in Mongolia. Would you like to sleep in a yurt?"

"Awesome!"

Alex put a hand on his shoulder. "I take that as a yes. Meanwhile would you like to try the sword? With your mother's permission, of course."

Peter looked up, his body taut with excitement. "Could I, Mom? I'll be very careful."

"He will indeed," Alex assured her. "But only if you agree."

Part of Joanna knew that her son could not be in safer hands, for Alex's skill was obvious. At the same time, part of her balked, all too aware of the danger in any unprepared movement with a sword, even a dull one.

"Please?"

She sighed, looking at Alex with a blend of worry, exasperation, and amusement. "Just don't get carried away. *Either* of you."

"Not a chance," Alex said firmly.

"Will you watch us, Mom?"

"Yes." Alex's eyes darkened. "Will you watch us?"

"Try to stop me."

Joanna sat on a grassy bank overlooking the lawn by the edge of the moat and watched Alex cup Peter's fingers around the grip, then guide him through a few movements. The sun was warm on her shoulders, and the moat rippled in waves of silver. As the rich scent of roses filled the air, Joanna felt contentment slip over her.

She smiled when Alex put down the sword, then traced movements in the air with an invisible weapon. Peter copied each thrust perfectly. Back and forth they moved over the grass, while Alex called out directions for imaginary thrusts and parries.

As the sun grew higher, Alex took off his shirt and helped Peter roll up his sleeves. They turned, waved once, then proceeded to ignore her, lost in a long-ago age of knights and chivalry.

Joanna looked away at the sunlit moat. As she did,

something shimmered at the edge of her vision and a shadow fell over the grass.

She blinked, gripped with a sense of panic, seeing the shadow of a long face with a pair of singularly sad eyes.

Instantly, Joanna was struck by a wave of pain. She tried to speak, but her body was frozen. Words filled her head, urgent against the clang of metal.

Ask . . . Angus. The book holds the answer to the sword.

Light shimmered and broke as Joanna sat transfixed. The woman bent closer, her eyes dark with royal command.

The sword. Find the words.

The pale lips moved, soundless, and Joanna felt her heart race. She seemed to be pinned to the ground, borne down by an oppressive despair that felt centuries old.

In his quiet office at Greywood House, Metcalfe bent over the computer screen, typed in two words, then sat back with a frown. As before, the cursor winked back at him mockingly.

Sighing, he finished his tea and tried two more commands with an equal lack of success. He was just about to stand up when the screen exploded to life, disgorging line after line of systems code.

The butler laughed softly and bent closer. "Now then, that's better. Let's see what we have."

His eyes narrowed. After two minutes, he found what he was looking for. He had accessed the network of the private hospital where Jacques St. Cyr was a patient. Punching several keys, he called up the latest nursing orders followed by a list of St. Cyr's recent visitors.

His eyes widened. "Bloody, bloody hell," he muttered, reaching for the phone.

29

Peter's face was pinched and very pale. "What's wrong with her? Why won't she answer me?"

Alex eased the boy behind him. "It's probably too much sun, Peter. Your mother will be fine in a moment. Meanwhile, why don't you find Marston and wheedle some special lemonade out of him?"

Peter didn't move. "Don't lie to me please."

Alex bit back a curse. "Very well, Peter. Your mother looks weak. We're going to need your help."

After a moment, the boy nodded. "I'll go." He took a shuddering breath. "Just—take care of her, will you? She . . . she's all I have now."

Alex sank down by Joanna and drew her rigid body against his chest. "She's all I have, too, Peter. And neither of us is going to lose her," he said fiercely.

How dare you come back?

Sunlight gleamed over the moat as Joanna dug her fingers into the soft grass. Pain shot through her forehead and anger surrounded her, black and heavy. She tried vainly to move, but the weight was unbearable, driving her down into the restless past.

Betrayed.

How dare you both come back?

Movement came beside her, but Joanna barely noticed. Her hands were locked on the cold earth, her body

318

shaking. The smell of sweat, horses, and burning torches was all around her.

She gasped as words hammered in her head.

We are betrayed! Make haste and hide the papers lest they be discovered.

She heard shouts. The clang of metal. She moved blindly through a tunnel of darkness without beginning or end.

The sword will claim Our secret. It will carry Our message South, to Our cousin, the Queen. And We will wait here for her answer, praying for release from this endless hell of captivity.

Joanna felt a rush of cold air. Pain exploded through her head. The tunnel grew smaller, squeezing, pressing, taking her down into darkness.

"Joanna?" Alex's face was grim as he stroked Joanna's face. "Can you hear me?"

He cursed, hating the pallor of her skin and the tension in her body. With unsteady fingers he pulled her against him, sensing the same chill hostility they had felt in the attic. "You can't have her," he said furiously. "This time she is my world. I won't be caught again, captive of your dreams." He spoke from some dim corner of memory, almost unaware of the hoarse vow he made while he bent protectively over the woman he loved. The woman he had lost in another time, separated by honor to clan and sword and queen.

Never again. In this time she would be his honor and his country. "Joanna, talk to me, damn it!"

She moved in his arms, shuddering. "A—Alex?"

"Right here."

"Is she gone?"

Alex's hands tightened. "Is who gone? No one else is here. I sent Peter inside to Marston."

Joanna frowned. "Why?"

"Because you scared the bloody hell out of us, sitting here like a statue."

"There were shouts. I felt something—a woman. She

was angry, Alex. But so cold and alone. She said something about the sword and her hopes for a release from captivity. It—it must have been Mary."

"Sweet God." He pulled her closer, running his hand over her back until some of the tension left her shoulders.

Wind eddied over the hillside, raising waves across the moat. A wall of clouds raced over the abbey roofs. Joanna shivered.

"What is it?"

"She wanted something, Alex. Desperately."

"It was the sword that she wanted. And her freedom."

Her eyes widened. "You saw her, too?"

"No, but I felt her." His jaw hardened. "I have no doubt that it was Mary's ghost."

Joanna thought again of the presence in the Long Gallery. "The armoire—one of the insignia is crooked. I was thinking of it, Alex, when I saw her." She caught a shaky breath. "We've got to open that armoire somehow."

"We will. But not now." Alex held her still when she tried to sit up. "You're not going anywhere yet. Peter will be back with some of Marston's special lemonade, which includes a generous dose of whisky. You're going to drink it. Peter was half scared out of his mind when he saw you like that."

Joanna frowned. "It was as if I was caught inside a tunnel, locked away from light and warmth. It went on forever." She began to tremble again.

Alex cursed, pulling her closer as Peter ran over the grass. "Here's a whole glass. Marston said it's his special, special kind." He frowned. "What does that mean?"

"That it's the good stuff," Alex said darkly. He held the glass to Joanna's lips. "Drink it."

She took one swallow and coughed wildly. "That's *terrible.*"

"Low on flavor but great on stamina. Finish it," Alex ordered.

Joanna took another slow drink, then reached for Peter's hand. "I'm fine, love. Sorry if I frightened you."

"Lord Greywood said you had too much sun. That's all, wasn't it?" There was a note of desperation in the boy's voice.

"Lord Greywood was right. It was just the sun."

"I told him not to lie to me," Peter said fiercely. "Then he told me *he* was worried, too, so I went inside for the lemonade." Peter wrinkled his nose. "There was a noisy lady in a funny red hat asking Marston a lot of questions. When she left, Marston was muttering a *lot.*"

Joanna laughed. "One of the stragglers from the tour. Poor Marston."

"Poor Marston, nothing. The man is made of iron," Alex said.

Perfectly on cue, Marston strode regally over the lawn bearing a large hamper, from which he produced strawberry cake, minced tarts, and a bottle of chilled champagne. "I trust you are feeling better, Ms. Russell?"

"Much better, Marston."

"It was the sun?"

Joanna gave a crooked smile. "So it seems. But what is all *this?*"

The butler smiled at Alex. "I believe this qualifies as a special occasion." He handed Peter an iced glass of lemonade and a large slice of strawberry cake. "Eat up, Peter. You'll need your energy if you're going to study with Lord Greywood."

"*Am* I?" Peter looked eagerly at Alex.

"I don't see why not."

"I'd like that," Peter said quietly. "And I'd like to watch you make a sword."

"It would be an honor." Alex's eyes twinkled. "Perhaps your mother would like to watch, too."

"Would you, Mom?"

"I think I could be persuaded."

"I'm sure I can think of a way," Alex murmured. "Now drink the champagne Marston is holding out."

Joanna took the glass of perfectly chilled Krug. "Any more of this and I'll find myself stumbling over the armor."

Peter's eyes widened. "You mean you'd be *drunk?*"

"Maybe I already am." Joanna looked soberly at Alex. "That would explain why I felt so odd."

Alex touched his glass to hers. "You had a difficult morning with the tour and last night you had no sleep. It's set you on edge, that's all."

Peter frowned. "Why didn't you have any sleep?"

"The wind was very loud. It . . . disturbed me," Joanna said. "Then I was late for the tour this morning."

"I can sympathize." Marston glared at the empty courtyard. "That female in the red hat was enough to make anyone feel unwell."

"You *were* muttering a lot, Marston." Peter studied the butler. "My mom does that when she's angry. Did you mutter when the ricasso on the sword wasn't the way you wanted it?" he asked Alex.

"Oh, I muttered all right. That and a few other things."

"I like it better when she mutters than when she gets quiet and rubs her eyes." Peter studied his mother. "Then she pretends nothing's wrong. She usually does that when it's late and she thinks I'm asleep."

Joanna flushed. "Peter!"

"See." The boy gave a mischievous smile. "I can be very quiet when I want to."

Marston hid a smile. "A good habit to cultivate, young man. But I believe that hulking fellow glaring at us from the terrace is your uncle Michael come to take you riding."

Peter jumped up, cake and lemonade forgotten. "Over heeere, Uncle Michael!"

Marston's voice fell. "Lord Sefton also wished to speak to you, Lord Greywood."

A look passed between the two men, unseen by Joanna as she gave Peter a quick hug. "You'll be good? And nothing reckless. Remember what Aunt Kelly said about keeping an eye on Uncle Michael?"

"I promise."

Joanna's eyes darkened as she watched her son race over the soft grass to the terrace, where he was swung high up into Michael Burke's arms.

Alex's brow rose. "So he's to keep an eye on Uncle Michael, is he?"

"He's going to hold back so Michael doesn't take the jumps at full speed."

"I detect Kelly's hand at work here. A very clever woman. So is her most beautiful friend." Alex pulled Joanna into his arms for a slow and very thorough kiss.

Marston cleared his throat. "Don't mind me."

Alex didn't, deepening the kiss.

Paper rustled. Glass clinked. "I see nothing and hear nothing. The perfectly discreet butler."

Alex's lips moved over Joanna's. His hands slid to her waist.

"Absolutely, completely discreet." China clattered.

Alex muttered but didn't quite raise his head. "Go away, Marston."

"Alex!"

"It's quite all right, Ms. Russell. I'm well used to it by now." The butler smiled irrepressibly as he picked up the hamper. "I know a man in love when I see him."

Alex looked down at Joanna. "I plan to sit here in the sun and kiss the woman I love." His smile wobbled. "If she'll let me."

Joanna's eyes darkened. "She will."

Marston chuckled. "A very nice thought. Just don't be too thorough about it. I doubt 'Uncle Michael' will like to be kept waiting."

Alex's head bent. "Tell him to go knit a baby sweater," he muttered as his mouth closed over Joanna's.

"What are they doing out there?" Michael Burke glared over the lawn toward the abbey's moat.

His wife smiled complacently. "Kissing."

"Humph."

Kelly patted his back. "You're just grumpy because you lost the bet. I told you they'd be together before the week ended, and I was right."

"Humph."

Behind them, Peter was helping Marston put away the

last of the picnic things. Suddenly, Kelly stiffened. Her hand slid to her stomach.

"Kelly?" Michael was behind her instantly, rubbing her back. "Sweet God, don't tell me that it's time!" His face went pale.

"False alarm." She smiled crookedly. "It's over now."

Her husband frowned. "Kelly?"

"I'm fine." His wife turned to wave at Peter. "All done?"

Peter nodded. "Marston says we can have a scavenger hunt up in the abbey's attic next week."

"Heaven protect and preserve us," Michael murmured.

"Maybe we'll see the abbey ghost," Peter said eagerly. "Can we go riding now?"

Kelly looked at her husband. "Dimitri can take us on ahead if you need to speak with Alex."

Michael shook his head.

"Oh, go on with you. Find Alex and talk about whatever dire things you've been wanting to discuss all morning."

"That obvious, was it?"

Kelly straightened his collar lovingly. "Only to me, my love." She rose, kissing him softly, while Peter watched impatiently.

"First my mom, now you two." His nose wrinkled.

"Better get used to it, Peter," Michael said without looking away from his wife.

"You mean all that kissing stuff?"

"Exactly." Michael chuckled. "I have the feeling you're going to be seeing lots of it."

Peter shook his head, mystified. "Yuck."

"You'll rest."

"I'll sit," Joanna said. "I want to go through some records about Mary Stuart." Sunlight poured through the study windows overlooking the moat.

"No, you'll *sleep*. Right here beneath this blanket," Alex said firmly. "And you *won't* get up until I come back."

Joanna smiled, touching his cheek. "Bully."

"Damn it, I'm concerned about you."

"I know." Joanna sighed, tugging the soft quilt around her. "I'll sleep. Just don't be too long."

"We'll get into that armoire some way or another this afternoon, and tonight you and Peter will come to Greywood. I thought maybe you'd like to watch me. While I work, that is," he said diffidently.

"Making a sword? We'd *love it*. Is it going to be a rapier or a period replica? What metals have you chosen for the design? Can I help you with the inlay?" She gave a cheeky smile. "I *seem* to recall some Gypsy lore that the maker of a sword must remain celibate during the period of his work or the sword will be ruined."

Alex chuckled. "Sleep. We'll discuss swords and celibacy later."

With a sigh, Joanna curled into the blanket. "I love you, Alexei," she whispered. "I've loved you for years." Her fingers found Alex's just before she closed her eyes. "Maybe even longer than that," she whispered.

Michael was standing motionless at the window in the library. Sunlight glinted off his dark hair, playing over the fine lines at the corner of his eyes, and his face was hard.

"You've had some news?" Alex helped himself to a glass of steaming Lapsang Souchong tea from the tray Marston had arranged on a Regency side table.

"I'm afraid so." Michael frowned out at the moat. "Marston just had a call from your man at Greywood. It seems he managed to hack into the network of that private hospital in Surrey. The stroke Jacques St. Cyr suffered came under very mysterious circumstances and was possibly chemically induced. The hospital is running blood tests now."

Alex went very still. "How is he?"

"He's still alive but barely."

"What time did it happen?"

"Early evening. I made a few phone calls, but it seems that no one in the adjoining rooms of the hospital heard or saw anything unusual. Which means that these people are damnably slick." Michael frowned. "I don't like the feel of this, Alex. Stay close to Joanna and her son. We'll keep the boy with us until you come for him."

Alex nodded. "It's very near now, Michael. All of it, right there in front of me. Sometimes I can almost see the whole puzzle. The lost sword. The Cameron Bible. All those stories about a hidden treasure. Jacques believed they were true." Alex jammed his hands irritably through his hair. "Damn it, why can't I put the pieces together?"

Michael put a hand on his shoulder. "You will, and you'll find the sword, too. But what then? How can you turn the sword over to the Estavian government?"

Alex sighed. "How can I not? Orlov was right. Honor is honor, Mikhail. But first I have to know where to find the sword. Has Sir Gordon phoned?"

"I'm afraid he's gone missing. Metcalfe phoned his office as you asked. They said Sir Gordon left this morning on an extended trip to the Far East, and there was no scheduled date for his return."

Alex cursed tightly. "There goes our last clue. It was supposed to be the key to everything." Slowly Alex's eyes narrowed. "The key to everything," he repeated softly.

His jaw hardened.

It was so close now. Why couldn't he see the last piece?

After Michael left, Alex watched Joanna as she slept, one hand curved around the pillow. Sunlight pooled over her hair, glinting in streaks of gold and copper fire. He did not touch her though he hungered for the taste of her lips and her low, shuddering sigh.

His Gypsy blood burned, sensing things that other men would have ignored. But Alex had learned very young that such wordless instincts were precious. As an artist, he courted the stirrings of his unconscious, for these fired his finest work.

What was his unconscious trying to tell him now?

Biting back a curse, he stood up and saw Marston

waiting by the door, his face grim. "You are going out, my lord?"

"Sometimes you're too knowing for comfort, Marston. Are you sure you don't have a Gypsy or two somewhere in your family tree?"

"Sometimes I wish I did."

Alex's smile didn't quite reach his eyes. "I'm worried, Marston. Not that I know why. I'd like to ring Metcalfe."

"You can use the phone in the study."

Alex's intuition of danger grew as he waited for Metcalfe to answer.

"Greywood House."

"Metcalfe, is that you?" Relief filled Alex's voice. "Are you all right?"

"Quite, my lord. Is something wrong?"

Alex grinned sheepishly. For once the old blood sense was wrong, probably the effect of being in love. Desperately and hopelessly in love.

"Just a feeling I had. Any calls?"

"Three from your office, one from Hong Kong. Another two from the Estavian mission. I believe that makes four from them so far today."

Alex snorted. "They don't give up, do they? Any more news on St. Cyr?"

"I'm afraid his condition remains the same."

"Anything from Sir Gordon Mount?"

"No, my lord."

Alex felt a stirring at his neck. The third clue would have been the key. Without it, they could search forever and still not find the sword.

He frowned.

The key.

Once again, he had the sense of dim images twisting around him. "The key. Of course."

"My lord, I—" There was a rustling on the line, then a muffled thump.

"Metcalfe?"

No answer.

"Metcalfe, are you there?"

The line clicked once, then went dead.

Alex's face settled into hard lines of anger. Darkness burned through his blood: *danger*. He ran to the kitchen. "Marston?"

"Is there anything I can do for you, my lord?"

"Keep ringing Greywood. Something's wrong over there, and I'm going to take a look. Meanwhile, keep close to Ms. Russell. See that she stays here at the abbey. Whatever you do," Alex said grimly, "do not let her leave until I return."

"I understand, my lord. Consider it done."

Greywood House was silent. Deathly silent.

The key.

When two are one, together paired, the enchantment will begin.

Alex ran down the front hall. At the kitchen, he stopped, cursing as he tripped over a table upended by the door. Then he saw the chaos beyond.

Two chairs were broken in two. Shattered china covered the floor, and flowers were dumped across the cabinets.

"Metcalfe?" The alarm in his blood screamed. The key was here if only he wasn't too late.

"Metcalfe, where are you?"

Something creaked behind the glass partition at the far side of the kitchen. Picking up a butcher's knife, Alex crept through the broken glass until he came to the side of the partition.

Metcalfe was struggling to rise, blood streaking his brow, his clothing all awry.

"Stay still, Metcalfe. Let me get some ice for your head."

"I—I tried to stop them, my lord."

"Steady now. Don't talk." Alex pulled a bottle of cooking sherry from the mess. "Drink this first."

The butler complied, and his hand tightened on Alex's arm. "There were two of them. They wanted to know where you were, when you would be back. I told them nothing. No matter what they did."

Alex bit back a curse, knowing Marston's stubbornness might have cost him his life. "What happened then?"

"They were looking for something. A key, I think. They went through every drawer. When they couldn't open the door to your study, they were furious." Metcalfe touched his head gingerly and winced.

"You did all you could, Metcalfe. More than I would have asked. Can you manage on your own here for a few minutes?"

The key.

"Perfectly." Metcalfe smiled shakily. "Just see you leave that bottle of sherry when you go."

Alex headed for the stairs. Already his mind was racing.

He found the old rocking horse in the nursery, lit by a bar of sunlight. The key gleamed, hanging from the hand-painted mane.

He told me he wanted you to have something to remember him by. Geordie Hamilton's words echoed through his head.

Something that would last forever.

Alex felt his blood roar as he stared at the chipped toy his father had made for him so long ago.

He even hammered the key around its neck.

He reached out slowly, remembering his father's stiff formality and the silence he let speak for his heart.

Here was the key, emblem of the love that his father could never express.

Alex's fingers traced the chipped paint, the staring eyes, the rough, handmade key to a door that had been forever closed.

He nearly cried out at the explosion of images. He saw it all, the misted Highlands, the desperate messages, and then the shouts of angry soldiers.

English soldiers.

Alex sank to his knees, arms to his chest, while the memories battered through him.

The key to my faith has no lock and no limit. Like the blade itself, it burns and shimmers.

So real, he thought blindly. As real as the regret and fury he had tasted then as Angus Cameron, torn by honor from the woman he loved. He could almost hear the claymore whispering to him, calling him back to a forgotten duty. A cursed duty at war with his heart.

Then the blood sense made him look down. A paper was shoved in a crack just behind the horse's ear. Alex's fingers trembled as he opened the yellowed sheet and read his father's careful slanting script.

The last riddle: the Heart, which is the Key to Forever.

Only when given does the heart prosper. Only when shared does love take wing. When man and woman stand together, hearts entwined, the riddle will be solved. Like scabbard and sword, their power will rise beyond all evil.

Love is the magic and the key. Find the still, sweet yearning in the heart and cherish it well, you of Cameron blood. This is the hardest secret and the greatest power.

Let the heart lead the way. Then and only then will the real treasure be yours.

Hear who would hear.

Alex swallowed as he studied the slanting words. His father must have copied the old words from the Cameron notebook, leaving a trail for Alex to follow. Alex could sense his father's bitter regret and his hope that the sword might never be found, for if found, it would one day have to be turned over to a government he abhorred.

But he had left his son this final clue along with the key.

Alex felt the sword now, felt its silent silver call from high in the abbey's Long Gallery. And he prayed that Sir Gordon hadn't found the sword first.

* * *

Rachel McTiernan looked up from her notebook and frowned. "Did you hear that, Harrison?"

"Hear what, my love?"

"A thump. Over near the old tunnels."

"Couldn't be." Her husband frowned down at the dirt-encrusted edges of an old amphora and shook his head. "Must be thunder. No one's allowed in those tunnels. It's far too dangerous."

Rachel's eyes narrowed. "I suppose you're right." When the odd sound was not repeated, she sighed and turned back to her meticulous reconstruction of the stone circle that she and Peter had recently surveyed.

30

DIMITRI DROVE fast, talking all the while with Peter. "After your ride, I will show you how to use the cards. A trick to make the ace appear, then a trick to make the fours disappear. You will like this, no?"

Peter nodded eagerly as he sat in the backseat next to Lady Sefton. "I'm not very good at cards. My mom says it's because I have an honest face."

"To have honest face is good, Peter Russell. This is right, Lady Sefton?"

"Very right, Dimitri." As Kelly slid her arm around Peter, she saw that his eyes were growing heavy. "Would you like to rest for a while?"

The boy nodded. "Just for a little. Don't let me miss anything."

Oh, to be young again, she thought. "I wouldn't dream of it."

Peter's head drooped. Within minutes, he was asleep. Kelly surreptitiously rubbed her back.

"It hurts you, no?" Dimitri watched her from the rearview mirror.

"Sometimes."

"More than that, I think." His brown eyes crinkled. "You do not speak of it. You do not like to worry that big husband of yours."

"Very fanciful of you, Dimitri." Kelly winced as they took a sharp turn, and she noticed that he lowered his speed after that. "Tell me about Alex. What was he like in Russia with his mother when you first met him?"

Dimitri's eyes sparkled. "The boy marches into our camp like fat White Russian general, all boastful talk and him scrawny as young pup. But his eyes, how full of fire. He runs away from his mother, angry at the whole world." Dimitri's voice fell. "Mostly at the father who lets him leave England and the country which does not permit him to return. A great shame. Some will say he lost many years in Estavia, but my father sees the fire in Alexei's eyes. He teaches him when no one else can, makes him contact his mother and tell her he is safe. Then begins his training at the fire, learning to bend and shape and curse a blade into life." Dimitri shook his head. "He is mad, that one. Wilder than even my father as a boy. The way of the sword is strong in him, and he accepts nothing less than the best."

Kelly savored the exotic tale. "But what happened when he finally returned to England? Alex doesn't like to talk about those years."

The big man shrugged. "Good but also bad years for Alexei."

"What about Jacques St. Cyr? Are he and Alex enemies because of Nathalie?"

Dimitri made a derisive sound. "Is fault of St. Cyr, who is hard as frozen horse dung. Still, he is father. Alexei takes something more precious than sword from him. When Alex and Nathalie marry, it is very sudden."

Kelly sighed. "St. Cyr is still bitter. And Alex has never really forgotten."

"Is not good memories for him. Her father is very angry. Books thrown. Police called. Alex and Nathalie go off to Greece for six months for father to cool. But he does not. Only more anger. And then . . ."

"Then she left," Kelly said slowly. "That much of the story I do know. And that the shadows are still with him."

The big Gypsy sighed. "But some shadows come before light, no?"

"Yes," Kelly said, remembering her own time of shadows and the man who had rescued her from their horror. She frowned as they rounded a curve. "What's that?"

"Car in road. There is broken tire, I think."

"You mean a flat?" Kelly frowned. "Is someone bending down by the rear wheel?"

Dimitri slowed the car. "I stop and give them help."

Kelly sat very still. "Perhaps we should wait, Dimitri."

"Is trouble. We must help."

"Dimitri—"

Kelly's protest was lost in the creak of the door. Her eyes darkened as the big Gypsy strode toward the car slanted across the road.

A black Citroën.

Then Kelly stiffened. Three men were moving out of the trees.

Joanna awoke to a growling wind. The abbey study was veiled in shadows, all light swallowed by a bank of angry racing clouds. She blinked, then burrowed back beneath the blanket with a smile.

Alex.

The lies were done. There would be no more waking with dark memories. From now on it would be Alex's warm hands that coaxed her from sleep.

But where was he? Joanna looked at her watch. He should have been back by now. She slipped on her shoes and picked up the phone, dialing her parents at the dig site.

"Sussex Roman Site."

"Mother, it's Joanna."

"Hello, my love. Are you coming by for dinner? We're having clay-roasted chicken with rosemary and basil tonight. Harrison is doing the honors. I thought you might like to ask your young man. Lord and Lady Sefton also."

Your young man.

Joanna felt a crazy grin spread over her face. "I'm not sure I can. Something has come up. Peter will be coming with me to Lord Greywood's."

"Lovely. I liked the man on sight. He has good hands."

"Humm." Her mother was right, Joanna thought.

"He makes a fine lover, I expect."

"Mother."

Rachel McTiernan laughed complacently. "Shocking, isn't it?"

"Has Peter returned yet?"

"It's far too early. He was to go riding with Kelly and Michael."

"Yes, but—"

"Stop worrying, my love. The boy has got to spread his wings sometime. So do you," her mother said pointedly. "I'm sure Peter will be fine. That nice Mr. Dimitri was with him after all."

Joanna sighed. "I suppose you're right. It's just that some strange things have been happening."

"Not here, they aren't. Look, Joanna, I'm afraid I'd better go. I can see two of the new volunteers having trouble with the new wall—" Abruptly, her voice caught. "Good heavens."

"Mother? What is it?"

"It's an ambulance. It's—" The phone fell with a clatter. Joanna heard sounds of movement and falling papers.

"Mother, answer me."

The phone struck something hard. Joanna heard a new voice. "This is Officer Pettit. Who am I speaking with?"

"Joanna Russell. I'm the daughter of the McTiernans. Is something wrong?"

The officer cleared his throat. "Peter Russell is your son, I believe?"

Joanna felt the telephone shake in her fingers. "Yes, he is." *Dear God, not Peter. Please, please, not Peter.*

"I see. You had better come as quickly as you can." Thunder rumbled in the distance. "I'm afraid there has been an accident."

* * *

"Marston?" Alex gripped his car phone, squinting as a bolt of lightning struck the giant oak in Greywood's circular drive. Static hissed in his ear, then faded. "What's happening there?"

"I tried to phone you at Greywood, my lord. There was no answer."

"The line was cut," Alex said tightly. "How is Joanna?"

"She left, my lord."

"Left? *When,* damn it?"

"No more than five minutes ago. That blasted woman from the tour was here again. When I came back, Ms. Russell was running for her car. She said something about Peter and an accident at the dig site. Dear Lord, I trust the boy is not seriously hurt."

"Peter." Alex felt as if a hammer had slammed down onto his chest. "Oh, God, no."

"One more thing, my lord." Marston sounded confused. "The woman from the tour—she simply vanished. But after she'd gone, I found—"

"You found what?" Alex's voice was hard.

"The armoire's doors had been forced open, and there was a panel removed from the back."

The sword. They have it now. Alex cursed softly. The images were too sharp to doubt.

"Shall I call the police, my lord?"

"First call Michael Burke at home, Marston. Tell him to meet me at the McTiernans' dig site. *Then* call the police."

Rain splattered over the courtyard and rocked Greywood's towering elms. Alex slammed the car right, fishtailed on a patch of mud, then careened onto the main road. The car skidded wildly, but he held the turn, his eyes grim as he roared north into the rain.

Fingers of lightning flashed over the abbey. Thunder rolled across the valley, past the broad tree-lined drive, past the Witch's Pool and the roses clustered along the moat. At a high window near the roof, light whirled and circled, then focused on a point before the magnificent old armoire.

"Will she come?"

Adrian Draycott's voice was grim. "We can only hope."

"But now they have the sword."

"With the binding spell gone, there is an opening. Good or bad, the strongest will claim the sword now. That is the danger."

Two shapes took form, wreathed in gold light. The man was broad at the shoulder, clad all in black save for the lace that fluttered at cuff and collar. Behind him stood a woman, her beautiful face set in lines of worry.

"What will happen now?"

Adrian Draycott's ghostly features flickered. "That will be up to them."

"But the past is *done!* Why can't they let it be finished?"

"Is the past ever truly finished?" Frowning, Adrian traced the fleur-de-lis and the crooked dragon carved on the armoire.

"We made it so," the woman beside him said. "With our faith and our love."

Lightning clawed at the sky, and the trees began to pitch and heave. Adrian sighed. "So we did."

"Unless you act tonight, people will die. People who have rendered service to your beloved abbey."

"Do you think I can forget?" The abbey ghost flung up one hand, lace agleam. The air seemed to shake. "Lest you forget, I, too, am bound by rules, Gray. My power is held to the abbey itself. I cannot go beyond it."

Gray Mackenzie, the woman he loved, studied the shattered panel of the old armoire. Her dark eyes filled with excitement. "You may not, but *she* may."

"This is madness, Gray."

"She has stayed here too long, Adrian, haunted by a message that was never conveyed. Send her now. Free her. Let her go in search of her long-lost message and the claymore that held it."

Lightning flared, bathing Adrian's hard features in cold light. "You are wise beyond my deserving. It would be possible, I suppose. But she must be summoned and then convinced."

"I shall convince her," said Gray, "as one woman to another. But first we must find her."

Together they stood before the armoire, their hands linked. Slowly, a heaviness filled the room. Sadness swirled around them like clouds.

"Who stands whispering to me?" The voice came first and then the figure itself. A tall woman, she wore her black gown with stiff pride. A headdress of lace crowned her auburn hair. Her shoes were black, of Spanish leather, and her hands cradled a prayer book and rosary. "Has my answer come?" she whispered. "Has the Cameron returned with the sword at last? Or has he betrayed me like all the others?"

"There is another Cameron come, my lady," Gray Mackenzie said softly. "Great death will be done tonight unless you intervene."

"I am but a captive here, betrayed. Cursed to wait and wonder."

Adrian spoke now. "You are free to go, as you have always been free. There are no gates that can hold you now."

Cold air seemed to spin through the room. "Free. But how? And where shall I find my answer?"

"Your sword and its scabbard shall lead you."

The heaviness in the room grew. Outside the window, rain clawed angrily at the roof.

And then the pale queen nodded, her face suffused with excitement. "I feel them now. They are close, and my answers with them. We bid you thanks, Lord Draycott. We shall bear you Our goodwill always."

Her grave form moved past the armoire, past the fine old paintings and the cut velvet curtains. As lightning exploded through the sky, she merged into the abbey's thick walls, then bled away into the night.

31

JOANNA SQUINTED through the rain, searching for the narrow turnoff. Finally, she saw the light swinging wildly above the weathered sign to the Roman dig site. She eased into the tight turn, her wheels tossing up mud from a bank already deeply grooved with rain. Holding her jacket over her head, Joanna ran to the stone house that served as her parents' office.

"Mother?" she called. "Is anyone there?"

Lightning cracked, illuminating a figure behind the desk. The big chair swiveled slowly.

Joanna frowned when she saw the person sitting in the darkness. "Sir Gordon? But what are you doing here?"

A shutter banged in the wind. "Protecting my investment. Getting repaid for too many years of taking orders from Jacques St. Cyr." Calmly, the solicitor flipped on a light.

"Where's Peter?" Joanna hissed, her nails digging into the wood of the door. "What have you done with my son?"

Sir Gordon rose from the chair. "I have done nothing to Peter. He is very like you, isn't he? Very clever. Very imaginative."

"If you've hurt him, I'll kill you."

"Peter is fine." The solicitor frowned. "Though for how long, I cannot say."

"What do you mean?" Joanna threw herself at him, hammering at his chest.

339

He scowled as he caught her fists. "Peter is in the house with your parents. For now he is safe."

"And you've come after the claymore."

Sir Gordon smiled faintly. "Not at all. We already have the claymore. It was in the armoire all the time."

Behind Joanna the door creaked. She caught the drifting hint of perfume, a mix of lavender and roses.

"Ah, Sir Gordon. I see that you've welcomed our new guest."

Joanna turned. Her eyes narrowed.

"Do you recognize me without the hat, Ms. Russell? And without that rather common accent? Unfortunately, both were necessary. I did not wish to be noticed during your tour."

Joanna stared angrily at the woman in the hat who had been so talkative during the morning tour of the abbey. "What do you want?"

"But surely, Ms. Russell, you already know that." The woman's lips curved. "I want the Cameron claymore and the treasure hidden inside it, of course."

"There's no proof that the sword holds anything."

"It is *fact*," the woman hissed. "I have the proof of it right here." She held out a square of parchment yellowed and brittle with age. "This came from inside the armoire. The document witnesses that a priceless object is hidden inside the sword. The signature is that of Mary Stuart herself. Now perhaps you will not be so skeptical."

"I don't believe any of this. Who *are* you?" Joanna was bothered by something about the woman's face. Something that was almost familiar.

"You mean your darling Alex didn't tell you?" The cool lips curved. "I am his wife, of course. Nathalie St. Cyr. The daughter of Jacques St. Cyr."

Alex's fingers tightened on the wheel. He cursed at the rain that fell in heavy sheets, covering the road.

He thought of Peter's face, eager and keen as they parried over the abbey lawns. He remembered his burst of boyish laughter when he mastered a move and managed to corner his teacher.

Keep him safe, Alex prayed fiercely. *And keep his mother safe along with him.*

"You're *Jacques's* daughter?" Joanna didn't mention the rest, too stunned to consider that information yet.

"My father and I had a rather abysmal parting of the ways. Over money, as always." The keen eyes glittered, and Joanna saw how much they were like Jacques's eyes. "How dreary he could be."

"He never mentioned you."

"No, I don't expect he would. He wasn't exactly delighted when Alex and I were married. I don't suppose I was thinking very straight myself. Alex was such a healthy male animal, with all that lovely sexual energy just waiting to be tapped. And he was bitter, which opened him to my influence." Her eyes hardened. "Not quite open enough, as it turned out. But all that is past history now. We have far more important things to discuss tonight." She gestured to Sir Gordon, who lifted a box from the floor.

Joanna recognized it immediately. "The scabbard," she whispered.

"But of course." Nathalie St. Cyr carefully lifted the jeweled metal from the box. "And now the other package, Sir Gordon."

The solicitor carefully lifted a bundle onto the table.

Joanna's breath caught as light spilled over the curving hilt of an ancient Scottish claymore.

"This one is quite real, I assure you," Nathalie said smugly. "The envelope holding Jacques's last clue was empty, so we checked the armoire after you two spent so much time up in the Long Gallery. The expression on your face during the tour told me you suspected the sword was there."

"How did you find it?"

"We simply cut open the doors of the armoire, removed the panel, and *voilà.*" Her eyes hardened. "Dear Alex is not so clever as he thought."

"Why do you hate him so?"

Cold laughter rang through the room. "Because I was supposed to manipulate *him,* to use him as I chose against my father. But I discovered that Alex Cameron had too much steel for that. In truth, he and Jacques were very much alike. Alex refused any money from his own father. Greywood Foundation and all its assets were built up by him through his own planning. You didn't know that either, did you?"

Joanna shook her head.

"He wanted only to be an artist. A poet in steel. He vowed to make his own success without any help from his family. And that is exactly what he did." Nathalie's lips pursed. "How stupid he was, scrimping every day. No money for cars or clothes even though his doting father would have sent him anything he wanted. Unlike *mine.*"

Joanna frowned. "So you walked out on him?"

Nathalie shrugged. "An inelegant phrase but an accurate one. I hadn't selected him so carefully just to languish in poverty until he could make a success of himself, damn him! But I realized there were ways to make the separation profitable to me." She laughed tightly. "I told Jacques that Alex had lied to me, mistreated me. I even made the bruises to prove it. My dear father was livid." She laughed again. "It suited his pride to hate a competitor, of course."

"You bitch," Joanna breathed.

The woman eased a revolver from her pocket. "Am I? Perhaps. But now, Ms. Russell, you will open the sword for us and find its treasure."

Joanna swallowed. Wild laughter built in her throat. "I *can't.* The clues make no sense."

Nathalie St. Cyr's black eyes narrowed. "Very well. I only hope you will be equally calm as you watch your son and your parents being buried beneath ten tons of earth." She moved to the door, and a tall man with an expressionless face stepped inside. "Ms. Russell, meet Pavel Orlov, chief trade officer of the Estavian government. At least that's what he *says* he is."

The man crossed the room soundlessly.

"Bring her," Nathalie ordered.

As they walked through the rainy darkness, Joanna clutched her purse tightly, shivering. Sir Gordon Mount walked at her side, a gun to her back, while the Estavian followed several feet behind, scanning the nearby paths.

"Murder, theft, and intimidation," Joanna said tightly. "How could you do these things?

Sir Gordon shrugged. "The end always justifies the means, Ms. Russell. And I have waited a very long time to taste my revenge against Jacques St. Cyr. I suggest you come up with answers quickly, because Nathalie is not a patient woman. Simon Loring learned that to his misfortune."

"Simon was working with you?"

"It was his idea. He found Nathalie and convinced her to help." The Englishman shoved her forward. "Move."

Joanna stumbled, and as she struggled to right herself, her hand brushed her purse. She felt a sharp, unfamiliar outline. Her fingers slid over cold metal.

The receiver that Alex had given her.

Hidden by the darkness, Joanna found the small button and pressed down as Alex had instructed, praying that the reception would be adequate. "Very clever of you, Sir Gordon. Now you have both the scabbard and the claymore you stole from the armoire." She spoke clearly, filling in the gaps and hoping that Alex would understand. "But what makes you think I can open the sword for you?"

"You are very clever, Ms. Russell. Jacques was most confident you could solve his riddle. Otherwise he would never have left you those clues."

"And if I don't? Are you going to kill me and everyone else at the dig site? Will it be my parents first followed by Peter?"

Sir Gordon laughed tightly. "Don't forget about Lady Sefton and the man called Dimitri. Solve the secret for us and you will be free."

Joanna eased the receiver higher in her purse. "*You*

might say that, but what about the others working with you?" She thought wildly, trying to provide Alex with as much information as possible. She pointed to the man named Orlov, who had moved to check a row of steps. "What will Nathalie St. Cyr and this man Orlov say?"

"All the Estavians want is the sword. They are obsessed with how they can use it to control the arrogant Lord Greywood in certain business ventures he has proposed for their country. There was some sort of agreement with his father, and they are determined to force Greywood into providing them the best possible political assistance here in England. His inside information is nearly worth the price of the sword. Not that the Estavians will ever be allowed to have it," he added coldly.

"You can hardly split the discovery with Nathalie and offer it to Orlov's people at the same time."

"We can *offer* anything we like." The solicitor shrugged. "The details will be worked out."

"The end justifies the means again? And what about us? You'll never let us go, knowing all we do."

"You will stay here until we have what we want." They were nearly at the far side of the camp now, their way lit by a row of narrow electric lights, haloed in the rain.

Joanna stiffened. "Not *here!*"

"Keep moving," he ordered.

"That's the old tunnel system. Sweet God, it was hacked out by amateurs in the forties! It's a death trap. You can't take us in *there.*"

Orlov moved forward, his face unreadable. "It will serve its temporary use."

"Coward."

For a moment, his hands clenched on Joanna's arm, and she was terrified he would feel the outline of the receiver. But he only shoved her forward, cursing. "Open the sword, Ms. Russell, or their deaths will rest on you."

Joanna released the receiver just as he pushed her down the muddy track and into the abandoned tunnels.

* * *

Alex's hands shook with rage on the steering wheel as he listened to the ragged voices drift in and out of the static.

"—clever of you, Sir Gordon. So now you have both the scabbard and the claymore."

"—you going to kill me and everyone else at the dig site?"

Sweet God, was Orlov in on this with Nathalie St. Cyr?

Alex cursed harshly as the pieces of the puzzle slammed home. He had had his own suspicions about Nathalie's possible involvement, but he had never suspected Orlov.

He glanced grimly at his watch—fifteen minutes until he reached the dig site. Joanna had cleverly laid out all the details for him, including the warning about the old tunnels. She was frightened but managing to stay alert.

He jabbed out Michael's number on the cellular phone. The last thing they needed was for an angry ex–Royal Marine Commando to charge into the middle of things without knowing the exact situation.

Alex frowned at the darkness and the sheeting rain, thinking. Thinking desperately.

32

THE NARROW chamber was thick with dust in the criss-crossed beams of three flashlights. Nathalie St. Cyr crouched beside the blanket carrying the Cameron claymore and the beautiful jeweled scabbard. She muttered as she shoved the long blade into the scabbard, then dug wildly at the hilt. "Open. *Open,* damn you."

Frowning, Sir Gordon pushed Joanna down the incline.

"Shoving and hammering will only break the sword," Orlov said sharply. "Then neither of us will have what we want."

Nathalie rose, cursing softly. Joanna's face went white as she saw Dimitri stretched unconscious in one corner. Beside him sat Peter, Kelly, and Joanna's parents, their hands behind their backs. "Dear God, let them go. I'll do whatever I can for you—just let them go."

Thunder hammered through the sky as Nathalie laughed. "Find the treasure and then we'll discuss it, my dear."

Sir Gordon shoved Joanna down beside the blanket and gave her the scabbard. "You must be quick," he hissed. "Her patience will not last long."

The sword was magnificent, its long blade marked by only a few patches of tarnish. Light played over the cold silver almost as if the metal were alive.

Joanna's hands trembled as she studied the priceless old sword. "Hold up that light," she said fiercely. If there was an answer, she would have to find it now. "Let me have a better look."

She remembered Jacques's note. *When two are one, together paired, the enchantment will begin.*

Frowning, she studied the shape of blade and hilt.

Metal gleamed, and the dented hilt showed the scars of hard use in battle. The grip was long, made to accommodate two hands in a thrust of stunning force. *Claidheamh mór,* it was called. The name suited its ancient power.

Joanna slid one finger along the blade, wishing that the cold metal could whisper all its secrets.

Had it truly been used in the defense of Mary, Queen of Scots, when ruthless men had tried to assassinate her while she was being held at Draycott Abbey? Had she repaid her stalwart protector, Angus Cameron, by hiding a treasure in the sword?

Joanna turned into the light. The blade was perfectly balanced and its hilt was smooth to her touch, but there were no fine jewels or gold to satisfy the old legend. Yet for a moment, as light played over the blade, she felt the sword vibrate deep within the metal and she seemed to hear the clang of steel on steel.

The ruby on the scabbard winked in the lantern light as Joanna thought of the biblical verses she and Alex had seen on the page of illuminated text decorated with the tree and the dove.

But where shall wisdom be found? It cannot be gotten for gold, neither shall silver be weighed for the price thereof.

She frowned, struggling to remember the rest, and then as she touched the single exquisite gem, the line came to her.

For the price of wisdom is above rubies.

Her breath caught as she fingered the scabbard.

The *ruby* was the key. She touched the scabbard, then

slowly traced the dragon and the fleur-de-lis on the sword.

This dragon did not appear to be crooked. Could that be significant?

A gust of cold air moved through the room, digging at Joanna's hair and rushing over her fingers, almost as if it were searching for the blade below her hand. Goose bumps rose over her skin. Had a shadow moved at the edge of her vision?

She shoved away the wild thought. She had no time for hallucinations.

The page marked in the Cameron Bible had been Job, chapter 28. And the last verse about the rubies—yes, verse 18. Could the numbers be some kind of code?

Carefully Joanna slid the claymore into its scabbard, then touched the two tiny rivets above the ruby.

"Nothing's happening. Open the sword or they will all die," Nathalie said furiously. "Make it *work*."

Joanna noticed Orlov moving toward Kelly and Peter in the corner, and her heart lurched. She *had* to open the sword.

As she crouched in the cold dirt, Joanna felt some desperate instinct guide her hands over the sword.

For the price of wisdom is above rubies.

Almost of their own accord, her fingers moved over the rivets, lifting one and pushing the other. Two times, eight times. Then the lower rivet: one time, eight times, like the numbers in the Bible.

Somewhere deep inside the scabbard, metal turned. There was a hollow click, and Joanna felt the hilt vibrate.

But before she could complete the proper movements, Nathalie St. Cyr cried out, grabbing wildly for the scabbard. Joanna tried to block her, but the sword tumbled to the hard earth.

"Damn it, what have you *done?*" Orlov shoved Nathalie back as she cursed in anger. "You will open the sword now." He picked up the sword and thrust it into Joanna's hands.

Joanna frowned. "It looks as if it might be broken."

"Then fix it," he ordered coldly.

"Yes, fix it!" Nathalie screamed. "Soon everything will collapse in here, walls and all. I saw to that earlier today. If you fail, you will all die here tonight."

Joanna's eyes narrowed on the Estavian, who merely shrugged. "She is right. It is just as well for us to cover our tracks."

"A big bang and then no evidence left, you see?" Nathalie gave a high laugh.

So they mean to kill all of us, Joanna thought. *No evidence.*

Behind them a rock skittered down the entrance passage. Alex stumbled out of the darkness, his face bruised and his hands bound behind him.

Orlov turned. He frowned at the man nudging Alex forward with a gun. "He came alone?"

"Yes, Your Excellency. There was none other."

"You fool! He is too clever to come alone. There must be others. Go back and check."

"What's going on here?" Alex seemed confused. "Kelly? Why are you on the ground? And you, Orlov— What are you doing here?" Then his eyes focused on the woman at the wall with a flashlight in her hands. Joanna saw his body stiffen with disbelief. *"Nathalie?"*

His ex-wife frowned. "Shut up, Alex. Your beautiful Ms. Russell must not be disturbed while she works with the sword."

Alex blinked at Joanna. "You have the claymore? I don't understand."

"The treasure is inside the sword. It was more than a legend, you fool." Nathalie St. Cyr played her flashlight over the blade, which shimmered in the bright beam. "Open it, damn you!"

Joanna closed her eyes. The numbers of the biblical verse had worked once. She would try them again.

She gripped the long, curved hilt, twisting twice to the left and eight times to the right. She held her breath, too dazed to wonder where her intuition had come from.

Beside her the wall began to shudder.

"Nathalie, what did you do?" Sir Gordon growled. "We'll all be killed in here!"

Nathalie St. Cyr's eyes were dark pools of madness. "I destabilized the beams enough to make our work tonight easier." She ran one red-tipped nail over Peter's cheek. "Do you understand me, Ms. Russell? You'd better work faster, hadn't you?"

Joanna bit back her fury, looking down at the sword. She pulled gently at the scabbard and felt it begin to shift.

Without warning, the earth rocked again, and they were suddenly plunged into darkness. Joanna had a blurred impression of cold air and the sound of Alex cursing. She dropped the sword, and a body hit the ground. Something hurtled past her feet.

A beam of light cut the darkness, and Joanna saw Orlov struggling with Alex near the wall.

When she turned, Nathalie and Peter were gone.

The ground was still shaking as she grabbed Sir Gordon's flashlight and plunged blindly into the musty tunnels after her son.

33

"WHERE'S JOANNA?" Alex whirled around, searching the darkness. Orlov lay unmoving on the dark earth.

"She—she went into the tunnel." Harrison McTiernan pushed stiffly to his feet as Alex cut his ropes. "That terrible woman took Peter and the sword."

"What about Sir Gordon?"

"He must have bolted when the lights went out."

Alex cursed. He looked down at Kelly Burke, whose face was very pale. "How are you doing, love?"

"Fine," she said, but her lips were tight with pain. "Only I think it might not be too long now . . ."

Sweat broke out on Alex's brow. "Michael is on his way. Don't worry, he'll make it."

Rachel McTiernan took Kelly's hand in a strong grip. "Lady Sefton is going to be just fine. Harrison, go fetch some blankets. Take that nice Mr. Dimitri with you and bring us back a pot of boiling water."

"Shouldn't she be in the house?" her husband asked.

Rachel shook her head. "No time." The earth walls shuddered, and she patted Kelly's hand briskly. "They taught you about breathing, didn't they?"

"More than I wanted to know."

"Good. We'll be starting on that in a minute. Just relax, because we're going to get you up that passage and into the van that's nearby. We'll manage fine there. Harrison will escort that unpleasant Mr. Orlov up and lock him in a storage shed."

Kelly stiffened as a wave of pain shot through her. "Oh, God, where is Michael?"

"He'll be along soon. Meanwhile, we're going to focus on breathing." Joanna's mother smiled calmly. "I've delivered more than a few babies, my dear. Out in the wilds of Crete, I'm considered quite a miracle worker."

"You are?" Kelly smiled tentatively. "So what are w-we waiting for?"

Harrison concealed his surprise and helped Dimitri to his feet. "Can you stand up, Mr. Dimitri?"

"Just Dimitri, please." The Gypsy nodded, his face flushed. "And yes, of course. Will be honor to help with baby of Lady Sefton."

Kelly looked at Alex. "What about you?"

"I'm going after Joanna and Peter."

"But the walls—what that crazy woman did—"

"Just see that you take care of my beautiful godchild," Alex called back.

Joanna could hear the walls shifting as she ran through the tunnel, listening for voices. Dust drifted everywhere, veiling the beam of her flashlight. She had to fight to keep from sneezing because any sharp noise would give away her presence to Nathalie St. Cyr, and Joanna knew that surprise was her greatest weapon now. There was an old trench somewhere to her right. If she remembered correctly, it branched once, then led back to the main tunnel.

She played her light carefully over a dark wall of earth, where the tunnel narrowed sharply. Joanna shivered when she saw that the trench opening was far smaller than she had remembered, barely a crawl space.

Fighting back her panic, she slid inside, the flashlight gripped in one hand as she pushed herself through the tight passage. Thirty yards to go, she told herself, trying not to think of the tons of earth shifting above her. Instead, she kept Peter's face in her mind as she pulled herself forward, breathing hoarsely. Only a few more minutes, she told herself.

If the walls lasted that long.

"Stay there. Don't move an inch."

Peter's face was very pale in the beam of Nathalie St. Cyr's flashlight. "I *won't*."

"You'll be damned sorry if you don't." Nathalie sank to the passage floor and studied the Cameron claymore, pushing at the hilt until she heard a hollow rattle. "Damn it, why won't the bloody thing open?"

"Maybe you have to press it a certain way," Peter said tentatively.

"Did your mother tell you that?"

Peter shook his head. "No, but that's what she would do. She always says to think a problem through until it makes sense."

"The perfect little mother," Nathalie said mockingly. "And the perfect little son. Too bad you'll both die if I don't get this damned sword open."

Peter started to say something, then his hands fisted shakily behind his back. His mouth was tight with fear as the woman shoved angrily at the old claymore. Then his eyes widened. Two feet down the tunnel he saw an opening in the wall. There in the shadows Joanna was crouched, one finger to her lips. His whole face brightened, and he nodded covertly.

"Damn it, hold the light on the sword!"

Reluctantly, Peter moved toward his half-crazed captor. As he did, the ground heaved, dirt and small stones raining down from the ceiling.

Nathalie laughed wildly. "Frightens you, does it? Makes you see how close you are to dying." Laughing still, she bent her head and clawed savagely at the hilt without noticeable effect. "Damn all the Camerons and damnation to Mary, Queen of Scots, too!"

For a moment, cold air skittered through the tunnel. Nathalie looked back, frowning. "I've seen her, you know. She calls out in my dreams. She demands what is hers, but she won't have it. The treasure is mine!"

Peter watched, his face tense with strain.

"Hold the light closer, damn you."

He bent forward, his hands shaking as a wedge of earth dislodged from the ceiling and thundered onto the floor.

"Steady, you fool." Nathalie slapped his hand, then raised the sword. In the shifting dust, the dragon seemed to turn its head and crawl along the great blade.

"Maybe you should twist the hilt," Peter said quietly. "That's what my mother did."

Down the passage, Joanna crept silently closer.

"Maybe I should. Once to the right and twice to the left, wasn't it?" Her head bent, nearly concealed by a cloud of dust as the walls swayed and the wooden beams creaked in angry protest.

Joanna motioned Peter to move toward her.

Slowly, he inched backward. He was nearly at the fallen mound of earth when Nathalie looked up. "Where do you think you're going? Get back here." Then her eyes narrowed. "Only this time bring your perfect little mother with you." Her voice hardened. "*Now,* Ms. Russell." Her pistol leveled. "Before I shoot him the same way I shot Simon Loring."

Alex heard the voices, tantalizingly close. He ran harder, desperately devising a plan to divert Nathalie's anger onto himself long enough for Peter and Joanna to escape. But as he rounded the corner, his hope gave out.

The tunnel was blocked by a solid mass of earth where the ceiling had given way.

"Joanna!" he cried wildly into the heaving dust.

"Alex can't help you now, can he? No one can help you. Not until you show me the key to the sword."

Joanna's face was streaked with dirt, and blood covered her hands, cut in maneuvering the rocky tunnel. "Let me see it."

Nathalie grabbed the light from Peter's trembling fingers. "The little fool can't even hold a light steady."

Joanna looked up and winked at her son, who gave a shaky smile in answer.

"Move, damn it!" Nathalie jabbed the gun against her side.

"I'm trying." Joanna worked the rivets gently, feeling the metal move, then lock in place.

"Just *open* the bloody thing."

Joanna tried to imagine the hidden inner workings. A spring perhaps. Maybe a cross pin that had to be dislodged when the hilt moved against the scabbard.

Gradually an idea came to her. She felt sweat streak down her face. "Hold the hilt," she ordered Nathalie.

"The boy will do it."

"No, it has to be *you*. He's not strong enough. Something's locked inside, don't you see?"

Her heart was pounding. She prayed the woman would agree. They hadn't much time left.

"All right, damn it. But remember my pistol's right here."

"Take the grip. No, there above the hilt."

Nathalie held the cold steel, now coated with dust. Her fingers tightened.

"Pull when I tell you." Joanna eased to a crouch. Her hands moved over the hilt. "When I say three, I'm going to twist and you'll have to pull as hard as you can."

"Now you're being sensible, little mother."

"One." Joanna looked at Peter and nodded slightly. "Two." She looked at Nathalie, whose eyes were focused on the sword. "Three."

Joanna shoved to her feet and released the scabbard, sending her captor back against the wall with violent force. "Run!" she screamed to Peter. Ignoring her, he ran forward and swept up the sword, followed by the dust-covered scabbard.

"Run!" Joanna cried, pushing him into the smoking tunnel.

Behind them the air filled with falling dirt. Nathalie screamed in fury as Joanna caught Peter's hand and stumbled forward over the jagged piles of fallen earth and rock.

The beams all along the tunnel shuddered, then shifted in a horrible groan of earth and wood. Nathalie was thrown back into the darkness, and her light winked out.

Joanna felt wildly for the wall. "We're going to make it, Peter. Stay close."

"We'll pretend it's an adventure, OK?"

Joanna's throat tightened. "That's right. It will be our very best adventure."

The walls shifted beneath her fingers, and Joanna bit back a cry. It was several hundred feet back to the tunnel mouth. Dear God, how were they going to make it in time?

As she ran, pulling Peter beside her, she saw light gather to her right. Then through the dust she saw Alex, coughing as he ran toward them.

"You have the boy?"

"Peter's fine. But there's no more time. These beams are going to give out any second."

"Go ahead." Alex's face was grim. He turned his beam onto the swaying passage as aftershocks filled the air. Peter began to cough, his fingers tight on Joanna's.

Alex looked at Joanna, his face very hard. "Go."

"Alex, I—"

"Go."

The last beams shook, straining beneath the weight of tons of earth. Alex ran to the wall and braced the main beam with the full weight of his powerful body. "Go *now*."

Forcing back tears, Joanna turned and stumbled forward into the churning dust, Peter clamped to her side.

Behind them, deep in the earth, they felt a low tremor begin, growling malevolently as it raced toward them.

34

Stones fell on their heads. Peter was crying.

Joanna shoved the tears and dust from her face, struggling upward as the earth pitched around them. Then she felt cold air strike her face from somewhere above.

"The opening—it's there, Peter. Go on, love." She shoved upward, pushing him toward the faint opening where she saw stars twinkling high in the night sky.

His head was through, then one shoulder. Joanna cried in relief as she felt him climb free.

Then the storm broke in angry fury. Walls of earth shook free, and suddenly, she was pinned in the hot, choking darkness.

"P-Peter." She coughed, reaching out blindly and finding only earth. "I—love you," she whispered.

The world seemed to blur. Dimly, as if from miles away, she heard Peter crying above the hammer of her own heart.

Darkness all around . . .

Did you feel the same, Mary, when you were betrayed? Did the sword save you from one threat only to bring you a greater darkness?

Then soft laughter stirred the dank air and dim light seemed to gather amid the drifting dust.

Remember me.

The words moved through Joanna's head as cold air whispered over her face like ghostly fingers.

Remember how I waited for my freedom. I trusted their promises. Let this never be forgotten . . .

"I'll remember," Joanna whispered. Her throat burned. Her chest was a mass of pain. Through the shifting dirt, she heard angry, desperate words rasped in a rough, foreign tongue, and a string of oaths. And then her name.

"No more shadows. You're not running away from me ever again."

Calloused fingers groped, circled her wrists, and pulled savagely. Pain slammed through Joanna's arms where Alex fought to lift her up, out from beneath a wall of fallen earth. She felt the desperate strain of his muscles and the stiffness of his fingers.

Suddenly, she was free, struggling from the dust, breathing cold, sweet air and wrapped in Alex's hard arms while Peter shuddered and cried and laughed beside her.

The rain had stopped. Stars winked fiercely against the velvet canopy of the storm-washed sky.

Unspeakably beautiful, Joanna thought, too tired to move. She coughed raggedly, braced against Alex's shoulder while she cradled Peter close.

"How did you get out?" Peter asked Alex shakily.

"I found the side trench at the last moment. Five seconds later, and I'd still be inside there. Odd, I almost felt as if someone were guiding me."

Mary. Joanna felt something twist inside her.

"Mr. Cameron is a hero, isn't he?"

"Yes, a definite hero." Tears skidded down Joanna's cheeks as she stared at Alex's face, black with dirt and lined by a jagged cut across his brow.

Silence fell, rich and dark and sweet with life after the churning death of the tunnels.

"I was afraid. But you came," Peter whispered. "Both of you."

"Always," Joanna said fiercely.

Alex pulled them both closer. *"Always,* Peter. I promise. No matter where you are or what kind of trouble you're in. That's what fathers are for."

"I didn't cry," Peter said proudly. "Not until the very end. I knew the angry lady wouldn't like it. She didn't make it out of the tunnel, did she?"

"I'm afraid not." Joanna felt Alex's arm move around her shoulders. "She was caught in the cave-in."

Out in the darkness puddles of water shimmered beneath the electric lights. The hills were faintly visible in the distance, black against the deep indigo curtain of the sky.

Joanna suddenly sat forward. "What about Kelly?"

"Safe with Michael. Your parents are with her, too. I don't think it will be long now."

"But—"

Then the cry of a baby pierced the night, fiercely human as it announced itself over the last groans of drifting earth, as life will always follow in the wake of death.

Peter sat forward, his eyes bright with awe. "A baby."

Alex smiled. He found Joanna's hand, and their fingers locked tightly. "Michael will be bursting at the seams, every inch the impossible doting father."

Minutes later, Dimitri came running out of the darkness, his dusty face creased in a huge smile. "Alex—Ms. Russell, I am stepfather! Me, Dimitri! Boy will be Ian Montclair Mikhail Dimitri Burke!" he said proudly. "Doctor is on way, but who needs? Mrs. McTiernan and I manage just fine."

"I suppose Kelly helped a little," Alex said, chuckling. "And I believe the word is *godfather*. I see we'll be sharing the responsibility. How is Mikhail looking?"

The Gypsy clucked his tongue. "Not so good. Very pale. I think he goes somewhere to be sick. Mrs. McTiernan, she gives him something to drink."

Abruptly another cry split the air, high and shrill, louder than the first.

Alex looked at Joanna.

Joanna looked at Alex. "Twins?" she whispered.

"Of course. Lady Sefton knew all along, but it was to be surprise for Mikhail," Dimitri said, beaming as if he were the father in question.

"I'll just bet it was a surprise," Alex said. "Twins. Heaven help us."

Then they were all laughing and all crying, arms linked in a tight hugging embrace. Overhead, the stars were sharp as glass where the moon sailed above the trees.

It was a very beautiful night indeed.

Epilogue

"BLAST IT, is the whole *country* coming here?"

The twelfth viscount Draycott scowled at the line of cars crowding the drive in front of the abbey. It was a sunny day three weeks after the tunnel cave-in, and camera crews were already descending, silver high-tech cases in hand. "I thought there were only to be a few friends of Joanna and Alex."

"I wanted them to feel comfortable. Especially Joanna. You know how vulnerable she is." Kacey Draycott frowned at her reflection in the tall cheval glass. "I only hope that this man Alexei Cameron is serious. He has a reputation as a world-class playboy, my love."

Her husband's brow rose. "Are you asking me to check out Alex Cameron?"

"Not exactly. Just talk to him. Be sure he's serious." Kacey Draycott shook her head. "I've always had the sense Joanna had some tragedy in her life. She's been so quiet and reserved. I don't want to see her hurt again, Nicholas."

"At this point I don't know if I'll be able to talk to anyone. There are already thirty cars down there, and the place is crawling with photographers."

"Oh, didn't I tell you?" His wife smiled as she worked at fastening a strand of matched pink pearls that had been an anniversary present from her doting husband. "Jacques St. Cyr is coming, too."

"St. Cyr? That guarantees a three-ring circus. When did the man get out of the hospital?"

"He's made a remarkable recovery. Joanna has been going to see him every day. She and Lord Greywood said it only seemed right for St. Cyr to be here when the Cameron sword was opened, because he was involved in finding the sword."

Nicholas Draycott snorted. "And I suppose St. Cyr just *had* to invite a few more friends, who just *had* to invite several members of the press. Blast it, Kacey, it's a zoo down there, and we just got back from France. I was looking forward to spending some time alone with you."

His wife turned in a swirl of silk and traced his hard jaw. "So was I, my love. But it seems a small enough thing after all they've been through. And they have taken such good care of the abbey in our absence." Her hands slid along his chest.

His eyes closed as her lips moved over his warm skin. "How long do we have?" he asked hoarsely.

"The opening of the sword was to begin at noon. It is now"—silk rustled—"eleven oh-four."

Nicholas Draycott smiled down into her face, his long fingers freeing the silk bow that fastened the dress he had bought her in Paris the week before. "Just enough time."

"But Nicholas, I haven't finished getting ready. My face—"

"Is radiant as always."

"And my hair—"

"Exquisite. Like Burmese silk. I want to feel it spill over my chest." His expression grew determined. "It was wonderful to be with Dominic and Cathlin in France, but we never had any privacy. And I'm not going to wait a minute longer . . ."

Silk whispered, then pooled over the floor. Nicholas made a low, hard sound as he stood looking at his wife's body, still slim after their first child. As beautiful as the day they had met, when she had locked him in a stall in the old stables. His lips curved at the memory.

"What are you smiling at, impossible man?"

"At the way you locked me in the stables."

"I had a perfect right."

"So you did."

"You were arrogant beyond imagining."

"I still am. Michael Burke says my only hope is the touch of a good woman, and *he* should know." His lips met the coral tip of one perfect breast, veiled by sheer silk. "I don't suppose you know any good women who might be available for the next half hour or so?"

Kacey's fingers eased over his chest. "Did you have any particular type in mind? French accent? Black hair?" She snagged his belt. "Green eyes perhaps?"

"Blond. With eyes that put a tropical dawn to shame." Nicholas skimmed her warm skin, feeling the wild skip of her pulse. "The only one for me in this lifetime or any other," he whispered, his voice suddenly very sober. "Believe it, Kacey."

"I believe it." She let her fingers answer and then her lips. Warm and open, making him groan when she touched him with all the confident skill learned in a lifetime—

And maybe more.

Silk rustled. The bed creaked.

"Nicholas, my camisole!"

"Forget the camisole. I'll buy you a dozen more. In fact, I insist upon it, since this one is criminally beautiful."

His leather belt hissed free.

"I'll take you shopping myself," he said hoarsely.

"With greatest pleasure. Starting tomorrow."

Neither noticed the loudspeaker blaring parking directions to the steadily increasing traffic along the abbey's sunlit drive.

"Ms. Russell, how good to see you!"

Metcalfe stood in the middle of Greywood's bright kitchens surrounded by a sea of copper pots, freshly cleaned silver, and yards of damask tablecloths. Smiling, he pushed up his sleeves, maneuvered a copper pan into the oven, then strode over to shake Joanna's hand. "Lord Greywood just returned this morning. He was looking very tired, but he brought Elena's parents back with him. They are staying with Dimitri, I believe."

"I'm so glad to hear it." Joanna toyed nervously with her hair as she stared around the kitchen. "Elena must have been thrilled."

"Quite."

Joanna bit her lip and crossed her arms over her chest.

"He is upstairs," Metcalfe said helpfully.

"Oh."

"He was going to clean up, then rest briefly before the ceremony at the abbey."

"I see." Joanna frowned at a copper kettle.

The butler's eyes flickered over her trench coat. "Is it showing signs of rain again?"

"What? Oh, that. No. That is, you never know." Joanna played with the end of her belt. "If he's resting, I'd better go. This was probably a bad idea. I'll come back when he—"

"If you'll forgive me, I think seeing you would do a world of good for his lordship. He's been irascible as a caged bear these last weeks since the unpleasant incident at the dig site."

"He has?"

"Absolutely. He doesn't eat and he doesn't sleep. Paces like a restless cat, complaining about everything."

"He does?" Joanna said hopefully.

"I'm afraid so. He hasn't . . ." Metcalfe hesitated. "He hasn't spoken with you?"

Joanna's face was very pale. "No, he hasn't." Her fingers linked, twisting nervously. "He's only sent messages through my parents."

"Oh, dear." Metcalfe drummed his fingers on a gleaming copper soup tureen. "I suppose he was worried about settling this business with Elena's parents. He made a quick trip to the U.S., then flew straight on to Munich and caught a train north. Yes, I'm certain all this has to do with Elena."

It was a lie, and they both knew it.

"Look, Metcalfe, I'd better go. Just tell him . . ." Joanna swallowed. "Tell him anything you like."

The butler took a step in front of her and squeezed her shoulder gently. "May I offer some advice? Go up and see him. Just for a few minutes. I'm sure there's a perfectly good reason for his silence."

Joanna shook her head. "I . . . can't, Metcalfe." She shoved her hands into the pockets of her coat.

"Someone needs to do something. If the man stays in *this* frame of mind, I will have to consider handing in my resignation."

Joanna looked shocked. "You couldn't. Greywood would never be the same without you! Surely things aren't that bad?"

Metcalfe shook his head. "It's past time that *someone* took him in hand. The master bedroom is the last door on the right at the end of the first corridor. I suggest you give him hell."

Joanna's eyes took on a determined glitter. "Maybe you're right, Metcalfe."

Alex Cameron rubbed the knot of tension in his neck as he stood at the broad windows overlooking Greywood's banks of fragrant lavender. His eyes felt as if someone had poured sand into them and he was bone tired, but he knew he wouldn't be able to sleep in spite of the forty-one hours of straight traveling he had just endured.

He frowned, trying to focus on the memory of Elena's face when her parents had stepped out of his car an hour ago.

Yes, that was good. Very good.

But the memory didn't take away the pain that had been gnawing at him for the last three weeks.

Give her time, he told himself angrily. *She was pushed around once before. She was threatened and manipulated and terrorized. Give her the space to make her own choices for a change. You owe her that much.*

Frowning, he tossed his shirt onto a chair, then stripped out of his flannel trousers.

Yes, even if it left him twisted into tiny pieces inside, Alex was going to do the right thing for once. No charm, no husky persuasion. No long, drugging kisses that would push Joanna Russell into seeing things his way, which was getting married as fast as possible.

The problem was that Alex hadn't known doing the right thing would be so bloody painful.

No matter what Joanna decided, he wouldn't let Peter's father bother her. Alex had made a quick visit to Texas, where Jason Harris was employed as a marketing analyst for a high-profile investment company.

They had had a nice chat. A nice *long* chat.

Alex smiled, rubbing his bruised knuckles, remembering how much he had enjoyed knocking out the man's two front teeth, cutting off a stream of filthy curses. Now Alex had every confidence that Mr. Jason Harris would cause no further disruption in Joanna's life.

He winced as he rubbed his neck. His two lower ribs still ached from the "misunderstanding" he had had with a pair of Estavian border guards who hadn't been keen on releasing Elena's parents in spite of the signed emigration documents that Alex had shown them. They had delivered a bruising kick to Alex's ribs before he managed to subdue them.

Alex was actually glad for the pain, however. It almost took his mind off Joanna.

Her luminous eyes. Her husky laugh. The soft little sounds she made when he—

Cursing softly, he kicked off the rest of his clothes and headed for the bath.

He was stiff and jetlagged, and he wanted nothing more than to fall into bed and sleep for about a week, but first he was going to scrub off the dust of the Estavian border.

He was just testing the temperature in the shower when the phone rang. Cursing, Alex slung a towel low around his hips. So much for telling Metcalfe to hold his calls. The butler had been glowering at him for three weeks now, dropping little hints about how quiet things were at Greywood without Peter and his mother.

But Metcalfe didn't understand. Joanna needed time

to make her own decisions, and Alex damned well wasn't going to crowd her, especially when he couldn't shake a feeling of guilt for causing her to be involved in such danger.

The phone call was from the Estavian ambassador, who was clearly nervous.

Good, Alex thought. Nervous, he liked.

"Yes, I quite understood. Of course I accept your apologies." Alex stood frowning at the giant elm at the end of Greywood's sweeping drive. The ambassador sounded genuinely desperate to prevent any diplomatic repercussions from the incident with Orlov. "No, there will be no need for you to extend a written apology with the personal signature of your president. I understand that this was all Pavel Orlov's idea. Yes, taking him home to Estavia seems the best answer. I'm quite happy to see the matter brought to a close, too." Alex frowned, massaging the throbbing pain near his lower right rib. So containment would be the order of the day: Orlov would take all the blame and English–Estavian relations would lumber forward, undisturbed.

Alex didn't know whether to feel relieved or disgusted.

"I see. I'm glad you think so. I agree that this should not go any farther."

With his eyes locked on the green lawns, Alex did not hear the door to his bedroom ease open or a slender figure pad silently over the carpet.

"So you've decided to accept my plan for the electronics factory and the mining venture? Excellent. I'm sure we can come to mutually satisfactory terms."

A shadow fell over his shoulder.

"But you'll have to agree to one thing first. I have the names of three families that are to be freed from preventive custody."

A silence.

"The charge? Smuggling contraband consumer goods. At least that was Orlov's term for it." Alex waited tensely. "So that was Orlov's doing, too, you say. More leverage against me if his plan failed. I'm glad to hear that you will act so quickly. Once I have confirmation of their release, I am certain that we can act equally fast." After a pause, he said flatly, "No, I'll need their release *first.*"

Alex stiffened as something slid over his neck. He turned, eyes wide. "What—"

Joanna cut off his startled question with a slow, open-mouthed kiss across his jaw.

"Er, what was that you said, Ambassador?" Alex swallowed, trying to concentrate as Joanna's warm lips brushed his neck. "Oh, fine. Yes, I'll look forward to receiving your letter of intent." He made a hard sound. "What? No, I'm fine. Just fine. It's a little hot down here, that's all."

Joanna's lips curved at his explanation. Her hands eased lovingly over the rigid muscles of his bronzed chest.

"Of course, that would be fine."

Her fingers closed over the end of the hastily tied towel.

Alex swallowed again, feeling fire shoot through his lower body. "I'm not certain how wise that would be."

The white fabric stretched.

"What? No, there's no need for you to deliver your apologies in person, Mr. Ambassador."

Not while the most exquisite woman in the world is about to drive me to a state of permanent meltdown.

Alex bit back a groan as Joanna pressed slow, trailing kisses down his chest and across his rock-hard stomach. "Thank you. No, that would be far too hard." He ground his teeth as Joanna's fingers moved lower. "Painfully hard, actually."

"Painfully hard?" she whispered. The towel loosened.

"Ah, I'm not certain I can wait that long."

Joanna smiled as the towel fell to the floor.

"Er—sorry, Mr. Ambassador. Got to go. Important call coming in."

Alex dropped the phone blindly and caught Joanna's face.

"Important call, am I?"

"That and a lot of other things." His face hardened. "Don't, Joanna. God help me, don't."

She went very still. "You don't like it?"

Alex grimaced. "I *love* it."

"Then why didn't you call me? It's been almost three weeks."

Alex jammed a hand through his long hair. "Joanna, I'm trying to do the right thing here."

"You call ignoring me the right thing?"

"I'm not ignoring you; I'm giving you space. With everything that's happened, I thought you deserved more time. Damn it, Joanna, I don't want you to feel obliged to—"

"Obliged to what?"

"To *marry* me!"

"Marry you," she repeated softly. Her hands linked behind his neck. "Why would I feel that? After all, you only had your way with me five years ago, seduced me, and discarded me."

His eyes flashed. "Damn it, we didn't—"

"And then," she continued implacably, "you did the same thing three weeks ago. I tumbled into your web, the most gullible of victims. I hope this isn't going to be some kind of habit with you, Lord Greywood."

Alexei grimaced as she nestled closer against his chest. "Joanna, I didn't want to press you for a commitment so soon. And Nathalie—I told you so little about her. I suppose I wanted to deny it ever happened."

"Forget Nathalie." Her hands slid along his chest. "Press me," she said huskily. "I won't break."

A shudder went through him. *So much for high and noble intentions, Alexei Turov. Your mother told you it would be like this, reckless and blind. The only important thing in the universe when it struck.*

Love.

He said the word in Russian and Estavian and Romany.

Then he gripped her face and brought his mouth down on hers, open and searching and red hot, until neither one could breathe.

"This is definitely going to be a habit with me," he said huskily, reaching behind him to the desk. "You'd better get used to it, Russell."

Then his eyes darkened. He took out a ring from an ornate gilded leather box. "Marry me, Joanna. Dog my steps. Challenge my logic. Test my willpower every day of my life. Make me forget all my hard-earned words of English when you smile that dazzling smile that makes my heart crack in two." He slid a heavy handmade ring onto her finger. "Say yes. It's pathetic to see a grown man beg."

Her fingers slid through his long hair. "There are other women, Alex. Women with fine titles."

"I like your name just fine," he said softly, repeating the words she had said to him five years before on a deserted tropical beach.

"But you speak English. I speak American."

"I like the way you speak just fine." He kissed her hand just below the ring she now wore.

When Joanna looked down, her breath caught. Three gold ravens were linked, holding a superb three-carat ruby. "Oh, Alex—"

"Say yes."

"But—"

"Yes."

"But when—"

His mouth crushed hers, searching and sweet. He didn't pull away until her eyes were radiant and hazed with passion. "Well?"

"Yes." Then she said the word in Estavian and Russian and very colloquial Romany. "Did I get it right?"

He could only nod.

"Dimitri taught me. He thought I might need to be able to say them." She cleared her throat. "Just in case . . . someone asked me"—she swallowed—"to marry him."

"You mean a big, ignorant half-Gypsy who's too stupid to know the most precious thing in the world when it's only inches away from him?"

"I think that might be the one," Joanna said softly.

Alex's forehead slanted down onto her head, and he took a long, shuddering breath. There was no way in hell he was going to give her any more time just in case she changed her mind.

"You're wearing too many clothes, Russell. Let's get this ugly thing off." He fumbled with her belt. "Why are you wearing a coat when there's not a cloud in the sky?"

Joanna smiled lazily. "Actually, it was going to be my secret weapon."

"A raincoat?"

"Just in case you'd forgotten your offer." She caught back a husky laugh. "To marry me, that is."

Alex muttered several words of savage Romany, rolled his eyes skyward, then opened the last buttons of Joanna's coat. He went absolutely still when he saw what she was wearing underneath: absolutely nothing.

"That's a devastating secret weapon you've got there." His voice was hoarse. Only the golden links of a raven necklace gleamed against her pale skin.

He swallowed. And swallowed again. "Good sweet Lord, is it."

Her lips curved with a hint of wantonness. "What about giving me time?"

"To hell with time."

"And what about all that talk of doing the right thing?"

"This *is* the right thing." Alex fumbled with the knot in her belt, disgusted to see that his hands were not quite steady.

Joanna gave a smile of radiant happiness. "I understand that Sir Gordon was caught trying to catch a flight out of Jersey. Two days ago he confessed to his involvement, right down to helping Nathalie and Loring plan their attack on Jacques. Nathalie was that talkative woman on my tour, did you know?"

"Ummm."

"It was Sir Gordon's idea to have the ambulance go to the dig site and report that Peter had been hurt. He knew my mother's call would get me there immediately."

"Ummm."

Joanna frowned. "Jacques is taking it all rather hard, of course. I think as he recovers he feels more and more responsible for what happened."

"Ummm." The knot wouldn't budge, Alex noticed to his utter disgust. Or maybe the problem was that his usually reliable coordination had become seriously unbalanced ever since a smiling Joanna Russell had walked into his bedroom.

"Peter's been asking every day when we're going to have our honeymoon. He says that now you have the license, we can sleep in the same bed."

The knot finally slid free. "That boy is nine going on ninety, I think."

"Does that bother you?"

The raincoat slid over her shoulders.

Alex toyed with the necklace and smiled when he saw her swallow at the direction his gaze was slanted. If he had to look at her much longer, he was going to go mad. "Peter? Not at all. I'm just not sure I'll be any match for him. I found two gray hairs this morning."

Joanna's fingers slid downward. She found his rising heat and claimed him between her searching fingers. "I think you're a match for just about anything, my lord."

Alex's eyes darkened. "Shall we find out?"

"I thought you'd never ask."

The desk was behind her as he lifted her fiercely.

"The bed—"

"We'll never make it," Alex said hoarsely. "Besides, I'm not feeling honorable anymore." The raincoat pooled over the polished mahogany desk as he traced a wet path over her breast with his tongue. "I love you, Joanna," he said hoarsely. "Love was the third key. The key that lasts forever. My father knew that. Somehow he reached out over time and taught me that final lesson."

Joanna swallowed as he found her silken heat. "But Alex, what about finishing your current sword? I seem to recall reading that Gypsy custom required, er, lack of female companionship"—her breath caught as his fingers parted her with exquisite skill—"u-until the blade is finished, I mean."

"The blade was done last week," Alex said, smiling darkly. "It was just an excuse to give you some extra time. But your time is up."

Joanna made a soft, restless sound as he eased her back against the cool wood and pressed inside her.

"I think," she said huskily, pulling his lips down to hers and wriggling to seat his velvet blade even deeper within her, "that our time is just beginning."

"God help me," Alex whispered. Then he forgot everything but the sleek pull of her, the husky sound of her laughter. Honor and duty were finally fulfilled as he made their bodies one. Love was all around them, shimmering and forever.

Now the sword sang its dark songs to him no more.

Sunlight glinted off the moat, and the wind whispered through cascading centifolia roses as Jacques St. Cyr slowly moved down the granite steps to convene what would prove to be one of the most talked-about events the international art world had ever witnessed.

He stopped to shake hands with Nicholas Draycott, looking very tanned and fit in a white linen jacket, one arm draped around his smiling American wife.

On his way to the tent set up on the abbey lawn, St. Cyr saw Peter playing cards with Dimitri and stopped to give a bit of advice.

"Palm your ace like this, *mon fils. Comme ça,* just beneath the wrist, with the gentlest of movements. Keep them looking at your other hand—something very obvious. *Et voilà.*"

Peter gave his own demonstration, much to Dimitri's delight. "Very well done, Peter. Now I never beat you again. Even I do not palm so well as this."

Michael Burke stood nearby with his radiant wife. Both bore pink-cheeked infants, drowsy beneath white eyelet caps.

St. Cyr's brow rose as he took in the contented scene. *"Eh bien,* I do not as a rule find infants attractive, Lord Sefton, but I must say that these two are exceptional. No doubt the credit belongs to your beautiful wife."

Lady Sefton smiled faintly. "Oh, Michael made his contribution."

"Any time you wish to discuss a commission, please phone me," St. Cyr said. "I have a very fine Norman sword that I would like your opinion on."

Kelly Burke's brow rose. "But what about Joanna?"

Jacques smiled. "I expect that Ms. Russell will be far too busy to have any time for my small concerns," he said calmly, leaning on his ivory cane.

He shared a look with Lady Sefton as the lady in question moved over the grass hand in hand with Alex Cameron. The two were twenty minutes late and a million miles away.

"It took them long enough to find each other," St. Cyr said softly.

Kelly's eyes widened. "You planned this. All of it."

"Not quite all," the Frenchman said, his eyes on Joanna. "When dealing with people, one can only hope. I knew there would be danger, and so I took precautions. But not enough," he added darkly.

"But Joanna told me the envelope containing the third clue was empty. Why did you do that?"

St. Cyr gave a very Gallic shrug. "If I was no longer present to substitute the real clue, it meant my enemies had won. I had my doubts about Sir Gordon, you see. In that case, the rest would be up to Alex's and Joanna's skill. I certainly wasn't going to give the final clue to the same men who had tried to kill me."

"Very clever," Michael Burke said.

"Not clever enough. I held a funeral for my daughter last week, though her body was never found. Probably I lost her years before the cave-in. That same night I nearly managed to have Alex and Joanna killed. No, not clever at all," he said grimly.

Kelly touched his arm. "Perhaps it's time to forget."

"Only if they will let me," St. Cyr said.

As flashbulbs popped and videotape whirred, Alex and St. Cyr walked toward each other. Their faces were hard.

"St. Cyr, I don't know why I shouldn't give you one

good uppercut to the jaw and leave you unconscious here on the grass."

"You would have every right," the Frenchman said quietly. *"Alors . . ."* He raised his jaw, presenting a perfect target.

Alex gave a disgusted laugh and gripped his shoulder instead. There was a fresh explosion of flashbulbs followed by clapping as Alex ran his arm around Joanna's shoulders and pulled her close. "How can I do that to the man who brought us together? But tell me one thing. Why the angry scene at Greywood on the night of Joanna's reenactment?"

Jacques gave another Gallic shrug. "You would not trust anything I had to say, I think. Our hostility goes too far for that, especially after Nathalie and her deceit. So I decide that telling Joanna she absolutely must *not* go with you is the best way to make you accept her."

"Reverse psychology," Alex said in disgust. "And like a fool I fell for it."

"You both did a superb job," St. Cyr said seriously. "But now perhaps we should put the ladies and gentlemen of the press out of their misery, *non?"*

With a great flourish, Jacques opened the polished box and took out the exquisite scabbard. Beside him, Alex raised the Cameron sword.

Then both men stood back while Joanna slid the two together and gently twisted the gilt fittings.

Something moved deep inside the sword. There was a low vibration as the hilt slowly turned.

When she pulled the scabbard from the sword, a small hole darkened the side of the great claymore's grip.

"Mon Dieu," Jacques whispered, surreptitiously crossing himself.

The cameras snapped in earnest, and the reporters surged forward in a mad wave as Alex carefully removed a sheet of vellum wound in a tight scroll inside the grip.

Images burned through his blood in mad waves of color. He had a rough sense of what the lines said even without opening the sheets.

He also knew the document was priceless. Only after

experts had carefully opened the fragile sheet and examined its contents could the full story be released to the press.

"Well?" a man in a jaunty bowler called. "What does it say, Greywood?"

"It appears to be some kind of document, but I'm afraid we'll have to leave the details to the experts. After all this time, I don't want to have the page crumble to dust in my hand."

"Document? What *kind* of document?" a man in red suspenders called eagerly.

"As I said, it is a very old piece of paper. More than that I cannot say now, gentlemen."

There was a ripple of eager voices followed by another burst of flashbulbs.

Jacques St. Cyr nodded slowly as Alex cradled the precious vellum. "Something tells me that you have an idea what that sheet contains, Greywood." His voice was low, meant only for the three of them. "A very literal page of history, I suspect."

"I have a hunch it's a letter from Elizabeth thanking Mary for their private meeting. After that Elizabeth graciously agrees to release her cousin from custody, providing Mary will relinquish all rights to the throne of England," Alex murmured. "If my instincts are correct, it is a legal contract, signed and dated, witnessed by one Angus Cameron." He paused. "My ancestor."

"Good heavens," Joanna breathed. "A document like that would set history on its ear. But what happened to all their plans?"

"Betrayal happened. Lies upon lies, hidden for centuries," Alex said grimly. "They came so close, those two queens. Perhaps as women they would have found a gentler resolution to their differences. But greedy men intervened and these lines were probably intercepted before they could ever be put to use. Elizabeth was persuaded to forget she had ever written them."

"And Mary had to die," Joanna whispered, remembering the chill that had come over her in the Long

Gallery. A chill that had come from a death that should never have taken place.

As Joanna stood with the wind combing through her hair and the sun warm on her shoulders, she seemed to feel the same presence beside her again. But this time there was lightness and resolution and the hint of low laughter. Her breath caught. "Do you feel it, Alex?"

His eyes narrowed. "Not cold anymore. Different. Almost a sense of relief."

"Her work is finally done," Joanna said softly. "She knows she can rest now that we know the truth." Her fingers met Alex's and tightened. "Tell me I'm not imagining all this."

"There's one way to be certain." He caught her hand and moved toward the abbey.

"You will explain to me, perhaps, these cryptic things you speak of," St. Cyr murmured. "A poor old man like I, with a weak heart, makes a bad one to keep secrets from."

Alex took his shoulder for a moment. "Very well, come along, you cunning old fox. This is one story I think you'll enjoy."

Darkness swirled. Light shimmered over the framed portraits, Chinese porcelains, and the great armoire.

"Hurry, Adrian. They're *coming.*"

A man moved out of the shadows. "There, it is done. The past is sealed, and she is entirely free. They will find nothing of her here, no trace at all."

"Very well done, my love. But I think we should go."

The abbey ghost smiled smugly. "Nor will they capture any images with their infernal machines."

"Their cameras? What have you done now, Adrian Draycott?"

"Just a bit of magic. In their photographs, all they will see of the sword is flares of light, like tiny flames. I've had quite enough of their blasted interference here at my abbey. Perhaps this will teach them all a lesson." He scowled. "The Evil Viscount indeed."

Gray laughed softly. "Perhaps it is time they learned to cease their meddling. But we had better be gone, Adrian. This man Alexei sees things few other men see."

Adrian frowned. "He sees far too much. But leaving suits me perfectly. I know a delightful spot beside a row of lavender. I think you will be seduced by my newest roses."

The figure beside him smiled. "Shameless man." Her voice fell. "Beloved man. As if you don't seduce me with one simple look . . ."

She caught his fingers and tugged him toward the portrait haloed in a beam of sunlight.

Her hand rose. She turned, laughing softly, her golden gown swirling around her. And then she shimmered away, lost among the light playing over the fine pigments.

The air was filled with the rich scent of roses. Light rippled, playing through the quiet room. There was a low cry, like the kind made by a large cat.

Then in a swirl of black velvet, Adrian Draycott, too, disappeared.

But the eyes that stared back from the portrait seemed to glint knowingly, a warning to any who would threaten the peace of this weathered old abbey.

And the eyes in the portrait were far too real to be a mere static image.

Far too alive.

Far too happy.

Author's Note

JOANNA AND Alex.

Dear me, how I miss *these* two already!

Passionate and proud, they released their secrets layer by layer while I watched breathlessly. I won't be at all surprised to find them back in a future book—along with Joanna's wonderfully incorrigible parents.

If you are as fascinated as I am by dashing knights and the complexity of all that extraordinary armor with its pauldrons and gorgets, greaves and sabatons, you will find a wealth of wonderful details in Charles Ffoulkes's *The Armourer and His Craft* (New York: Dover Books, 1988), which even includes authentic excerpts about armor from medieval documents.

The world of the sword and the way of elegant combat continue to obsess collectors today. Like Joanna, the true connoisseur must do more than simply observe these fine works of art. Only with firsthand experience at using the sword can one appreciate the careful design and lasting mystique of these centuries-old weapons. Today swords that predate the Renaissance are extremely rare, and authentic Scottish claymores are rarer still. These ancient, two-handed swords of old Scotland derive their name from the Gaelic *claidheamh mór* or great sword and were widely used in the fifteenth and sixteenth centuries. In battle they were wielded in explosive overhead strokes to instantly hew down an enemy. Authentic claymores are extremely rare and fetch phenomenal prices when they come up at auction. A sword of great legend such as the Cameron claymore would command an untold price, especially in view of the historical documents concealed within it. Those particularly interested in the code of honor and dueling through the ages will find Alfred Hutton's excellent book, *The Sword and the Centuries* (New York: Barnes and Noble, 1995), filled with anecdotes.

Gypsies?

For centuries Gypsies have been considered with fear and scorn, set apart by language and custom from the settled peoples of Europe. For an unforgettable first-hand look at the problems of contemporary Gypsies in Eastern Europe, see Isabel Fonsecca's powerful study, *Bury Me Standing* (New York: Random House, 1986). An older book on the subject, *The Gypsies,* by Angus Fraser (Oxford, England: Blackwell Publishers, 1992), presents a good introduction to the complex story of Gypsy migrations in Europe, where over sixty different dialects of Romany speech continue to be spoken today.

Oh yes, if you are interested in Alexei's singular skill of palm reading, try *Palmistry and the Inner Self* by Ray Douglas (London: Blandford, 1995), which presents the palm and its various marks as a window to the inner soul. Fascinating reading. Of course, Alex knew this without having to read *any* books.

As always, I welcome your letters. If you would like information about upcoming Draycott Abbey books and a copy of my current newsletter, please send a stamped self-addressed envelope to me at:

111 East 14th Street, #277K
New York, New York 10003

You can also reach my web site on the internet at http://www.comet.net/writers/skye. I love hearing from you!

Happy reading,
Christina Skye